PRAI
Winner of the R
by th

"[Robin D. Owe
passion, exotic futuristic settings, and edgy suspense."
—Jayne Castle, *New York Times* bestselling
author of *The Hot Zone*

"Will have readers on t___ ___ ___ Another terrific tale from the bril___ ___ ___ 't
miss it."

"[This] emotionally ___ ___ s,
family dynamics, and ___ ___ e;
and dusts it all with hu___ ___ al

"Maintaining the world-building for science fiction and
character-driven plot for romance is near impossible. Owens
does it brilliantly."   —*The Romance Readers Connection*

"Dazzling . . . Robin D. Owens paints a world filled with characters who sweep readers into an unforgettable adventure with
every delicious word, every breath, every beat of their hearts.
Brava!"   —Deb Stover, award-winning author of *Always*

"A taut mixture of suspense and action . . . that leaves you
stunned."   —*Smexy Books*

"A delight . . . Hits all my joy buttons."   —*Fresh Fiction*

"[Owens's] creativity shines."   —*Darque Reviews*

"I keep telling myself that [Robin D. Owens] just can't get
much better, but with every book she amazes and surprises
me!"   —*The Best Reviews*

GHOST KILLER

ROBIN D. OWENS

BERKLEY SENSATION, NEW YORK

THE BERKLEY PUBLISHING GROUP
Published by the Penguin Group
Penguin Group (USA) LLC
375 Hudson Street, New York, New York 10014

USA • Canada • UK • Ireland • Australia • New Zealand • India • South Africa • China

penguin.com

A Penguin Random House Company

GHOST KILLER

A Berkley Sensation Book / published by arrangement with the author

For information, address: The Berkley Publishing Group,
a division of Penguin Group (USA) LLC,
375 Hudson Street, New York, New York 10014.

ISBN: 978-0-425-26983-1

PUBLISHING HISTORY
Berkley Sensation mass-market edition / February 2015

PRINTED IN THE UNITED STATES OF AMERICA

10 9 8 7 6 5 4 3 2 1

Cover art by Tony Mauro.
Cover design by George Long.
Interior text design by Kelly Lipovich.

To all my readers who followed me to Denver
and the Old West, thank you!
And to new readers,
welcome and may you enjoy all the worlds you visit in books!

COUNTING CROWS RHYME

One for sorrow,
Two for luck;
Three for a wedding,
Four for death;
Five for silver,
Six for gold;
Seven for a secret,
Not to be told;
Eight for heaven,
Nine for [hell];
And ten for the devil's own sell [self].

The autumn winds blow bleak and chill,
   The sighing, quivering aspen waves
      Above the summit of the hill.
      Above the unrecorded graves,
   Where halt, abandoned burros feed,
And coyotes call—and this is Creede.

—CY WARMAN, "A QUIET DAY IN CREEDE,"
   FRONTIER STORIES, 1898

ONE

DANGER COMES, ENZO howled, running through the bedroom door. Not the doorway, the door. Even a ghost Labrador should not have all the hair on his body standing out.

Clare Cermak's heartbeat kicked fast and she shuddered in the bed of her lover. She pulled the sheet high, even though the room was—had been—warm and sunny this morning.

Enzo leapt for the bed and landed on her, in her, sending the coldness of his being into her legs. His dark doggy eyes showed fear. Before she could say anything, those "eyes" began to morph into bottomless black mist with jagged white streaks . . . signifying that the Other spirit who took over her happy companion would be speaking to her. Enzo was her spirit guide; she hadn't quite figured out what the Other was, but when he/it came, she felt like an expendable pawn in an unknown chess game.

You are not, quite, expendable, the Other "said." The words reverberated in her head, but more, seemed to knock heavy molecules of air together in soundless explosions through the room. Zach, facedown beside her, began to stir and she wasn't sure whether she wanted him to hear what the Other said or not. This was the first time she'd been to his apartment, the first night she'd spent. She cherished the togetherness that the Other could splinter.

Judgmental eyes fixed upon her. *Not, quite, expendable,* the Other repeated. *Your work has been . . . adequate . . . for your first two projects, since you accepted your gift.*

Clare had heard her psychic ability to help ghosts pass on to the hereafter called a gift, but she considered it a curse.

We have paid you well for your gift, the Other, still standing face-to-face with her, said.

Yes, she'd inherited millions, and for each major ghost she'd aided, had received income. But she'd also lost her previous life as an accountant, which she'd loved.

You are ungrateful. The Other's skin of his muzzle pulled back and showed the teeth bigger than what she saw, supernatural teeth.

Beside her, Zach groaned and rolled over, pushed away his dark hair from his forehead and opened blue green eyes. The Other stepped to put a paw square on his chest and Zach grunted.

It is well you are together, Clare Cermak and Zach Slade, the Other said dispassionately. *One of you might survive, should you walk into this danger.*

A rapping came on the door between Zach's former-housekeeper's apartment and the rest of the mansion. The Other and Enzo vanished and Zach sat up, put his warm, muscular, and *solid*, arm around Clare. He looked down at her. "I heard the Other. You *will* survive."

Clare realized she trembled. Mostly with cold, she assured herself.

"What did the bastard say?"

She shook her head in denial of the fear spearing through her, swallowed so she found more spit in her dry mouth to speak. "Danger comes."

Zach grunted, rolled off the bed and pulled on some sweat pants, yelled to the person still pounding on the door, "Just a damn— Just a minute!"

"Probably Mrs. Flinton," Clare said, speaking of his landlady, the very wealthy owner of the mansion. She'd offered the apartment to Zach the first day he'd been in Denver and interviewed with Rickman Security and Investigations.

Clare dragged on her bra, turned yesterday's panties inside out for now and put them on, slipped into her sundress. She had no clothes here.

Zach had already snagged his cane and left the bedroom. He'd gone to the door in the little hallway just outside and perpendicular to the bedroom. Clare heard him open the door slightly. "Mrs. Flinton?"

"I'm so sorry to disturb you. So, sorry," her voice quavered. Usually the woman exuded vim and vigor.

"Sorry to disturb me? That's a first," Zach teased. "Come on in. I think you need to talk to Clare, right?" he said in a casual tone that amazed Clare. She still had trouble breathing steadily. But he'd been a deputy sheriff and was used to adrenaline dumps. That didn't happen often when you were a certified public accountant at a nice, safe job for a prestigious, maybe stodgy, firm.

"Yes. There's trouble." A drawn-in breath. "An evil ghost."

The last three words stopped Clare in her tracks, to take a breath. She'd only been a ghost seer for seventeen days and didn't have the experience to handle an evil ghost.

But Mrs. Flinton continued to talk in a whisper. "I have tea and pastries in the breakfast room, if you wish to join me."

Clare didn't want to pretend this discussion would be pleasant over tea and pastries. She stomped her fear into the carpet as she joined Zach and Mrs. Flinton in the hallway.

He slanted a look at Clare, stepped back, then opened the door wide for his landlady. For the first time since Clare had met her, Mrs. Flinton actually looked and acted elderly, face sagging with worry, mouth quivering.

"The tea—" Mrs. Flinton protested.

"I have food. I'm a P.I. and I discuss cases in my apartment. We can talk in the living room." He turned and stalked the few steps to where the short hall opened into the main living space.

He sounded more accepting of his change of career from

a deputy sheriff in Montana to a P.I. in Denver, due to a gunshot wound, than he had when Clare had first met him.

His living room was a manly room for speaking of danger, as opposed to the parlor, which was decorated in cheerful yellow chintz with filmy white curtains.

The woman pushed a roller walker into the room, leaning on it. She crossed to one of the big brown leather chairs, leaving the sofa and the other chair on this side of the room for Zach and Clare.

Clare felt too nervy to sit. "I'll put coffee on, why don't I?" She crossed to the small pullman kitchen that was separated from the living room by a half wall that was a counter with stools in the main space.

Mrs. Flinton, who'd unaccustomedly slumped, perked up, her pink-lipsticked mouth smiling. "Coffee!"

Clare angled back to her. "Are you supposed to have coffee?"

"I would love some." Mrs. Flinton tried a wobbly smile.

Since the older woman evaded the question, she probably wasn't supposed to have coffee. But Clare needed it and thought Zach did, too. She sent Mrs. Flinton a stern look over the counter. "You'll be having herbal tea."

Mrs. Flinton pouted, then sighed. "I suppose you're right. Though what I really need is a martini."

Zach chuckled as he lounged on the couch. "Not going to have that, either."

"Bloody Mary?" Mrs. Flinton raised penciled-on brows.

"Nope. No alcohol here."

Sniffing, Mrs. Flinton said, "You are wrong. We stocked your liquor cabinet, and I know my housekeeper has given you wine from my cellar with your meals." Another sniff. "Wine my doctor says I can't have."

The return of her upbeat personality and the dripping of the coffee as it filled the pot soothed Clare enough for her to slide into the living room with a pleasant expression and sit next to Zach.

Mrs. Flinton's face crumpled when she saw Clare and

tears began to roll down her cheeks. There was nothing for it; Clare rose and moved over to perch on the arm of the woman's chair, patted her on the shoulder. "Maybe you'd better tell us what's wrong, Mrs. Flinton."

"Please call me Barbara, especially since I'll be imposing on you so much." She whisked out a lace-edged hanky and dabbed her eyes and her cheeks.

Zach said, "Just tell us, Barbara."

Straightening to ramrod stiff, not looking at Clare, Barbara said, "Yes, I suppose I must. It's about another ghost seer."

Clare drew in a small breath. Maybe she'd have help in dealing with this evil ghost. Any help would be great. "Another ghost seer?"

Mrs. Flinton continued, "Yes, I have a little bit of several psychic gifts, but Caden has just one, like you, and we're thinking it must be ghost seeing." Her fingers crushed the handkerchief until the delicate linen disappeared into her fist.

Clare's gaze met Zach's. He nodded, as if confirming he was in this with her. As he always had been. She was lucky.

"Caden?" she asked, her voice a little higher than usual. "And who is 'we'?"

"We are me, his great grandmother, and my daughter, Caden's grandmother, who believe in psychic gifts, but not his parents."

"Parents," said Zach neutrally.

"Caden is seven." A quivery sigh followed by a rush of words. "It seems his gift is coming too fast and too soon."

Clare recalled when her own gift descended—freezing in the hottest summer of Denver, the weird going-insane feeling, and, yes, people who didn't think she saw ghosts, including herself. Terrible stress. "Oh my God," Clare breathed. Despite any danger, she could not refuse to help.

"Yes, dear." Mrs. Flinton cleared her throat. She sniffed wetly, raised big, blue eyes to Clare. "Even though in our family we don't have the effects that seem to apply to yours— the lethal coldness and threat of insanity, it's not good. There's a powerful and bad ghost out there, and he's young."

Clare flinched. The tea kettle shrieked. Avoiding Zach's gaze, she went behind the counter to the stove on the far wall and turned off the burner. She fussed with the loose leaf tea of twigs and blossoms in a little basket. Grabbed a half minute to lean discreetly against the fridge.

"Pour your coffees first, dear," Mrs. Flinton instructed. "Otherwise the water will be too hot for the herbs and ruin their efficacy."

Waiting until her hands were steady, Clare poured mugs of coffee for Zach and herself. Just the smell of rich, dark caffeine strengthened her. He always took black, and she added a little sugar from the bowl on the counter, and real cream from the fridge to hers. With her chin high, she took a mug to him.

He looked at her straight, all acceptance of life-threatening trouble, and as if judging whether she could also face that up front. She firmed her lips and dipped her head. As much as she'd bobbed and ducked in the past, trying to evade her gift, now was not the time to drag her feet.

The bottom line was that an endangered child wouldn't let her ignore her power to move ghosts on. Hopefully she had enough mojo-whatever to kick an evil one out of this world.

Giving them all time to think about what should be said next, what plans had to be made, Clare put her own mug on a magazine on the coffee table, went back for Mrs. Flinton's tea, then handed the delicate china cup to her.

"Thank you, dear," Mrs. Flinton said, and cradled the cup in both hands as if cherishing the warmth.

Clare sat next to Zach and even leaned against him a little. He was much nicer than the fridge, and knew about trouble and danger. Leaning against him, accepting his expertise, didn't automatically mean she was dependent on him.

Putting down his mug, he took the lead, as she'd expected.

"Trouble," Zach prompted.

Mrs. Flinton's hand holding the teacup shook and she put it down. "Yes. I know Caden's in trouble and my granddaughter and her husband *don't* believe that. They are good, solid—"

"Unimaginative—" Zach said.

"Rational—" Clare began herself.

"Yes. Both of those." Mrs. Flinton blinked rapidly as if to keep more tears from falling. Her eyes appeared even bluer and she whispered, "I've heard . . . that an evil ghost is very dangerous, even to the living." She stared into the distance, turning so pale that her carefully blended makeup stood out on her face.

Clare shivered. Zach slid his arm from the sofa behind her to wrap around her shoulders.

Since Mrs. Flinton already knew about Enzo, Clare called him. "Enzo?"

The ghost Labrador simply appeared, sitting between Mrs. Flinton and Clare, angled to watch them both. *Oh, no!* Enzo whimpered. *This is bad. This is VERY bad.* He shuddered, straightened, and turned his eyes on Clare. *But we will do it! I will help. I . . . I am SURE we can kill the bad ghost!*

Her formerly staunch phantom dog didn't sound sure.

"Yeah," Zach said. *He* didn't sound too alarmed and rubbed Clare's shoulder.

Clare *was* alarmed. Enzo had spoken of evil ghosts before. She knew she wasn't experienced enough to fight one.

Mrs. Flinton began to hiccup in distress. Clare stood and walked around the coffee table to pick up her teacup and hand it back to her. "Drink it down, Mrs. Flinton," Clare said. Luckily her voice didn't betray her inner qualms.

Nodding, Mrs. Flinton sipped, then gestured to the elegant Hermès bag attached to her walker. "Please retrieve my phone. I have something I want you to view."

The cell in a sparkly lavender case was easy to find.

"I recorded a call from Caden on SeeAndTalk. Please take the phone over to Zach so you can both watch."

Clare did, sitting thigh-to-thigh with Zach. She thumbed on the app and held it so they could both see.

"Hi, Great-Gram," a blond-haired boy with Mrs. Flinton's eyes whispered.

"Hello, Caden," Mrs. Flinton's voice came.

The boy glanced around. "I gotta be fast." His expression tightened, pinching his features. "They don't believe me, Gram! I tell them, and tell them, but they *won't* believe. They say I'm making it up." He gulped. "I'm not, Gram."

"What's wrong, Caden?"

"There's a ghost here in town. A real bad one. I think it was lurking or . . . you know that scary place where East Willow and West Willow Creeks meet? Near the bottom of the dirt Bachelor Loop road? The place where Mrs. Treedy killed her husband and herself last month—"

"How do you know about that, Caden?"

"I know I wasn't s'posed to hear, but all the kids did. That scary spot isn't sitting there no more. I think it mighta been a crazy ghost and got stirred up." He shivered. "I went there and now it's like a nasty old oily spot and feels like dirt and gravel in the wind." He began hyperventilating.

"Calm down, Caden, and tell me."

"I'm sorry, Gram. There's a ghost! A big, bad ghost and it's out to get me!"

"Get you how?"

The thin boy shuddered. "Suck my soul out of my body and eat it."

A harsh breath from Mrs. Flinton. "Caden, love?"

His lower lip thrust out, his brows came down. "I can *too* see ghosts. I told you. And you said you believed me!"

"I said that, and I meant it," the woman assured.

"Well, I *do* see ghosts, though usually not old, old ones like this one. And I don't see this one as much as feel it, and it feels really awful. As if it has teeth, crunch, crunch, crunch, and wants to eat me. My bones, crunch, crunch, crunch. And my, my inside spirit or . . . the rest of me."

Clare jerked. Zach's arm came around her and Enzo trotted over and laid chill on her feet.

"All right, Caden—" Mrs. Flinton began to soothe.

"Gram!"

"Shh, Caden," Mrs. Flinton said. "Listen to me. Are you listening?"

The boy bobbed his head.

"You can't live in fear. And the best way to stop doing that is to live moment to moment. Just concentrate on getting as much joy out of every minute you can. Do you understand me?"

"Don't worry about the future?"

"That's only making you more afraid, so don't do that now. I'll be sending you help. I promise."

That is good advice, Enzo sent to Clare mentally. *We must remember it.*

Yes, it fit in with Enzo's character well, and Mrs. Flinton's, not so much with Clare's. But with all the situations she'd been experiencing in her new career, she should consider it a motto to strive for.

"Caden?" called a young woman's voice on the recording.

"Gram, Mommy and Daddy don't believe me." Tears began to trickle down his face. "It comes most at night. I'm afraid to sleep. Help me, Gram."

"Caden, where are you and what are you doing?" called the younger woman.

The screen went black. Clare glanced up to see Mrs. Flinton's shoulders hunched and shaking as she wept into her handkerchief. Her muffled voice came. "It's hard to enjoy every moment when you fear, but I *do* fear. I did my best so Caden wouldn't." She uncurled, dabbed at her nose. "He trusts me, I must take care of him."

Zach cleared his throat. "When did Caden's call come in?"

Mrs. Flinton wiped her eyes and blew her nose and her spine straightened to ramrod. "This morning. I checked with my granddaughter, Caden's fine and at school." Her breath rasped in and out. "I knew I could count on you, Zach, and on Clare"—Mrs. Flinton sent her a look of appeal—"to help me. So I waited for you. As long as I could. I have a favor to ask you—" Mrs. Flinton began in a shaky voice.

The door from the mansion opened and Tony Rickman, Zach's boss at Rickman Security and Investigations, walked in carrying a large tray holding covered dishes. Clare smelled bacon and eggs.

"I'll take care of this, Godmama Barbara," Mr. Rickman said, striding the few paces to the coffee table and lowering the tray. He then turned to Zach and Clare. "I have a case for you both."

TWO

"WHEN I CALLED you, Tony, I didn't mean for you to interrupt your workday and come over," Mrs. Flinton said with starch in her tone.

Mr. Rickman went to her and kissed her cheek. "I'm here to take charge—take care of my godmama." His mouth flattened. "And young Caden. We don't know all the particulars," the man stated flatly. "This case could include a physical threat as well as . . . ah . . . non-physical. As your other cases have, Clare."

She nodded but wasn't reassured. Her insides continued to tremble with the thought of facing an evil spirit.

Zach raised his brows at Clare, his expression calm. She'd always been wishy-washy about "consulting" for Rickman Security and Investigations and using her psychic gift. Was a little wary of Tony Rickman, too. Bad enough that The Powers That Be, the universe, whatever, dropped cases of ghosts that needed to move on in her lap, let alone another, human source. She also didn't want her name to get out as a medium. The more people who knew she could communicate with ghosts, the less a secret it was.

"Do we accept this case?" Zach asked.

Clare shrugged then said, "You don't have to pay us—me—Mrs. Flinton. You saved my life . . . or at least my sanity."

"I agree," Zach said.

"You work for me, you get paid," Mr. Rickman said. "And you will both work for me on this."

Zach leaned down to whisper to Clare, "He's a control freak."

Thinking back to the few things she'd read in her great-aunt Sandra's journals—the previous holder of the "gift"—Clare said, "I'm not sure there *will* be a physical element to this . . . or . . . whether regular people are in danger." She rubbed Enzo's back with her foot.

Enzo thumped his tail. *Bad ghosts CAN hurt people! Especially people who can see them, like you and Caden. It will try to get your spirit and eat you first.*

An image from him brushed against her mind—that she didn't think he meant her to see—of some screaming clawed being ripping the spirit from her body, and, yes, *eating* her with dozens of razor-like teeth.

She shuddered, swallowed hard, then swigged some coffee to wet her mouth that had gone dry. "So bad ghosts can hurt people," Clare repeated aloud. "But that doesn't mean there's a human villain, does it, a physical threat?"

Enzo sat up. *Ghosts can influence people.*

"Ghosts can influence people," Zach repeated. So he heard Enzo.

"We need you to go to Creede, Colorado, today," Mr. Rickman said, taking control of the conversation again.

"That's where Caden is?" Clare asked.

"Yes," both Mrs. Flinton and Mr. Rickman said in unison. Mrs. Flinton sniffled.

Mr. Rickman pulled out a big, square handkerchief from his trousers pocket and handed it to her, shot a glance at Clare and Zach. "Eat," he ordered.

Zach leaned over and took off the silver domes. Sure enough, thick bacon, soft scrambled cheesy eggs, and buttered English muffins sat on two plates. Zach lifted one and shoveled the eggs in his mouth.

That was a man of action for you, ready to fuel up at a moment's notice while her throat was still dry and closed from fear. Clare savored her coffee.

Tony Rickman arranged his big body in the chair near them.

Mrs. Flinton said, "I called my granddaughter and asked if Caden could spend some time with me, get him out of the town, and was politely told to keep my nose out of their business." She sighed and didn't meet anyone's eyes. "They have serious ideas about how to raise their son, and it doesn't include any 'fancies or fantasies' I might 'put in his head,'" Mrs. Flinton stated calmly, though her hand trembled a little bit as she drank her tea.

Beside Clare, Zach stiffened. He had a marine general for a father who probably held the same beliefs. Those Clare herself had recently cherished until she'd been violently shown that psychic powers, and ghosts, existed.

"Godmama Barbara's right." Tony Rickman stared at Clare and Zach. "The LuCettes won't send Caden here to be influenced by her without supervision." Now Mr. Rickman gave a wintry smile. "And they won't send Caden to me because they don't want him around a military man, and they distrust my wife Desiree, thinking she's a flake."

Clare rather thought that, too.

"If I go down there, I'll only alienate them . . . more," Mrs. Flinton said. The older woman's mouth pursed, showing fine lines. "They wouldn't welcome me." Her lips pressed together and she shook her head as she gazed at Clare. "My own psychic power is not strong enough to help."

Tony Rickman grunted, "Good."

Placing her teacup on a side table, Mrs. Flinton said, "Caden is right." She sighed. "His parents won't believe him. Will only think he's having nightmares, which is how they explain his gift. I *do* believe him about a threatening ghost. Do you?"

"Yes," Clare and Zach said at the same time.

Yes! Enzo hopped to his feet, paced and circled the room, tail thwapping the air, sending a chilly draft through the room. Mrs. Flinton and Clare watched him, Zach ate, and Tony Rickman crossed his arms over his chest and studiously avoided looking at the spectral Labrador.

Enzo came back and sat near Clare's feet, but mostly in the coffee table, looked sorrowfully at the food, then back at her. *This is dangerous, Clare. Every spirit the bad ghost eats makes it bigger and eviler. I don't want it to eat a boy. We must protect him.*

"I don't want it to eat a boy, either," Clare said.

Zach crunched down his bacon. "We won't let that happen," he said with complete assurance.

Clare didn't know how they could prevent it, didn't know enough, but Zach was used to acting fast, thinking on his feet, and solving problems. She sent a thought to Enzo. *I don't know how to MAKE an evil ghost move on. Do you?*

His color cycled from substantial grays to nearly translucent. *Maybe.* He looked up at her earnestly. *We will try and we will do it!*

She blew a breath out, glanced around the room. Zach was totally on her side, she knew that, and he might be able to come up with scenarios that would work if—when—she shared what she knew. Her shoulders had tensed when she realized she didn't think she could do this without him.

Keeping her tones light, she asked, "Mrs. Flinton, can you give me any tips for sending a ghost on?"

The older lady shook her head. "I'm sorry, I can't. I see ghosts, of course, and communicate with them occasionally if they please, but I can't help them transition to their next life."

Clare nodded. She hadn't thought so. Her gaze swung to Mr. Rickman, who looked sterner than ever. His jaw flexed and his gaze drilled into hers. "Terminate it with extreme prejudice," he said.

Even she knew that meant "kill."

"I've never done that," she said.

He jerked a nod, but from his attitude he expected her to learn how to do so.

They locked stares until Mrs. Flinton said, "Creede is a four-and-a-half-hour drive. If you leave now, you could reach it mid-afternoon, well before dark." Her chin set. "That's important. I want Caden protected, and they won't let me take him, and they won't come visit me as a family. My granddaughter and grandson-in-law have a motel in town, and they live on the premises. This is a busy time of year for them."

"Major hunting season's coming up," Zach said.

"Yes. And Michael also has a business for processing game. They make a good bit of money this time of year."

"And not so much during the winter," Clare said. "When the tourists are mostly gone."

"No. Many businesses close during the winter. But Michael and Jessica are stubborn about self-sufficiency, among other things."

"Self-sufficiency is important. Even for those who have family money or trust funds," Clare said.

"They love their life," Mrs. Flinton said.

Lucky them.

"And that's important." Mrs. Flinton managed a slight smile. "Loving your live and living each minute."

Rickman stretched his big body and stood and Zach rose a millisecond after his boss, still holding his coffee mug. "We'll get right on this," Zach said.

Clare got to her feet, too. "I need to go home and pack."

Mrs. Flinton pressed her hands together. "How long do you think it will take for you to . . . move this thing on?"

Destroy it, Enzo said.

"Destroy it," Clare muttered, tensing all over again. "I don't know. You know I have very limited experience."

"This ghost is probably subtly affecting the whole town, Clare, influencing people to more violence. More sensitive folks will have nightmares and hear . . . experience . . . things. Awful," Mrs. Flinton said.

Mr. Rickman rolled his hand. "Give me a shot at how long this will take, Clare."

"It shouldn't take more than"—she looked at Enzo—"two weeks."

The dog's forehead wrinkled but he didn't contradict her.

Clearing his throat, and looking out the front window, Mr. Rickman said, "There's a big tourist event, car show—Cruisin' the Canyon—Friday through Sunday in Creede." He rolled a shoulder. "I have a classic car, thought about attending. Gonna be a lot of tourists in the town this weekend . . . to be influenced by this monster, maybe in danger."

So soon! All the blood drained from Clare's face. She felt it going, along with her knees that wobbled, then gave out, so she plunked back down on the couch.

Zach lowered his coffee mug. "If a supernatural murderer is anything like a regular one and looking for a big score—" He shrugged.

"A lot of people to play with." Her lips had gone cold. "Maybe even deaths to feed him," she whispered.

This is not good, Enzo said, then steeled himself and gave a determined bark. *We are a TEAM, we will do this. We will stop the ghost and be HEROES!* He hopped up and down.

His cheer overcame her fear . . . for a few seconds.

"How soon can you leave?" Rickman asked. "Or do you want us to charter a flight, arrange a car?"

"I can do that." Mrs. Flinton's chin lifted. "Money can't buy everything, but it can make things a whole lot easier. And it sounds as if every hour might count."

Mr. Rickman grunted, looked at his highly engineered watch. "It will take a little time to set everything up, make all your travel arrangements."

"Creede has an airport?" Zach asked.

"Yeah," Tony Rickman said.

Zach narrowed his eyes. "How populous is the town?"

"About four hundred full-time residents," Mrs. Flinton said.

Angling his head at his boss, Zach said, "A private charter arriving and the people on it would be news for a small town." He looked at Mrs. Flinton. "News that would reach the ears of your granddaughter and her husband, would let them know we're coming and piss them off. Better if we went under-cover, at least at first while we get the lay of the land."

"You're right," Tony Rickman said. His mouth flattened. "Alamosa is about an hour-and-a-half drive from Creede. We can fly you into Alamosa and rent you a car there."

"Sounds good," Zach said.

Mr. Rickman turned on his heel. "I'll have my assistant set it up: the flight, the car, the stay at the motel. Hopefully they aren't booked for the weekend."

"I must finish this by Friday, the weekend at the latest," Clare said through cold lips. All of her was cold. Again. As usual. She'd had eight days to help her first ghost transi-tion . . . on. Then had helped her second in five days.

Yes. She'd kept track. Three and a half days to destroy a ghost-seer-eating ghost. The process of which, the whys and wherefores, the *hows* she knew nothing about.

"Clare, how soon can you leave?" Tony Rickman repeated.

She jerked from dread-filled thoughts. Blinking, she shrugged, looked at Zach. "An hour?"

He gave a quick negative shake of his head, a motion she thought Mr. Rickman and Mrs. Flinton missed. Since Zach didn't want to speak up, she trusted him and amended her answer. "Sorry, more like two hours."

"Right. We'll send a car to pick you up at your place in, say, two-and-a-half hours."

"All right."

Mr. Rickman's hand went to his inside suit jacket pocket and he pulled out a wallet and a platinum credit card, and offered it to Zach, who put both of his hands on the curved handle of his old-fashioned wooden cane. "Sorry, can't take that."

"It's a business card for you and your expenses," Rick-man bit off.

"So it has 'Rickman Security and Investigations' on it," Zach pointed out. "Which the family—what's their names?—would recognize. All the locals might."

"All right." The card went back into wallet and pocket. "The family is—"

"Jessica and Michael LuCette," Mrs. Flinton said as she rose and moved toward them with her walker. Now she appeared calmer, close to her old sprightliness. She angled her head at Tony for a kiss on the cheek. He bent and complied, put an arm around her thin shoulders and squeezed. "We'll handle this," he said in a grim tone, meeting Zach's gaze.

It occurred to Clare that that shared male look might mean Rickman would send out his security force. Zach had told her most of Rickman's employees were ex-military special operations kind of men. She wondered what they thought they could do about a spirit-eating ghost. She had no illusions whatsoever that *she* would be on the front line of this battle. A battle she didn't know how to fight, let alone win.

She drank down the rest of her tepid coffee.

Mrs. Flinton said, "Thank you, Clare. I have full faith that you can . . . destroy this evil revenant."

Great. Clare put her empty cup on the coffee table, stood, and kissed the woman's cheek. "I will do my best." She said it quietly, but it was a vow. Zach moved around her and kissed Mrs. Flinton, too. "We'll do our best and we'll save Caden."

"And Creede," Tony Rickman said, putting on his sunglasses. "My take on evil is that it doesn't like to limit itself to one person or one town or one valley, even."

Zach smiled and put his arm around Clare's shoulders. "Clare saves the world." He sounded completely confident she could do it.

Clare saves the world! Enzo echoed, wagging his tale and grinning, like he thought she could do that, too.

She thought her spirit would be torn from her, shredded, and eaten by a ghost.

THREE

WHEN MRS. FLINTON and Mr. Rickman left, the atmosphere of the apartment continued to buzz with tension. Though Zach appeared casual, and that might have fooled Mrs. Flinton, the second the door closed behind the others he strode to his bedroom and hauled out a suitcase. Clare followed him, but Enzo vanished.

Zach packed clothes for autumn and the fast-arriving mountain winter quickly and efficiently.

Since Clare didn't want to deal with all the dreadful questions in her head, she asked one of the least important. "Why do you need more time?" It appeared like he'd be done packing and ready to go in under a half hour.

"I need to see my mother." His mouth twisted. "Say good-bye to her if this is going to be such a dangerous mission."

Clare swallowed hard. "Of course. Do you want me to come with you?" They'd just visited Geneva in the mental health facility the night before—to discover more information about Zach's psychic abilities that had passed down through his mother.

Now Zach slanted Clare a sardonic look. "Yeah. Of course

I'd like you to come with me, but it's more efficient if you go pack. I think this is something I've got to do myself."

She shifted from foot to foot, swallowed, and took his hand. "I consider us a couple, Zach, an exclusive couple."

His brows lifted. "Yeah, we're a couple. A couple of what, I don't know, but an *exclusive* couple. We're in this together." He glanced away, rubbed the back of his neck.

Tilting her head, Clare spoke a thought that just surfaced. "Have you gone to her before when you've taken on dangerous cases?"

He winced. "Yeah." He withdrew his hand from Clare's and she reluctantly let him. Stretching his arms high, he worked his shoulders. Clare heard a couple of pops. "I don't like doing it because she always seems to know—" He stopped.

"A touch of precognition, like yours?" Clare asked.

"I guess." His brows remained lowered. "It's never good. If I brought you, and she thought you were in danger, too . . . I don't know what she'd do. She likes you and she remembered previously meeting you. That's a big deal. I've got a feeling it's not going to be one of her good days."

Straightening her spine, Clare said, "Since my cases haven't been . . . easy, I've made my will. It's the responsible thing to do. What about you?"

"God." Zach turned, stripped, and headed for the shower.

All thought drained from Clare's brain as she watched him. "God," she murmured herself.

Zach turned with irritation on his face, but she wasn't much looking at his expression. Yes, he remained lean from his wounding months ago, but the sheer sight of him had her tingling. She admired his frame, his sleek muscles slowly filling out.

Essentially male. Especially since his body reacted to her gaze, becoming erect. She wavered unsteadily on her feet, her breath catching, her breasts plumping, her own body responding to his. Hot, she was so hot! She whipped off her dress, flung off her bra and panties. Wetting her lips, she curled a finger. "Come on over here, Zach."

His eyes lit and he grinned, sauntered toward her. His limp did nothing but squeeze her heart, remind her that she was his first lover after his injury, and something special spun between them.

Something sizzling, needy . . . and more than passion.

As he drew close her head tilted back so she could see him better, wait for him . . . this once . . . soon she'd pounce on him and be wild . . . follow her gypsy blood and show him how she wanted him. How she wanted him to take her.

His right arm came around her waist, jerked her to him and, my God, they were skin to skin. Sensation ruled, the roughness of his lightly haired body rubbing against hers as she lifted her arms to clasp them around his neck. Her breasts rose, her nipples rasped from his chest, the feel of his arousal hot and hard, long and thick against her stomach, that part of him as smooth as she. Her blood pounded through her, so she thought nothing, only *experienced*. Only craved.

Her vision went blurry. She smelled his breath as his mouth touched hers, tasted him as he thrust his tongue through her lips, probed her mouth. She moaned with desire.

He bent her back and back, arching her, his body over hers, then he released her and she lay on the bed. She widened her eyes, staring. Now his flushed face showed wild triumph and *he* gazed at the apex of her thighs, her sex revealed to him, damp, needy.

Yanking a drawer open, he sheathed himself with protection, and she blinked, trying to draw in the sight of all of him, struggled through the flood of sensations to even speak, and could only find one word: his name. "Zach."

She raised her arms, formed the sound again. "Zach." This time a plea.

A chuckle ripped from him, a grin, then he grabbed her, positioned her, plunged into her, and the sunshine around her dimmed with the veil of red lust.

God, he felt good! Better than last night, than early this morning. The looming threat in the back of her mind making this joining incredible.

Now his expression became strained as he surged and withdrew, focused on her . . . himself . . . them. Sexual need clawed at her, demanding the spiraling, gasping climb, the arching of her own body for more, more, *more*. She whimpered each breath, clutched him, set her fingernails into his back, needing the thrust of his body, the withdrawal, the pounding back into her.

Yet her climax caught her by surprise, between one breath and the next, exploding through her, scattering her to the stars and the universe beyond, flashing brilliant colors behind her closed eyelids.

He shouted, lunged into her and stayed, then collapsed on her and they held each other.

She lay there, her mind spinning, her breath rasping. As her arms encircling him went limp, she trailed them down his heaving body, then let them lie on the bed.

After long minutes, and too soon, he rose from her. She managed to focus her eyes before he disappeared into the bathroom, saw the strong lines of his back, his muscular butt. Gorgeous man. Virile. More man than she'd ever had before, more than she'd have been able to handle before her gift had dropped into her. Not a man she'd have wanted before—too rough, too many shadows. He'd have scared her and challenged her, and she'd been happy in her rut.

Now she couldn't bear the thought of not knowing him. Her heart gave a massive thump as more of her mind cleared from the amazing sex and reminded her of the morning events and the deadly situation they'd become entangled in.

She could lose—not him, she hoped, never him. Lose her life, that would be more acceptable than losing him, and now she knew how very much she cared for him. More than sweet and sweaty passion, more than affection, slipping too easily into love.

An awful mewling sound came from her, thankfully covered from Zach's hearing by the pulsing of hard, noisy water streams.

Sitting up gingerly as she shoved the frightening thoughts from her brain so she could simply function, she stood and turned her mind back to the logical thread of conversation and the point she'd been trying to make before lust had swamped her. The accountant in her came to the front. She couldn't let this important conversation go.

Slowly she walked into the bathroom. She liked showers with Zach, and she *did* need one, but though their sexual interlude had been relatively quick, they had a deadline to meet.

The frosted glass of the enclosure revealed only the bronze color of his body and the shape of it. She took a wet maroon washcloth he'd left on the sink for her and cleaned up, figuring angles.

Zach shampooed, and the scent of tea tree oil wafted out. She wondered if that had been his choice, or if the bathroom had come stocked like the furnished apartment and liquor cabinet.

Finally deciding to be blunt, she cleared her throat and projected her voice. "Having a will is important."

He flinched but said nothing. She rinsed the washcloth, wrung it, and hung it on the towel rack, then tried initiating the discussion again. "Zach," she called. "A will?"

Without looking at her, he began scrubbing and her body took notice, so she turned her back away from the vision of him.

His voice raised over the pounding water. "My mother will get my disability and retirement funds. Not that she needs the money."

"Did you note her as your beneficiary?"

He grunted. "I don't recall. Probably."

"If not, your assets would be inherited by both your parents, and considering your mother is in a mental health facility, no doubt your father would receive them on her behalf."

"No. I don't want the General to have control of my money and dole it out to her."

"Who else would you like to manage your funds for her?" Clare asked.

"Goddammit to hell." The sound of water stopped abruptly.

"Distant cousins on Mom's side, I guess, as trustees for her. Though I haven't checked any of them out lately. Not for a couple of years." The door opened and she heard towel-rubbing. Then he walked around to face her and his blue green gaze lasered to her and latched on.

She raised her hands. "No. Absolutely not. Don't make me responsible for your mother." She bit her lower lip when he continued to stare. "What about Mr. Rickman?"

"I'd trust him with her life. He isn't a money man. You're a money woman."

"If you must," Clare said, "go to my old firm, Burgess, Sturgis, and Heaps."

He stared at her. "Seriously? They're named that?"

She gritted her teeth, loosened her jaw, then said, "It's an old, traditional firm. They are very well thought of in the financial community."

Zach smiled at her, a simple, sincere smile that made her heart squeeze in her chest. "They must be tops if they hired you."

"Thank you."

He flung the towel over the bar and strode from the bathroom.

Clare couldn't leave the thick cotton that way and folded and straightened it. When she entered his bedroom, he was dressing in nice slacks and a linen shirt.

She made the bed. It would be better to strip it and re-make it, but she didn't know where the extra sheets were and it was *his* bed, not hers, and time ticked down.

Zach went to a hidden wall safe and opened it, put a gun in his bag. Not the weapon he usually carried, which was on the table on his side of the bed, not even the second one that he called his clutch piece, but a third weapon. He swung the bag to the floor. "Take that with you, and I'll meet you at your place as soon as possible. Can I park my truck in your garage?"

"Of course." But she stared at the piece of luggage. "I don't have a concealed weapon permit. What if I get stopped by the police?"

"Clare, you never go over the speed limit," he said with condescension.

"I do, too!"

"What, by two miles an hour? And you live close to here, not more than fifteen minutes away."

"Oh, all right."

"Gotta go. C'mere." He'd finished dressing, including his ankle and leg brace, his holster at the small of his back, gun, and a sports jacket.

She walked into his embrace, felt his strong arms close around her, and felt safe. For all too short a time. Tilting her face for his kiss, she enjoyed the press of his lips on hers, his tongue sweeping along her lips, leaving his taste on them.

Though he'd been gone from the plains of Montana for a week, the tang of sage remained. A smell and taste she'd always associate with Zach. She became aware of his slight arousal, again, how satisfying, and her own inner muscles clenched. How soon she'd become accustomed to frequent, excellent sex.

He rubbed her back up and down with his big hands, caressing her, soothing her, murmuring in her ear. "We'll get through this."

Her stomach tightened, but she tried not to reveal her nerves. "I'm sure," she lied.

With a stare under lowered brows, he said, "Later." One side of his mouth lifted. "Use your new keys on the way out. The alarm code is one-two-four-three-five-seven-six."

"All right. An easy sequence to remember."

He picked up the curved-handled old-fashioned wooden cane and twirled it, smiled, and turned away. She saw his shoulders tense and he marched from the bedroom and out of the apartment. She wanted to go with him, but since he thought that would upset his mother, she wouldn't.

Though he was wrong if he thought to spare his mother pain, because he wouldn't. Geneva Slade had never gotten over the death of one son; Clare could only imagine how another dark loss might overwhelm her.

* * *

Enzo awaited her when she got home. He sat in the large entryway next to the stairs with cocked ears, though his cheerfulness subdued. His tail wagged a couple of times, but she heard no swish, just felt the standard chill radiating from her ghostly pet.

You are really going to do this, Clare? he asked.

She inhaled a quick breath, let it out choppily. "I am not going to let a boy be eaten by an evil ghost."

Her phantom dog rose and trotted up the stairs. *You will need the big knife, then. I will show it to you.*

"Knife!" For one brief instant, courage blazed inside of her. A weapon, she'd have a weapon! Then her stomach jolted and her throat closed again. She had no clue how to use a big knife.

But Zach would. If the knife was, say, a long dagger, it might be used as a sword. Zach used his cane as a weapon; he could teach her cane moves, couldn't he? She was sure he knew how to use a regular knife.

"Is the knife . . . supernatural?" she asked Enzo, following him up the stairs, turning right toward her bedroom. Perhaps if the weapon *was* supernatural, all she'd have to do was hold it and let it lead her to the evil ghost and dispatch it. Like the fairy tales Great-Aunt Sandra had told her as a small child. Fairy tales. Fiction.

Of course it wouldn't be that easy. And in fairy tales, the prince or princess had to overcome great obstacles. And if you weren't the *right* princess, you could die. Clare bit her lip.

Her gift passed through the family, too. And her successor to the awful thing was her niece, Dora, who wasn't quite as young as Caden LuCette. Like him, Dora was untrained and, unlike Caden, Dora *would* experience the Cermak's gift—deadly cold, the threat of insanity and death if she didn't accept her psychic power. Though her parents, Clare's brother and sister-in-law, would probably accept Dora and her gift.

Clare! Focus! You can't daydream! We can do this. The knife will help!

Clare shook herself to find she stood in the tiny office she used for her ghost seer cases. Atop the battered desk lay her old laptop from two years ago. She'd framed maps on the walls: a huge one of Denver on which she'd shaded the worst areas for ghosts of her time period; one of Colorado; and one of the United States. Some smaller maps were reproductions of old ones, Denver in 1887, 1890, 1893, 1903. Those last three years were later than the time period she was sensitive to, 1850–1900, and ghosts, the American West . . .

CLARE! You MUST pay attention. Enzo had hunkered down near Great-Aunt Sandra's large carved chest, a gorgeous piece of various woods fanning out on the front around a small half-circle that had always seemed like the sun and rays to Clare.

Enzo pointed his paw at the chest. His eyes appeared to be more liquid . . . and he hadn't been as much of a cheerleader this morning.

He seemed to have recognized the danger and mixed in a too-real determination with his optimism. That was *so* not a good sign. He'd always been a happy dog, even when she'd been going insane . . . even when she'd been dying because she refused her gift.

After drawing a big breath in through her nose, she went to the chest. Once she opened it, incense would waft from the box and more grief would come at the sight of the colorful cut-velvet scarves and caftans of her dead great-aunt.

She lifted the top, saw the richest of Sandra's "working" clothes, smelled incense and the spicy perfume that both Sandra and Clare herself loved, and tears backed behind her eyes.

Sandra had been a ghost seer like Clare. Unlike her, Sandra had had a psychic medium business. The portion of the fortune Sandra had inherited from the previous ghost seer, and the riches she'd made herself from her work, the gifts of the universe after a successful closed case—transitioned ghost—and investments, had gone to Clare, along with the family psychic gift.

On the whole, Clare would rather have remained a mid-level certified public accountant in a solid Denver firm.

Clare had packed up a closetful of such clothes and sent them to her sister-in-law in Williamsburg, Virginia, for costumes, until told to quit. Now Clare lifted the folded garments, feeling the soft brush of velvet against her palms, and she swallowed the tears. Her childhood had been so drama-ridden and crazy and always-on-the-road-to-*somewhere-else* with her parents, that when she'd set up her normal life, she hadn't visited "weird" Great-Aunt Sandra. Clare deeply regretted that.

Especially now that she'd be facing something that could eat her spirit and she had less than sixteen days of training. Carefully she stacked the clothes aside; these were heavier, beaded, more embroidered, better for blocking the unearthly cold generated by phantoms.

Snuffles came and she turned to see Enzo pawing at the clothes, sticking his whole head into them, and disturbing nothing. Clearing her throat, she stared at the pale wood of the bottom of the box and said, "The knife's in here?"

Enzo sat back and nodded, a slight excitement in his eyes. *It's hidden. Like a puzzle box, Clare. You know about puzzle boxes.*

She nodded. She'd liked them once, before her first ghost seer case. She knelt before the hope chest, leaned over, and swept her hands over the wood bottom, then the sides, but saw and felt nothing. No ghostly vibrations or emanations.

Sinking back on her heels, she stared at the front's fancy wood inlay, the carving around the lip, and at all four elegant corners of the chest. "Hmm."

A frigid nose ran up and down her arm, along with a smear of ice. Enzo. She glanced at him from the side of her eyes. His shadows had solidified a bit, settled into the multi-gray aspects of ghost Labrador instead of a flat gray. Maybe he was coming out of his funk, which would be great, because his humor really helped her since she had a naturally serious personality. *I could give you maybe a little hint.*

She raised her brows and smiled. "Maybe." Her hands went to the front of the chest first, the fan of many woods from the small light wood half-circle at the center of the bottom. Nothing except the slight feel of the seams. She pressed the "sun." Nothing.

Enzo sat beside her, radiating pleasure, his muzzle slightly open. Good. Letting her vision go slightly out of focus, she checked the bottom carving, found a slightly worn spot and worked her fingers around it, under it, pulled, and heard a click. Looking into the chest, she saw bundles of papers . . .

Love letters, Enzo said sadly. *Before I was with her.* Enzo had been Great-Aunt Sandra's dog when Clare had been a tween. She'd gotten the impression that he'd stayed with Sandra as a companion, but hadn't been her mentor or spirit guide. Apparently that had been John Dillinger, since, according to Sandra's journals, she had specialized in ghosts from 1905–1939.

Clare looked at the letters tied with a ribbon, set them aside. Older, dark brown leather colored books made her breath catch. "Journals?" she asked. "From Great-Great-Uncle Amos?" With a smile she turned to Enzo, and found the Other.

They might help. We have encouraged those of your blood to record what must be, the Other said, *but not many are in English, mostly Hungarian.*

"Oh."

The thin red one is of the weeks that the gift descended upon Orun, your great-great uncle Amos's older brother. Orun refused to BELIEVE and died from the cold. The Other's smile twitched Enzo's muzzle in a not-doglike scary way. *You remember that.*

"Since it was three weeks ago, yes, I recall that part of this inheritance."

The Other snorted. *Time grows short before people come. You must get the knife.*

"Is the knife supernatural?"

The Other's back rippled as if in a shrug. *You will see.*

But you cannot kill an evil ghost of your time period without it. There is a price for using it. He paused and actually clarified, *You may ask me when that time comes.*

When, not if. Clare's mouth dried.

And it must always be kept safe and hidden and with you, or Our agreement with you is broken. You would not like what happens if the bond is broken through your carelessness.

"Oh. Oh!" Rules, good. More pressure, terrible.

She was *cold*, more from the icy touch of fear she got when looking into his eerie eyes than the freezing waves emanating from him. A loud click sounded, the top of the chest opened, and an ivory silk bag about fifteen inches in length fell. Clare shot out her hands and caught it and the hidden panel of the chest sprang back shut. Probably the Other's doing.

She could feel a metal sheath in her hands and the hilt of the knife looked lumpy through the cloth. Even as she reached for the faded red tassels that tied the top of the silk cover, her doorbell rang.

Hide it, Clare! Enzo was back, staring at her with worried eyes. She ran to her bedroom walk-in closet, grabbed the piece of luggage she used for a week's trip, and shoved the knife in the main pocket. Good thing they'd fly by private plane. Looked like she'd have to book chartered flights in the future to dispatch evil ghosts.

Her door knocker pounded. Hurrying to the door of the small ghost seer office, she closed the room off, went to the hall intercom, fumbled, and then pressed "front door."

"Who's there?" she asked.

"It's me," said a woman's voice with an accent she'd never been able to place. "Desiree Rickman."

Tony Rickman's wife. What was she doing here?

"I consider you a friend, Clare."

Clare wasn't sure she felt the same way.

"I'd like to talk to you before you leave. I'm worried about you, Clare."

She wasn't the only one.

FOUR

CLARE WENT DOWN the stairs, grumbling. She hadn't changed clothes, hadn't taken a shower, and now she'd meet the most stunning woman she knew all disheveled and with the feel of dried sweat on her skin.

She arranged her face in an acceptable curious expression, looked through the peephole, saw the smaller woman and no one else, and opened the door.

Desiree Rickman gave her a smile loaded with charm. "What a fabulous house."

"I just moved in two weeks ago." It seemed like yesterday . . . or a year ago, so much had happened. Her gorgeous Tudor-style brick house built in the 1920s cost her more than she'd ever thought she'd pay for a place. She absolutely loved it. Stepping back, she said, "Come in."

"Thanks. I won't be here long. I just brought your plane and car rental papers."

"Oh." Clare led the way to the main living area with a tall and beautiful curved window made of many small panes, *the* main selling point for her . . . though she'd liked the bedroom balcony, the lovely backyard, the remodeled kitchen.

Desiree, a dazzling mixed-race woman, wore sunshades and moved in that prowling way that Clare began to understand belonged to professional operatives. The woman went toward the window. She was totally aware of her body and what she could do with it. Clare still had trouble with her beginning yoga lessons.

"This is wonderful. And we'll be able to see when Tony arrives."

"Your husband is coming? Wait, that's the wrong question. Mr. Rickman doesn't know you're here?"

Desiree winked. "No. I took the papers from his receptionist-assistant."

Clare just stared at her. "You people have my e-mail. Don't you think it would have been perfectly fine to send me the documents and I could download them to my tablet? Or, if necessary, print them out?"

With a chuckle, Desiree said, "You sound like Samantha, his assistant." Then Desiree sobered and the skin around her eyes tightened. "I heard there's trouble in Creede with Godmama Barbara's family."

As usual, Clare couldn't figure out how much to say to Desiree. Clare didn't even understand where the puzzle piece of Tony Rickman's wife fit into the whole picture of Rickman Security and Investigations. "Yes, there's trouble in Creede."

"I wanted to offer my help, in case you need me. Is your ghost dog around?"

Here I am, Desiree. Like most male beings, he fawned around her legs, but Desiree stayed focused on Clare.

Aww, she can't see me, or feel me, Enzo said.

"No, she can't," Clare said and decided Desiree could handle blunt. "I'm not sure how helpful you'd be if you can't sense ghosts."

Desiree went still and hard. "Are you discounting me because I see auras?"

A month ago Clare would dismiss anyone who hinted they had psychic powers. Today she simply said, "No." After a pause she added, "I'm resentful because Enzo, my phantom dog, says yours is a gift of life and living." Another pause. "And mine is a gift of the dead and death."

"Awww." Desiree moved quickly and hugged Clare. It felt good, comforting. The woman released her and said, "Point me to your dog so I can try to see him again." Clare just knew Desiree would persist in trying something forever. For a beautiful woman, she was a little goofy.

Clare gestured to Enzo who stood, head up, tongue hanging out in his grin.

Desiree squinted, then walked straight through him and back and shook her head. "Nope. No aura. No coldness. He *is* cold, isn't he, like all the literature says?"

"Yes. And I think your husband senses ghosts, at least he acted that way when Enzo and another one was in his office."

"Oh, that's rich!" Desiree zoomed in with another hug. All right, maybe Clare could get used to this. And she *did* need friends. Most of her other friends had been from work, and those had faded when she'd been going back and forth to settle her great-aunt's estate in Chicago. Then she'd inherited those tidy millions and decided someone else could use her good job. The ghost seer thing had hit . . . and she'd understood that her work friends wouldn't deal with it any better than she had, would think she was crazy if she tried to explain her new life.

"Thanks," Clare mumbled, patted the smaller woman on the back. Clare was five foot seven inches, and she thought Desiree might be five four.

Desiree retreated an arm's length. "I'm so glad we're friends."

"I am, too."

"But, Clare, honey, your aura is all squidgy."

"Squidgy," Clare repeated.

Frowning, Desiree scanned her. "Very tight to your body. Some muddiness in your colors, not as clear. Are you frightened?"

"I'm scared shitless a ghost will eat me and I'll become part of it and do terrible evil."

"That's a possibility?" Desiree asked.

"Yes. I don't know how long you've been able to see auras—"

"All my life."

"But I just came into my psychic powers twenty-two days and three hours ago." On the way to the airport in Chicago, after finishing probate on her great-aunt's estate, preparing that house for sale, and dividing the furniture and planning how it would be moved.

"Oh, dear. That's . . ." Desiree's mouth opened and closed, then she finally said, "Tough."

"Yes."

"I absolutely want you to call me if you need me."

Clare didn't know what the woman could do against a supernatural foe . . . if her psychic power could be used offensively as her body could.

"Thank you," Clare said.

"Tony's here!" Desiree nearly sang. She glided from the room toward the entry hall and the front door. Clare followed her. Desiree opened the door without a thought of security . . . probably because she believed she could handle anything out there. Clare joined her in the doorway.

A black Mercedes with dark tinted windows parked in Clare's driveway on the other side of her car, and it *was* Tony Rickman. She thought that he often ran after his wife, whom Zach called a loose cannon. The car door closed and Mr. Rickman walked around the vehicle. Clare couldn't read his feelings. He strode up to them. "Clare. Desiree, I thought I asked you not to come."

"Clare's my friend, Tony."

"Right, but she treats me like her boss."

"With respect," Clare said stiffly.

"Call me Tony."

Clare hesitated, then nodded. She still wasn't sure at all about working for him, even as a consultant.

He nodded back to her, then said, "We can bring the car around to take you to the airport sooner. One of my guys will be flying the plane."

The latter was rather interesting, but didn't Tony notice Clare wore the same thing she had earlier? "No," she said. "I haven't packed yet." She hadn't even *showered* yet.

"Where's Zach?" Tony asked.

"He's not here," Desiree said.

Clare wondered how the woman knew. Desiree smiled at her. "He'd have been down, protecting you from me. You don't need any protection from me."

"Of course not," Tony said drily. "Clare is not the sort to go on harebrained quests." He stared at Desiree, still expressionless, but like when she'd seen them together before, she thought they loved each other deeply.

"Where *is* Zach?" More demand than question.

Clare straightened her spine, stared into the lenses of Tony's dark glasses. "He's visiting his mother." The Rickmans were in the security business and had hired Zach, they'd have checked him out before offering him a job and discovered his mother was in a mental health facility in Boulder.

"Oh," said Desiree in a sad little voice.

"Oh," echoed Tony. His shoulders rolled as if releasing tension.

"Zach doesn't think the . . ." Clare struggled for a term ". . . leave taking . . . will go well. I'd rather you not be here when he returns. And I have a lot to do before then."

"Understood," Tony said, reaching out and curling his fingers around his wife's upper arm. "We won't impose. You got all the papers?"

"Yes."

"All right." Desiree smiled. "It should be a good week for the fall color, the drive from Alamosa isn't hard, and you should pack for winter, as well."

"I know."

"Have you ever been to Creede?" Desiree asked.

"No."

"We go there a couple of times a year." She elbowed her husband, who showed no indication that he'd felt her. "All work and no play makes this guy a grumpy man."

Fleetingly Clare wondered what he—they—did for play.

Desiree grinned. "We rock climb."

That was just crazy.

"All the restaurants and hotels should remain open through the end of the month."

"That's good."

"It is. More options."

Tony tugged at his wife, gently. "The car will be here in a while. You make sure you call, Clare, if you need any help."

She still didn't think there was anything he could do. "I will."

Before they left, Desiree planted herself in front of Clare, the woman's expression turning serious, perhaps even deadly. "I want you to call me every day," she stated, slipped a card from her pocket. "My numbers are here."

Clare tried a smile and took the card. "I'm hoping it will be only four days."

Desiree nodded. "I understand you want to send the ghost on before Friday and the beginning of the Cruisin' the Canyon event." Desiree shrugged. "But who knows how long it might take? We all know, though, that plans turn to shit."

"We haven't done much planning," Clare grumbled, disliking that part. It was pretty much find the ghost and kill it somehow, all too vague.

Enzo appeared, sitting and panting beside her. *I am sorry that she is not coming with us. She might maybe be able to help.*

Interesting the phantom dog might think so, but Clare wouldn't put anyone she liked in the way of an evil ghost, especially if they could only "maybe be able" to help. She was torn as to whether she wanted Zach with her. Well, she definitely wanted Zach with her, but didn't want him hurt at *all.*

Desiree still watched Clare with concern. "You take care." She held out a hand.

Clare took it, caught the slight unfocus of Desiree's eyes.

No doubt she scanned Clare's aura again. The other woman nodded, appearing more satisfied than she had before. But this was a female operative, who'd faced death—probably often. Clare set her shoulders. She'd faced death, too, twice, in each of her previous cases. Of course, only death had threatened, not some spirit-sucking-evil-turn-you-evil-too thing. She swallowed.

"One last item," Tony Rickman said. He tipped his sunglasses down, stared at Clare. "You know Creede is the only town in Mineral County, so it's the county seat. If the ghost manages to eliminate Creede . . ."

"But no pressure." Clare raised her hands palms up.

Tony barked a laugh, slid his glasses back on. "You'll do, Clare Cermak."

Desiree hugged Clare. "Call me if you need me."

The couple turned and walked back to the Mercedes hand in hand and Clare's heart twinged at the thought she might never see them again.

Clare had showered, tidied up the house, prepared it for her being away, and packed before Zach arrived, looking tense. He bussed her lips, glanced at his watch, and said, "The car will be here shortly, are you ready? Get any time to research Creede?"

Since he seemed to want to avoid talking about his mother, Clare said nothing, but she took his wrists, opened them wide, and stepped up to him, hugging him. Yes, his muscular body thrummed with tension. He grunted and air escaped him and his arms came around her, holding her gently. "I'm not fragile," she murmured into the top of his chest. Not like his mother.

His hand slid over her head. "No, you aren't."

She looked up at him. "I'm actually very strong."

"I know it." He dropped his head, sniffed at her. "You smell great."

"I'm clean."

"And you're wearing that great spicy, exotic, woodsy-whatever perfume we like."

"Yes. And no to your earlier question, I had no time to research Creede."

"Right. Got a beer?"

"Absolutely. Do you think they serve food and drink on the plane?"

"Probably. I had a good breakfast, did you eat?"

"Not much." She patted her tote. "I have granola bars in here."

"That's going to be sufficient for you, seriously?"

"No, but I just can't eat yet, I'm too wired."

He set a hand on her face. "You have to fuel yourself." He blinked, then slid his hand down her torso. "How are your ribs?"

"Okay. Still hurting from that fall four days ago."

"Dammit!" He pulled away from her, paced the entry hall and stalked to the kitchen. "I don't like this. Not one little bit. If it was anyone except Mrs. Flinton—"

"We'd still be on our way. Neither of us is going to ignore danger to a child."

"No."

A car horn came from the front. Zach scowled. "They're early."

Clare managed to twitch her lips upward. "The sooner we go, the sooner it's done."

Zach just swore under his breath.

The private plane was amazing. Small and beautiful inside and out. Clare had no problem believing the pilot was ex-military; all his movements looked sharp and efficient. He told them the total flight would take about an hour, that there was food, beer, and wine in a cooler, that Wi-Fi was available for the flight, gave them a two-fingered salute and took their luggage to stow.

Clare sat in the beige leather seat behind the table and brought out one of her great-aunt Sandra's blue journals that should discuss rules of being a ghost seer in it.

Zach looked at the food and chose a large submarine sandwich, but only sighed at the beer and took a cola instead. "I'll be driving."

Clare's stomach rumbled. "What kind of sandwiches are in there?"

"Another bacon avocado like mine, an everything, tuna salad, chicken salad—"

"I'll have the chicken salad and some fizzy water."

"Gotcha."

They ate in silence, Zach cleaned up and looked out the window and brooded, and Clare pulled out her tablet, set it on the table, and went online to an encyclopedia site for a brief overview. "Gee, Creede reads like a who's who of famous people: Bat Masterson, Soapy Smith, Poker Alice . . ."

"Huh." Zach stopped staring out the window—she didn't think he was paying attention to the view—and turned to look at her. "Soapy Smith, conman of the West." He shook his head. "The ghost can't be him, he was killed in Alaska, I think. Shot. Ran a gang, though, as I recall, there and in Denver, so he probably ran one in Creede, too." Zach frowned. "Your cases have been about notorious or legendary men." He reached out and took her hand. "And either you or Enzo once mentioned that the ghost would be a mass of 'negativity.' Who's the most notorious guy in Creede, or what's the most negative thing that happened?"

"Good point." Clare scrolled through the article then simply stopped because her hand shook so hard.

Zach said, "What? Or who?"

"Robert Ford was shot, murdered in Creede, June 8, 1892," she recited the info seared before her eyes. "Three days after a terrible fire."

"Fire, major negativity. How many died in the fire?" asked Zach.

"I don't know. Then murder."

Zach said, "The name Robert Ford sounds familiar but I can't place it."

"The article said Robert Ford was the member of the

Jesse James gang who shot Jesse James. He and his brother. His brother committed suicide."

"Hell. Murder. Suicide. Murder. What happened to the guy who killed Ford?"

Clare fumbled her phone and the website back on, scanned it. "He was sent to prison here in Colorado, but when he got out, he moved to Oklahoma City. There he got in a street fight with a policeman and was shot, but that event is out of my time range."

Zach shook his head. "Nothing but murder and suicide in this whole situation."

"The timing's there, but it's long. Ford killed Jesse James ten years before he ended up in Creede. Ford's brother committed suicide three years after the murder of James, seven years before Ford's death. The death of Ford's killer is out of my ghost seeing time period, in 1904."

"Still a helluva string of events stretching back and forward."

"Yes."

"We still need more info," Zach stated.

I suppose I must help you a little more, the Other said disapprovingly.

FIVE

SINCE ZACH STIFFENED in the luxurious chair beside her, Clare knew he heard the Other, too. Whether the spirit's voice echoed hollowly in his mind like it did hers, she didn't know.

"Thank you," she said aloud and humbly, trying to *feel* humble and squashing all irritation. The Other could read her emotions easily.

In the form of Enzo, the Other stalked up and down the short aisle, appearing more interested in its surroundings than Clare or the project.

It snapped its head toward Clare in no move a living dog would make, pierced her with its icy gaze. The phantom dog nostrils widened as if she smelled bad. *Listen closely. You must discover the ghost's core identity and address it by name, so that you can destroy it. You must find the trigger that caused the core identity to reach critical mass and begin to devour other phantoms.*

"Core identity?" Zach asked.

But the Other turned to mist and dissipated, not even leaving Enzo.

"Well, that was weird," Zach said.

Clare sighed. "Yes. Short and not so sweet, but at least we have goals."

"Tell me about this core identity business."

She tapped the blue journal in front of her, one of her great-aunt Sandra's. She'd spent time flipping through the pages of loopy penmanship to find a half-page story about an evil ghost Sandra had easily dispatched with the knife in a couple of hours. Clare reckoned she wouldn't be so lucky.

"I'm still not sure about the nature of ghosts," she said slowly. "How much of the real spirit of deceased people is really there."

Zach grunted. "The previous ones you helped, Jack Slade and J. Dawson Hidgepath, seemed like real people."

"Yes, but there are also fragments." She waved a hand. "That might not matter. Anyway, from what I understand, a powerful evil ghost is a magnet of negativity, perhaps a challenged individual—"

"No political correctness crap," Zach interrupted. "I believe there are bad people, evil people."

Clare lifted her chin. "There are also confused people who make bad choices."

"And some of those bad choices can make them into vile folks, irredeemable, who like doing horrible things to good people."

She swallowed at that thought—because Zach had sure seen a lot more of such people than she.

Clare said, "All right. I agree." Like all the other conversations this morning, this wasn't a discussion she cared to have. "Whether the person was evil or not, sometimes the worst of a person can linger, and the ghost can turn bad—"

"I remember that was a concern. Will it always be a concern?"

"I think so. Because the . . . limbo . . . that ghosts survive in is awful."

"Got it. Keep going."

"The original ghost or negative shade—"

Zach snorted.

"—acts as a magnet for all sorts of other stuff and gets bigger and bigger—"

"Like a wad of flypaper."

"I suppose so."

"All right. I think I got it. So there will be a bunch of ghosts, probably from your time period, and we'll have to figure out who was the first."

"Or just one ghost with layers, but we must discover his name."

"Huh. As for the trigger, Caden gave it to us."

"He did?"

"He mentioned a murder." Zach shook his head. "But I don't think it could be that."

"Why not?"

"Creede has been around for at least a century, right? No matter how small and sleepy a town is, it probably had a murder in all that time—at least in the general area of the ghost."

"I suppose." She thought. "Caden said, 'a murder-suicide.'"

"Yeah, I recall, but I'm thinking that might not be enough to trigger something that eats little boys, either."

"No?"

"People kill, people commit suicide. Why? What's the motive? I bet if we can put a finger on the exact motivation for a murder-suicide, say the 'core reason' for the deaths, the basic, uh, sin—though I don't believe in sin—we might get somewhere. Say, like the seven deadly sins: greed, anger, pride, lust, envy, sloth, and gluttony."

"I don't think I've ever heard of a person killing due to gluttony," Clare said.

"Maybe not."

"And that's an interesting list, or rather, how you listed the sins, the self-indulgences, the emotions that control you and that you don't control."

"Yes, it's a matter of control, self-control and discipline," Zach agreed.

"So you listed them, how? The ones you think could be the basis of murder or suicide?"

"Yeah, I guess I must have."

"Uh-huh. And how would you order that list for your own weaknesses?"

"If I'm going to bare my soul, woman, I want you on my lap." He unfastened her seat belt and lifted her to sit on his thighs. Nice.

"And I expect the listing to be mutual."

She nodded. "That's only fair."

"So . . . anger first. Still pretty angry about losing my career. Pride. I admit I'm proud."

"Don't like to ask for help," she murmured. That had been the cause of a bump in their relationship the night before.

"I suppose," he said. "Envy that others are doing what I can't anymore."

"Reasonable." She patted his chest.

"Lust, greed, sloth, and gluttony," he ended.

"You've managed your lust well." She kissed him and he opened his mouth under the brief press of her lips, his tongue dampened her own lips, and, yes, she felt lust uncurl inside her.

He drew back and said, "Now, you."

"Well, I want to say that I haven't seen any sloth or gluttony in your makeup."

"Sloth is a big deal for you." He stroked her hair.

"Yes, I think so. Or refusing to be responsible, or putting self-gratification over every other thing, because my parents do that. See the world, experience whatever piques them, move on a whim."

"And drag their children along when they do that."

"Not anymore," Clare said.

"Your list, Clare? Your weaknesses?"

"I'm sure you could guess," she said primly.

"Probably as well as you would have guessed mine."

"Probably."

She said, "All right. Hmm. Envy first, for the reason you gave. I no longer have my career, my life as I shaped it. Pride, lust, anger, greed, gluttony, sloth."

"I haven't seen you be gluttonous."

"You haven't seen me with a bag of chips and any kind of dip, salsa, guacamole, hummus, chutney, soft cheese—"

"I get the picture."

"Chips do not last long in my house."

His arms slipped under her thighs and he lifted her. "Nope, I'm not feeling the gluttony." He looked over at the cooler. "There were chips in there."

She salivated. "Really, what kind?"

"Um, barbeque, I think."

"I don't care for flavored chips. I think even more chemicals are coursing through your body than usual with them." She paused. "Though I will eat them in a pinch."

He squeezed her, whispered in her ear. "Then we'll have to use our mutual lust to work off your gluttony."

She laughed and relaxed, almost feeling normal. "Sounds good to me."

In Alamosa they picked up the rental truck that Rickman had arranged, Zach changed clothes into something more casual, and they were on their way. Like most of the trips they'd taken together, they didn't talk much, and Clare let Zach sink into his preferred driving mind zone.

Within a few minutes of passing the foothills of the Rio Grande Valley, they drove into winter. First rain splattered against the windshield, then as they rose in elevation the precipitation turned to misty snow. No one else seemed to be moving in the entire world.

"The valley and the river are a whole lot wider than I thought," Clare said.

Zach smiled. "Well, it *is* the Rio Grande. You're just used to creeks and close canyon walls on both sides like those in the Front Range near Denver."

She shifted in her seat, tired of sitting. "That's true, but the rock-faces look a lot alike." Tall and jagged on her right. And they passed one of the standard "Falling Rock" signs.

Zach slammed on the brakes. The seat belt grabbed Clare as they fishtailed, then slowed to a crawl.

"What?" she asked.

"You don't see them." Now Zach's tones flattened.

"No." She wet her lips. "Crows? The ones only you see that are a prophecy? The psychic trait from your grand-mother?"

"Yeah. Four. According to the Counting Crows Rhyme I was taught as a child and that matches the predictions, four is for death."

"Oh. Not good. You're sure?"

His hands ran up and down the wheel, then the car picked up speed. "Just before I met you, when I first came to Colo-rado from Montana, I saw four crows."

"Death followed?" Clare asked in a small voice.

"Yeah."

She let out a shaky breath. "I'm sorry."

"So am I." He paused a minute, then she felt his glance. "You never looked me or my shooting in Montana up on the Internet, did you?"

"No. You told me about it, why should I?"

Shaking his head, he said, "Every other woman I was in-volved with would have."

Her stomach sank.

"Every other woman would have wanted to see the whole damn thing, followed the whole story—that my new partner and I pulled over an ex-cop from Plainsview City." His lips thinned. "My partner wasn't like you, she was sloppy."

Clare wasn't sure why he'd changed the subject, but stayed quiet. Surely that last bit was complimentary. She didn't tend to be sloppy.

"My partner was a local, she knew the guy and his fam-ily, she went up to him and asked him to step out and he did. She was offering to drive him home when I came up. I'da let him in our vehicle, let her drive him home. But she hadn't checked him for weapons. I didn't either." Zach stretched his shoulders. "The guy had a gun and I saw it and we scuffled and he shot me. An investigative television reporter from

Billings was there for another story, close enough to hear the shot, apparently." Zach's twitch of the lips upward wasn't a smile. "It was a circus. I was shot, the sheriff's department's training and processes and practices were scrutinized. Some of the guys I worked with had never liked me and this made it worse." Another shrug. "So it goes."

Clare put her hand on his steel-like thigh. "I'm sorry," she repeated. Then added, "We all make mistakes."

His smile turned sardonic. "Truth." He exhaled, long, but not a sigh. "I was on my way out of Montana when my partner came to apologize. She seemed to have to do that like every other week. She was with her new partner, one of the guys who didn't like me." Zach's gaze cut to Clare again. "As backup. Now *that* woman was dependent. Always needed backup."

Clare got an awful feeling she knew why this story had come up at this time. "Was?"

"Yeah. I saw four crows as they left."

"Four for death."

"Yeah. The sheriff called me—he's a stand-up guy— apparently I was the last one to see them before their car crashed in a bad thunderstorm."

"Oh." She hadn't heard all the details before.

Nicer to look at Zach than the wet asphalt, the snow coming down, though they were still in the valley. If *their* car went off the road, they had a couple of yards before they ran into the rock cliff on their right, and even longer to the drop-off to the river on their left.

"So the Crow Rhyme prediction was right in that instance, and you anticipate it being correct now."

Zach made a sound, then cleared his throat and said, "You—and Mrs. Flinton and, hell, my own Gram when I was a kid—seem to think I have a thing."

"A psychic power of precognition."

"I know that word, too."

"Well, if your precognition and the Counting Crows Rhyme is true, we've been warned. We're ready, and we'll see if that prophecy is immutable," Clare said.

"Uh-huh." Zach picked up the speed.

A few minutes later Clare looked at the nav and un-clenched her fists. "We're coming up to Wagon Wheel Gap."

"Ghosts from your time period?"

"Yes. It's been blessedly ghost free so far."

Zach sped up further. "No one's on the road."

"I noticed. Absolutely no rush hour traffic."

"That's a good thing, for sure."

They passed a few houses, and Clare looked left beyond Zach to the wide valley and dimly sensed there could be an apparition or two at a couple of tourist ranches they passed by. To their right was the canyon wall and another "Falling Rock" sign.

Soon they turned off the main highway to Creede and Clare shifted in her seat. "The valley narrows from here. There was a series of towns, down around here was Ame-thyst and South Creede, then Jimtown or Gintown, which is the current business district, then up the canyon was String-town and old Creede itself at the convergence of East and West Willow Creeks—"

"—where Caden said there used to be a scary feeling," Zach added, breaking into her factual delivery. So she liked facts. Facts were logical. They didn't change. Well, they shouldn't change, though she'd learned historical facts were more mushy than others. Definitely more amorphous than nice, clean bookkeeping figures.

"Yes," she agreed. The GPS beeped and told them their destination, the LuCettes' motel, was coming up on the right.

"Let's head clear through the town to the former scary place," Zach suggested.

Clare's teeth clenched and she had to loosen her jaw before asking, "Why?"

"Best to see the layout of the town, what's here and now."

In a stifled voice, Clare said, "All right. I've already programmed it into the system." She changed the desti-nation.

He reached out with his right hand and slipped his fingers

behind her head, massaged the knotted muscles of her neck. "Easy, Clare. How's the ghost situation?"

She tried to relax so his fingers would do a better job, and glanced around. "It's . . . it's okay." She frowned. "I don't sense anything."

"Not even Enzo?"

"No, he hasn't been with us since we got in the car."

"Though he got in the car, too."

She shook her head, liked the tug of some of her hair caught on his fingers. "I still don't know much about how ghosts travel, especially Enzo."

"We might need to find out how fast ghosts travel. Especially how fast the evil phantom might get to the motel with Caden from the confluence of the Willow creeks," Zach said, slowing at the stop sign. He angled his chin at a sign in front of them. "Historic Creede, here we go." He took a right.

Clare tensed, and he tugged her hair. "I'm driving, you don't have to deal with ghosts pressing around the car, and the minute they get too bad, we'll turn around."

She pulled her head away from his fingers and he put both hands on the wheel. "I don't know how I'm going to do this, get rid of a threatening ghost," she whispered hoarsely. "I don't know nearly enough."

"But you packed some of your great-aunt Sandra's journals."

"Yes, one where she destroyed a ghost that drove people mad." Clare swallowed. "We know such ghosts have that negative core."

"Probably was murdered, committed suicide, or was a bad dude in life," Zach said.

She found her hand twisting a strand of her hair. She'd never done that under pressure as an accountant. Not even at eleven fifty-five p.m. on April fifteenth.

"I'm extrapolating from what Enzo told me, getting it straight in my mind."

Zach's lips formed a half smile. "Getting the rules down, so we can plan."

"I sure hope so."

"We'll figure the whole thing out," he said. His voice was steady, but his jaw flexed as if he had doubts, too. "There, straight ahead, see the cliffs that all the postcards show? We're coming up on the business district, historic Creede."

He drove slowly, and Clare stared; more, she extended all her senses and felt . . . nothing. Rolling down the window, she let in the snow-fresh air. It had melted away and left wet streets. She stuck her head nearly out the window.

"What," asked Zach.

She wet her lips. "Nothing. I *feel* nothing. No ghosts at all. No lingering shadows or shades of emotions from ghosts that have left, no ghosts out of my time period . . ."

Zach's hands flexed on the wheel. "That's not good."

"No."

Uh-oh, said Enzo, his head resting on Clare's right shoulder.

SIX

ENZO CONTINUED, *THERE ARE no ghosts. It's eaten ALL OF THEM!* He howled, a long and lonely, despairing howl that raised the hair on the back of her neck. Zach's shoulders hunched.

I AM THE OOOOONLY GHOST IN TOWN!

"Stop it," Zach snapped. "You don't want to attract its attention."

Enzo leapt through the seat and Clare—no mistaking when a ghost passed through her—and huddled in the passenger seat well, draped all over Clare's feet and lower legs and her tote bag. Her feet chilled and even the outside air seemed warmer. She rolled the window up and braced herself to pet her ghost dog.

When she touched a ghost, the chill was worse—at least double, maybe even quadruple—she didn't know the multiplier. Cold, cold, cold. When she'd helped previous ghosts on she'd had to initiate contact, merge with them, and it had been a race to send them on before the cold froze her heart.

She leaned forward and petted Enzo's head. He nuzzled her palm and licked her hand. "I only need you to answer some questions, then you can return to Denver before dark, if you like."

I am your companion. I will stay with you.

"We'll protect you," Zach said.

We will protect each other, Enzo replied staunchly.

With a last pat on her phantom Lab's head, Clare withdrew her numbed fingers and turned to Zach. "You hear Enzo well, then?"

"Yeah."

He didn't seem to want to talk about that, either, so Clare let it lie. She met her dog's big eyes. "We'll protect each other," she agreed.

His tail stirred chill air in the car. *Yes, you will kill the big, bad ghost with the big knife!*

Zach's gaze cut to her. "Knife?"

She cleared her voice. "I've been meaning to tell you about that."

"Big knife." Now he smiled.

"I'm also hoping that you'll help me with defensive moves or something."

His smile stopped and his expression turned grim. "A knife. For killing evil ghosts, right, Enzo?"

Yesss. A hiss that went outside the range of her mental hearing and hurt her head.

"Where'd this knife come from?" Zach asked.

"I didn't know I had it," Clare said. "It was in a secret compartment in Great-Aunt Sandra's work chest. The Other showed me how to find it. I haven't looked at it yet."

It is a very powerful weapon, Enzo assured.

"The Other, huh. He say anything else?"

In a small voice, Clare replied, "Only that there was a price to pay to use it."

Zach growled, "Of course there is." She heard a definite inhale and exhale from him, then he continued matter-of-factly, "There's always a price to be paid for killing."

Just that told her that he'd killed, probably in the line of duty when he was a peace officer. "I'm sure."

"The confluence was where Caden said the murder-suicide was. Huh."

"What?"

"Most murder-suicides are usually in the home. Personal. Private. Intimate."

"Oh."

"Sharp kid, he's given us solid background to work with."

"Yes, that's a help."

They got into the canyon proper and Zach's breath caught at the same time hers did at the striking rock formations.

"Amazing," Zach said.

"Yes. Incredible rocks and gorgeous views, even more so with the aspen turning gold."

They drove past the firehouse built into the side of a hill, the mining museum, and the community center—also underground—passed ponds on their right where Willow Creek was, then bushes masked the running water. The asphalt road gave way to packed dirt with some sharp rocks and Zach slowed, taking more care.

"This was Stringtown," Clare said. "It was up against the canyon walls, though I think the stream moved some. There was both a fire and a flood in 1892, the year of Robert Ford's death, and the fire took out most of Jimtown."

"Jimtown?"

"Jimtown or Gintown."

"I'd suspect the latter was the first name, then it slid into respectability."

"Probably. We're heading for the Bachelor Historic Driving Loop. It starts where the creeks join."

"Lots of history. Still no ghosts?"

"No, and it's creeping me out." Because there should be plenty in such a mining town. How soon she'd become accustomed to catching sight of shadows from the corners of her eyes.

Ahead of them the road split. On the right above the confluence of the streams, it became a large parking area before snaking up another canyon. On the left, it narrowed and headed around a rocky cliff.

"This is it," Clare said at the same time the nav did. She turned it off. The roads were sparse enough that they wouldn't be needing it.

Zach pulled into the lot where the point of the cliff twisted into a spar, thrusting into the sky. He parked near the three covered tourist information billboards, farther away from the triangle of land piled with rocks that dropped off into the junction of the streams. Where Caden had said the scary spot had been.

Zach got out and so did Clare. Drawing in a big breath of cool and misty air that had nothing to do with ghosts and everything to do with oncoming winter, Clare stretched. Naturally, she'd gravitate to the billboards, but she set her shoulders and followed Zach toward the point of land in a Y with the arms embracing them. Mid-sized sharp boulders were stacked near the drop-off, no doubt in an endeavor to keep people from standing at the very edge and falling into the shallow but tumbling stream.

Bushes mostly concealed East Willow Creek, the one against the canyon wall.

"Feel anything?" Zach asked, swinging his cane a little like he might be dowsing, sensing energies or something.

"Do you?" she shot back.

His smile was quick, sincere, lethal. "I asked you first."

So she gingerly walked around, closing her eyes now and again.

"Don't do that," Zach said roughly. "Not when I'm here to help you." He took her arm and began to walk her around and she kept her eyelids shut. "Stop. Here." She scowled. "Just the faintest tingle."

He let go of her and when she opened her eyes he was several feet ahead of her and squatting. They were behind the billboards. "Look here," Zach said. "No grass here and there should be. Patch of bare ground, probably a lot of trampling went on."

Clare's stomach dipped and her throat tightened. "You think that's where the murder-suicide took place."

"That's right." He stood and walked back up to her. "Let's look at this outcropping." So they did. Straight on it blended against the rest of the cliff; from the east side it wasn't too imposing, just part of the cliff. And when Clare looked at it at one particular angle, when it was framed between two other jutting rocks, it appeared to be a triangular witch's hat.

"If I were an evil ghost, I'd hang out here."

She answered through cold lips. "If you were stationary. From what Caden says, it's not stationary."

Zach's brows raised. "It isn't here right now?"

"No."

"Damn good. I don't want you confronting it until we know more."

"Thanks."

At that moment a police siren screamed for several seconds, then cut off. Zach's head had jerked up, his nostrils flared. "Another unit has joined a previous one." He turned away from the east entrance to the Bachelor Historic Tour, angled his chin. "It's up the other road. Not too far. What's up there?"

Clare shook her head. "The other end of the loop. Some famous mines."

"Let's go." He waved toward the car door, but didn't take her arm. Keeping his gun hand free.

"Are you sure—"

Without glancing at her, he said, "I'm sure that if there's been a death that the damned Counting Crows Rhyme predicted, I want to know about it. I want that relief. God help me, I hope it's already happened."

"Oh. Yes." Clare swallowed and got back in the car.

They hadn't gone more than a half mile before Zach stopped where two silver full-sized trucks blocked the road. Definitely a death scene. He could feel it in the strained atmosphere even inside his cab.

A sheriff's deputy glanced at them and began to walk

toward them. Zach swung out of the truck and matched the deputy in gait and attitude. The man relaxed, then frowned a little at Zach's cane.

"The road is closed," the younger man said.

"I can see that. Just curious." He scanned the area, couldn't see much, but the setup had him shaking his head. "Looks like you have your work cut out for you."

The guy grunted. Zach handed him his card—one of his cards from his former life, hoping that it would prompt the man to talk. "I retired a month ago."

"Zach Slade from Montana, eh?"

"Yes." He offered his hand.

"I'm Johnny Linscomb." He shook Zach's hand.

"What's up?" Zach asked.

Linscomb removed his hat and ran his hand over his buzz cut. "Terrible accident."

"Accident?"

"Yeah. Falling rock. Happens. Plenty sharp." He looked at the cliff and Zach followed his gaze, then around the road. Yes, many shards of rock splinters.

"Helluva thing." The deputy shook his head. "Hit one of the guys in the head . . . spike to the brain. The other died of a fragment straight through the carotid artery, God. Freak accident. Really weird. What are the odds?"

Clare might know them, but Zach sure didn't. He shook his head along with Deputy Linscomb. "Most I've ever seen rockfall kill is when a boulder hits a car."

"Weird." The deputy liked the word.

Strange, unexplained deaths while an evil ghost was on the loose? Zach didn't believe in this coincidence. "When did it happen?" he asked. He had to know if the damn Counting Crows Rhyme still had good radar.

"Not too long ago, an hour, maybe. They were found quickly. We aren't that slow around here."

"So," Zach leaned a little on his cane, trying to frame the words he wanted to say. Something had triggered the evil ghost; could this incident be tied in with all the other weird woo-woo? Negativity seemed to be the snag. "Are they upstanding members of the community who'll be missed?"

The deputy looked startled. "Funny you should say that. They're from out of state and were poachers."

"Poachers?"

"Yeah, they had a small game hunting license, for bobcat— or rather the owner of the group license did. He's not here. We called him and he's on his way. Apparently these two left on their own, said they were going to view the mining museum or something. Not hunting season yet." The man's lips thinned. "They got a lynx, a protected Canada lynx." He spit out the words. "Not a bobcat."

Zach blinked. "Lynxes have long ear tufts and bigger paws than bobcats."

Linscomb slanted him a look. "That's right. You know that. *I* know that. Did these dim bulbs? Dunno. But they weren't on the up-and-up, that's for sure."

Shaking his head, Zach said, "Tough job. Sorry you have to do it."

"That's the work." His gaze went to Zach's cane, then away as a man walked with even more authority toward them. "Can I help you?" he asked in a peremptory tone.

Zach toughened his own stance into one that said he'd been on the job. The guy's eyes narrowed, he dipped his head. He was a couple of inches taller than Zach and thinner and younger. "Or do you think you can help me." Not a question.

Zach figured talking about an evil ghost would get him nowhere. "Sorry to interrupt your work, Sheriff," Zach said, offering his hand. "Zach Slade, in town for a while."

"Mason Pais. You'll be here how long?" The man's grip was firm, the shake was short. His fingers felt a little cool.

Zach didn't say he'd be there as long as it took. "A week maybe."

"Enjoy Creede," the sheriff said, dismissing him.

"Thanks, I will. I'll leave you to it. My lady and I can check out the Bachelor Loop tomorrow."

"Have a good stay," Linscomb added.

"We'll do that." He gave them a half-salute, and walked back to Clare, swinging into the old cop stride, no matter that it tired his leg.

He figured either Linscomb or Pais would check him out, maybe before he and Clare got to the LuCettes.

Zach sure as hell hoped he didn't see any more sets of four crows, but he doubted that hope would come true.

He told Clare briefly what had happened, but made it evident that he wanted to think about the situation and discuss it later. He got the impression that she did, too. He reversed to the last large turnaround spot, then drove back into town.

The LuCettes' motel was a medium-sized U-shaped building of dark wood that had been treated to withstand the mountain elements. What looked to be a small swimming pool behind a fenced area had been covered for the season. A boy sat swinging in a little playground, watching their car as they pulled into the sparsely populated parking lot.

Zach heard Clare catch her breath. "Caden."

"Looks like."

SEVEN

ZACH PARKED AND they exited the car. He took the time to stretch the kinks out. The boy stopped swinging and came to the edge of the grass. He squinted at Clare, glanced at Zach sideways. Without looking at the kid, Zach bent down and massaged his left calf and ankle, adjusted the brace a little. When he straightened, the boy was staring at Clare and taking small steps toward her. Definitely Caden. Cute kid with something of Mrs. Flinton's bone structure he'd have to grow into.

Clare said, "Mrs. Flinton sent me."

Caden bulleted into her, hugging her tight. Clare's hands fluttered, she held the boy for a moment, then crouched.

"Gram sent you. She *did*! And you're like me, aren't you?"

"I'm a ghost seer," Clare said so quietly that Zach could barely hear her. "And, yes, I'm here to help you." Though she put force into the words, Zach caught the edge of doubt, hoped the kid didn't.

Caden gulped. "You won't let it come after me? Won't let it eat me?"

"Absolutely not."

With a sigh, the boy stepped back.

Zach caught a movement through the window of the motel check-in, and said, "Let's keep who we are quiet. Tell
your parents if they ask. And, yeah, we'll help you. We have
a ghost-killing knife."

As expected, the boy came around to greet Zach. "Can
I see it?"

"Caden?" The door opened and a short, curvy, blond
woman came out.

"Hi, Mom!" Caden's cheer sounded forced to Zach. "Our
new guests are here."

"I see that."

Clare turned to the woman and held out her hand with
one of her professional smiles on her face. "Clare Cermak."
She tilted her head in Zach's direction. "My partner, Zach
Slade. We have reservations."

The word *partner* had zinged to him, actually to his dick.
Clare might mean it in a business sense, but his gut reaction
had been that she was claiming him as her man. Oh, yeah,
he liked that.

"I'm Jessica LuCette."

Caden walked back to her, face bland. A kid shouldn't
have to hide his feelings like that from his mother. Zach
and his older brother Jim hadn't . . . only when the General
was around. But this granddaughter of Mrs. Flinton didn't
support her son.

As the General hadn't supported Jim and Zach, and
enough about the ancient history of his childhood. This was
here and now and they had this boy to save. Zach snagged
his cane and limped heavier than usual around the car.
Yeah, pity came to Mrs. LuCette's eyes and he used it to
distract her from any judgments she might have made about
Clare. Zach didn't think she'd seen the hug between her son
and Clare.

The women had finished shaking, so Zach put his hand
out. "Pleased to meet you." Her grip was sturdy and short.

Zach smiled ruefully. "We're ready to check in." Mrs.

LuCette turned for the door. Caden, after a wide-eyed look at them, followed her.

Zach used some of his professional charm on her, and got her chatting about Cruisin' the Canyon. He didn't bring up the murder-suicide or any other rough topics. She didn't volunteer anything about her family or Caden, and he didn't ask.

He lifted out the suitcases, slammed the trunk, and rolled his own to the door, because he didn't think he'd need his free hand for his weapon.

So far, the town had been quiet, but not as slow as it would be in winter. Some of the businesses had closed already; most would shut down at the end of the month until late May or June.

Tourists from local towns or Denver might have driven down to see the fall color and stay. Clare had told him that Bachelor Loop was well known to have beautiful shows of golden aspen. From experience, an accident like the one they'd stumbled on—which a tingle at the back of his neck that snaked down his spine told him was no accident—would only close the road for a couple of hours.

No accident, but a murderous ghost. He rubbed his nape. He was really going there with cause and effect. A bullet of belief had lodged in him that a supernatural entity caused those deaths. He gave a passing thought to other freaky deaths he'd seen in his career, then rolled his shoulders. Those were past. This was *right now*, and he had to help Clare, protect her.

He sure didn't like the sound of a ghost that ate people, particularly ghost seers. Clare was a rookie in the business. Sure, he'd seen her help specters pass on, and she'd handled herself well, but he didn't like that a novice swimmer was being thrown into the deep end of the lake.

As soon as the door closed behind them and they were in the clean, tidy, and rustically furnished pine-paneled room, he said, "Show me this ghost-killing knife." He was curious, and he wanted to see what would do the job.

* * *

With her bag still standing on its end, Clare unzipped a large compartment and pulled out the silk bag. She sat on the bed and picked at the fancy knot that tied two red silk tassels together. Zach stood leaning easily on his cane and watching her, which made her even more nervous.

"It feels like the sheath for the blade is about six inches long, and the handle is at least five. That's over the knife-carrying limits for Denver, right?" She cleared her throat.

"Certainly, but we're not in a big city and don't know whether the blade is sharp enough to do anything except dispatch ghosts."

"Oh. I hadn't thought of that." The knot finally wiggled loose and she straightened the drawstring. Then she opened the bag, reached in, and gripped a handle.

She froze.

"What?" asked Zach.

Forcing her lips to move, she said, "The handle feels *right* in my hand but also . . ."

"Also?" Zach prompted.

She wet her lips. "Bone. It feels like bone." She'd hunched over, so now she straightened her spine, inhaled, and scowled. "I've learned the feel of bone in the last five days."

Zach's brows went up and he nodded.

Slowly she pulled out the knife, her palm sweating a little. Sure enough, the two knobs of a bone showed first . . . a large bone. A little squeeze of her stomach had her thinking this was a *human* bone. She'd handled those in the last week, too.

The whole hilt was bone; the curved blade remained snug in the sheath.

"Nice sheath," Zach said.

"Beautiful," Clare breathed, recognizing cloisonné work, enamel over metal, and decorated in an intricate pattern that pleased her eye—a blue, green, gold, and black wavy Hungarian pattern. With her free forefinger, she traced a sinuous golden line from tip to hilt, received a little sizzle along her nerves. Obviously a magical sheath, wide enough to accommodate the curve of an equally magical blade. The whole thing no doubt one of those gifts of the universe Great-Aunt Sandra wrote about.

A smile edged Zach's mouth. "Intricate but not too girly."

She lifted her chin. "I will have you know that the two or three ghost seers in my family before Great-Aunt Sandra were men."

"Two or three? That's not an exact figure, Clare," he joked.

Clearing her throat and not meeting his gaze, she said, "My great-great-uncle Orun didn't make it. He didn't accept the gift and died. Froze to death."

"Clare." Zach sat next to her, took her hand. Her fingers were cold, not from ghosts, not from upcoming winter, but from simple fear.

Her glance grazed across his face before she continued, "It was bad for me, but worse for him."

Now Zach moved his arm to around her shoulders, squeezed her, and warmth radiated to her from his lean and muscular body. "How could it be worse for him than for you? I saw what you went through."

Leaning her head against his shoulder she met his eyes. "Yes, I nearly died of cold in the hottest ever Denver summer. But Orun inherited the ghost seer power in one of the coldest Chicago winters."

"I see what you mean." Zach squeezed her again and his arm dropped lower so his hand curved over her left breast.

"Ah, Zach, do you recall I have a blade on my lap?"

"I think I'm more interested in something soft than something sharp."

"You don't want to see what will kill a ghost?"

His lips came closer and closer, brushed the corner of her mouth. He took the sheathed knife and tossed it onto his horizontal bag, then lay down and carried her with him. They both rolled on their sides to face each other.

So fascinating, this man, to her. Strong, fierce features, the touch of bronze in his skin, his black hair with tints of dark mink brown. She feathered her fingers across his brow, down to the edge of his cheekbones, smiled. "I like looking at you."

He chuckled. "No woman in my life has said that."

It was on the tip of her tongue to tease and mention his mother, but his mother was no teasing matter. Instead she laced a Hungarian-Slavic accent into her voice and said, "I am coming to appreciate the unusual."

He wrapped his arm around her and pulled her close enough that she felt his arousal. "That's my blooming Clare Cermak, leaving her tight, rational seed-shell."

She put her arms around his neck, pressed even closer so her breasts flattened against his chest. "Having to leave my shell, much to my dismay," she admitted. "And pretty much kicking and screaming." She moved her mouth closer and closer to his, until she could smell his minty breath and could warm his lips with her own exhalations. Desire twined and spiraled between them, her heart sped up, her sex clenched, mind and body recalling the pleasure that this man could give her, would give her, without even asking for it.

With the tip of her tongue, she traced his lips, liked the shudder of his body against hers, showing she affected him. She wanted him more than just in her, and she realized he *was* more to her. He was close to her heart, the need for him rooted inside her so that if he walked away, she would tear. Her arms convulsed around him, yearning for that closeness that she'd felt with no other. No standing one step away from a relationship with Zach Slade.

Then his mouth slanted against hers, his tongue probed her own, and he tasted wonderful as he always did, and this time her heart gave an actual little lurch as she knew she was falling in love with him. She hadn't ever been deeply in love before.

Thrilling.

Terrifying.

"My sweet Clare," he murmured.

His hands had gone to her breasts, cupping them, molding them, his thumbs brushing across her nipples that had turned ultrasensitive and had her lower body pushing against his, which wrung a low moan from him.

She sank into the kiss, closed her eyes, and soaked in the pleasure of Zach's taste and smell and the length of his body next to hers. Cherished this one moment.

Then she pushed against him and rolled away, off the bed and onto her feet.

"Wha—!"

"You have too many clothes on."

His eyes gleamed. "You do, too."

She grinned, wiggled her brows. "Let me help you with that issue."

"Ah. All right."

He sat with a smooth flex of excellent abs, smiled, and waited.

Clare moved before him, matched his gaze, loving his blue green eyes, loving, more, the sparkle in them. She set her hands on his shoulders, measured the muscle of them, the strength, the breadth. "Fine, fine shoulders," she found herself saying.

His smile widened. "Glad you like them."

"You are one prime male, Mister Slade."

A shadow passed through his eyes, perhaps a thought of his disability, though, to her, that meant nothing but that he'd hurt and healed. Not without flaw, on the outside. And she knew some of his flaws on the inside—like a reluctance to let anyone help him in tight emotional spots, even his lover.

His hands settled on the curve of her hips and she nearly jolted. "You're too quiet. I'm not sure I like it when my woman is too quiet. She might be plotting my downfall."

Her brows rose and she gently knocked his hands away and he let her. "You're right there, Mister. I'm going to make you . . . crazy. Crazy with lust."

"You don't have far to go."

"Good." Her fingers moved to the top button of his blue and gray flannel shirt. For a moment she flattened her hands against his chest so she could feel the soft material over the hard muscular wall of his body.

"Fine chest, too?" Zach asked.

"For sure." She got to work on his buttons, not too slowly, not too quickly, just a steady rhythm that they could both appreciate. Now and then she'd put her hands inside his shirt and stroke his lightly haired chest, liking that texture against her palms, too. He sat still, but his breathing sped up.

She reached the top of his well-worn jeans and unsnapped them, slid her hands around his waist, pulled out the bottom, and finished working on the buttons, her fingers brushing his abdomen, his thighs, his erection. She wasn't ready to give them both the pleasure of stroking his sex yet.

Putting her hands inside his shirt, she slid them up his strong torso. His body was hot, and hers was definitely getting there. The more she touched him, the more her own sex dampened, clenched, demanded his shaft. Again she moved her hands to his chest, trailed them upward to trace his collarbone, then removed his shirt. She folded it and placed it atop his bag.

Zach made a choking noise.

She met his amused eyes.

"These things have a proper order," she said in her most prissy tone.

"Baby, you *are* driving me crazy."

"Hardly, yet."

"Uh. Do you think you can take your sweater off, too?"

She wore a thin burgundy cashmere sweater, and had put on black, lacy, *and* comfortable underwear for him. Studying him from lowered lashes, especially the thick length of his erection, she tilted her head. "I don't think it's time for me to disrobe."

"Baby, lose the clothes."

"No." She took a step back.

EIGHT

"I LIKE LOOKING at you," she repeated.

He sighed and his chest went in and out and accented more muscles. He remained a little thin from the shooting that had ruined his career and disabled him. He'd be even more incredible when he regained that muscle. Oh, yes.

Stepping back to him, she put her thumbs on his nipples and scraped them.

"Good God, woman!" He jumped to his feet, six foot two to her five foot seven.

"You like that. Nice to know." She reached for the zipper of his jeans and slowly drew the tab down; she couldn't bear to hurt him.

His breath was still rapid, but had gone unsteady.

Finally, his jeans were open all the way and his hard arousal in white boxers pushed through pale denim.

If she dropped his pants, she'd have to mess with jeans around his shoes, so she knelt at his feet.

"Oh, man."

"Woman here."

"Don't I know it. Sexy woman."

"Not tonight," she said. "Later."

He swayed, steadied himself, and removed his holstered gun and bent to put it on the nightstand.

She waited, then went to work on his cross-trainers. She untied the laces, lifted his feet out of them, one, then the other, stroking the soles of his feet. The right one arched and flexed away from her touch; the other couldn't. She placed each foot on the floor, went to work on his left ankle and calf brace and took it off, then his socks, folding them and putting them in his shoes. She rubbed his feet. He groaned and looked like he might topple backward before she got his jeans and boxers off, so she stood and stuck her thumbs in the waistband of his jeans and pulled them down, lifting them away from each foot.

Then she rose slowly, and on the journey, rubbed her body against his, her cashmere sweater teasing his abdomen and chest, and her hand went naturally to his erection, curved around it, hard, hot, thick behind his boxers. She tested his length, watching his straining expression and the barely controlled wild in his eyes, then she skimmed her fingernails along his shaft.

He made an incoherent sound, dragged her close, one hand clamped on her butt, the other curved around her neck, and he angled her head and ravaged her mouth with a deeply surging tongue.

Her knees weakened, her mind spun, and, oh, God, she wanted him in her, thrusting like that, sending her—them both—to ecstasy.

His hands swept under her sweater, flicked open the back of her bra and freed her breasts. He palmed them, caressed them, stroked until the feel of the soft brush of her sweater on her back and sides, his tougher skin on her nipples and breasts, made her quiver with need and her panting matched his.

She had barely enough thought for her fingers to go to the top of his underwear and yank them down. He moan-laughed in her mouth but didn't stop her as he lifted his knees, and one of them insinuated itself between her thighs and pressed on her needy, melting sex and then he was naked. Her hand curved around him and she held tight, pumped a couple of times until he broke her grip, spun her, and she fell on the bed.

"My. Turn." She thought those were the words he said; her mind had fogged and his voice rumbled.

Then his hot hands were at her jeans and they came off along with her panties and socks and tangled around her shoes, trapping her feet—ah, how she ached for him, but he slid away from her hands as he dealt with her shoes and socks. A few seconds later he *pounced*. His hands opened her thighs, and he plunged into her and filled her. And completed her.

Her fingers pressed into those fine, fine shoulders; his hands went under her butt and tilted her up, and the sweet, sweet, *sweet* friction had her whimpering with yearning for the hovering orgasm. She circled her hips, rocked with him, and her ears cleared when she heard him muttering her name. "Clare, Clare, Clare." He lunged into her again and again and then release hit her, spun her through space and time and the universe and he was with her.

He groaned and shuddered and then lay atop her, breathing roughly next to her ear, and she became aware of her cashmere sweater bunched between them, recalled the sensation of it against her skin as they'd loved together, and trembled. She hoped that had pleased him, too. "Cashmere," she said, and her mind did a loop of *that-came-out-of-my-mouth*.

"Yeah, excellent." Zach stroked her side and she felt his fingers through the thin material.

"Ooooh," she purred.

He lifted away from her, and she frowned at the loss of him. Then her sweater was stripped off and she thought it went flying—no way to treat a—her bra, thankfully, was untangled and dropped, the sheets were pulled down, and she was stuffed in between them.

"I don' haff to sleep. I'm not—"

"Shh. We had an active night and a stressful day. Just rest your eyes."

"Rest my eyes. I'll be up all night if I sl—"

"Rest," he crooned.

Slipping into sleep should have been warm relief, but a black and roiling threat tinted the soft clouds billowing around her.

Clare woke up when Zach turned the bedside light on. She propped herself on her forearm and glanced at the curtains, but they were room darkening and she couldn't tell the time of day by the light. "I'm starving," she said, then noticed Zach staring down at his basic black piece of luggage and the bone-handled knife on it.

"Okay, you want to look at the knife now."

He shook his head. "No, I want to shower." His mouth turned down. "I've already checked the shower out, it's part of a tub, not a separate enclosure. Sex might be iffy."

"Go ahead."

"Fine. I shower and dress, you shower and dress, we find a place to eat, then return and look at the knife."

"Maybe you show me some fighting moves?"

He eyed the room. "Maybe. And maybe we should find someplace outside to practice."

Enzo appeared sitting right on top of Zach's bag. *The knife will draw the ghost.*

"Crap," Zach said.

Clare jackknifed to sit. "Uh-oh."

Again Zach looked around, expression grim. "What must we do to confuse the ghost—"

If the knife is out of the silk bag, it will draw the specter. Enzo curled over and licked the sheath.

Eww, frigid ghost drool on something she'd be handling. She thought she saw frost form on the metal. Surely that couldn't be good for it.

Zach picked up the hilt, grabbed the bag, and stuck the knife in it, though he didn't tie the tassels. Now that Clare squinted at the ivory material, she saw small round circles containing different patterns of solid and broken lines, perhaps some kind of protection? "Is there a particular knot that we must use, like the one I untied?"

Sandra knew three. Enzo's forehead furrowed. *But I*

think there are more. His head drooped. *The Other will know and could teach you.*

Clare looked at Zach. "You know any fancy knots?"

His face went stony. "No."

She sensed he lied, and considered the circumstances of their relationship.

He wanted exclusivity and so did she. He wasn't done with her and she still wanted him, and more than his body, and they were getting pretty darn intimate. She remained cautious about taking more than she gave, becoming dependent on him. She'd always firmly believed in equality in relationships, and with her previous lovers, that hadn't been any problem.

But if she propped herself up on him because of his strength and courage in the face of all this unusual *stuff* going on and he walked away, she could fall and fail and die. So she couldn't do that. She'd have to equal his strength and courage, and that felt like a huge challenge.

The issue right here and right now was whether she'd call him on his lie. "Okay, Zach, hand me the sheath and I'll tie it the best I can. And do me a favor, don't lie to me."

His lowered lashes flicked up, surprise showing on his face.

"If you don't want to talk about something, say so. Just don't lie. And I will give you the same courtesy."

"Sorry," he said gruffly, not looking at her. "My brother and I practiced some knots together."

"I understand." She rose and walked to him, hand out for the bone knife.

"I'll do it. You go take a shower."

"All right." She walked into the bathroom containing simple fixtures . . . and lush towels.

A few minutes later she'd dressed in jeans, shirt, and thermal vest and Zach was taking his shower. She stared at the red tassels that were knotted even fancier than before. She stroked the multilayer Chinese-looking knot and thought of Zach, and his grief for a lost big brother hero that never went away, and was awed at such love.

Her family seemed to love more lightly.

Walking to the window, she peeked out between the curtains. Clouds had rolled in again and the sky sleeted small bits of white. Seemed like late afternoon to her, and her stomach rumbled. She definitely needed to eat.

Zach came out of the bathroom, wet hair sleeked against his head, and giddiness flushed through her that this virile man desired *her*.

She said, "I think after we eat, instead of returning here, we should drive up and down all the town streets, those on the hillside, too. Like you said, get a feel for it." Her lips thinned. "Not only the old and historic portion but what's here now. What the evil apparition threatens."

Zach nodded. "Good idea."

The hamburger at Pico's Patio was one of the most delicious Clare had ever eaten, probably because she was so hungry. As she ate, Zach studied the diners. He was better at judging who was a tourist and who was a local than she.

Back in the car, they drove through the gray evening, up and down the three long streets in town and those on the ridges, and found the road to the airport and the medical center in the south of town. They admired some incredibly beautiful and unique homes that often occurred in small mountain towns, and came across the turn to the cemetery.

Zach took it, and a simple white church came into view, as well as the road up a gentle slope. The hillside cemetery was easy to spot with the two wooden poles and a top plank announcing it, old and new gravestones, and a miniature white church. The prairie grass, still summer yellow, hid the muddy ground.

He stopped. "Shall we walk?"

"Seeing if there are no ghosts or apparitions or specters or shades here, too?" she grumbled.

But he'd gotten out of the car and circled to open her door, held out a hand. "It's peaceful and pretty and I haven't been in an old cemetery for a long time."

"Day before yesterday?" she reminded.

"I didn't walk around that one, and it was for a reburial, not the same," he said firmly, taking her hand with the one that didn't hold his cane. Since Clare didn't see another person, Zach might also figure they were safe. Well, at least safe because they'd just hit town and people hadn't heard of her or what she could do. In this particular case, unlike the last one, he wouldn't be on the lookout for a hunting accident. Yet.

"Enzo," she called. She could use some cheering up.

I am here! He gazed around, tail wagging. *It's pretty. Though the hills are not too steep so I can run through them and sniff bones.*

Clare gasped and coughed. She *was* getting better about the collateral *stuff* she dealt with in her new . . . vocation.

Oooh, look! A dog house just for me in the cemetery! He headed straight for the small white church with a red roof.

Zach chuckled. "What a dog."

She angled a glance at her lover. "You can see and hear him well, even without contact with me."

"Yeah."

They walked and looked at new and old tombstones, some of wood that wouldn't last, some overgrown slabs, some graves in little fenced in areas.

"Nothing?" Zach asked.

"No."

Enzo zoomed up to them, his expression sad. *No. No lingering tiny bits of personalities at ALL. They have been EATEN. I will be eaten.*

"No, you won't," she and Zach said together. Enzo moved close to Clare. So close he was inside her right leg, chilling it.

"Nothing of Robert Ford?" Zach asked.

Clare blinked. "You were looking for him?"

"Sort of."

"He's not here."

"His remains were exhumed?"

"Yes, and taken somewhere else. I remember that, though I don't recall where. Missouri?" She reached in her jacket pocket for her phone and Zach squeezed her hand. "No need."

"And they didn't bury him here either."

"What? No?"

"No. The rumor on the Internet is," and until she looked at original sources like the contemporary newspaper, the *Creede Candle*, whatever was on the Internet would be suspect, "that the good town people didn't want him buried with them in the cemetery, so his gravesite was somewhere else. It seems he shot up the town and the new streetlights and was run out of town. He came back a couple of months later and was killed soon afterward."

"Shooting up a town sounds familiar."

"Yes, like our first ghost, the gunfighter."

"Wild West," Zach murmured.

Clare returned to the current project, shaking her head. "Ford came back."

"And he died."

Enzo shook his head. *Bad men don't learn fast. They make the same mistakes over and over again.*

"That's true," Zach said. "Now what mistake would our current ghost have repeated? That's the trigger, repetition of some mistake, issue, problem."

"I'm sure you're right," Clare said. "If we need to see Robert Ford's original burial spot, I'm guessing it isn't too far away . . . I'm sure I read about the location—" Again she touched her cell.

"It doesn't matter right now."

"We don't have a lot of time." And that thought squeezed her breath in her chest.

I can find the Ford place, I can! Enzo enthused. He took off running.

"We'll work on the riddles tomorrow," Zach said.

"I was hoping there would be a definitive biography of

Robert Ford, but there isn't. I think the best I can do is something on Soapy Smith since they both were in Creede at the same time."

"Right." Bad men competing seemed to light more interest in his eyes and she thought he filed the idea away as he turned her toward him and said, "Calm down. Let me help. You don't have to do this alone—either figure out the trigger and the core identity of the ghost, or the phantom's name, or fight it."

She let him hug her, closed her eyes and hid from the world, from the dead, with her face against his chest and listening to his heartbeat instead of the whistling breeze. She rested there for a while. "Thank you. I'm glad you're here with me."

His arms tightened, but he didn't reply. After a minute, she pulled back and they walked the gradual incline of the hillside. At the northeast base of the cemetery, she saw the town expanded with new streets right next to the graveyard. "Who would want that?" she muttered.

Zach smiled. "Restful neighbors."

"For you, maybe."

"An Old West silver mining town without ghosts," he said, as if thinking.

Clare sniffed. "Just last month I wouldn't have noticed them."

"Are you sure? I bet you would have sensed them. Might have sensed them all your life, but since your drama-loving, always-moving parents bothered you, you just thought they were part of your life. Maybe that was another reason you became a very . . . controlled . . . and rational accountant."

She kissed his jaw. "That's very insightful."

"Uh-huh. The gift came through your gypsy blood. From your mother's side, right?"

"Yes, like yours, another thing we have in common, though you have the Celtic background."

"Yeah." Now he sounded rusty, as if he ground out the words. "The damned wiffy Scot-Celtic blood." His expression shadowed into one of his regular broods. "*Not* through my father's Native American blood." He tramped back toward the car and the gate, thumping his cane. "Though I know nothing about those ancestors, and don't think my father, the General, does either."

"You are who you are," she said, projecting calm.

"Would have been really awful if I got a double-whammy of woo-woo stuff."

"So," she said. "Here we are, confirming there are no ghosts, not even in the cemetery, and that we have no clues."

He gave her a smile that looked too practiced to her. "We have each other."

"Well, that's right. Now let's go get that knife and you can give me lessons or something."

A fast-moving gray phantom ran up to them, through them. "I think Enzo likes running through us," Clare said. "Did you feel him?"

"A little chill," Zach admitted. "Dogs love to run, of course he'd like going through us. He knows you don't like it."

"Rebellion," Clare said.

"Teasing." Zach tugged at a lock of her hair. It had gone completely frizzy in the humidity. She tried to squish it down with both hands, but, as always throughout her life, it sprang back up.

"Good thing I brought my best conditioner."

"I like it this way," Zach said.

Enzo zipped through them again, leapt and twisted in a move that a normal Lab couldn't make, and sat in front of them. *I found the hole where a once-dead person was but who isn't there no more. He hasn't been there for a long, long time.*

"All right," Zach said. He leaned down to pet Enzo, but his hand went straight through the phantom dog's head. Enzo wiggled his butt. *I felt that, Zach. Nice warm hand!*

"I felt it, too. Cool air."

Enzo hopped to his feet and rubbed against Clare. *Clare's touch is BEST.*

So she reached down and petted his head, feeling like she stroked dry ice, her fingertips searing . . . though they didn't burn red. Still, she'd been the one to touch, so the cold was worse.

Ooooh, lovely Clare. Thank you, Clare! Enzo licked her hand.

"You're welcome."

Zach angled so he could clasp her frigid fingers in his own. The man's muscle mass, lean as he was, still generated a lot of heat in general, and now his hand felt amazingly warm. He smiled at her. "Enzo's right. Clare's touch is the best."

Enzo trotted in the direction he'd come. *Follow me!*

"Across hillsides, I don't think so, dog," Zach said. He didn't raise his voice, but Enzo stopped and ran back to them.

"No one's in the grave, we'll check it out later." Zach squeezed her fingers and they turned to walk back to the car.

"Sounds fine to me."

We are going to look at the knife. Enzo's back rippled. *It is a good but powerful thing.*

"Sounds like it will kill a powerful, evil ghost, then," Zach said.

Yes. Enzo gave Clare big, dark, doggy eyes. *I was hoping Clare wouldn't have to fight a bad ghost for a long, long, long time.*

"You and me both," Clare said.

As they stopped at the car, Zach opened the door for her, then kissed her on the temple. "You'll be fine."

That he yet believed that boggled Clare's mind. And that he was the optimist of the two of them. Just plain odd.

NINE

CLARE HAD OPENED the room-darkening curtains to reveal the view of the town and the hill on the far side that showed a dotting of houses with their lights on. The rain had started again and sputtered against the window, making the pine paneling and the earth-toned room cozy.

Time to really look at the knife.

Zach placed the silk bag holding the knife in its sheath on the end of the bed that Clare had made before they left for dinner, then he unpacked while she made coffee for them both. Enzo sat in the chair by the window, keeping an eye out for the evil revenant, though the phantom dog had told them that he hadn't sensed the powerful entity.

When Zach had stretched out with his back against the headboard, holding a thick white pottery mug that was standard to many hotels and diners, Clare took the cloth tube in her hands. The new knot Zach had tied was deceptively simpler and took her longer to undo. Finally the red tassels hung straight and she opened the drawstring, drew out the sheathed knife.

All her senses ruffled—a faint, high chime at the top of

her hearing, the musky scent of unknown incense, most of all a feeling of déjà vu when she clasped the weapon by the hilt, as if she knew it better than just the few minutes she'd touched it before. As if it knew *her*, and what kind of strange thought was that?

She glanced at Zach. He sipped his coffee and held her eyes. "Yeah, I heard the chime, got the smell, too."

Enzo had tensed, but he turned his head, snuffling, and projected, *Of course the knife will feel right to you. It is yours from Sandra, and Amos before her, and Nuri before him, and Simza before him.*

"An ancestral blade." Zach sounded amused.

"Yes." She continued to look at Enzo. "How did you know all of that?"

I know a lot that Sandra told me, and sometimes, sometimes, the Other will let me know and say stuff. Not often though.

Clare nodded. "I'd prefer hearing data from you than it."

That got her a slightly lolling tongue before the wraith Lab turned back to the window. His body twitched. *I can sense it. The evil thing. Distant, though.*

"Then let's study the blade fast," Zach said. "Rather take my time, though."

So would Clare. With her left hand, she touched the intricate enamel and gold pattern. "Where did this come from?" She aimed the question at her dog.

His back hunched smaller. *Made special for the blade, old, old, old. Too many questions will bring the Other.*

Zach's white cotton-socked right foot nudged Clare's hip. "We don't particularly like the Other," he said, though Clare thought the being bothered her more than her lover.

"No," she agreed. "We don't."

"Unsheathe the blade."

Curling her left fingers around the sheath, she pulled with both hands. The six-inch curved blade came easily and her eyes widened at the ivory of it. "It's the same bone," she said flatly. "But the handle is glossier, smoother."

"Oils from people handling it more," Zach said. "Interesting." He put his mug on the bedside table and scooted to her. "What kind of bone?"

"Whose bone" is the right question, Enzo said, not *quite* sounding the Other, though his natural mental tone had deepened.

"Whose bone?" Clare parroted.

The ancestress who consented to be a ghost seer for us. The Other turned Enzo's body to face her, sitting up straight, but his dog ears were lifted and angled as if he still listened for the evil ghost. *It is a blade made from Vadoma's big leg bone.*

"Her femur," Clare said, emphasizing that for herself.

"The pommel must be the end near the knee," Zach said.

"Okay, that's creepy." She removed her fingers from the hilt—and they came reluctantly as if her hand liked holding the knife—gave it to Zach to scrutinize and took the few paces to her coffee that she'd left on the sink counter outside the bathroom.

"Ouch!" Zach said. She whirled to see him staring at a slice on the pad of his index finger that looked like a paper cut.

"Why did you test the knife with your finger?" she asked, exasperated.

"I didn't." He scowled at the blade. "I barely touched it. It cut me. And it sucked the couple of drops of blood right up." He made a loud slurping sound.

"Ick."

The blade is hungry, Enzo said.

Clare drank coffee that tasted more bitter than it should have. "Why do I think I'm not going to like this next part?"

You must tune the blade to your personal essence before it will kill ghosts for you, the Other said.

An atavistic shudder ran through Clare, nearly causing her to spill her coffee. "Let me guess, the blade is bone and it will need blood. My blood."

The spectral dog inclined his head. *Soaked in your blood.*

"Soaked!" Clare gasped and heard Zach growl a protest.

You must pay that price, the Other intoned.

"This ghost seer business is getting more and more expensive," Clare snapped.

We have always paid you well. The Other turned back to look out the window, dismissing her. *You have not looked at the knife. You should do so. You should know your weapon. The evil ghost feels the blade, is confused about that feeling. It will cast about before it understands how to find it. You have, perhaps, twenty of your minutes.*

"Hmph." But Clare marched over to where Zach sat, stared at the leg bone of her ancestress, and gulped. "Looks in pretty good shape. No dark spots or soil stains or whatever like . . . like I've seen on bones before."

"Very clean," Zach agreed.

"Pretty steep curve," she noted.

It is as we requested her son to make it, the Other commented.

More ick.

She sat next to Zach, and he lay the blade across her knees. It was pristine ivory, only about an inch and a quarter wide at the hilt, then was fined down to a blade that began curving to a point at the end. "It's a . . . powerful . . . looking knife," she said doubtfully.

"Yes," Zach said.

"If you like that sort of thing."

"It's sharper than a bone knife should be, and I'll bet it keeps its edge well, too."

"Magic," Clare stated. "It wants my blood." She sighed. "I don't know how I'm going to soak the darn blade in my blood. Especially here. Maybe if I had a medical person draw a pint or whatever, but explaining that would be tough."

"Yeah," Zach said, though he had a considering expression as if he were several steps ahead of her in figuring out the process, which wouldn't surprise her a bit since he knew weapons and she didn't.

"I may as well give it a taste," she grumbled. "Prime it so it knows more is coming." She set it next to the outside, fleshy part of her arm, not daring to get it near a vein in her wrist. Barely pressing down, the thing sliced deeper than she wanted and she gritted her teeth at the pain and watched the blood disappear around the blade.

"Give that to me," Zach said roughly. He wrapped his fingers around hers and lifted the greedy, bloodsucking blade a little.

"Thanks."

"I've got a first aid kit in my suitcase."

Clare sighed again. "The way my cases have been going, I should have thought of that, but I didn't. Next time."

"I hope not."

The ghost begins to search. Put the blade away now, said the Other.

"You have a real bad notion of time, Other," Zach said.

It is smarter than I anticipated. Every time the knife is out of the silk shell, the ghost will sense it more quickly.

"Come to find it more quickly," Zach said.

Yes. The Other stared at them, at her, now, with those depthless, judging mist-eyes. *That will be true of all evil ghosts in your future.*

"Joy," said Clare flatly. She curved her fingers around the hilt and sheathed the bone blade. Zach took the long knife from her, slipped it back in the silk tube, and tied the tassels. Clare was glad when she could no longer see it.

The phantom Lab hopped off the chair and onto the bed with them, no longer the Other spirit, but her companion, Enzo, again. Clare crossed over to the window and pulled the curtains, shutting out the dark and the rain that had turned to spitting hail. Shutting her and Zach and Enzo into the warmth of light.

She went back and petted Enzo and he dropped his lower jaw in a slight smile at her, licked her icy fingers. "You don't have to stay, Enzo. Go home to Denver. I give you permission."

No, I must stay. The Other was very clear. And I WANT to, because we must WIN. We will NOT be eaten.

Zach stood next to her with a bandage and a roll of gauze. "We're not letting any stupid ghost eat you or Caden."

The Other said it was smart.

"No. An evil being, whether human or not, isn't smart if it attracts attention to its crimes. That's when people come after it to stop it."

"To destroy it," Clare said.

To kill it. You will KILL it, Clare. Enzo sounded more cheerful.

Her mouth dried up. "Yes. Sure."

The rest of the evening, Clare sat next to Zach and watched football and desultorily researched as much as she could find on Creede, Robert Ford, and Soapy Smith, marking dates that she'd like to look up if the archives held the newspapers.

The History Colorado Center and the Denver Public Library, of course, had the most material and what she found online didn't seem easily accessed. As much as it pained her, she'd consider hiring a research assistant if necessary, if she could find a good one who'd work fast and efficiently.

She needed information before she had to confront and fight the ghost. She needed the phantom's name.

Whining wind shook the windows along with eerie shrieks. She couldn't tell whether she was the only one who heard it—well, she and Zach and Enzo, who lay draped over their feet.

After the game, Clare set aside her tablet to charge and cuddled with Zach, who kept her warm. Even with the lights out, and Zach at her back, she couldn't sleep. Instead her consciousness descended into a gray state of not-life. That faded into darkness until she shook with the sound of a death cry and the seeping of something—water?—that clogged her lungs then became a flood engulfing her. She saw a thin thread of bright red blood.

She choked, coughed, woke. Zach lay still and sleeping behind her. Trembling with fear, with cold, she carefully slipped from his loose grasp, crawled from the bed. In the dark, a bar of ivory glowed on the television table in front of her—the knife.

Enzo? she whispered with her mind.

I am under the bed, he whispered back. *It is not safe for me in the ghost dimension.*

Not if there was real red blood adding color to that place.

She heard him gulp. *Are you going out? It is not safe out there. Nowhere in this town is safe.*

Clare stopped, finding herself at the door, her hand on the handle, not recalling moving there. She didn't even have shoes on, or a robe over her flannel pajamas!

Low, persistent growling came from the courtyard of the motel. The hair on the nape of her neck rose in atavistic horror. Inside she trembled. Hell, her hand on the door lever shook. But she *could* sense it, the evil ghost, how it stalked and paused at each door. How it stopped in front of theirs. Enzo sat *in* her legs and shivered with her. Perhaps she masked him from the ghost. She didn't know. She didn't know too awful much. Universes of things she had to learn before she should fight this ghost.

Her mouth dried. The handle turned icy under her fingers. In panic mode, she couldn't move, frozen in every sense.

High-pitched keening sliced into her mind. Not one muscle twitched.

Then, screaming, human screaming, young boy shrieking came. "No, *no,* NO!"

Whatever threatened outside her door whisked away, zooming in the direction of Caden's cries, and Clare wrenched free of horror. "No!" she yelled herself, but it whispered out.

"What's going on!" Zach's rough demand grounded her further.

"It's after Caden. It . . . it . . . wa-wasss . . . h'r . . . ri-right . . . outs'de . . th . . door . . . bu-but—" She couldn't speak for the shivering.

Zach joined her, gun in hand. He looked great, strong, solid, large.

And he couldn't fight this, not like her. Then he dropped the gun and grabbed the knife in its ivory silk tube, swept an arm around her waist, and simply lifted her and moved her aside.

The heat of him snapped her all the way back. She pushed the lever, whipped the door open, gasped at the cold of the night as well as the lingering frigidity of the ghost, and yanked the knife from Zach's hand.

WHAT ARE YOU DOING?! demanded the Other, who'd taken over Enzo.

She didn't bother to answer, just rushed over to the LuCettes' living quarters where lights went on. Caden continued screaming, and some massive gray white swirling mass with *black* lightning roiled around the door.

TEN

SHE SHOULD YELL herself, let out all her fear and her anger and her determination in some war cry. She didn't know one. She leveled the knife, silk tube and all, and charged at the thing, speared it on one of its frayed edges. Darn it, she must do better!

HURT! Hurts! What is this? Ghost . . . layer . . . ghost . . . killer. NO! It whirled to her, the mass hit her, the freezing, blinding snowstorm of it.

Must. Keep. Moving. She couldn't feel her feet, her hands. Pretend they were there. Slash! Stab!

Don't do this! the Other thundered in her mind, all rolling and roaring, drowning out the faint mind wisps of the thing she battled. The whispers that slid across her skin like slime, speaking of sin. Of hunger. She thought she felt the nibble of little sharp teeth gouging into her.

The door to the apartment opened! Oh, no!

"What's going on!" This shouted in male and female voices.

Zach cursing, really cursing, using words she hadn't heard from him before. The knife swept from her hand.

No! No! This time a high-pitched Enzo, pushing out the Other? Would no one shut up so she could fight this thing?

I will bite it. I will! Enzo jumped into the nightmare snow whirl. Black lightning struck around him, struck him.

Clare surged into the thing, too, hands clawed. She fought and breathed in ice, and since her mouth was open and snow fell into it, she *bit*.

Loud, hideous shrieking or sobbing. Maybe Clare'd hurt it again! The storm moved *through* her, worse, worse, worse than any ghost she'd felt before. One voice became a multitude, whimpering or furious, or screaming. She doubled over as a sharp shard-like a hook dragged through her. Just closed that visualization down, blanked her mind. The specter wasn't going to use her own fears on her.

"Robert Ford, we know you!" Zach's harsh voice impinged on Clare.

The icy hook ripped as deep, wild grief flooded her—emotions from the ghost . . . then . . . guilt?

Then the thing was out of her and she shook, head to toe, and as she did, small icicles fell from her.

Her vision cleared enough for her to see Caden collapsed on the floor, hands over his ears, shuddering.

Alive.

A man scooped him up. Square body type and rawboned, red blond hair cut short, he was younger than Clare and Zach.

"Clare." Caden held out his hand to her, tear tracks showing on his face. "Clare, you saved me."

Just breathing hurt; standing was a challenge.

"Clare?" snapped the man.

"We *will* talk, Ms. Cermak," a pale Mrs. LuCette said. "Come in." Her round chin set. "Bring Mr. Slade and that . . . that . . . thing he is carrying."

Clare shuffled in. Zach's arm came around her waist and it felt like a hot iron bar. Not quite searing, but uncomfortable. Slowly she straightened her spine, bit by bit until she no longer stooped and she could move a little faster, away from Zach.

Mrs. LuCette indicated a country-style sofa of blue and white plaid and Zach helped Clare control her fall to it.

"She came to help me. And she *did*. She made the evil ghost go away." Caden cried, his tears shading his eyes all the bluer and magnifying them. Snot ran from his nose. Poor child.

"What are you talking about?" Mr. LuCette asked.

"Gram sent them. Sent Clare, who sees ghosts like I do and *fights* them! I'm glad she's here." He stuck out his bottom lip.

"I thought we agreed we wouldn't talk about this anymore." Mrs. LuCette frowned.

"No. You told me I couldn't. I didn't say I would. That's not the same."

Caden's parents glared at Zach and her. Clare could feel the heat of their anger.

"Is it true my grandmother sent you?" demanded Mrs. LuCette.

Clare managed to drop her chin and heft it up again in a difficult nod.

Zach said, "That's right. Mrs. Flinton's worried about Caden and we believe she has cause."

"We don't," rasped Mr. LuCette. "We don't like her interference in our parenting, and we don't like her odd notions."

Zach said, "Something strange is definitely going on in this canyon—"

"You're wrong there," said Mr. LuCette. "Nothing happened, but Caden had a nightmare and went screaming to the door, and you were outside."

Clare could feel Zach's irritation, too—as if some of her normal senses had shut down or been scorched away—her hearing went in and out—but other, unusual, senses had kicked in.

"You mean the number of deaths here lately is usual." A statement, not a question from Zach.

"I don't think we need to talk about this before Caden." Mrs. LuCette and her husband shared a glance.

"We're asking you to leave," Mr. LuCette announced. "We don't want you staying here in our establishment."

"I should have a say in this, too," Caden protested. "I like them and I want them to stay."

"You're seven," Mrs. LuCette said, "and not an adult, with an adult's *mature* judgment." Obviously she didn't think Clare or Zach had mature judgment.

Zach waited a few seconds before he answered. "I think you should take time to consider your choices. Send Caden to his grandmother, leave town yourselves . . ."

"No," Mr. LuCette stated.

Caden began weeping.

"He's overtired. I'll put him back in bed," said Michael LuCette. "Don't be here when I come back."

"Consider us gone," Zach said in a hard voice. Then he softened it and said, "Good night, Caden. Hasta la vista." He stood. Clare didn't think her knees worked, like so much else in her body. "We'll be at the Jimtown Inn."

The world swooped around her as Zach picked her up. Wow. He carried her outside and to the car—she didn't know how, but his gait did feel odd—opened the door, and stuck her in. "You just sit here. I'll handle everything."

"I . . . can—"

"Sit. Be quiet."

He hopped in the driver's seat just enough to turn on the car and heater.

So cold. So scared. The cold would fade; Clare thought the scared would live in her bones forever. Such a coward, she was. She closed her eyes, but saw the white and swirling mess again, and this time in the jagged black lightning flashes—or light-eating streaks—heavily lashed brown eyes stared at her. Creepy.

She heard Zach coming back, rolling two bags. So he must have put on the shoe brace and the ankle and leg brace and wasn't using his cane. The trunk opened and a few seconds later closed and he came to her again. He took her foot in his hands and slipped a sock and shoe on it, did the same with the other, then threaded her arms through her jacket.

"Thanks," she said, or meant to. Her mouth formed the word but nothing came out.

He kissed her forehead, put her tote in next to her feet. She saw her purse in there . . . and the knife. He swung her legs around. She had to snap out of this, contribute, be an equal partner, *not* be dependent. But reality seemed one pace away from the mists moving around her, as if she'd stepped into the ghost no-where and could look out, but not get out. She had to think.

Nothing came to mind.

Zach shut her door and joined her in the front. "I repacked your suitcase, so it won't look like you did it. Double-checked that I have everything of ours. We're ready to roll."

Okay. But she'd only thought that and hadn't said it.

They drove through the streets that were punctuated with few lights from homes and businesses along the way. Clare's continual trembling calmed to a shudder now and then. She tried, tried again, and said through cold lips, "I don't know what's wrong with me."

"Shock." He sounded furious.

"Oh." A thought shimmered. This felt a lot like when she'd been denying her gift and going mad as scary ghosts haunted her . . . and like freezing to death. Yes, that was the downside of her gift. If she didn't accept it, she'd die. But she had! A spurt of anger heated her. She had accepted that she had a gift to see apparitions, to help wraiths move from this world—this gray featureless world—and onto whatever was next.

And she'd *worked* at her new, unwanted, vocation. She *had* helped ghosts pass on. Yes, the downside of *not* helping was to go mad. No choice in any of that, but she'd come to value her gift, and she'd certainly done the best that she could. She should not be sitting here, stressed to the max, like a bump on a log. She should be acting.

Zach stopped in the business district just below the canyon and helped her from the car, slid her tote over her shoulder. She couldn't turn her head to see it. Her vision had narrowed too much. Must still be in shock. Get over it! But though her mind struggled, it couldn't quite leave the gray.

She managed to leave the truck under her own power, stood, and followed Zach past a lavender door and up an extremely steep flight of stairs wide enough for only one person. Yes, she recognized a turn-of-the-twentieth-century hotel when she was in one. They took the first door on the left, with the name "Holy Moses," . . . one of the local mines.

Zach opened that door, too. "Sorry," he said gruffly. "This is the only room available, and the bathroom is down the hall."

Clare looked down the hall, not more than fifteen feet away. There were only five other doors. Small hotel.

"No problem," she squeaked.

Zach's smile lit his eyes and triumph seeped warmly through her. She'd accomplished a two-word sentence, very good.

Clearing her voice, she entered the small room. "How did we get this room so fast?"

"There was a mix-up I didn't tell you about. Samantha, Rickman's assistant, booked the most 'atmospheric' hotel for us. This one. But even though it was built in 1905, it's on the site of other buildings that were here earlier. Noted for its ghosts. By the time Rickman corrected her error, and told her to get us reservations at the LuCettes', it was too late to cancel, so I let it stand."

"Uh huh. Getting to know you, Zach. Having this room was also backup."

"And we needed it, didn't we?"

Nodding was easier now. There was an old painted wooden vanity with a mirror in a curvy frame immediately to her left. She put down the tote. "Another place I couldn't usually stand because of spooks, huh?"

"That's right. I'll get our stuff."

Clare thought of the nearly vertical stairs. "I don't need anything tonight."

Zach's face hardened as if he thought she tried to spare

him the truth. "Nothing else but you," she said. She tried a weak smile. "We're already dressed for bed."

His stance eased. "Right. No one's here at the hotel to check in with." He nodded at the vanity. "They left the outer door and this room door unlocked for us." He shook his head. "Trusting folk, but all the businesses around here are closed. It's too late." He looked at the bed set into an alcove just its size and grunted. "Double bed."

"All the better to be close to you," Clare said. Yes. Thank heavens, her mind was coming back online. She leaned over and pulled out her purse.

Zach walked over to take it from her and she wouldn't let him. "I need it."

"Why?"

She sniffed. "My feet must be filthy. I have damp wipes."

"Of course you do."

He stepped in and wrapped her close. "My God, Clare. My God."

"You saw it, too," she said.

"I'm not sure what I saw or felt. But there was some *thing,* and damn, I fought it, too."

They stood for a few minutes until she shifted foot to foot. "My feet feel grimy." She pulled away.

Zach plucked the purse from her loose grip and handed her the wipes. Then he poured her a mug of water from one of the bottles he'd pulled from her tote, glad that his hand was steady.

A splash of water hit his shoe. Nope, his hands were shakier than he'd thought. God. He'd almost lost her. Lost Clare. Panic sweat began to dry on his body. Regular sweat, too. And the standard exertion sweat when he fought the— thing, the snowstorm from hell—when he'd strained his physical limits to run with his disability, to carry Clare when his foot didn't work right.

The panic sweat had come first, because of his fear for Clare. "Are you sure you want to sleep in those pajamas?" Knowing her, she should have another set or a nightgown or something in her bag. She wouldn't pack just one thing, even for five days. Though he figured she *could* close the case in five days—four now, counting all day Friday—she didn't have that faith in herself. And packing was one of the few things she could control in this whole situation.

"Clare?" She sat, pasty white with an overlay of her own drying sweat, scrubbing and scrubbing at her right foot as if she'd started the action and couldn't think of anything else to do. This was not his Clare—dull, unresponsive.

When he'd offered to get her bags, he'd thought he'd grab some small amount of breathing room, of thinking room, for himself. Now he wasn't sure if she really understood he was in the same room as she.

Putting the mug of water back on the small coffee tray on the vanity, he stepped up to the bed and took the wipe from her, sat next to her, and cleaned her left foot, too. They were scraped from running across the gravelly sidewalk to the LuCettes'.

When her soles were as clean as he thought they'd get without a shower, he pulled the covers down and encouraged her to tuck herself in. Then he turned off the lights; took off his shoes, socks, braces; and spooned against her.

God. He'd almost lost her. The thought cycled around and around, churning his whole system. They'd become too close; he couldn't lose her now without damage to himself, and he wouldn't want it any other way.

The four-letter "l" word hovered in his mind, but he shied away from forming it even mentally. Too soon. Too quickly.

But he couldn't lose Clare.

She worried that she was dependent on him. That she wasn't an equal partner in this relationship. That he didn't allow her to help him, and that made her lesser, or him more stubborn, or something.

Just last night they'd argued and he'd had to do some heavy thinking about his past and *his* psychic woo-woo Counting Crows Rhyme predictions thing . . . and his lost brother. Tough relationship stuff. But, by God, he'd take all that gut-twisting emotional relationship business instead of this ghost killing crap any day.

He *needed* Clare . . . needed her support . . . needed her to help him make sense of the supernatural world, hers and his, that they lived in now . . . and thinking of that, he opened his eyes to see a faint ivory glow from the vanity, emanating from the cloth tube of the knife.

Tonight had scared him shitless. Those awful sounds, rumbling growls as if some beast hunted, the child's screams. Clare's actions.

He didn't think he'd been so scared in his life—at least not since his childhood when his brother Jim had been shot in a drive-by because Jim had thought Zach had angrily gone off from their new home on the military base.

No, Zach didn't want to think of that. When he'd depended on that sixth sense he and Jim had shared, knowing where the other was, and that had failed. Except *that* memory loomed in his mind and his heart, echoed in his body as his first big mistake, his first failure.

His parents had promised him that the next time they moved quarters to a new base, he'd have permission to leave it. They'd reneged. Angry, he'd left—but hadn't gone off base, though he said he would. Jim, older at sixteen, *had* gone off base.

Zach had thought the psychic link he'd shared with Jim would let his brother know where he was. But it had failed. Then came a long and agonizing wait until they learned Jim had died. Their family had been smashed to smithereens.

Yeah, his first whopping life mistake.

The second one had gotten him shot and crippled earlier in the year.

He would *not* fail to protect Clare, would *not* lose her.

When he closed his eyes, etched on his inner vision was that whirling mass of *something*. He'd felt the evil, the awful hunger to *feed*.

He didn't know what Clare had seen, heard, sensed. To him, it had looked like a whipped-up white-out ball of a snowstorm, rotating fast with bits of sharp-edged rock, big like the spike that had gone into the throat of one of the hunters, and small like gravel, and shiny bits of pointy metal, razors . . . or teeth. Maybe teeth, supernatural teeth.

And maybe he was letting his imagination get the better of him. Who'd ever heard of metal shark-like teeth in a ghost, or a snowstorm?

But now he heard the wind pick up outside . . . wailing like a lost soul . . . like many ghosts that had been eaten by one voracious spirit.

Clare shivered in his arms, and he took a soft, small feather pillow and put it over her ear and hugged her closer, until they touched.

He was so scared his dick was limp, a first this near to Clare.

And he hadn't told her of the crows he'd seen on their short journey from the LuCettes' place to here in the middle of the night. The one crow—sorrow—he had plenty of sorrow and worry for Clare and Caden and all of Creede right now. Check one prediction off the list.

Two sets of four crows.

Four for death.

He shivered at that one.

Clare murmured and wiggled closer and he wrapped his arms around her and felt her, warm and alive. She'd be back to her vibrant self tomorrow. He hoped.

He wouldn't allow death to take her. He'd find some way to protect her, no matter the cost.

ELEVEN

ZACH WOKE EARLIER than Clare, but still kept her in his arms. The morning was too quiet, even for the deserted business district of a small town soon after dawn. No bird-song. Clare's house had trees and birds greeting the sun in the morning. So did his apartment at Mrs. Flinton's.

No birds here, and there should have been. The inn was barely two stories with trees along the south side of the building and one in the front, close to their west-facing room.

They hadn't paid any attention to the thermostat when they'd come in, and the room felt too cool. And if it was too cool for him, it would be chilly for Clare, who'd be sensitive to cold for the rest of her life.

He rolled from the bed and Clare grumbled, her expression scrunching. Her arm flailed as if searching for him, then tucked in under the quilt. He liked that she wanted him near, but it made his heart squeeze at how close they'd become. Even in the low morning light, an ominous feeling lingered.

Padding over to the thermostat, he turned it up, then eyed the 1905 room dimensions. Small, with small furnishings.

The room held only the double bed, the vanity, a table and a chair, and an antique wood and porcelain wash basin next to a screen in the corner. The television was mounted on the wall over the table. He dragged on a pair of jeans and, moving quietly, he opened the outside door to the balcony just enough to step into the more than bracing air. Since it was only a few degrees above freezing, he couldn't stand out here long. The steep hills shadowed the empty street, and Zach sensed the shade was more than thick clouds blocking the rising sun. The crazy ghost had smudged the town. He blinked and thought he saw ominous layers, as if last night had just been another coating.

Nope, no birds. And, thankfully, no crows.

Goose bumps rose and his nose twitched at an odd smell . . . maybe a hint of sulfur. He didn't think it came from him, but hell, he needed coffee and a shower for sure. Sliding back into the room, he welcomed the heat. With a last glance at Clare, he put on some clean sweatpants, took the bathroom key and his kit, and headed for the shower.

Zach knew small towns. He'd worked as a deputy sheriff in lightly populated counties for more than half a decade, moving west from the eastern seaboard cities where he'd started his career as a cop.

There'd be a place where the locals would gossip during breakfast of the events of the night. Both this place, the Jimtown Inn, and the LuCettes' motel offered breakfast along with night stays, and the restaurant here was open to the public for all meals until next month.

The chef here had a better rep. If Zach were local, he'd come here . . . unless rumor and gossip were rampant about what had gone on in the early morning at the LuCettes'. Then folks would go there to get the scoop.

Interesting that the LuCettes hadn't called the sheriff while he and Clare were there. But Zach's gut clenched at the thought that Caden's parents really hadn't experienced much other than their boy's screaming from a nightmare and Clare and him coming to their door looking wasted.

Could the LuCettes' senses be that dull?

Even in his prior career, even before the shooting, he'd been aware that inexplicable stuff happened. Weird stuff.

Now it looked like he was becoming an expert on weird stuff.

Maybe none of the people staying with the LuCettes had noticed anything unusual either. When he'd driven away, he'd counted twelve cars. Be interesting to see how many were there this evening.

While he considered things, he wondered where the local cops—Mineral County sheriff deputies—ate to keep their ears to the ground, their fingers on the pulse of their town. Even better would be to know where they traded info, but Zach figured that would be in the county building—the courthouse and sheriff's department—diagonally across the street from this hotel, where he couldn't easily eavesdrop.

When he returned, Clare was up, had made the bed, folded his clothes from yesterday, and placed them atop his suitcase. She wore the fluffy hotel robe, still looked more fragile than he wanted. "Good morning," she said.

Just words. She didn't think the morning was any better than he did. "Good mornin'."

She brushed a kiss over his lips, snagged the bathroom key from his fingers, and left.

A few minutes later, he heard several voices in the hallway through the thin plank door. A couple of them held Texan accents—and Clare responded to morning courtesies with the other guests.

He opened the room door for her so she wouldn't have to stand in the tiny hall and use the key. She walked in, her face flushed above the thick white hotel robe. He nodded to the two large people as they passed his and Clare's room and headed singly down the stairs.

A little nosey, Zach stood by the open crack of the room door. The Texan tourists spoke of the good breakfast they anticipated and the classic car they'd brought up for the Cruisin' the Canyon show. As their voices rose from the nearly vertical staircase, they commented on how they might want to drive Bachelor Loop and see the old mines . . . and where the hunters died.

The rumor mill was fast in this particular small town if visitors had already heard about the deaths. They must have picked up the gossip at dinner the night before, though Zach didn't recall seeing them at Pico's Patio, which he'd figured was where town people ate out.

He closed the door and turned toward Clare. "You look better."

"Thanks a lot." She grimaced. Then she sent him that flirty glance of hers, grabbed the clothes she'd laid out atop her bag on the luggage rack, and disappeared behind the screen in the corner. She tossed the robe over the top of the screen and rustling came to his ears. His blood heated just from imagining her nude. He cleared his throat. "I think your bedroom at your house could do with a screen. Do you have one?"

Her head popped around the side, showing a shoulder with no bra strap. His dick hardened. This not-quite-naked, not-quite-dressed tease show really worked. Her eyes sparkled. "I have three."

"We'll, uh, have to check them out." His mind spun a bit with consideration and input from his body. "Maybe a thin one, like one of those Japanese screens." Where he could see her outline as she undressed and dressed. He swallowed.

"I don't have a shoji screen." She walked out dressed in jeans and a tank under another very soft sweater, probably another cashmere one, in deep blue that showed off the auburn glints in her hair. "But I have one of those old-fashioned screens with gathered material." She tilted her head. "Muslin or linen, perhaps."

"Uh-huh." Clearing his throat, he said, "You really want to go down to breakfast?" Though it would be better for her than sex. Really. She still looked pale to him. He told his dick to subside. It didn't listen. Good thing his jeans were old and a little loose.

"I'm hungry, and the Jimtown Inn Restaurant is supposed

to have great food. We paid for breakfast, I'm sure, and there are probably specific hours we can eat." She pulled the robe off the screen and hung it on a hanger from the short wooden pole with a shelf above that stood in for a closet. She turned and blinked at the door next to the window as if she hadn't seen it before. "What's that?"

"Door to the balcony."

Her face lit. "We have a balcony?"

"Yeah. We share it with the other two rooms that face the front, the Commodore and the Jackpot. We can look out on the busy nightlife of Creede."

"Nice." But she didn't check it out. Instead she came and kissed him on the lips. He smelled her ginger-orange travel shampoo and mint toothpaste. Perked his dick up more. Hell with it. He pulled out his dark blue flannel shirt and let it hang outside his jeans; the bottom was square cut, no tails.

Clare raised her brows and gave him a cheeky grin. "Let's eat."

He nodded and picked up his cane, opened the door for her, and let her precede him into the hall that barely held two people side by side. She went down the stairs first, then through the door to the restaurant that had been locked when they'd come in the night before. When he caught up with her, he put a hand on her arm to slow her down before she was much into the big, empty outer dining room so he could check it.

The chamber appeared to be the original hotel lobby, converted to a more profitable room as part of the restaurant. He kept their pace slow as they moved toward the chatter coming from the wide doorway to a second room, dipped his head to murmur in her ear, "I want to sit near where the locals congregate."

Her eyes showed surprise, then she nodded. They walked into the second large room, this one with tablecloths, silverware, cloth napkins, and juice goblets at the ready. The Texan couple sat next to one of the windows. Closer to the back of the room and the huge carved wooden bar was a large round table that held several people who seemed less touristy in dress and attitude.

The hostess came up to them. "You must be the Slades in the Holy Moses Room."

"That's us," Zach said. Clare frowned but didn't contradict him. Zach indicated a table next to the one that held residents and the waitress led them there.

They'd no sooner ordered the morning's special omelettes before a man walked through the front door of the restaurant. The locals focused on the newcomer who wore dark jeans, a plaid red flannel shirt, and an insulated vest. His expression raw, the man took the seat that his friends had saved for him.

He folded into the chair, ran his hand through his thinning silver hair. "Christ, what a morning. Day's already shot to hell and gone."

"What's up, Bill?"

Bill's mouth turned down. "Pais wanted to see me."

"The sheriff?"

"Yeah, about my group hunting license for bobcat."

Another man in a gray plaid shirt grunted. "Envied you that when you got it in the draw."

"Yeah, thought I was lucky. They jerked the license," Bill said with bitterness.

"Jerked it because of those jerks Ross and Burk," added a third man, thin with a wrinkled face and an edgy smile.

"Yeah. Christ. Now I can't even use it when hunting season starts." Bill rubbed his face. "I can't believe Ross and Burk went out."

"Wanted to see how their new rifles worked, most likely," said a solid woman who'd just nodded to Bill when he'd come in and continued knitting some pink thing. She pursed her lips and shook her head. "Heard them talking about that at Pico's Patio night before last. Not to speak ill of the dead, but Ross and Burk cut corners, all five years they've been coming up here, Bill, and you shoulda known that."

"City people," gray plaid sneered.

"Yeah, yeah." Bill flipped over a coffee mug and someone slid a carafe to him. He poured the drink and chugged it. With a sideways glance at the knitter, Bill said, "Not to speak ill of the dead, but, Jesus, they really screwed me over." More glugging of coffee. "Didn't wait until my license was good and got one of those damn Canada lynx that were just reintroduced instead of a bobcat. What a cluster—" He stopped abruptly when the middle-aged waitress appeared with a pad. "I'll take the huevos rancheros, Pearl. Sorry for the language, ladies."

"Everybody's on edge," the knitter said. Her needles stopped a moment and she rolled her neck. Zach heard the pop of vertebrae from where he sat. His gaze cut to Clare and her wide eyes showed she listened, too.

"Did you hear the wind last night?" The woman shivered. "I don't recall the wind being that rough at this time of year ever before. Really cold, especially after such a warm summer."

Gray plaid grunted. "No wind in Wagon Wheel Gap."

"Fierce and nasty in town," the thin guy said. "Didn't like it at all."

"Me neither," said the waitress. "Anyone want anything else?"

A chorus of negatives.

"I'll get those eggs. Sorry about your trouble, Bill." The waitress paused. "I heard Ross's and Burk's deaths were strange? Rockfall splinters." She shuddered.

"Fu—, shoot, yeah," Bill said. He rubbed his face. "One in the head, the other in the throat. I'll remember that for a long time. Glad I don't have to deal with their wives. Don't think I've ever had a decent conversation with the women. The sheriff is handling that, thank Christ."

"Strange," repeated the waitress.

The knitter stopped, swept a glance around the table. "Lotta strange stuff going on lately." Her shoulders hunched. "I don't like it. Maybe I'll go see my folk in Grand Junction." She glanced at the thin guy. "What do you think? Shall we go see my sister in Grand Junction?" He shifted in his seat, scowled, then finally said, "After Cruisin' in the Canyon." Mumbling, he added, "If stuff gets worse."

"Speaking of strange," gray plaid said, "I heard that the LuCette kid had screaming nightmares bad enough to make a couple of people check out in the middle of the night."

"Poor little guy," the knitter commented, her needles clicking away steadily again.

"That family has always had a bit of oddness in them," Bill said.

"Not the LuCettes," the knitter said. "The Flintons are the folks who have the touch of fey, and I won't hear a word against them . . . neither of them, the LuCettes or the Flintons. And I tell you that if little Caden is having nightmares, it's just another sign that something is off around here."

"Huh," gray plaid guy said, but Bill and the thin man shared a concerned glance.

Then the waitress came with great-smelling omelettes and placed them before Zach and Clare.

"Thank you." Clare's voice sounded strained though she smiled up at the server.

The local folks at the table next to them got up and left before Clare had finished her coffee. As they went out, a tall older man of about seventy walked in, scanned the room, saw them, came over to their table, and took a seat.

Clare appeared alarmed. Zach touched her hand. "Checking us out."

"That's right. Mason Pais, Jr."

TWELVE

"I RECOGNIZE YOUR surname as the same as the sheriff who worked the rockfall accident yesterday," Zach said.

"He's the fourth, Mason Pais the fourth, and following in my footsteps. I'm Junior . . . the second."

"You sound proud of him," Clare said calmly, though Zach noted she folded and refolded the linen napkin in her lap.

"I am. Very. He's the youngest sheriff in Colorado. Studied and trained for it since he was a kid and he's a good sheriff. Said he met you yesterday, that you're an ex-deputy,"—Pais glanced at Zach's cane— "and now a P.I. Don't know as there's anything here that needs a P.I."

Zach lifted and dropped a shoulder. "Who asked you to look us up?"

"Michael LuCette. His family has been here as long as mine has."

"Oh," Clare said in a small voice.

"Wondered if that was who was behind this little visit," Zach said. He reached into his jacket and pulled out his wallet, handed Pais his card.

The man glanced at it, stuck it in his back jeans pocket. "Zach Slade, Rickman Security and Investigations," he said.

"Yes."

Clare's backbone had stiffened to ramrod straight.

Pais frowned at her. "You work for them, too?"

She sniffed. "Not as an . . . operative. An expert consultant. Occasionally."

"Huh," Pais said.

"I don't have a card." Her tone indicated she didn't *want* a card.

"I've met Rickman and his wife," Pais remarked, keeping his voice slow and drawling, his attitude casual to tempt them to say more.

Clare took the bait. Her eyes warmed and she smiled. "Desiree Rickman is a friend."

Tilting back on two legs of his chair, Pais said, "She's a pistol, all right."

"We are who we say we are." Zach relaxed his body.

"And the Rickmans are associated with the Flintons who are kin to the LuCettes," Pais said.

"That's right," Zach replied.

Clare's lips thinned and she glanced at Zach. He shrugged.

After clearing her throat, she said, "Yes, Mrs. Flinton sent us."

During the small pause in conversation, the waitress came up with a carafe. "Coffee, Mason?"

He looked at both of them, but Zach said nothing and Clare kept her mouth shut, too, as she studied the man.

"Don't mind if I do, Pearl," Pais said to the server.

The woman gave him a mug and poured the excellent coffee. As soon as she left, Pais sipped, then shook his head, commenting on Clare's info. "Barbara Flinton. Now there's an original woman. Another pistol."

This time Clare said nothing. Zach knew she wouldn't ever admit to a stranger that she was a ghost seer. Not this soon in her . . . vocation.

"What do you want from us?" Clare said, her voice

wobbling a little. Zach reached out and covered her hands with one of his own, stilling them.

"How about the truth?"

Clare shot Zach another glance. He kept his face expressionless so as not to influence her decision.

"Or I could call Tony Rickman or Barbara Flinton."

"Mr. Rickman wouldn't say anything," Clare snapped back. Her lips thinned, tightened, and she looked at Zach again, then let out a slow breath, met the man's eyes and said in a very quiet voice, "Caden LuCette sees ghosts. I do, too. There's an evil one around and I'm here to stop it."

Well, that surprised Zach.

Pais's face went inscrutable. "I hear that you believe that."

Zach finished up his coffee. "And I've heard there have been too many deaths in Creede lately."

The man flinched infinitesimally, but Zach saw it. "Something else has happened." He kept his voice soft, too.

Clare gasped. "What?"

After sliding his gaze around the room, Pais clicked the front legs of his chair back on the floor, picked up his mug, swigged, then muttered, "One of our elderly ladies . . . who should *not* have been out on her own last night, fell outside. Cracked her head on the coping at the top of the flume, rolled into the creek. It's not deep at this time of year . . ."

"But it's freezing cold," Clare whispered. She'd gone pallid as if cold herself.

"Gone?" asked Zach.

"Yeah."

Well that was one "four crows for death prediction" done, and it hadn't been Caden or Clare, thank God.

Unfortunately, one more death prediction remained.

Clare raised her hand and Pearl bustled over. "More coffee, please, mine has gone cold."

"For sure, honey." Pearl hurried back and poured steaming, aromatic brew into Clare's cup. Both Zach and Pais gestured for a refill.

When she was gone, Pais said, "I just heard the news before I came in."

"It will get around quickly enough," Zach said.

"That's right." Pais sipped from his mug, eyed them, then leaned over the table and said, "Appreciate it if you didn't speak to the LuCettes."

Putting down her cup, Clare looked up at the former sheriff. "Perhaps you can tell the LuCettes—when you talk to them about us—that they should consider taking Caden away, or sending him to his great-grandmother's."

"I'll relay that warning," Pais said.

"Concern." Clare tilted her chin. "We can be concerned about a young boy." She paused. "If you have any influence with those who serve and protect, you should protect the LuCettes and Caden."

"I hear you." The ex-sheriff's observation of Clare intensified.

Zach heard the refusal in the man's voice and even more suspicion of Clare. Time to divert attention to himself. "And we can be concerned about an old woman who lost her life in odd circumstances," Zach added.

"I didn't say anything about the circumstances being odd . . . but the door to her house shoulda been locked, and her companion had fallen asleep, and old Mrs. Tewksbury shouldn't have been anywhere near the stream."

"Uh-huh," Zach said. He drank his coffee, still good. "A lot of people to be concerned about here, the whole town."

Clare frowned. "You will really watch Caden?" She sounded doubtful, glanced in the direction of the motel. Her eyes flickered as if she made plans.

Pais leaned forward, face hard and set, and said in a low voice that shouldn't carry past their table, "You two listen, and listen good. If you attempt to see Caden LuCette, I will personally get a restraining order against you." Pais's smile twitched tight. "It won't be hard to convince one of our local judges. And then we'll just run you right out of town," the ex-sheriff ended with satisfaction.

Clare's shoulders straightened and she glared at the older man. "Then you *will* watch Caden. You and whomever would run us out of town. Believe me when I say he's in danger." She didn't back down, and that pleased Zach.

"I'm outta here." Pais rose. With a last jerk of his head in a not-so-courteous-good-bye-nod, he stalked from the restaurant.

"You okay?" Zach asked.

Another sigh. "As well as can be expected. I hope *they'll*—the Paises, LuCettes, and whomever—will listen." She swallowed. "Too many deaths should concern them." She shook her head. "Another one, last night." Her brows lowered in concentration. "I think the flume with the stream runs behind this building."

"Yeah? You want to check it out?" Zach asked. He did.

"I suppose we should, and look around the rest of the town more, too, not just drive through it, and at least find the archives."

"Right." He stood and put his napkin on his plate, reached in, and pulled out his wallet.

Now her brows went up.

"Tip, Clare. What do you think this would have cost us in Denver?"

"Oh, all right. Leave her seven dollars as a little over twenty percent."

Clare checked the weather on her phone and they went up to get their outer gear. The highs should be in the upper fifties. Weather predictions were for a cold front the next couple of days and mixed weather—snow early and late mixed with rain mixed with sleet mixed with occasional sunshine.

Once outside and rounding the hotel, Zach noticed heavy clouds flattened the sky to a steady gray. They walked between buildings to the rear to observe the stream, nicely flowing in the bottom of a man-made, widely angled V, the flume. A foot-high rim of rectangular stone blocks set in concrete edged the top. Clare followed his gaze and winced.

"Yeah, trip, hit your head, fall and roll down into the

stream, drown or freeze to death. Easy." He paused. "A real good wind could push a tottery person off balance."

Clare looked upstream to the small metal bridges with open railings. Those wouldn't keep anyone from falling either.

"We don't know if Mrs. Tewksbury was tottery," Clare said halfheartedly.

"No. We don't know a lot of things." Zach took her hand. He'd decided the threat this case brought was primarily supernatural and his gun wouldn't dent the thing. If he'd had one of his weapons last night, he couldn't have drawn it under the circumstances anyway. Though he did note that the silk-sheathed bone knife *had* affected the monster.

"We don't know too many things." He tugged on her hand and they walked to the front of the hotel and the street.

Hills on the east and west contained the town, with the south showing a distant ridge, too. The highway opening out into the Rio Grande river valley wound southeast. Rocky promontories toward the north led to the mining canyons.

Clare sauntered with Zach through the business district and down to the town park that held the archives. Only the hardware store was open, the tourist places still shut for another hour . . . a couple of them even closed until next June. They all looked interesting.

The wind picked up, gathering clouds low over the canyon in big puffs with dark bellies. More likely they'd get caught on peaks and drop rain, sleet, or snow than they'd just blow away.

Mostly two-story brick buildings, painted and not, comprised the three blocks of the business district that catered to tourists. Their window and door frames were painted, like the lavender wood of their hotel, to attract the eye and promise delightful shopping. All of the buildings were built later than the fateful June day of Robert Ford's murder, since a fire had burned down Jimtown three days before—and some intimated that it had been set by Soapy Smith's men to torch Ford's dance and gambling hall.

They reached the corner where the street angled and Clare stopped, the crisp, clean air lifting her mood. "Just think, Soapy Smith could have set up his con right here. It looks like the spot where his Orleans Club was."

Zach chuckled and squeezed her hand. "You know how that scam worked?"

She stuck up her nose. "Yes, he'd buy little bars of soap, unwrap them, put a hundred dollar bill, a ten dollar bill, and maybe some one dollar bills around them, rewrap, then come out and hawk them. 'Soap for a dollar! Some have money inside. Take a chance, you could win big!'"

Zach snorted. "And Soapy's first customer would be a confederate who 'buys' the one-hundred-dollar-wrapped bar, opens it, and shows it to everyone." Zach shrugged. "Made more than one fortune that way."

"Yes." Clare tilted her head. "He had a gang here, so maybe I was wrong, he'd be rich enough not to run that scam."

"For some, rich enough *isn't* enough."

"No. I saw that often in my previous career." She turned around on the corner, admiring the silver-faced building, made from tin perhaps, with dark blue trim across the street.

With a roll of his shoulders, Zach said, "We talked about greed. I'm not getting a feeling that the motive is that particular one of the seven deadly sins. It's something else."

Clare turned her admiring gaze toward Zach, who raised his brows. "You're a good investigator."

"Thanks."

"Have you seen any more crows?" she asked.

Now his shoulders hunched a little and he said gruffly, "No lying, so rather not say."

Her mouth went dry; she swallowed, but it remained dry. "Four then, for death according to the rhyme."

"You remember that part of the rhyme."

"It's hard to forget."

Wanting to change the subject, Zach said conversationally, "We haven't seen Enzo today." He wondered if the ghost dog would be any use whatsoever in a deadly case.

Clare jerked a little as if he'd interrupted a deep train of thought. "No," she said in a stifled voice. "I haven't seen or heard from him since . . . since . . ."

"He jumped right into the ghost, ready to bite," Zach provided.

"Yes. I can't believe that I forgot about him!"

"Well, you would have known if he were, uh, consumed, right?"

She nodded. "I'm sure." Her next inhalation was long and even. "I'm going to . . . look for him."

"Right."

"Mentally," she said, as if he hadn't gotten it.

"Yes." He wrapped an arm around her waist. "The sidewalks look relatively new, bump free. I'll keep you safe."

"Of course." Her eyes went blank, and her lips moved in the word, *Enzo.*

I am here, Clare! the ghost dog replied. Zach actually heard him from a distance and a damn cold shiver trickled down Zach's spine.

Where's here? Clare's mind-tone sounded just like her voice. Zach kept his arm around her, scanning the sidewalk and the street. A couple of cars drove by, one woman walked her dog on a leash, but several dogs without people wandered around on their own business. That wouldn't happen in any other town Zach knew.

Are you in Denver? Clare asked Enzo.

Zach stared straight ahead, pretending that Enzo was right here . . . okay, pretending a ghost dog he was used to speaking with telepathically was close . . . Yeah, and that sounded so normal. For sure.

No. A slight whine from the ghost dog. *I am here in Creede.*

Are you hurt? Do you need me?

"Us," Zach murmured.

Us? Do you need us, Enzo?

The big scary ghost WITH TEETH frightened me and made me dissipate and when I woke up I was still where I was but the boy was there and he was scared too and we decided to be scared together and I slept on his bed, and he was okay and I was okay and he asked me if I would go to school with him today and I have never been to school and thought I might like it, so I am going. Okay, Clare? You have Zach, but Caden is little and has nobody. And we will be safe in school, I think. Okay?

Clare suppressed a tiny sob. Zach opened his mouth to protest to Enzo—alright, he'd say the words at the same time as he'd think them to the Lab—but she turned and looked at him, put her fingers over his lips. He frowned but she just shook her head.

That's fine, Enzo. It's absolutely best that you guard Caden. Her mind-voice sounded light with a trace of cheerfulness. The woman lied well with her mind, better than she did with her regular voice and her expression and her body language. Interesting talent. Maybe because she had experience ordering her mind. Zach'd remember that.

Thank you, Clare. See you later, Clare! See you later, Zach.

See you later, Enzo, Clare said. She turned and they stopped and she hugged Zach. Her head bent so all he could see was her pretty hair, and a bit of the delicate nape of her neck.

"Caden needs Enzo more than I do." Her voice sounded muffled.

Zach stroked her hair. "If you say so."

"It's good that the Lab is with him during school."

Zach paused. "I know what it's like being an odd kid in school, we traveled so much—"

"We traveled so much—" Clare said at the same time. "I remember other children not accepting my brother and me." She raised her face. Her eyes appeared a little damp, but her expression was so tender that Zach had to bend and kiss her. Let his lips sink against the slight plush of hers, touched them with his tongue.

She stepped back, linked her fingers with his. "It will be fine," she said.

In person, Clare was a very poor liar.

Hand in hand they strolled to a park and the yellow-painted with brown wood trim ex–train depot that functioned as the town museum. Taped to the inside of the window were the hours.

"Not until Friday," Zach said.

Clare sighed.

A tiny building across the park was the archives library and they climbed the three steps to look at the printed sign on that door. "Again, Friday hours, in the afternoon. By Friday—"

"We're not thinking of that now."

"No, I don't want to think of that," she murmured. She leaned close to peek through the door's window. Zach looked, too. Shelves. Nothing much to see.

"I called and e-mailed the contact person of the Creede Historical Society. She hasn't called me back yet. I'm not sure how to research this without access to original documents."

Zach nudged her. "You don't know how to run an investigation."

"No. I don't," she said in her prissy manner. That lifted his spirits a little, for she was getting back to her normal self. He hoped. There was still a pallidity to her skin that he didn't care for.

"We talk and we listen," he said. "We made a good start this morning when that guy who had the hunters staying with him came in and complained."

"He wanted to complain to all the world how they'd done him wrong," Clare commented.

Zach chuckled. "Basic human desire. Especially since they were caught doing something illegal that reflected on him. Explain, defend yourself. Complain. Usually works."

Clare frowned and her face pinched a bit. Dammit, she looked thinner than yesterday. Did fighting the ghost do that? Not good at all. He loved her curves. He loved the softness of her, especially her inner gentleness that had her believing in everyone's basic goodness, and he didn't want that to tarnish. He'd fight to keep that spark in her clean and alive.

He took her hand and pulled her down from the steps and back into the park that held the depot and the library. Then they crossed the street to walk back up to the Jimtown Inn. One of the proprietors of a shop saw Clare staring at the window and opened the place early, welcoming them in. They looked around, with Zach studying the shirts. The place had books by local Creede writers and photographers, and Clare picked up a couple that even Zach thought were seriously overpriced.

Once they hit the street again, rain had begun to spit and sputter and they walked a little faster.

"If this were . . . one of my regular cases," Clare began, staring forlornly at the closed archives across the street. "I could, perhaps, communicate with other ghosts, who might know the culprit."

"There are bound to be old timers here, descendants of those who stayed after the silver boom went bust," Zach said.

"Family stories get exaggerated as well as lose their detail, maybe even names get changed," Clare grumbled.

After snorting, he said, "What makes you think journalists of the time wouldn't slant the facts to make it a better story?" All right, some bitterness from his own experience after the shooting escaped. Investigative reporters from the big city of Billings had happened to be in town and had done a number on the whole incident.

She gazed at him with wide eyes. "You think so?"

"This was a rowdy camp, and during that time period those Wild West story pamphlets were published and journalists were like Mark Twain, who also wrote tall tales. Of course facts would be slanted in the newspaper. Always."

She sighed. "And that's pretty much all historians have to go on in this case, I think."

"Since a ghost from the past is definitely affecting the present, we need to discover some clues *in* the present."

Nodding, she said, "The breakfast gossip was illuminating."

"Actions of the ghost." He lowered his voice. "Murders of the ghost."

"I think so, too," she whispered back. "I'm so sorry we can't take Caden out of this."

Zach shook his head. "Can't do it. Everyone gets real tense if someone kidnaps a child. The neighborhood, the town, the cops."

"Not an option," Clare agreed, her mouth turning down. She stomped along the sidewalk for a few feet. When she gazed up at him again, her eyes held determination. "We distracted that ghost last night. We can continue to do so. We are more of a threat to it."

He caught her hand. On impulse, he lifted her fingers to his mouth, kissed them. "Not the greatest of alternatives, but one that could work. I like the way you think." He paused. "Maybe I can smooth things a little by cultivating the local cops. Let them see we're the good guys." Two of the sheriff's trucks were parked outside the county building.

Smiling, she squeezed his hand. "You like doing that."

"Yeah, it'll be a little rougher since the Pais guys don't appear to like us." Zach liked the zip of challenge. "I'm sure that in the sheriff's department, and even somewhat in the town, what the Paises say, goes."

He continued, "And I learned something important the night before last. Cops aren't my tribe anymore." He squeezed her fingers. "You are. Primarily you are."

Her smile at him was warm and some of the lingering darkness of the night blew away. Then she nibbled her lip as if in thought. "The supernatural tribe?"

At that he flinched, wanted to grunt noncommittally, but grudgingly said, "Maybe." He drew in a breath of clean, fresh mountain air you just didn't get in Denver, the hint of prairie grass, hills glazed with frost, wet rock. "I'm making a tribe with the Rickman Security and Investigations operatives."

"Uh-huh. That reminds me. We ordered body armor. Do you think it came in?"

"Body armor might have been helpful last night," Zach said.

"Yes. Though, in the end, I don't think it will stop an evil being from munching on me," she replied just as matter-of-factly as he had, and put a hand to her midriff.

"Your ribs hurt?" Though she wasn't touching them.

"It's . . . odd. Like the thing left an icy splinter in me."

He didn't like the sound of that. He studied her. She wasn't looking as good as she had yesterday morning, but a whole lot better than last night, or even when she woke. Infusing his voice with desire—not at all hard—he said, "Let's see if we can melt that ice."

"Yes."

THIRTEEN

THEY GOT BACK to the restaurant as it closed after breakfast hours. Some people filed out; a few lingered in the deep alcove of the main restaurant door. Zach nodded to the Texans as they took off across the street to the hardware store, then opened the closer door that led straight up the stairs to the hotel rooms. For curiosity's sake, he tested the door at the bottom of the stairs that led into the restaurant. It was locked.

He smiled. "Doesn't sound like anyone's in their rooms."

"No." Clare's answer was breathy and went straight to his groin, hardening his dick. He touched her back so she went first.

"This is the best idea we've had all day," he said.

"Yes." She hurried up the stairs and Zach thought her jeans weren't quite tight enough. Her ass was prime . . . yeah, he'd seen tighter, more muscular. Often. Even naked. But Clare's butt simply felt the best in his hands, the right mixture of soft-give and muscle underneath. And it looked great to him. His palms itched, and his dick pressed hard against the front of his jeans in demand to be cradled by her soft stomach, to be slid into her sweet wetness. To climb and shatter with her in orgasm.

God, his mouth watered. He took the steps faster.

She had to jiggle the key in the door and he caught up with her before she opened it, pressed against her so she could feel how hard he was, how much he wanted her. Yeah, absolutely perfect ass. Even more of his blood plummeted to his dick, and his mind dimmed with lust. He angled his hips, once, twice, rubbing against her.

She gasped, and another surge of pleasure wound him higher, because she sure wasn't gasping in fear this time. The portion of her angled cheek he could see was flushed . . . and . . .

He stood, simply stood and closed his eyes, concentrated on her. She trembled. His mouth dried, oh, man, he *needed* her. To be in her.

The door opened and she rushed into the room. He moved quickly after her, and that was damn good because someone else came out of one of the other rooms and she'd have been embarrassed if they'd been caught while he was rubbing up her.

She began to turn, but he stopped her, drew her back so his cock could settle between the firmness of her buttocks again. His fingers went under her jacket to the front of her jeans and slid inside, down her silky skin over her curly hair at the apex of her thighs and lower, to dip between her moist folds and caress her.

"Zach!"

He wasn't interested in answering her, so he only growled, continued to stroke her, felt her getting wetter, warmer, plumper.

His other hand went to the top of her jacket zipper and he slowly pulled it down, the evocative sound of undressing her making him all the hotter. She shifted a little against his fingers, leaned back against him. So it had an effect on her, too.

The thin cashmere sweater caressed the palm of his other

hand as he stroked up to her left breast and curved his hand over her budded nipple, let it thrust against her tank and sweater in the center of his palm, tease him there. He made her move against his fingers at her sex, and her reactions ratcheted his passion sky high.

His jeans were too damn tight and the rain had come back and smacked the roof and balcony as backdrop to their heavy, ragged breathing.

He thought she made little mewling sounds, too, but the blood began to pound in his ears, odd because he thought it was all in his dick. He couldn't recall the last time he'd been so turned on . . . okay, maybe the first time he was with Clare . . .

"Sex only gets better," he mumbled, aching as he withdrew his hand from her, grabbed her jacket, and wrenched it off, dropped it. He took the bottom of her sweater and tank with both hands and yanked up, threw the garments across the small room, flicked open her bra and tossed it, too.

"Oh. My. God," she whispered.

Her nipples looked thick and rosy. Some other time he'd suck on them. Some other time. Needy fire moved in his veins, along his nerves, demanding completion.

His thumbs found her skin again, the snap of her jeans, and slid them and her panties off. He couldn't help himself; he had to touch and squeeze that ass. Just. Incredibly. Right.

"Zach!"

She stepped from her clothes and away, turned, and came back, her fingers flicking the buttons on his shirt open. Then the shirt was gone and she pulled his tee off. He stopped her hands at his waistband.

"What?" she demanded.

"I think . . ." Not that he was thinking much. But somehow the deep yearning reached a peak and burst into something different than just sex to . . . more. Sharing intimacy.

"Tenderness." The word dropped from his mouth. Now he stepped back, still holding her hands, and locked gazes with her. A shudder ran through him . . . His body trying to overwhelm his mind, no, his heart. Not this time. He'd hold on to the sweet-painful edge of control to the very last instant. "Lemme show you tenderness."

A wild light in her eyes flamed, then banked; her expression turned completely open, defenseless, vulnerable. Her hands went limp in his, her body swayed to his and he almost, almost lost it. He swallowed. Raising her hands to his shoulders, he reveled in the touch of her fingers on his bare skin. He framed her face in his palms, again aware of their sensitivity, how smooth her golden skin was, then slid his hands into her thick, untamed hair, letting the strands move along the backs of his hands, the tips of his fingers. He caught his breath, scented her, and that added to all the other aspects that were simply *Clare*, his woman. His lover. His.

He tilted her head, angled his own, and pressed his mouth gently, gently on hers. She opened for him, as she'd always opened for him, body and emotions. Their breaths mingled, and just that thinned his control to a thread. He withdrew from her, watching her nude body still sway, her head still back, her mouth still open, and her eyes closed. His woman openly showing her desire for *him*.

With gritted teeth, he opened his belt, carefully unzipped his jeans over his straining dick, shoved down his jeans and boxers, and pulled off his shoes. Hell with the brace; he'd leave it on.

Her head slowly straightened, her skin that blushing peach under gold. So tempting, all of her.

She'd opened her eyes and the hazel of her irises, mixed green and brown with flecks of gold, were only a thin rim around her pupils. Her gaze dropped to his thrusting erection and she smiled.

He swooped. Just lifted her into his arms, took the few steps to the bed, put her on it. "Please." His whisper was hoarse. And was he *pleading*? Sounded like that. Who cared? "Let me look at you. Please."

Her breath sifted from her and she closed her eyes.

So beautiful, full breasts now flattening a little, curve of the stomach, hair redder at the junction of her legs than on her head. He looked between her thighs and his dick twitched and he had to yank his stare back to her face . . . her lovely face, the overall shape of her, the just plain *rightness* of her.

He leaned over her, touched her forehead, feathered his fingers down from her temple to the corner of her lips.

She smiled and he knew with sweet pleasure that she thought of nothing but him; no shadows darkened her mind.

He continued to trail his fingers over her body, cherishing her, the swell of her breast; the touch of her nipple on his palm again made his arousal stronger.

The room dimmed. Though the rain had stopped, clouds moved over any weak sun. Shadows artistically shaded her body, emphasizing her beauty. He straightened and just soaked in the sight of her until her own eyes opened and she stared at him, pupils still big, mouth soft.

Teasing himself, he lay down next to her. Propped on his side and his elbow, he caressed her some more, tracing her collarbone, drawing his finger down the center of her body. She stayed quiet. Back up and stopping to put his hand over her heart, the quickened thump matched the pulse in her neck. Her skin felt like silk under his fingers. Their gazes met and matched and as they looked at each other, everything else in the world dropped away. Only Clare was real.

With the lightest of touches, he stroked one nipple, then the other, watched them tighten more into small thrusting peaks. His mouth watered as he recalled the softness and the shape of her breasts against his lips, but he didn't want to move. The moment, the atmosphere of true intimacy spun around them, enveloping them in a bubble of special time.

The natural light flickered as the limbs of the tree tossed dark patterns over them.

"Just beautiful," he said.

She smiled, flushed darker, the pink of her blood under her tan making her even more striking. "You, too," she whispered. Her glance went to his erection and her fingers crept close and he caught her hand and raised it to her lips. "Let me."

Now her lips formed in a pout. "I have been. And you're being slow."

"Tender," he reminded her. He leaned down, close, closer until his lips barely skimmed hers, let his breath brush over her lips, inhaled hers. They breathed together, exchanged that life essential. God. Wonderful. Had he ever taken the time to go so slowly with lovemaking when he wasn't buried in a woman? He didn't recall. Didn't recollect sex with any other woman than Clare, not now. They'd all faded from his memory.

He put her hand on his face, needing her touch there . . . and she stroked his cheek and he had to close his eyes at her gentle caress, as if she cared, as if she'd *take care* with him. Cared what he felt and thought and *was*.

As he did with her. More than sex. More than a lover. Just plain more.

His hand flattened as he wanted to feel the touch of her skin against all his fingers and palm. So very smooth as he caressed her, ending again at the juncture of her legs.

They widened and her hips rose a little. He petted her, soft and gentle. As he met her gaze, he saw she remained focused on him. Her sex was damp, then wet as he drove her higher, watching her eyes fog, her body strain, caught up in the strive for climax. Her whole body flushed, tightened, tiny cries left her plump and parted lips.

He could hold on. Could do this for her, watch her, stringing out his own fulfillment, living instant by instant with steel need because she looked so beautiful, responded so freely to his touch.

Then she shuddered, gasped, and turned her head, her eyes wide and her stare fixed on him. She smiled.

And he lost it—the control and the wish to be tender. Evaporated in the steam of lust. With a grunt, he rolled to her, tucked her soft body under his and thrust into her hard. Wet, hot, tight . . . and her hum of pleasure rose to his ears and he felt big and hard and who cared about anything else. He had his woman under him, was *in* her, and would make damn sure she knew that no one would need her as much as he did. No one would give her more.

He groaned with each desperate plunge into her, each withdrawal too long. Her arms and legs clamped around him, she arched, her hips kept time and God that was good! Then her inner muscles clamped around him and nothing in his entire life ever felt that great. Throwing back his head, he shouted as he came. Another, quieter moan, as he subsided on top of her, lay against her, felt the dampness of sweat between them, his and hers.

His mind grayed and he slipped into a timeless place of complete contentment for a while . . . until her breathing slowed and began to sound forced. When he had enough energy to make the effort, he rolled and kept himself under her, let her cover him, and his own body went limp.

She felt boneless, too. So it had to have been good for her. At least took her mind off every damn fear she might have with regard to this job. And, no, he didn't want to even attempt thinking about this case. Let their brains rest, cherish the moment. *Live in the moment.*

Time passed until he realized they lay in muted sun squares and understood what they meant—the rain, snow, sleet was gone. He got up and took a quick shower, meeting no one coming or going. As soon as Clare had done the same, and they were both dressed, he opened the outside door.

"The day's cleared . . . at least for now. Come on out on the balcony. There's a fair number of people to watch."

"All right. Oh, there're tables and chairs. I could work out here."

"Yeah."

They both went to the lavender rail. Zach tested it before he let her lean on it. Now birds had gathered in the trees and chirped and peeped. Still no crows. All to the good.

The street below, especially in front of the hardware store in the only town of Mineral County, had gotten some traffic.

He watched people walk up and down the opposite sidewalk.

Following his gaze, she saw him take in the closed bar at the south end of the street, in what she now knew was the first brick building to go up after the fire in June 1892, and she studied the old buildings as he did, the tourist shops, the restaurant, all the way up to the next street and to the large, newer construction—the county building. Which would, of course, house the sheriff's department.

She sidled closer to him, leaned against his side. His arm came around her, giving her more warmth in the cool air. No one below looked at them, and she didn't hear any sounds from the rooms that shared the balcony with them.

Keeping her tone light, she said, "I bet I can guess what you're thinking."

He grunted. They stood another few heartbeats in silence and he looked at her. "What?"

"That you want to go look at the actual site of the accident where the old lady fell and drowned, not just the stream as we did together." Clare grimaced, not something she was interested in. "Then you'd like to talk to the sheriff again."

"I'd have to talk to someone in the sheriff's department to find out where the accidental fall took place, maybe run it by them so I could take a look. But those Paises, elder ex-sheriff and the younger current sheriff, weren't welcoming."

She gave a short laugh. "And you didn't like that."

He jerked a shoulder. "Who would?"

"But you want to be accepted by the local police."

"It sure would make finding things out here a little easier."

"You think clues in the here and now can lead to our historic ghost."

"Yeah."

"All right." She pointed at him. "And you think that Pais the elder, the ex-sheriff, would have talked to his grandson about meeting us and given the current sheriff his observations."

Zach stared at her, scratched his jaw. "Well, yeah, of course."

She pursed her lips. "You think we made an acceptable impression on Pais?"

One side of his mouth lifted. "Yeah, despite what he said, despite his threat, once he really thought about us, I believe he'd've revised his impression. I'm sure he's curious, and I think that they both will have done a deeper research run on us."

"Oh."

He leaned over and kissed her mouth, and she felt the teasing sweep of his tongue on her bottom lip before he withdrew. "You're squeaky clean."

"Except for being thought a crazy psychic medium."

One side of his mouth kicked up. "Well, yeah, except for that, and that's relatively recent." He slanted her a look. "I wondered why you brought that up with ex-sheriff Pais."

She shrugged. "He asked." Her lips curved in a wobbly smile. "I always stated my profession up front."

"You were an accountant."

"A lot of people find—found—accountants boring."

"Not me."

"Thanks. But though I *am* changing, I can feel it, I want to keep some parts of me as much as I was as I can." Her smile faded. "If that makes sense. Mason Pais, Jr., asked why I was here and I gave him a straight answer. One he might not believe, but one that reflected who I am . . . now." She sighed. "And I have to become used to being thought a crazy psychic medium. That's my life now, people doubting me. Evade or lie to them when they first ask and later they doubt me even more."

He kissed her. "You're one of a kind, Clare."

Another sigh. "I've been hoping that's not true. In any event, the elder Pais asked and I answered with the truth. Besides, I needed to emphasize that Caden is in danger and they should be watchful."

Zach's fingers curved around the thin top of the rail,

gripped, and released. "I'd bet good money that the Paises—or people they asked—contacted both Mrs. Rickman and Mrs. Flinton."

Clare just sighed, then checked her watch. "It's way after business hours, maybe a volunteer from the historical society has contacted me by e-mail and we can set up an appointment to look at the archives before Friday."

"That would be good," Zach said, but his stare remained focused on the county building.

"Go." She pushed at him. "I can look at those local books I bought, if nothing else." She could also consider how to blood her ancestress's darn bone knife. That was going to take some planning.

"Right." Zach pushed away, met her glance and stilled a second, curving his hand around her face. "Beautiful Clare." Another quick kiss. "Later."

"Um-hmm." She didn't follow him back into the small room. Instead she wiped off the damp remaining from the rain, snow, sleet, or the whole combination, from the table and two chairs on their side of the balcony. Soon she heard the creaky door to the hotel below her open, then saw Zach stride out with that old-fashioned cane he used. Because he was studying an old-fashioned cane defense system.

She *would* have to ask him for knife lessons. Darn it.

As soon as he vanished through the side door of the beige one-story county building, she went back into the room, and the heat of it contrasting with the outside air made her just stand and soak it up a bit before she marched over to the thermostat. Zach had turned it up. So thoughtful of him.

She got her tablet and checked the e-mail, nothing. She also checked her telephone because she'd left a message at the number printed on the notice taped to the archives window. No return call. Well, the people who helped out at the historical society with the records would have to be volunteering their time, doing it for a love of the history of their town and county, so no use getting upset at them for not being available on *her* schedule.

After taking care of those two small tasks, Clare rose from the table. She couldn't sit, couldn't settle down.

The amount of control she had over this situation was minuscule and she wanted to be *doing*, even researching, more than just looking at books that might not apply to her case, or scanning the Internet for more stories that were nothing but fictional legends.

So she paced the small room, arms wrapped around herself. She'd have included the balcony, but she didn't want the whole world to see how agitated she felt. Her ribs that had cracked in her last major case ached, and she could swear that she yet felt a twinge of where the ghost's ice splinter had lodged during the fight the night before.

This whole business emphasized the danger of her new vocation. She considered each of the last few weeks, and her few triumphs, as if it were a ledger sheet and had a bottom line of whether she'd achieved her goals or not.

First, if she hadn't accepted her gift, she would have died. She believed that implicitly since she had been dying, freezing to death in the hottest summer on record in Denver.

She had accepted it and survived. Credit.

Second, if she accepted her gift, but didn't use it to help ghosts, she'd go mad.

Currently her mind handled the ghosts in an orderly manner, and they appeared . . . acceptable . . . to her inner vision, dressed in what they wore, or cared to wear, during their lifetimes. But she vividly recalled when they'd come to her as they'd died, burned horribly, strangled . . .

Or, even worse, when white wraiths and shredded spirits pressed around her, wailing in her mind like banshees that wouldn't let another single thought into her head. She hadn't seen or heard or experienced anything except them.

No, not at all hard to go mad under those circumstances. As far as she knew, that particular circumstance lasted all of her life. If she didn't use her gift she'd go insane.

That had been close, but again she'd prevailed.

Worst of all, if she died or went mad and then died, the

family gift would go to her nine-year-old niece, Dora, who lived in Williamsburg, Virginia, and loved all things of Colonial America. Dora might be more flexible of mind than Clare, but she sure wasn't ready to handle the family gift-curse. Clare had spoken to Dora last week and the girl did want to discuss the gift and learn about it. So Clare could train her, eventually, not too soon. As far as Clare was concerned the looming gift-curse should not be allowed to besmirch Dora's childhood.

Without thought, she walked back to the table and her phone and scrolled through her contacts. When she reached Desiree Rickman, her finger hovered over the SeeAndTalk app.

Yes, she wanted to talk to someone. Desiree Rickman was an operative, physically impressive, both in beauty and the command she had over her body. A woman who could keep up her end in a fight. Not at all like Clare in that area. And Desiree believed in psychic powers, even more than Clare. That was a plus.

Most of all, she was the right gender.

Clare touched the app.

Before she could have second thoughts, Desiree's fabulous face with a curious and cheerful expression appeared. "Hi, Clare!"

Words fell from Clare's lips. "Do you know how to soak a knife in blood?"

FOURTEEN

WITH JUST THE slightest lifting of her brows, Desiree said, "Hmm. Maybe. Let's see the knife."

"It isn't flat."

Desiree nodded. "That complicates things."

It had for Clare. She'd considered the volume she might need to soak the knife. Not really much if it was just the blade, which was thin, but for the hilt? That was a good two inches or so. She wanted to give up no more blood than necessary.

"Let's see the blade," Desiree repeated.

Clare hesitated. The knife drew the ghost, but how likely was the ghost going to want to confront the blade? The specter hadn't liked the weapon the night before; Clare had sensed that.

As far as Clare knew, apparitions didn't get any extra-intelligence about supernatural things after death. Surely the monster didn't know Clare would have to . . . bloody . . . the knife before it could really hurt the thing. "Just a minute," Clare said.

"I'll wait."

Going with instinct, Clare opened the blinds behind the windows, pushed back the white curtains, and let in the sun. Then she stilled and listened . . . or sensed . . . the whistle of the breeze, the frost-white color of the light snow on the hills, the feeling of mad evil. The thing was up in the canyon, beyond Bachelor Loop, far up West Willow Creek.

From what she'd observed, ghosts could move in various fashions—glide, float, appear from one place to another instantaneously. But in the back of her mind, Clare sensed that this ghost liked to come with the wind.

She could do this fast. So she moved the tube containing the knife onto the bed and in the bright autumn sunlight. "Working on this now," she said, propping her phone close so Desiree could see.

"Oooh, pretty," the other woman said. "Nice silk sheath. The blade is sheathed, too?"

"Yes." Clare untied the first knot in the red tassels. Her fingers were becoming accustomed to the pattern Zach had made. "Ah, something you should know about the knife, um."

"What?"

"Um, it's bone."

Of course Desiree asked the question Clare had hoped to dodge.

"What kind of bone?"

Heat from embarrassment flushed Clare's skin and she blinked because it felt good. Despite the heat of the room, she'd been cold without realizing it, and, under the circumstances, that sounded dangerous.

"The bone is from one of my ancestress's femurs."

Even in the small app, Clare could see Desiree's eyes widen. "That is so cool."

Clare undid the last knot, hesitated. "Look closely and quickly because this is a supernatural knife. It will draw evil."

Desiree's brows climbed. "Wow." Her gaze sharpened.

Quickly pulling on the silk and the hilt of the knife, Clare separated the two, then yanked the blade from the metal sheath and held it in the sun. Now she saw the blade, too, carried a slight gloss that shone along it—from hands that had caressed the blade itself? From blood? From killing evil ghosts?

"Wow. Excellent," Desiree stated in a more professional tone. "Looks sharp, like it would do the job."

Clare jerked her head in a nod. "Yes, it should kill the ghost."

"Clare, it could kill almost anything else. Especially if it's supernatural."

After swallowing, Clare said, "Oh. I understand."

"And you need to soak it in blood?" Desiree confirmed.

Clare nodded. There'd been no hint of a breeze, but now she saw tree leaves dipping. "I must put it back." She grabbed the metal sheath with the mesmerizing blue and gold pattern, the silk tube, and slipped the knife in it, her fingers working to tie a knot. Not a very intricate knot. She'd have to study up.

The hair on the back of her neck, on her arms, ruffled. Yes, the ghost was headed this way but, perhaps . . . the sunshine . . . the lingering hurt from last night . . . a touch of fear slowed it. And it stopped in a comfortable place, the spar near the information boards at the confluence of the East and West Willow creeks.

Interesting that the entity considered that spot comfortable. Clare didn't think it was coincidence that a murder-suicide had occurred there.

"Clare, honey, are you there?" Desiree said.

Clare jolted away from the sensation of being north of there. "Oh, Desiree. Sorry."

"With regard to the soaking in blood thing. Whose blood?"

"Mine."

Desiree nodded. "I thought so. If you want my opinion—"

"Sure."

"I saw that you removed the blade from a sheath. Have you considered how liquid-proof the inside of the sheath is?"

Clare gasped. "That's brilliant." She tilted her head. "I'd have to find a way to brace the sheath and get a good flow into it . . . and enough light to see into the sheath so I don't let it overflow too much . . . then I'll work on soaking the hilt. Thanks, Desiree!"

"Wait, Clare—"

But Clare tapped her finger against the app and Desiree disappeared. Clare had a deep suspicion that if she even flickered an eyelash that Desiree construed as Clare needing help, the woman would be on the next private plane here. Clare didn't need to watch out for her, too. Regardless of all Desiree's martial arts or street fighting training and experience, Clare was pretty darn sure that Desiree would be helpless in the face of this threat and more a hindrance than an asset.

Desiree saw auras of those who were alive. She didn't even sense or feel the cold of ghosts. Her gift was for life. Clare had no idea if the ghost would be more dangerous to Desiree or not, but Clare sure didn't want to chance it. Not only was Desiree becoming a friend, but Clare thought she herself might have a fatal accident at Tony Rickman's hands if something happened to Desiree because of Clare.

Just as well both Rickmans were out of town, out of the situation. She sank onto the bed in the sunlight that was fading from a bright square back to a barely there shade of gray. Glancing out the window, she saw clouds rolling over the hills again, and she couldn't tell if that was natural or due to the ghost. Probably natural. Probably. Autumn could tip into winter and back and edge into Indian summer.

She let her eyes unfocus, calmed enough to try and clear her mind so she could perceive the ghost, hoping that the wraith itself was too busy-minded and emotionally wrecked to pick up Clare in return. Because she was still too close if it moved quickly.

Clare would have to weigh her options—how fast she might bleed into the sheath, something she had no clue about, though if it were a math problem with volume, she might be able to figure it out.

Not to mention what kind of tube or other container she might need for the hilt.

She recalled that the bone blade had liked blood, maybe it would speed up things, since it was supernatural and all. She found her teeth hurt because she'd clenched them.

But she *wouldn't* allow fear to overcome her. Breathing deeply and running through famous quotes about not letting fear stop her . . . she dredged up all the determination she could, headed for the table with the books she'd purchased, and began another, deeper, online search about Robert Ford, Creede, and the history of the year of 1892 in the booming silver mining camp.

Zach had just reached the door to the sheriff's office inside the county building when a deputy sheriff and the elder Mason Pais walked out.

Pais inclined his head. "Slade." The older man stood solidly at the threshold, the door open a crack behind them.

"Pais."

The deputy hesitated then left about his business.

"Something I can do for you?" the ex-sheriff questioned.

"Thought I'd ask if I could see the place where Mrs. Tewksbury fell."

"Not much to see," Pais said.

Shrugging, Zach responded, "Helps me if I examine the scene."

Pais's expression soured and he grunted but didn't move. Obviously he didn't want Zach bothering his grandson, the sheriff.

Zach didn't move either. Standoff.

The door opened wide behind them, and the younger Pais, the sheriff, stood as tall but not quite as broad behind his grandfather, then shifted so he could see Zach. "You working for Tony? Rickman?"

Leaning on his cane, Zach met the men's stares in turn, first the older, then the younger who held the authority here, even if the elder didn't seem as if he completely ceded it. "That's right."

The cop and ex-cop studied him with similar expressions,

probably figuring Zach might be more controllable if he worked for Rickman instead of a loose cannon. One or both of them might know Tony; one or both of them might have spoken with Rickman. Zach wondered what Rickman might have said about Clare. No one was going to treat Clare with disrespect when Zach was around. But he wasn't going to open that ghost-seer can of worms.

"There's not much to see," Sheriff Pais said finally. "But I wouldn't put it past you to follow the creek until you found our tape, so let me give you directions."

"I can run him out to the scene of the accidental death," Pais the elder said.

"All right," the sheriff snapped, then stepped back and shut the door.

Neither Pais nor Zach commented on the sheriff's attitude when they went to the parking lot outside the side entrance of the building.

As they walked out of the county building, Pais matched Zach's stride and they both eyed each other with the same cop stares. The guy reached the door to the parking lot first and held it for Zach.

Nothing to do but accept the courtesy and go out. "Thanks."

Pais paused with Zach, glanced down at his cane and his bum left leg. "I recollected what happened to you last year. Made news here, too."

"Especially in certain circles," Zach said, and he could talk of the incident without heat now, a plus.

"Cop circles. Yeah." The ex-sheriff adjusted his cowboy hat. "Reminded us all to keep on our toes."

"Got that."

Loud sobbing came from behind them. Zach turned and pulled open the glass door.

A small blond woman whispered, "Thanks."

"Hello, Linda," Pais said, and a note of . . . hesitation? . . . disapproval? . . . both? in his voice alerted Zach.

"Please accept my condolences on the loss of your sister and brother-in-law."

The woman made a futile gesture, gulped, and pulled out

a pad of tissues from her pocket. "I'm just here to take care of some of Lucy's bequests." She wiped her eyes and stumbled over the threshold. Zach reached out and steadied her. "Easy, ma'am."

"Yes. Thank you," she replied in a suffocated voice and nearly fled from them to a new silver BMW convertible.

Zach stared at Pais, who kept a stone face. Obviously the guy didn't want to talk about the woman, not even an offhand remark, and that particular attitude from this particular man sent prickles of interest down Zach's spine. Something to pay attention to here, note, and find out more about Linda later.

Pais indicated a big and battered gray truck several years old, a vehicle that might have belonged once to the sheriff's office. As Mason Pais, Jr., had.

Zach glanced toward the hotel balcony; empty, no Clare.

In less than ten minutes they were downstream standing within the police tape.

The sheriff was right. Not much to see at the site of Mrs. Tewksbury's fall. Zach scrutinized the area, shook his head, rose from his crouch, leaned on his cane. "No sign of anyone else except the old lady until you all arrived on the scene?"

"You're right. We got the call—"

"We?" Zach raised his brows.

Pais Jr. flushed. "The sheriff's office."

Zach smiled. "I bet you have a police scanner at home."

The man pulled his cowboy hat lower. "You would win that bet." He cleared his throat. "I happened to live closer than any of the men in this instance."

"Uh-huh."

"You examine the scene enough?" Pais asked.

"Yeah." Zach eyeballed up and down the creek in the flume, looked at backs of the houses that lined it.

Pais jerked his chin at a white house. "That's where Mrs. Tewksbury lived. No, I ain't gonna take you to talk to her companion, her daughter-in-law, who's all broken up about the accident and tendin' to blame herself."

"Nothing I like more than interrogating grieving people,"

Zach said. He went to the truck, opened the door, and hauled himself inside. The short trip to the county building passed silently, though Zach noticed a new silver BMW parked on the street near Pico's Patio. Lunch . . . and a little investigation . . . sounded good.

He thanked Pais and headed back to the hotel and Clare. When he walked back into the room, she sat on the bed looking at the big book of old time photographs of Creede.

"I take it no one from the historical society has called," he said.

"Not yet."

"So we don't have an appointment to view whatever offerings the archives and historical society has."

"No." Her eyes looked red, as if she'd been crying. He didn't recall her crying around him. Earlier in the week because of him and a tangle in their relationship, maybe, yeah, but not about anything else when he was with her.

She opened her mouth, closed it, looked away, her expression miserable.

He moved over to the bed and sat down, took her hand. "Talk to me."

Her gaze met his, then slid away. She bit her lip. "I'm a coward."

"No. You aren't."

"I'm not a fighter."

"Yes, you are. And a survivor. What brought this on? Must be the whole Robert Ford thing. 'The dirty little coward who shot Mr. Howard.'"

Clare grimaced. "Perhaps." She gestured to a book bound in sky-blue with a very fancy and colorful winged woman flying on it. Zach had seen enough of Clare's great-aunt Sandra's journals to spot one.

He sat next to her. "Tell me the problem."

She gestured to the journal. "Great-Aunt Sandra had one little story in there about an evil ghost. She dealt with it easily and in half a page."

"Not much for you to go on."

"No."

"As I understand it, her entries aren't necessarily chrono-logical."

"She had a lot of journals, one in every room, and would pick them up and write in them as she pleased."

"But she dated the entries."

"Yes."

"So how old was she when she encountered that evil ghost?"

Clare picked up the book, flipped to where the red ribbon attached to the spine sat between pages, and looked. "Forty-seven."

"And she inherited her gift at the age of—"

"Seventeen."

Zach grunted. "So she had thirty years' worth of experi-ence when she encountered that particular evil ghost."

"Yes." Clare's mouth still turned down. She fiddled a lit-tle with the ribbon bookmark, a sure sign of nerves.

"And was that evil ghost haunting a full town?" Zach asked.

"It was in Chicago."

"A neighborhood then."

"All right, no."

"A block."

She hefted a sigh. "A house."

He smiled at that. "A real haunted house."

"Yes."

"A family home, maybe. Not even a hotel like this or a theater where other ghosts might happen and congregate. So evil ghosts are composite things with core identities. Was your great-aunt able to discern the core identity easily?"

"Yes."

"Not at all like our circumstances," he said firmly, pluck-ing the journal from her hands. "Let's go eat."

"Downstairs?"

"Pico's Patio." He smiled. "We may have a lead."

FIFTEEN

HER EYES WIDENED and she scrambled off the bed. "A lead? What kind of lead?"

He rubbed the back of his neck. "If you recall, Pais the elder spoke to Michael LuCette. We don't know what Lu-Cette would have said about Caden, or if Caden was there, too. If Caden was there, he'd have told Pais everything he told Mrs. Flinton. And Pais acted a little suspicious when we met this woman at the county building. Made my cop instincts twitchy. I think she's at Pico's."

Clare glanced out the window. "Sun's out." She went to her bag and put on a thermal vest. "Crazy weather."

"Which may or may not be natural." Zach held the door open, locked it behind them, and descended the stairs after Clare.

She glanced back over her shoulder and lowered her voice, though her words floated back easily to him. "Are you going to ask her some questions?"

He strained his ears to check whether anyone might be in the building, heard nothing. But that didn't mean much, so he waited until he joined her and they both exited the hotel and strolled to their truck. He took her arm, just because he liked touching her.

Bending his head so his mouth was close to her ear, he said, "I think we'll just look around, see what's what, how she interacts with people, whether they gossip about her."

"To her face?"

"Some do."

Hey, Clare! Hey, Zach! Enzo sounded like his regular optimistic self when he spoke to Zach mentally. Clare flinched a little under Zach's hand.

Hey, Enzo! she sent back telepathically.

We are at LUNCH RECESS! I LIKE recess! I told Caden that you might come and see us! He would like to see you.

Clare shared a glance with Zach as he opened the truck door for her. Then she said, *I'm not sure—*

Seeing you would make him feel even safer than just having me.

Zach got into the truck and hit the ignition, spoke to Enzo himself. *All right, we'll drive by. You can tell him that we'll be doing that, but we can't come and talk to him. His parents and teachers wouldn't like that.*

Okay, Zach. Okay, Clare.

"Do you know where the elementary school is?" Clare asked.

"Yeah. I know where the Creede School campus is."

"Oh. Yes. Small town," Clare said.

"Very. And, like everything else, it's not far. We'll go slowly. So they can see us. Then we'll swing over to Pico's."

"Poor little boy."

"Yeah."

"All right, coming up on the left," Zach said aloud to Clare, then said mentally to Enzo, *We are driving by. It will be easy to see me, harder to see Clare. But tell Caden we're on his side. Always.*

I WILL! Oooooh, here you come. I SEE you. Zach got

the image of Enzo panting, his tongue hanging out of the side of his mouth.

"The playground for the younger kids is before the larger building."

"I see it." She leaned forward. Caden pressed against the chain link fence, small fingers curling around the diamonds. She put her hand on Zach's thigh and the ghost Labrador coalesced from shades of gray to a doglike critter to Zach's eyes. Caden waved.

Zach waved, then muttered, "Dammit."

"What's wrong?"

"Don't look now but that beat-up old truck just beyond the walkway belongs to Pais the elder."

She sniffed. "We're tourists, just seeing the town. And there aren't that many streets to drive up and down." She lifted a hand.

"Don't wave at Caden or Enzo."

"Oh, all right," she grumbled, smoothing her hair. A futile gesture, but Zach loved her curls.

They crept by at the slowest pace Zach could do, which was pretty damn slow because there wasn't any other traffic.

Thank you, Clare! Thank you, Zach. Caden FEELS better! He is happier, Enzo projected.

That's good, Clare said.

Zach looked at her; she was smiling. A tiny, gut-deep feeling grew. He was good for her. Better than some ghost dog that she couldn't fully relate to. He was better for her than Enzo.

Surprise trailed along with the realization. He hadn't known that he really had to be needed by someone. Or someone had to be better because he was in their life. Not a codependency thing, but a simple happiness that he was there. He could *feel* that from Clare and wouldn't like it if anything happened to that feeling.

At the next through street he turned right and just a block away was Pico's Patio. The silver BMW hadn't moved.

"Good, she's still here."

"How do you know?"

"That's her car."

Clare gasped. "Good grief. It must have cost a fortune. And so inappropriate for a mountain town."

"Definite status symbol," Zach agreed, taking the first parking place he could. Pico's Patio appeared busy today, too.

Hand in hand they ambled down the street.

"It really is a pretty little town," Clare said.

"No ghosts to bother you."

"No, and I should not be glad about that,"—her fingers flexed in his—"because the evil one probably ate them all and it's a part of him—"

Zach halted, turned, and put a hand over her lips. "Stop. Breathe."

Her full breasts lifted with a big breath, her shoulders shifted to relieve stress, and she smiled at him and said, "Live in the moment. Enjoy the moment."

"That's right."

She squeezed his fingers tightly with her own. "And in this moment the ghost is not near." Her gaze shifted, went distant, the gold flecks in her eyes brightening. "No, it's far up the canyons, a little scared maybe." An edge came to her smile as it broadened. "Scared of me."

"That's right." He returned the pressure of her hand in his. "In this moment, we investigate."

More like she watched and learned as he investigated, but he wasn't gonna quibble, stop her when she was on a roll.

With a decisive nod, she strode toward Pico's Patio. A few diners sat outside at a couple of tables. Clare hesitated. "Is she—"

"No." He let go of Clare's hand to touch her back, guide her through the door.

One glance at the bar showed him that Linda sat there, a little hunched over her food. The server behind the bar, an older guy and not one of the college students Pico hired for the summer season, had his gaze glued to a golf game.

Other people sat at the short bar, but none of them next to Linda. They were dressed like town residents in faded, well-worn everyday clothes.

The L-shaped bar took up most of the front room, with space for tables in front of the window that faced the street, and a small aisle lined with two-tops on the way to the back room. Zach drew Clare to the far corner table near the end of the short side of the L and watched.

Linda sniffed wetly. She appeared worse than when Zach had seen her no more than an hour past. Close to a breaking point, though knowing despair from the inside out, he figured she'd broken a few times already and glued herself back together.

He recalled Pais the elder's disapproval of her. Looked like others disapproved, too. Maybe she'd been hungry. Tired of her own company. Maybe she'd planned on testing the waters to see the emotional reaction of people to her. Bad idea, and Zach bet she regretted that now . . . and a suspicion he knew who, or rather *what*, she might be settled into his brain from the cues Pais and the others around her gave him.

In 1892, in a wild mining camp that had experienced flood and fire, *the* event that stood out for the town was the murder of Robert Ford.

This year, another event must have dominated the gossip of the locals, been *the* most important happening of the year, and he knew what that was.

The waiter who served them last night, a college kid from back east who worked summers here with his girlfriend, moved toward Clare and Zach. "Hey, welcome back!" he said heartily. Too loudly. Or the quiet was unusual and he'd pitched his voice to talk over the usual buzz of the lunch crowd.

His smile strained as he handed them the menus.

"Thank you," Clare said and smiled in return. Without looking at the menu, she asked, "I know you have some salads, what do you recommend?"

"The one with steak strips. Or the taco salad. But my girlfriend likes the Pico's Fiesta Salad, with a lot of fresh veggies."

"Sounds good." She handed him back the menu.

"I'll have the chicken tacos with the special picante salsa," Zach said.

"Drinks?"

"Water and iced tea," Clare said.

"Just water," Zach said.

"Gotcha!" With a lope, the young man was gone.

Clare stared at Zach across the table.

"What?"

She held out her hand and he took it.

"This just reminds me of the time we met."

Didn't remind Zach of that, except it was lunch. He glanced outside. Okay, it was sunny. Well she looked better and smiled and he wouldn't contradict her.

"Such an interesting man you were, and are. You attracted me, and you still do."

He grinned. "Oh, yeah. Interesting, intriguing, that's what I first thought. Now you're just plain fascinating."

She appeared surprised, and he thought she blushed for the first time since they'd met.

Leaning forward and keeping her voice to a murmur, she said, "You're looking at the lady at the bar in designer jeans and shirt?"

He nodded.

Clare's shoulders loosened in a sigh. "If there's a human component in this case, it could be so much easier." She turned her head and stared at Linda sideways. Clare's mouth pursed. "I can't see her being the kind of person who's interested in history, in Poker Alice or Robert Ford or Soapy Smith or Bat Masterson. In the Old West ghosts, my specialty."

Linda stood up, threw paper napkins on her mostly untouched burger, and announced into the quiet, "It wasn't my fault! None of it was *my fault!*" She stormed from the restaurant.

Those townspeople who remained seemed to sigh in unison. Ten seconds of full silence ticked by, then voices rose in a buzz of gossip. Zach could tell the tourists because they frowned like Clare. Everyone else knew what Linda referred to.

"What was that all about?" Clare asked.

"I think I know." His lips curved in a smile. "I think I know and I think I've got the motive for our ghost."

Her mouth dropped open a little and her eyes widened, then sparkled, and she looked at him with such admiration that he thought he could beat that damned ghost single-handed.

"One of the puzzle-parts," she breathed.

"Yes."

Looking uncomfortable, their waiter came up with their food. A screech of tires on asphalt sounded and the fishtailing BMW zoomed past the window.

"Good grief," Clare said. "I can't imagine being in a hurry here."

Slipping the plates in front of them, the waiter didn't answer.

Zach shook his head. "Grief takes all forms, you know that, Clare."

"Yes," she said quietly, focusing on her salad now.

Glancing up at the young man, Zach said, "She's the sister of Mrs. Treedy, the woman who killed her husband and committed suicide, isn't she?"

Their waiter nodded. "Yes, that's Linda Boucher. The murder-suicide was in June. My girlfriend and I had just arrived a couple of days before."

Zach frowned. "June sounds a little late for you to get here."

"We're both in the drama department, and Creede has a well-known repertory theater. We got to work with some people there for the season. They do community outreach. There's this one little kid who's awesome, though he tends to talk to himself."

Zach and Clare shared a look. Clare picked up her fork and fiddled with it. "I have a young friend in town. Caden LuCette?"

"Yes. That's him. Good little actor."

"Hasn't your school started by now?"

The waiter shrugged. "Not quite, and our mentors at college know what we're doing. We're cutting it close, but we love it here." He looked around, took a deep breath of the air that held smells of cooking, and the fresh scent of the mountains when anyone went in or out. "We're leaving on Sunday, only a few days more."

"I see," Clare said. She'd tightened up.

"You staying for the Cruisin' the Canyon?"

"Probably," Zach said.

"Then you'll also probably be eating here, so I'll see you later. Chrissy will, too." He winked at them. "I told her of the tip you left me last night and she's looking forward to serving you." He strolled off.

Now Clare glared at Zach. She had accountant rules about tipping, and, yeah, he'd left more cash on the table after she'd turned to leave. Busted.

Brows down, Clare glanced away from him to the waiter and back. "I'm feeling played."

SIXTEEN

ZACH JERKED HIS chin at the waiter. "By him or everyone else?"

"Yes. No one told us Caden acted."

"Mrs. Flinton might not know, or it didn't mean anything to her. Think about the video we first saw and that child. Did it look like he was acting?"

A pause while Clare stabbed into her salad, chewed crispy vegetables.

"No," she said. "Except maybe a little today, woebegone behind that schoolyard fence."

"He wanted Enzo to stay with him. I believe a ghost seer boy would think a ghost dog companion was really cool."

"Yes."

"And this can explain why people don't believe him as much."

Clare's frown remained when she looked at him straight again. "People don't believe he sees ghosts because it is not rational that people see ghosts."

"Still struggling with the disrespect thing," Zach murmured.

She ate some more before answering. "It will take time for me to accept people don't believe me, don't respect what I do, what I can do."

"You'll always be considered a fake or a con by most people upon first meeting you, before they *know* what you can do."

"That's right. And it will take time to become accustomed to that." She appeared to consider the matter while she ate more of her salad and Zach crunched through a great tasting taco.

"It's been three weeks and two days since I saw my first ghost." A lost note in her voice had Zach reaching for her hand again. Lost. Her former life, her former self.

She swallowed, didn't look at him. From the way she held her face he thought she might be beating back tears. Her voice was thick when she said, "I think I'm allowed to mourn a career of a decade, a career I'd planned and studied for, for at least . . . two months?"

The words flicked like a whip on his own raw spot, reminding him of the dark, dark days when he'd awakened in the hospital knowing his foot would never work right again. Knowing his own career as a field law enforcement officer was kaput. And he'd mourned that for a lot longer than Clare had.

It had taken meeting her, learning of her similar shadows, and some harsh words for him to yank himself into a new reality.

Better that he changed the subject. Making his tone as light as possible under the circumstances, he said, "You've gotta hand it to the kid."

She looked up at him with tears filmed over her pretty hazel eyes, and a distant look in them.

"Caden, you've got to hand it to Caden. Going the artistic route, the actor route." Zach managed not to wince. He didn't know actors. They were probably okay guys. Zach coughed. "Anyway, if Caden is an actor, maybe folks will cut him a break when he's found 'talking to himself.'"

"Talking to ghosts," Clare said.

Zach nodded. "Easier to explain. People expect stuff like that from actors and other folks in the arts." He smiled, squeezed her fingers, then withdrew his hand. Eating the tacos was a two-handed activity. "Though I suppose, as an accountant, you could be considered to be mumbling numbers."

She bristled as he'd hoped. "A good accountant *doesn't* have to mutter figures aloud."

He grinned. "Of course not."

Clare sighed, then went back to her salad. "Yes, for Caden, it *could* mask his gift."

She said gift as if she meant curse, and Zach didn't blame her. He didn't like his own "gift." Which reminded him that there was an outstanding Counting-Crows-Rhyme-prediction of another death, and that ruined the taste of his food.

"Yes." Clare nodded. "That scenario would work in a small town where everyone knew everyone and found you talking to yourself. It would be harder to pull off in a big city like Denver, I think, if you didn't stick to your own neighborhood for shopping, for instance."

"Uh-huh," Zach said, and wondered if that had happened to her. He'd been gone a little while after she'd come into her psychic power—between her first and second cases.

"In any event. I shall just have to become accustomed to my new . . . vocation."

And those were words he'd heard before and knew she said nearly as a mantra.

Her phone beeped and he smiled.

"What?" she asked.

"That first day we met. At lunch. We both got calls."

Her face softened. "Yes."

He waved a hand. "Go ahead, take it."

She took it from the special pocket on her purse. "It's a text. The best time to meet anyone at the archives is tomorrow afternoon."

"So it goes," Zach said, but his optimism began to wane. "At least we have a good lead, the motive of the perp."

"Perp."

"Perpetrator. So much easier to say than damned big and evil ghost."

"Yes. About that woman who just stormed out of here. What do you know?"

"What do I guess? We'll talk about it . . . somewhere else. After lunch."

"All right." She paused, licked some salad dressing from her lower lip that had Zach thinking about bed and sex again. Something that happened with amazing frequency with Clare. He remained glad she'd come along and proved his ankle might be bad but his dick worked just fine.

Meeting his eyes, her lips firmed, then she said, "I'd like to go up the canyon, all the way around Bachelor Loop, and see the mines."

Unlike their previous talk, people would have heard words like that from everyone who passed through.

"Is that where the perp lurks?" Zach asked.

"I think I need to get a feeling for the atmosphere," she said.

"Examine the scene."

"Yes."

"Sure. We'll head up there after lunch."

"This is more than scenic," Clare said. "It's gorgeous."

"Yeah, mountains of golden aspen look good, especially against the evergreens. Colorado autumn putting on a show." Zach nodded. "It's real nice. Something wrong?" he asked. She had the shadows in the eyes look again. "The mines are interesting, too. From a distance." He'd be iffy climbing rocks and messing around in mines. Hardly anything more dangerous than abandoned mines.

"It's . . . it's a little different. More . . . sterile."

Looked the same to Zach as trips into the mountains as a kid. Mostly his mother managed to nag the General into putting in for leave so they could have a fall Colorado vacation.

"Huh." Zach scanned the area, and saw no crows, so he

didn't have to try and figure out his own gift. But something in the silence or whatever reminded him of when he'd looked at the shadowy street early that morning and thought that he'd seen layers set down by the ghost.

He glanced at Clare. She'd take what he'd say seriously. Well, she usually took what people said seriously, but her mind had sure gotten blown open to "irrationality" in the last three weeks and two days, so she'd *listen*.

"Um," he said.

She looked at him instead of out the window, focusing that sharp attention. Yeah, he liked that.

"Maybe because all the ghosts are missing, it doesn't seem right to you. Maybe you sensed ghosts all your life, even if you didn't see them."

"You've said something like that before."

"Yeah, a lot of options." And what he'd say next was way out there. "Or if it isn't just you, maybe the world is used to a . . . coating of human spirits and it's missing."

"Huh," she said, looking more thoughtful than tense. An improvement. "That's an interesting notion, in a whole different direction, a more philosophical or spiritual or theological direction."

"I'm not just a pretty face," Zach joked.

"No, you're an interesting, compelling, virile man," she said, almost in an absent tone.

Zach's mouth fell open and he turned to look at her . . . again, no traffic this weekday afternoon of uncertain weather, but he should still have kept his eyes on the road. Never knew when a rock splinter might be coming your way.

He wrenched his gaze away from her, and back to the road. "Thanks, I think. That's a lot for a man to live up to."

She sent him a sweet smile. "You make it easy."

Okay, he was tripping right off the path over the cliff into the fall of love. No. Yes. Maybe. Close the door on that until it could be addressed later!

A hawk screamed and they both flinched—him at the sound of a bird, Clare at the sound of a shriek, he supposed.

"Is it near?" he snapped. "I'm ready to turn around and take you right out of here. Not sure what this truck can do on these roads, but we can find out."

"No . . . I think maybe we hurt it last night and it's still sulking, or brooding. It can't be accustomed to being hurt—or being seen or being fought, even."

"Good," he said with satisfaction. "The more we can scare it, the more hesitant it will become and the easier to defeat."

"I suppose so. And we'll continue to focus its attention on us and not on Caden, which is all to the good," she said. She looked out at the cliff face next to her window, at the winding road ahead of them, past him to the green and gold hill outside his window. "We're all alone. Time to tell me what you deduced."

"Like I said, Pais the elder and I saw Linda at the county building. He acted cool and disapproving and warned me off asking her questions or asking him about her."

"He did?"

"Basic guy body language, Clare. But he wasn't interested in her as a woman. He saw her as a problem."

"You'd know guy and peace officer body language." Clare nodded, accepting that point.

"And he'd told us that he'd spoken with the LuCettes, and that might mean he heard from Caden all about the nasty, scary spot at the confluence of the Willow creeks where the murder-suicide happened and how that nasty, scary spot isn't there anymore but a big, evil ghost is traveling up and down the canyons and into the town, scaring the bejesus out of Caden."

Zach picked up a sports bottle and squeezed a stream of water into his mouth. The road was dirt, and though he drove slowly, dust rose around them.

"Since I'm a suspicious kind of guy myself, my mind immediately went to the motive any cop would assign to a murder-suicide. Had already traveled that pathway and back a few times."

"Hmm," Clare said.

"Think about it, Clare. I know you're the kind to like to believe in the best of people, but—"

"A love triangle," Clare said.

"Yeah. Jerk sleeping with his wife's sister."

Clare sighed. "I don't understand why people take wedding vows and break them. Either don't take them, or do your absolute best to stick with them, or if you can't, get out of the marriage."

"I can tell you that I've seen the results of plenty of 'love' triangles and a lot of it is simple power politics, relationship game playing."

"Ick," Clare said.

Yeah, he could love this girl. Not a girl, a woman. He could love this woman. Talk about scary.

"This time it was sister vis-à-vis sister and wife vis-à-vis husband, I think. And, man, when I saw her, guessed who she might be, it was like that—" He snapped his fingers. "Love triangle, and Linda survived. Jealousy, resentment, betrayal. Those are the emotions stirred up by a sex trio that ends in killing. And one of those is *the* motive of our ghost. Why it kills who it kills, why it is *allowed* to kill who it can kill, maybe, if we go back to some sort of universal balance of good and evil and our philosophical bent."

"Betrayal." Clare whispered the word. Flinched. Said in a higher, less steady voice, "I think we should turn around now and head back to town."

Zach whipped the truck around and pressed on the accelerator. The ride got a whole lot bumpier. Clare held on to the door brace. "That word." She raised her voice. "That caught its attention."

"Ah. Wondered about that. We can hash this out when we get back."

They reached the hotel without the specter following them. Clare checked before they got out of the truck, though she'd kept her mind's eye on the wraith, ready to tell Zach to keep going if it felt like the monster followed them. They could at least keep it busy and lead it away from town.

Wonderful that Zach had figured out this new lead, but the more she considered the entire situation, the more she realized that she had to blood the knife soon to be able to defend Caden and Creede and the whole valley.

Do the job quick enough that the ghost wouldn't come upon her while she bled, and mess up the process . . . or worse.

As soon as they walked in, she went to her bag, zipped it open, zipped the lining open, and took out the tube containing the knife. She held it, the feel of silk and bone against her palm and fingers, the zing of *rightness*. Her fingers went to the knot.

Zach frowned as he watched. "What are you doing?"

Clare frowned. "I'm going to have to blood it sooner or later. Sooner would be better." She met his eyes. "You had an idea how to do that when we first heard, didn't you?"

"Not sure what you're talking ab—"

"Zach." Yes, she was clenching her teeth again. "I thought I told you how I felt about lying. Say you don't want to answer. Just be up front."

"Damn." He hung up his windbreaker. Walking up to her, he hugged her, rubbed his head against her. "Sorry, Clare. Not used to explaining myself."

"Or opening up and being vulnerable." She huffed. "Well, I've figured out how I want to do it. So you don't need to tell me how you would handle it."

"Got it." But he kept her close and swayed with her until she relaxed in his arms. "Clare, this case sucks."

"I agree," she said against his chest. "I don't see any other options than getting through it."

He kissed her temple, then let her go, and as he did, he drew the knife from her fingers.

"I *do* have to blood that knife, and I think I should do it as soon as possible."

"Now?" he asked. "Won't we need some stuff, like a tube to fill up with blood for the handle?"

Clare sat abruptly on the chair next to the table. "Well, there's an image I could have done without, especially since it will be my blood."

SEVENTEEN

"I'M OPEN TO ideas."

"What say we get a bunch of gauze or bandage wrap, draw some blood from you, and soak it, then wrap it around the hilt. For the blade, we can just put blood in the sheath."

The whole idea made her stomach quiver, but she said, steadily enough, "Yes, I'd figured that out."

"You're a sharp lady."

"Ha, ha."

"Probably be better if we did this in the bathroom."

"We?"

"I'm not letting you do this alone."

"The bathroom will barely hold the two of us."

"It'll be fine." He glanced at the window. "I'm thinking it would be better to do this during the day."

"Better in the sun," Clare added. "And since it seems sunlight might be in short supply the next few days, and it's a little wavery now, I—we—should get started."

"In a few minutes," he said.

"Why?"

"Because I want to nail down our ideas about motive."

"Oh, okay." She tucked the knife back into her suitcase. "The motive is betrayal."

"Betrayal. Most particularly sexual betrayal." His whole torso rippled in a more-than-shrug-not-quite-stretch. "The murder-suicide came about due to a love triangle." He scowled. "Better called a sex triangle."

"Oh-kay." For an instant she thought of her and Zach. No, she wouldn't put up with another woman in his life. The very idea sliced sharper than the bone knife, than the ghost. "So you think sexual betrayal is the motive."

"The motive for the ghost, yeah. We'll base our deductions on the supposition that it was that particular kind of betrayal, that event, which triggered the murder-suicide. I think we have to look at regular betrayal, too." He sat down next to her and the mattress sagged a little, tilting her toward him. She put her arm around his waist and he did the same.

"Regular betrayal?"

"Look at the hunters who got killed yesterday. *Punished* for their betrayal of their friend who had the hunting license, and for betrayal of the laws in hunting out of season, and in betrayal of nature, even, maybe, in killing a Canada lynx instead of a bobcat."

"Oh my God." She rubbed her arms. She shouldn't be cold. She was letting fear affect her. She'd have to learn how to get over it, move on, somehow. She wished fervently that she knew how to meditate better. That would work, wouldn't it? Eek! Letting fear distract her, too! "That . . . that just doesn't sound decent."

Zach brushed her hair away from her face, and she turned to see his eyes more bluish than green, and holding sadness. "It's a warped kind of justice. And the old lady? She wandered away from her companion and went out the door and shouldn't have."

Clare just stared. "That doesn't sound too much like betrayal to me."

"It depends on your point of view," Zach said.

The cold spread through Clare . . . maybe from that little

cold wound the ghost had inflicted within her. The spot that had been diminished but not quite vanquished by time and sex. She began to shiver.

Zach lifted her and put her on his lap, curving over her.

"That is *wrong*." She swallowed, then whispered, "And I think the ghost might be able to influence people." She swallowed.

"Some people," Zach said, rubbing his hands up and down her arms. "Not sure about the hunters, but that murder-suicide outside near where there was a 'scary spot' according to Caden."

"You think the ghost might have haunted that spot."

"You're the expert. But we met a couple of ghosts who didn't move around."

"It's moving around now."

"Maybe it got transportation skills when it grew bigger and badder."

"Maybe. But I don't think that blaming the murder-suicide on the ghost is right."

"That woman and that man were responsible for their actions, for sure." His voice went harder. "One didn't have to cheat, and the other didn't have to kill him for it. Nor did the sister have to cheat on her sister by screwing her husband. Three bad decisions."

"I agree," Clare said. "We do agree on basics." That helped diminish her fear, too. She could count on Zach.

She went back to cementing the whole kernel of the situation in her mind. "And the murder-suicide, whether influenced by the monster or not, stirred up the energy of the phantom, triggering the transformation of the ghost from a . . . regular wraith to something that can harm the living and . . . and . . . eat ghost seers."

He tipped her head so she met his eyes and he gazed at her from under lowered brows. "I'm—we're—not going to let that happen. It's one piece of the puzzle."

"A pretty big piece."

"It tells us why, but not who."

"It can lead us to who, can't it, who the ghost is? Some-one . . . angry at sexual betrayal?"

"It's been a long time, Clare."

"We'll work hard on finding out, follow every lead."

"Yeah."

She found that Zach gently rocked her. How lovely. She loosened her muscles, listened to his heartbeat.

He grunted. She let him and the silence wrap around her. "And you figured it all out from that chance meeting."

"Yeah. It was all there in her body language, the older Pais's body language, the little dialogue I heard. Then I confirmed it with you at the restaurant."

"You're an excellent investigator," Clare said with admiration.

"Thanks, ma'am." He squeezed her, looked at the clock on the wall. "And shall we check on Caden and Enzo as they head home from school? It's about that time."

"Isn't that stalking?"

"Just keeping an eye out."

"Yes." She set her teeth, then said, "We can stop by the grocery and pick up some bandages and gauze."

His chest and thigh muscles stiffened under her.

"Let's get this done, quick and right," she said. She angled her head and closed her eyes, searching for the ghost with her mind. The thing had retreated, once again, to the upper canyon. Clare sensed the weather whipped the wind wild there, where the shadows lay deep across the crevices of the earth. "We might get done before the knife attracts it."

"Are you doing what I think you're doing? Sensing the ghost?" Zach frowned.

She hesitated, then patted his chest and said, "I still feel achy inside from fighting it last night, and that seems to have made a bond—"

"A bond!"

"A tiny bond between us," she said, patting again. "Anyway, the ghost is far away enough that flying here will take time. Like I said earlier, I think this particular apparition likes to come with wind, and perhaps bring weather. We can work with that limitation and move fast," she said, infusing cheer in her voice.

Zach stopped her hand and stilled her fingers. "You've asked me to do—or refrain from doing—a couple of things that make you craz—that is, that irritate you. I want you to stop pretending to feel okay when you're not."

Sighing, she slumped. "We're very serious people, Zach. You brood and I'm just of a more sober character."

"It's this project. It's nasty and scary and sucks. You're a fiery gypsy."

"The last thing I feel like right now is a fiery gypsy."

"Glad to hear it."

Her head shot up as she looked him in the eyes and she barely missed hitting his jaw, which would have hurt both of them.

"I want real emotions from you, the real you. You don't need to hide from me."

"You want me to be grim?"

"I want you to be absolutely real with me. No games."

She sighed and nodded. "All right." She thought about arguing that thinking positively would affect the world in a positive fashion, but that new age philosophy spouted at her beginning yoga glass she'd attended a couple of times hadn't really sunk in.

She thought back to an old, old song. "Accentuate the positive?" This time her tone was naturally light just because she felt good. Sitting on Zach, having him care for her, remembering a silly, upbeat song.

"Eliminate the negative," Zach said. He set her on her feet and his expression could only be called wolfish, sharpening his features. "We damn well will eliminate that ghost. With extreme prejudice."

"Extinguish it," she said. "Great-Aunt Sandra used that word."

Zach's lips tightened and he inclined his head. "A good

word. Extinguish." It rolled off his tongue. He took her hand. "Let's head for the school and remind ourselves of the basic reason—the bottom line—why we're doing this."

"To keep Caden safe," Clare said.

"Yes, to keep children and old ladies and even moronic hunters safe."

They sat around the corner from the school and saw the building disgorge children, and Caden run to his bike. Enzo loped with the boy, fast, tongue lolling from the side of his mouth, ears flopping, acting like a real, live dog. He turned a half-circle, barked at her and Zach, then kept the boy company. Caden's face looked stormy.

"Someone gave him grief during school," Zach murmured.

She supposed he'd know boys' expressions more than she did.

Yes, Zach! Enzo's high bark trailed back to them. Since Zach tensed, she knew he'd heard it, too. *But I got THEM!* Enzo continued. *They are just boys and not men and not too tall. I moved INTO them and froze all their little balls!* He sounded positively gleeful.

Clare's mouth dropped open.

Zach folded over the steering wheel, roaring with laughter.

A last, fading question came from Enzo as he kept up with Caden who rode out of sight. *You will keep him safe tonight?*

Clare wanted to tell her ghostly companion that she'd like it if he helped her through the soaking blood thing she was about to do, but set her teeth against that.

Zach sent mentally, *We will keep you safe.*

He slipped his arm around her and drew her close, kissed her temple. "You don't need him," Zach said simply. "You only need me."

She frowned and he reached over with his other hand and wound one of her curls on his finger. "And, no, you are not dependent on Enzo or me." He tugged on her hair. "Or not unusually dependent. We're your team in this."

"Oh. I hadn't thought of that."

One more tug. "Keep it in mind."

"I will, let's head to the grocery store."

But as Zach pressed the ignition, a little niggling thought wouldn't be silenced that Zach really thought she was part of *his* team, and he was the captain.

They were back in the bathroom with gauze, scissors, a plastic tray deeper than it was wide, a funnel, and the knife, when the rest of the inn's guests trooped in, talking loudly about classic cars and Cruisin' the Canyon.

Zach smiled at Clare, keeping his body relaxed since she appeared wide-eyed and pale. At least she hadn't pasted on a fake smile. No pretense from her. He didn't like seeing fear in her eyes, but that wasn't nearly as bad as her hiding her emotions from him so he didn't know what was going on with her. Wouldn't know how to help.

She continued to stare at him, then her body eased a little, too. Clare believed he was brave . . . and it was true that physical danger hadn't worried him for years before the shooting, and for months afterward he'd thought that the worst had happened.

Now he knew he'd been wrong. If anything happened to Clare . . . that would be the worst. Dying would be easier.

"We'll be real careful with the knife," Zach said. He untied the tassels that were in a much simpler knot than the one he'd done the day before. "You looked at the knife today."

She stood a little straighter. "Of course. I needed to check the dimensions."

He grunted, not thinking that might be the whole story, particularly since he figured that she had the sort of brain that could look at an object the first time and be able to make mathematical calculations regarding its dimensions. He said nothing.

The tassels hung free, but the top of the ivory sheath was still gathered. Zach's nostrils twitched as he smelled the musky perfume and incense scent from it . . . The cloth still protected the knife. He scrutinized the pouch in the harsh light of the bathroom, noticed the odd characters woven into it. Little circles with lines in them that appeared vaguely Chinese, which was strange, since Clare and the ancestress of the femur were of Romani and Hungarian descent.

Then he felt Clare's gaze on him, realized she waited for him to pull out the knife, and take it out of the metal sheath, too. They'd decided that since he was handier with a knife in anything other than cooking, he'd do the honors of cutting her veins open. Especially since the knife itself seemed a little twitchy.

Oh, yeah, he was sure looking forward to that.

Meeting his eyes, Clare set her left arm on the rim of the old-fashioned sink. Zach's gut clutched as he saw the tracery of blue lines under her golden skin. So close to the tendon. His jaw clenched. He would have to control the knife.

"Ready?" he asked.

Her lips tightened and she nodded. Then a horizontal line deepened above her nose. "The ghost is far enough away."

Zach nodded, too. He pulled the weapon from the ivory tube, set the tube on a shelf next to the hair dryer, then snicked the bone knife from the metal sheath and handed the blade to her while he arranged the sheath in a contraption of clamps they'd designed. Inwardly he scowled because the curve of the knife meant the metal sheath had to be wider to accommodate it than if it were a straight blade. That meant more blood going into the sheath.

Clare shifted her balance and the heavy plastic they'd covered the floor with crackled. Zach stuck the small funnel in the top of the sheath, took Clare's hand and positioned it.

"Do it fast." She wet her lips, frowned. "I think the ghost is beginning to feel the draw of the knife. I . . . sense . . . it is casting around for what is . . . affecting it."

"Right." He took her arm, placed it over the funnel, held

out his palm for the knife. She transferred it to him, though her fingers appeared reluctant to let the thing go.

He got another little shock that zipped from his hand to his toes, rocketed up to the top of his head, and left his ears buzzing. He had the distinct impression that the electricity could have killed him if the knife hadn't already tasted his blood.

Inhaling slowly and steadily, he put the tip of the knife against her vein. A terrible, high-pitched sound *ping*ed, the knife dipped deep, and a stream of blood that seemed *propelled* from Clare's vein rushed into the funnel.

Clare had squeaked with pain and Zach didn't look at her, couldn't look at her, had to control the knife. With great concentration he pulled it from her skin. The cut was deeper than he'd wanted. He put the knife down on the silk, noted with a sideways flick of his eyes that no blood showed on the blade or the cloth.

Both of them watched as her blood drained into the sheath . . . the gold outlining the blue and green and black pattern began to glow . . . tinted a burnished red. Then the funnel began to fill and Zach drew it up until the very end remained in the sheath. He grabbed a small roll of gauze and put it in the funnel, watched with more queasiness than he cared for as white turned deep red *supernaturally* fast.

When saturated, he transferred the funnel and gauze to the tray and Clare moved her dripping arm.

This whole procedure took a lot less time than it should have, making the hairs on the back of his neck rise as the atmosphere began to hum with tension.

No, that was the knife. *It* hummed.

EIGHTEEN

ZACH STARED AT it. Yes, like the sheath, the knife glowed. . . not ivory, but bone white with a hint of electric blue aura. Maybe. What the hell?

Clare made a choked sound and his head jerked back to her. Under the gold of her skin she was pale. Her pupils wide, even in the bright light, and he noted smudges under her eyes that hadn't been in evidence before this. She, too, stared at the knife.

IT'S TIME! yapped Enzo, suddenly appearing. Zach flinched and jiggled Clare's arm, which nudged the funnel. He snatched at it, kept it from falling and spilling the precious roll of blood-soaked gauze.

"Enzo!" Clare cried, sounding relieved.

"Got it," Zach said. The sink plug was in, so any blood that made it into the basin would not be lost. Zach lifted the funnel, held it in his right hand. With his left he got another roll of gauze, put it in the top of the sheath to siphon up enough blood that they wouldn't spill any when the blade returned.

That's enough blood, said Enzo.

"That's good," Zach said, over the mental voice of the dog and the continuing humming of the knife. He put both white-edged-with-red gauze and the funnel into the plastic tray.

"Why is it making that sound?" Clare asked, gaze still fixed on the knife, though her head had tilted toward the ghost dog.

It is tuning itself to you, Enzo said. He sat too quietly for the character he was.

"What's wrong?" Zach asked.

Instead of answering the question, Enzo fixed his shadowy eyes on Clare and said, *It must know ALL of you. Every sense. So now it is vibrating to the sound of you.*

"Huh," Zach and Clare said together.

It knows the taste of you already and wants more.

"Uh-huh," Clare said faintly. She swallowed. "I got that impression."

Enzo's head lowered until he couldn't look at either of them . . . or they couldn't see his eyes. *Did the Other tell you . . . or did I tell you that the knife needs to cut a piece of your hair, too?* His tail wagged back and forth, once.

"Cut my hair!" Clare's voice sounded nearly as appalled as she had been when told of the blood deal. She took her arm from along the sink, upended it over the plastic tray, shook it a little so a few drops fell, but it looked as if the thin cut was done with bleeding.

Put the flat of the blade on your puncture and it will heal better and faster, Enzo offered.

"Is that so," Zach said drily.

The dog turned his head quickly to look at Zach, must not have liked his expression, and returned to a droopy pose of staring at the floor.

Zach braced for the knife, picked it up again, suffered the shock zinging through him, and handed it to Clare. She nodded to him, continued to look at Enzo, sucked in a breath through pursed lips, and lowered the blade. It twisted in her hand, edge down; Enzo yelped, Zach reached for it, but Clare's knuckles whitened on the handle and she stopped the motion, turned it back. "No, you don't!" she said through gritted teeth. With a slow and steady hand, she placed the flat of the blade over her wound.

She hissed. So did the knife. When she lifted the blade, a red mark like a singe showed on her skin.

"Dammit," Zach said viciously. The more he saw of this knife, the less he liked it.

"Please move aside, Zach, so I can get to the sheath in the vise," Clare said.

Zach did so, moving through the phantom dog, feeling a little chill.

"Enzo, can you move, too?" Clare asked.

Hunching down, Enzo crawled away. Something was wrong with the Lab, but this wasn't the right time to confront the beast. Instead, Zach watched Clare as she inched to the knife sheath, angled the weapon down. Then her hand yanked forward and the blade slid fast into the sheath. A little distressed sound escaped Clare, her fingers loosened her grip around the hilt, and she dropped her hand.

The bone of the handle turned slightly rosy. And pulsed like a beating heart.

Or some odd vampiric thing that gulped down blood. The slight sound of glugging came.

"I guess we shouldn't wrap the hilt with the gauze yet," Zach said. That had been the next step in their plan.

"It's probably better that we wait until it stops . . . throbbing," Clare said faintly. She glanced at Enzo. "What do you think, Enzo?"

He snuffled. *That's right, Clare.*

"What's wrong, dog?" asked Zach. Feeling the urge to comfort the Lab, he lifted his foot and pretended to stroke the dog's back with it.

Enzo heaved a sigh, damp eyes coalesced in his dark eye sockets, and he said, *I was sent away. She SAYS she doesn't believe in me, but even though Caden and I was careful SHE knew I was there. I think she feels me.* He snuffled, his ears twitched, and when his voice came again in Zach's head, irritation laced the echoey tones, *I think SHE feels the cold of me and she called me Caden's imaginary compan-ion and she sent me AWAY!* Now the dog sat up, angled his head toward Zach, then Clare. *I am NOT imaginary.*

"No," Clare said. "You are a great companion."

Enzo subsided back onto the floor. *I wanted to stay with him,* the dog said.

"You wanted to guard him," Zach said.

The dog's tail wagged, this time twice. *Yes. Clare has the knife and you to guard her and both of you believe in ghosts. The little boy doesn't have anyone to stay close to him but me . . . and now doesn't have me, neither.*

"I understand," Clare said.

Zach's jaw clenched. She continued to put other people's—being's—needs before her own. She'd wanted *her* compan-ion with her, but her spirit guide hadn't come until he'd been sent away from Caden. She was too generous—generous to others to the detriment of herself. That should stop. They'd talk about it later.

She bent down and petted Enzo, comforting him, even though Zach knew the freezing cold of phantoms was worse when she initiated contact than when they touched her. At least Zach himself could touch her with warmth, give her warmth . . . heat even. They could ignite an inferno between them during sex. Oh, yeah, he always liked thinking of sex with Clare.

She straightened and gasped. Zach followed her stare to see that the bone handle of the knife appeared the slightest hint of—rosy with life? Now that was an uncomfortable thought.

"I think we can wrap the handle now," Clare said. She swept up the tray with the gauze before Zach got to it. When she slid the blade a little from the sheath, it was white, but shone as if it had been polished. Yeah, damn vampiric knife.

Zach stepped forward, held the metal sheath so Clare could start wrapping the rest of the blade. Being Clare and ultra-cautious, she started about an inch down on the blade, then rolled the gauze upward. Though the edge of the blade was sharp, the knife didn't cut the gauze. In fact, the edge sucked up the blood fast, turning white before she'd even reached the bottom of the handle.

He watched her circle the gauze carefully, overlapping every round at least halfway. Efficient. Another quality he prized in Clare. Finally she reached the knobs at the end, split the gauze in two, and wrapped them.

They'd gotten enough gauze.

She stepped back, mouth turning down.

Zach smelled the blood, too, more than when she'd shed it, and now the handle looked like a red and raw treat a real-live Enzo dog might like.

Clare wobbled and he stepped up and put an arm around her. "I don't like this," he said.

Her mouth kept the downward turn. "I don't either . . . but duty."

"Yeah, yeah, yeah. Damn, I wish the bathroom was part of the room and not down the hall."

"It's a short hall."

"Long enough, and the door and lock are flimsy enough that we can't leave this place while the knife is here."

She chuckled, stood straighter, and leaned on him. "I think I'd trust the knife to defend itself."

"Maybe." Zach glanced at Enzo. "What do you think, dog? Would the knife defend itself?"

Enzo sat up; his eyes went wide and his image wavered. *Don't leave the knife alone. It might get in trouble.*

"I don't like the sound of that," said Clare, frowning.

"Neither do I," Zach agreed. He went over to the toilet and sat on the closed wooden top and drew Clare onto his lap. It was sit there or on the floor. "We'll just wait. Talk to me about your research."

"Uh. Well, we don't know everything the archives has, but it's bound to have copies of the newspaper, the *Creede Candle*. And I found a story written by the editor of the paper at the time about the murder of Robert Ford in an old book I could download." She snorted.

"What?"

"You were right about newspapermen. Cy Warman definitely had an angle, an ax to grind. The story, at least, goes off on a tangent on how Ford had threatened him and the staff of the newspaper instead of telling more about the murder."

"Ha."

"Of course he wasn't there. He was across the street in his offices when he heard the shot. Do you know the story of Ford's murder?"

"I didn't read up on it, no."

"The circumstances are interesting," Clare said.

Zach had discovered that Clare found a lot of dull history fascinating. But this was death and murder, and fell within his notion of interesting, too, so he prepared to listen closely.

"One of the dance hall girls had died the night before and some of the others had started a subscription to get enough money to have her body taken up to the hill in a wagon and buried."

"Huh." Zach figured that though Clare had said "dance hall girls," they were really prostitutes.

"Yes. And the woman with the Subscription List was in Robert Ford's business tent—you remember the fire had just occurred three days before?"

"Yeah, yeah."

"Ford had several tents." Clare's brow creased. "From the pictures, I think near the parking lot of the county building. *Not* at the marker we saw this morning."

"Uh-huh, get on with the story, Clare."

Enzo yipped. His eyes had brightened as he gazed at Clare and listened.

"Well, she was there with the list, and Ford saw that Soapy Smith had put down that he'd pay five dollars."

Zach's lips twitched. "And Ford, of course, upped his amount higher than his rival's."

"Yes, he did. He put down ten dollars. And he quoted the Bible. He said, 'Charity covereth a multitude of sins.' Then he went back to talking to some other people, friends and girls. Soon after that Edward Capehart O'Kelley came in with a . . . nonstandard shotgun and called, 'Hello, Bob.'

When Ford turned around, he was shot in the neck and lower jaw. I guess it was a gruesome mess."

"With both barrels, it would be," Zach said, thinking of all the ways a shotgun could be "nonstandard," which was probably Clare speak for "someone-did-something-to-the-shotgun-that-I-didn't-understand-or-that-I-can't-remember."

She grimaced. "Bad enough that they wouldn't photograph his corpse, like they did for Jesse James and for Soapy Smith on the cover of another book I bought."

"I'd imagine," Zach said.

Clare raised her intent eyes to his. "There were a lot of people in the mining camp, and there were people in the tent with Ford. Some people would have stayed and settled here."

"Some people did, but it's been over a century, Clare, and we talked about old-timers and their memories."

"Yes, but I started thinking of stories and history, and thought the archives might have some old oral histories from decades past, perhaps even from an eyewitness."

"Long shot, but a good idea, and maybe the archives does."

We will do this! Enzo cheered.

A last, long slurping noise stopped Clare and they both turned to look at the knife. The gauze wrapped around the hilt was white again—even whiter than originally.

"Do you find that creepy?" she said.

"Oh, yeah."

With a sigh, she stood, straightened slowly, and put a hand to her ribs. Since she never mentioned any pain, Zach kept forgetting she'd cracked them last week. He had to do better at taking care of her.

Walking over to the shelf, Clare picked up the little manicure scissors, slid one side under the gauze, and snipped away. The bone handle appeared less blue-gray-white and more ivory, and, like the blade, glossier.

When the gauze had all curled into the sink, she took a tissue and swept it up, folded everything in another wad of tissue, and stuck it into the hanging cosmetic case on a hook on the back of the door.

"Huh." Zach scratched his jaw. "Probably a good idea to keep the wrappings."

Clare nodded. "I don't want to throw them away here." She frowned. "You think they should be considered medical waste?"

"I think we should burn them," Zach said flatly.

That would be good. Enzo nodded.

"All right. When I get home." She swiveled to the knife and plucked it from the sheath, dropped her head, and cut a small piece of hair near the nape of her neck. The knife hummed again. Sounded satisfied to Zach.

The rest of her wildly curling hair hid the shorn place as she tossed her head, then she tucked the lock of her hair into the ivory tube and paused. "The ghost is coming." She gasped. "It stopped. I don't know . . . I can't feel . . . I think it's a whirlwind of emotions, fury, bitterness . . ."

Zach snatched the knife from her, wrenched the metal sheath from the clamp and shot the knife home into it, grabbed the silk tube, and stuck the weapon in the cover. His fingers fumbled a little as he knotted the tassels. His ears popped as the atmosphere changed and the whole thing slipped from his hands into the sink. It hit with a muffled tinny sound.

Enzo barked.

Voices in the hallway stopped. Clare winced.

All right, it might have been odd to others that two people were in a small bathroom together.

Clare snatched the knife up, held it upside down, then swept a gesture to the sink, the floor.

Zach raised his brows.

She waited until creaking doors—five of them—closed. The inn was full, then.

"No blood," she whispered.

He scrutinized the room, then nodded, too.

Opening the door a crack, Zach examined the hallway. Nope, no one had faked going in and now waited avidly to see who came out of the bathroom. Good. He opened the door wide. When Clare passed him and went through it, he saw that she'd tidied up the shelf, removed the cobbled-together vise, and the bathroom showed nothing unusual, appeared innocuous . . . except for a lingering Enzo.

No telling who'd heard the clinking and who'd heard the dog.

Turning off the light, he locked the door and tested it, then watched Clare carefully walk the few paces to their door at the head of the stairs. She minded her steps more than he did.

As soon as they were in their own room, he said, "What's wrong?"

She sank down on the edge of the bed and said, "I'm hungry."

"Okay, let's head out for an early dinner, then, at Pico's Patio."

You should take the knife with you, so it can bond with you even more, Enzo said, walking through the door. His tone held a hint of a metallic hollowness that clued in Zach that the Other spirit seeped into the ghost Lab.

"Oh, all right," Clare replied with annoyance.

Zach eyed her. "You need protein."

"I think I'll have the steak tacos tonight."

Zach's mouth watered. "Sounds good. You coming, Enzo?"

The phantom wagged his tail, lifted his head. *I come. I know my duty, too.*

"I don't want you to think of me only as your duty," Clare said. "I thought we were friends."

Enzo leapt onto Clare's lap, part of him vanished into her torso. *We ARE, Clare.* He licked her face. *We ARE. I love you, Clare.*

"I love you, too, Enzo."

Letting his head drop, Enzo whispered mentally, *I am just scared.*

"We're all scared," Zach said.

Big doggy eyes stared at him. *You, too, Zach? You are scared, too?*

"Only smart to be scared of something that can hurt you."

That is RIGHT. Then Enzo repeated, *Only smart to be scared of something that can hurt you.*

"I'm sorry that this case and being with me is scaring you, Enzo," Clare said. Her shoulders slumped a little. "I know that you weren't scared with Great-Aunt Sandra."

No, Enzo said, *but she was old and didn't have any adventures.* He hopped off the bed and ran through the outside wall. Their truck was parked on the street near the front of the hotel, one story below.

"We *are* having an adventure," Zach said. He bent down and kissed Clare on the temple.

She stood up, held the knife by her side. "If I'm going to be carrying this thing around, I should check out some cargo pants. Her nose wrinkled. "They usually look scruffy." Lifting the ivory silk up, she poked a finger through a loop Zach hadn't noticed. "This would fit on a belt, if I had one."

"I have one," Zach offered. He'd wanted to take that thing away from her, protect her from the ghost and the knife and whatever else might threaten her.

She gave him a sharp glance, then went to her purse and reorganized the pockets, moving whatever she'd had in the outside one into the main compartment of her bag, stuck the knife in the outer pocket, then drew the strap over her shoulder. "How does it look?"

"Like a sheathed knife."

"What would it look like to a regular civilian type?" she asked.

Zach shrugged. "I don't know. Like a covered dog bone."

"Good enough."

They walked out into the fading day and the minute they hit the cool outside air and Zach saw gray clouds, he stepped aside from Clare.

"What?" she asked.

"I've got a bad feeling."

She grimaced. "I've had a bad feeling for two days."

NINETEEN

ENZO LOOKED OVER the side of the truck bed. The Lab lifted his nose, sniffed. His ears raised, too. *The air smells bad.* He gazed north toward the canyon, then his whole body pivoted until he faced northwest. *The scary crazy ghost is that way.* Enzo shook. *Too close.*

Zach didn't know what lay on the far side of the ridge, but the solid hill between them and the ghost reassured him. Still, he checked his weapon tucked in his SOB—small of back—holster. Easy access, good. Then he opened the truck door for Clare, went around to the driver's side.

Once they got into the restaurant, Zach saw the table he liked was taken. No good place to sit where his back wouldn't be vulnerable, so he went to one of the two-top tables in the narrow part of the room across from the bar, turned the chair so the back was against the wall, and sat perpendicular to the table. Not a great way to eat anything on a plate with utensils, so he'd decided to order a simple burger.

Clare had relaxed and was munching her first taco when the front door slammed open and a high-pitched voice shrieked, "Clare Cermak, ghossst sssseer." The last two words were hissed and slurred.

Startled, Clare dropped her taco. Zach rose from his seat.

It was Linda Boucher, and she looked strange, pale, her skin damp. That might be because she moved with awkward lurches inside a whirling snowstorm. Now and then teeth seemed to rip at her clothes, or razor slashes cut her. She didn't bleed.

She'd continued screeching curse words at Clare, came straight for his lady.

Zach passed Clare. Then she shot around him, arm stretched out, knife in hand—still in the silk sheath. She lunged for Linda.

Enzo howled and the hair on Zach's neck and arms raised. The dog leapt through Zach, through Clare, sending her angling toward the bar. Teeth bared, Enzo jumped into the heart of the storm. His jaw closed on Linda's neck. Her head snapped back, hard enough that there should have been a crack. Nothing.

Clare's momentum had her striking the woman in the side and Linda spun. More from the circling storm, Zach thought, than Clare's blow. Clare rushed by her and tendrils from the snowstorm whipped out at Clare.

Linda Boucher crumpled. Lay on the floor, dead.

But Zach sort of figured she'd already been dead when she walked in. Just great.

There was a smell of death, the voiding of a body, yeah, but it looked to Zach that the fluids had already dried on her jeans, not as if they'd just been expelled.

Clare turned, readying the knife again, stopped and swayed, staring at the limp woman. Clare's mouth opened but no sound emerged.

Enzo yowled again, long and despairing. The ghost shattered . . . but took Enzo with it, wrenching a cry from Clare. Zach moved fast, caught her, propped her up, ignored the turmoil of people around the fallen woman.

Clare's breath caught on a choking scream-sob and she panted as if she needed air. He looked where her gaze had fixed and saw huge two-feet-wide staring, disembodied purple-irised eyes. He shuddered along with Clare as they became the focus of that alien, dispassionate gaze.

You did not do well, stated the Other in precise tones of contempt. *Enzo has been swept up in the ghost's energy.*

Clare moaned, her fingers clutching at Zach's arm. She began to duck away from the thing, then turned and faced it.

I would have done better with more training. More information, she stated.

The eyes stared unblinking. *The ghost is not tightly compacted. I have managed to place a shell around the consciousness that is Enzo. The shell will erode within twenty-four hours. You must speed up your learning curve.* The eyes sparked. *I continue to tell you this, yet you do not comply.* Pale silver lids veiled the eyes, then they vanished.

More screams erupted around them as people surged from the back room, then realized the woman was dead and backpedaled. Zach squeezed Clare and said, "You might want to get out of this place and go to the truck for the time being. Otherwise I'll need you to stay with the rest of the patrons."

She nodded. "Thank you for giving me some time and space." She closed her eyes for a few seconds, but tears leaked from under her lashes. "And thank God Enzo hasn't . . . perished."

"We'll get him back."

"Yes." She hugged Zach quickly, went back to the table to get her purse and stashed the knife, and pushed through the crowd to the door. No one stopped her. Zach separated witnesses from others, and moved them all into the back room in opposite groups. He confiscated any electronics that might have been recording audio or video over deep protests, but with the owner's, Pico's, backing.

Zach stayed with the fallen body in the narrow aisle between the bar and the table where he and Clare had been eating. Soon the sheriff, and likely the elder Pais, would show up.

Now, he looked at a mini-tablet that he'd taken from their waitress who had been coming toward them from the back room on his left. She was the girlfriend of their waiter at lunch, would be leaving Creede soon, and had had her mini-tablet recording. To remember the ambience, she'd said, and probably had the most complete video of the event.

Everything had happened so quickly, he wanted to see what he might have missed . . . and what he might have to explain. The quality of the video was terrible, because of the ghosts involved, he reckoned.

Linda Boucher strode through the door, static around her. She didn't move in the whirlwind snowstorm that Zach had seen, thought Clare had seen, too.

Door slamming behind her, Linda began to spew filthy words—"ghost seer" was unintelligible unless you knew what she might be saying. She fixated on Clare. Hands in claws, reeling and jumping more than striding, the woman went for Clare.

Zach saw himself stand. Clare turned, reached down and came up with . . . nothing. Her hand looked whiter and longer but apparently the ivory silk sheath didn't film well. She stood and rushed beyond him.

Linda screamed and reared back for no good reason— that was when Enzo had launched himself at her—then Clare's hand struck her side, Linda pivoted, Clare zoomed past.

The woman fell and Clare stood a couple of yards away, looking like she might topple, too. Her hands dropped and she stared like everyone else at the dead woman. Zach moved to hold her, they both looked toward the ceiling, eyes glazed.

Now sirens screamed for a minute, then cut off. Sure enough, both Paises came through the door, the sheriff first, cowboy hat low on his forehead, expression grim. "Slade," he said to Zach. "Pico told me you were here. Want to give me a rundown?" he growled. He gestured for the two deputies to go through to the back room.

While Zach reported, Pais the elder ambled over to the bar and picked up the mini-tablet next to Zach, and ran through the loaded video.

"Do you know why Ms. Boucher would have attacked Ms. Cermak?" Sheriff Pais asked.

"They'd never met," Zach said. "I held the door for the woman this morning as she left the courthouse . . ." He nodded toward Pais the elder. "Mason Pais, Jr., was there. That's the only interaction I had with her, myself. She happened to be here when Clare and I ate lunch, and we saw her sitting at the bar."

"I heard about the scene at lunch," the sheriff said. He hunkered down over the body, felt the wrist, looked up at Zach. "You touch her at all?"

"No. I helped my lady get composed, then moved folks away. Not sure who, if anyone, might have touched her. I wasn't paying attention."

Mason Pais the fourth scowled. "You're a cop."

Zach shrugged. "Not anymore, and I was more concerned with Clare." He wondered how cold the body was . . . colder than death? Colder than a woman who'd been out in the chill evening, then died, should be? Ice cold as if the temp was below freezing?

Both Paises squatted near the body and Zach moved away to give them room.

"Odd," said the older man. He laid the back of his hand against her face, then touched the urine and defecation stains on the woman's jeans. Looking up at Pico, he said, "You said Ms. Cermak hit her and she fell."

The hefty chef and bar owner shrugged. "Something like that. Everything happened so fast." He cleared his throat. "She died so fast. I dunno."

"She *is* dead now," Pais the elder said.

"Goddamn strange," the sheriff said with near violence.

"Check out her neck," the other Pais said.

Grunting, the sheriff put his hand behind the sprawled woman's head, then stilled.

"What is it?" Zach asked.

"Got a head wound in the back. Blunt force trauma." He stared at Pico. "Did you see Ms. Cermak hit her from behind?"

Pico shook his head, then his whole body seemed to follow, jiggling fat. "No, the other lady hit her in the side." He pressed his hand to where his waist might once have been. "Then Linda whirled and the lady who was eating my food ran past her and then Linda fell." He gave a decisive nod. "I'm sure of that. Ms. . . . Cermak? . . . just stood and looked at Linda like we all did."

"Cermak didn't touch Linda after she was down?" the sheriff demanded sharply.

"No, Francie"—Pico gestured to the mini-tablet—"ran to Linda first, yelling her head off for me." Pico jerked his chin at Zach. "Him and his lady were closer to the door."

"Uh-huh," Pais the elder said. Putting his hands on his knees, he straightened slowly like his joints gave him problems. "A deputy and I will talk to Ms. Cermak, sheriff."

The sheriff's mouth thinned, then he nodded agreement. Zach stepped forward. The elder Pais pointed at him. "You can come along, but I'd appreciate it if you stayed out of our conversation."

"I'll do that as long as I feel it's in our best interests that I do," Zach said. He went to the door and opened it for the elder Pais.

Clare was very careful with her replies to Pais, Jr.'s, questions, with her breathing. She appeared shaken. The man didn't ask her about the knife, whether she had anything in her hand, and she kept quiet under Zach's frowning attention. They'd opened the truck door and soon the sheriff and one of the deputies had crowded around.

This wasn't the first time Clare had been questioned by the police about events, but she seemed too fragile, and Zach put a stop to it after he saw a body bag hauled out of the bar and restaurant, put in an ambulance, and driven away.

In a shaky voice, Clare agreed to go to the sheriff's department in the morning and Zach closed the door, keeping her away from the others. As they split up, he raised his voice. "You should have more answers in the morning so you can ask better questions." The sheriff took off his hat and hit it against his leg, a gesture that seemed habitual for him—one that would remove dust in the summer and snow in the winter—then turned his back and returned to the entrance of Pico's Patio.

Pico filled it, arms crossed and sulky. Zach couldn't tell whether the man would let them back in his establishment or not. Good thing the hotel restaurant and other seasonal places were open since he and Clare already had run through two local eateries—the LuCettes' and here.

"Back to the hotel?" he asked her as he fired up the engine.

She leaned back, her cloudlike hair framing her face, shook her head. Her eyes had closed. "Can we just drive? South? Out of Mineral County and back down to South Fork or whatever. Maybe find a spot to look at the Rio Grande?"

Night was falling as well as the temperature, but Zach said, "Sure."

A few minutes later he heard a choked sound. Clare was crying. He stopped in the wider valley, pulled over. Only a few lights from ranch homes dotted the area.

"Clare, honey . . ."

She turned to him and he held her as she wept. "I know you're scared for Enzo, but—"

"I killed her! I killed that woman! She was part of the ghost and I hit her with the knife and I *murdered* her."

"No!" He whipped out the word so she'd lift her face to him and she did. "No, you did *not* kill the woman. I believe she was already dead when she walked into the place."

"Wha- Wha- What?" Clare blew the word out on a breath.

"She had trauma to the back of her head. I saw it. Definite dented skull."

"Eww." Clare made a disgusted face.

"Which was what probably killed her. You went at her with a sheathed blade in a cloth cover. Hit her a glancing blow in the side. I'd say you would have bruised her. If she'd been alive. And it will be really interesting to see what the coroner has to say about whether there is a pre-death injury to the side. There was a video."

"There was?"

"You recall our waitress was recording stuff? She'd asked our permission to film us? 'Getting a pastiche of atmosphere of my summer job to remember it by'?" he quoted the girl.

Clare took a tissue from her pocket and wiped her face, blew her nose. "Yes."

"She recorded most of the action. Linda Boucher coming in and yelling and aiming for you."

"Oh." Clare swallowed, drew away from him to settle back in her seat; tension dripped away from her. Her brows came down. "I don't think anyone heard her call me a ghost seer except us . . . and Enzo . . ." Her voice cracked.

Yep, that was another sob; more tears ran down her cheeks.

"We'll get him back."

She nodded but her expression indicated doubt. Hell! Zach's hands clamped around the steering wheel. He *would* damn well get that dog back. He *would* protect Clare, at any cost. Dread and darkness pressed on him. He knew in his bones this case had turned bad, gone to deadly for him and his.

One small thought gave him relief. He'd caught up with his Counting Crows Rhyme precognition. As of this moment, he'd foreseen no more deaths. He let out a breath.

Clare cleared her throat. "Zach?"

"Yeah."

"You said that Ms. Boucher was dead when . . . when she walked in?" Clare's voice went squeaky.

He nodded. "I believe that."

She gulped. "So, like, we're . . . we're . . . dealing with *zombies* now?"

TWENTY

HE HADN'T THOUGHT of the situation from that angle.
Zombies. God. What next? No damn Counting Crows
Rhyme for zombies, unless it was "the devil's own self."

"I didn't sign up for zombies," Clare said.

Clare's statement flicked his sense of irony at the whole
mess of the last month. He snorted. "Clare, baby, you didn't
sign up for any of this. It was thrust upon you."

A small pause and a change of the quiet, then a slight
giggle. Her lips quirked, and she sent a sideway flirtatious
look. "I like your thrusting, Zach."

He coughed a laugh, grinned at her. "Ditto." He hit the
ignition. "Want to go back to the hotel and try out more of
my thrusting abilities?"

She gave him a wavery smile. "I *want* to go home to my
wonderful historic house in Denver and up to my lovely
bedroom and into the sleigh bed my great-aunt Sandra
gave me and slip between my thousand-thread-count sheets
with you."

"Sounds good to me. We can make it in five hours. Or

call someplace now and charter a plane back to Denver from Alamosa." He put the car in gear and continued southeast through the valley to the larger town.

Her smile tipped to wry as she glanced at him and folded her hands on her lap. "You don't know how to do that, order a plane up in a half hour." Her brows went up and down. "Neither do I."

Zach flexed his fingers. "We'll learn."

She sighed. "I'm sure. We both have the money to do that now. And heaven knows I can't take the wretched knife on a regular flight." She glared at her purse that lay in the wheel well by her feet and had since before he and Pais had come to question her. To Zach's relief, she hadn't mentioned the weapon. "Yes, I want to go home." Her chin lifted, set. "But I can't."

"We can't."

"We can't. I didn't get to eat my food, and I'm hungry." She put her hand on her stomach, then moved it to her side.

"Do your ribs hurt?" Zach asked before he realized she'd touched the opposite side of her previous injury. "Damn, that hellish ghost got a piece of you, didn't he?"

With a grimace, she rubbed her hand over her side. "Yes."

"Dammit. You need a doctor? Maybe we should go back to the hotel and I can look—"

"I'm hungry, Zach. I want to eat. Let's go on into South Fork and have a meal."

"All right." He pressed on the gas.

Lightly, she said, "I'll look at my side in the ladies' room, and if it seems bad, I'll let you look at it, too."

"Always a great date with you, Clare," he said.

She blinked. "We really haven't had any dates, have we? We met a couple of times for lunch, and I took tea at Mrs. Flinton's—"

"I'll take you out when we get home," he interrupted. He preferred not to think of that day at Mrs. Flinton's when he'd cut off the budding relationship with Clare, didn't want her thinking of it, either. She was with him now, exclusively with him, and he didn't want any damn uncertainty in her mind about that. Geez, he couldn't believe they'd never even eaten out together. Flipping through his recollections, he had to frown. Nope. One time they were on the way, but had decided in favor of sex instead. Seemed like they always decided in favor of sex instead. All fine and good, but he needed to treat her better.

He asked the navigator system for the best restaurant in South Fork, then used the hands-free phone to call and have them hold a table for them. Clare smiled and ducked her head, then looked up the menu online so they'd be ready to order the minute they walked in.

As they ate fabulous steak, Zach kept the talk on books and films and a few carefully chosen anecdotes from his past, mostly from his days as an adult. He had a few good childhood memories, as he supposed Clare did, but for both of them childhood had been tough, in different ways.

Before they'd been served, Clare had checked herself out and when she returned, her manner seemed lighter. She'd said she had surface scratches and some bruising but nothing nasty. Zach would examine her later. They still had gauze and bandages from the first aid kit they'd bought, along with some antibacterial cream. When he was a cop, he'd carried a heavy duty medical kit in his personal vehicle. The way their cases were going, he'd better make sure he had one now, too, as well as Clare keeping one in her Jeep.

After they'd eaten, they walked out into the night, fingers linked, relieved from the pressure and tension that saturated Creede. Zach felt no threat here that had him wanting to keep his free hand available for his weapon. When they turned back up toward the valley and the canyon, got away from town, the sky burst with stars and a huge moon. Despite the falling temperature, Zach opened the sunroof.

"Incredibly gorgeous," Clare murmured, tipping her head back to look. She still seemed at ease, so they'd made the right choice getting away from Creede. "Eeek!" Reaching

GHOST KILLER   185

down for her purse, she pulled out her phone, put in the nu-
meric password—which she'd given Zach—and began tapping. He thought he saw her searching the Internet.

"What?" asked Zach.

She looked over at him, the moonlight leeching her face
of its golden tone and casting it in dark and shadows and
twilight. Zach preferred to look at her in the day, Clare of
the sun-kissed skin.

"You know there's always a time element with regard
to the appearance of ghosts and when they are ready to
move on."

"Yeah."

"So I thought about the moon."

"The moon."

"As far as I can tell, the best time for a ghost to move
into the next-whatever is specific to an individual—the an-
niversary of an event, or the time of day, or the month or
something." Disapproval at the variety laced her tone. "So I
was wondering about the moon phase when Robert Ford
died."

"Good idea to check out."

She nodded and went back to working on the little screen,
shoulders hunched. Not paying attention to the beauty of the
night, the moon reflecting on the Rio Grande, the scent of
crisp air free of pollution. He understood her need for information, for control, but—

"Put that away as soon as you have the info and enjoy the
moment, the night, don't go surfing—"

She glanced up. "You're absolutely right. Just one minute." A few flicks of her fingers later, several clicks of screen-
shots or saved info, and she stuck the phone back into her
purse.

"Anything interesting?"

"Hard to tell, but the day of the full moon in June 1892
was the tenth, two days after Ford died."

Zach tilted his head to indicate the moon visible through
the roof. "We're close, too."

"The exact time of the full moon is tomorrow morning at 9:15 a.m., but it won't be visible since it sets before then." She paused, glanced at his strong profile. "You know what this timing thing means?"

He spared a quick look and a smile at her. "What?"

"Despite what we do, the ghost can't go on until it's the right time."

His mouth flattened. "That sucks."

"Yes." Her own inhalation felt shaky. "So I'm hoping it's the phase of the moon or something else so we can extinguish it *now*."

"That sounds fine to me." His head cocked and he looked at the moon through the sunroof. "Looks pretty full now."

"Yes, and just plain pretty." She sighed, and leaned back into her seat, turned and smiled at him. "And, yes, you're absolutely right. I should enjoy the beauty of the night and being with you. Have I told you how glad I am you're with me?"

He felt his face warm. "Thanks. I like being with you, too."

Another sigh. "That's good, because I'm beginning to think I am a high-maintenance kind of woman . . ." She was quiet for a couple of heartbeats. "Or, rather, the situations I've gotten into . . . the circumstances of my new career . . . are challenging. Not only for me, but for you, too."

He shrugged a shoulder. "I can handle it."

"Yes, you're very capable." Her admiring tone went straight through his heart and sent heat sliding down to his dick.

She put a hand on his thigh and he felt sensations from that touch in his favorite muscle, too. He covered her fingers with his.

Clare felt the strength and the sheer competence in Zach's hand on hers and more tears stung, so she had to swallow them. She had absolutely no doubt that Zach could handle this case; it was her own puny skill she worried about.

She'd lost Enzo. The ghost had gotten him and she hadn't been able to prevent that. Along with the grief of losing her companion, the anxiety about being without a spirit guide, was the fear skittering along her nerves just under her skin that she'd be the next one to be consumed.

This case had brought out the coward in her, though she thought she had dealt with, *could* deal with, villainous humans more easily than a ghost. If she had her choice, she'd still be denying psychic powers . . . especially in herself.

"We'll get Enzo back," Zach said again, patting her hand. She liked hearing that but was pretty sure the retrieval of Enzo would be up to her, and that wasn't a certainty at all.

She and Zach sat in silence . . . until she saw a shadowy man's aura in the distance. Her stomach clenched. She shouldn't see a *real* man this far away, let alone a ghost.

"Zach?" Her voice came thinner than she wished. She cleared her throat. She *was* a strong person, she *could* do this. "Zach, there's a ghost up ahead, a cowboy or a rancher or something, leaning against a fencepost."

Zach's fingers tightened over hers. He slowed as his gaze scanned to the left and the valley, back to the road, to the right and the rising land. As usual, there'd been few cars on the road, no vehicle lights either ahead or behind them now. "I see him," Zach said, slowing even more. "That is, I see a gray smudge next to one of the fenceposts. We're coming up on Wagon Wheel Gap, right?"

"Yes. It was settled before Creede." She paused. "He might be able to give us some information."

Zach grunted. As they drew near, the man tipped his cowboy hat to Clare, straightened. Zach made a U-turn in a wider spot in the road, driving up next to the phantom. He was dressed in the clothes of a guy who worked with horses—chaps, sturdy shirt, cowboy hat—all in shades of gray easy to see in the light. Definitely a ghost from Clare's time period.

Inexplicably, she was glad to see him—maybe because seeing a regular ghost wasn't nearly as bad as fighting a terrible one.

"Stay in the vehicle until I come around," Zach said, hitting the warning blinkers.

She'd unlocked her door and had been opening it. Despite his caution, she'd have hopped from the truck, but Zach made her think twice and she reached into the large side-pocket of her purse and took out the knife—a tight fit. If she continued to carry the thing around, she'd have to move up to her next larger bag, one with less compartments.

He didn't open the truck door or hold out a hand to steady her for the long step down. Despite the fact that they'd stopped for a supernatural being, he took no chances and kept his gun hand free.

When she exited, she saw he held his cane like the weapon it could become in his hands. She hadn't pressed him about knife fighting yet, but she should.

The cowboy tipped his hat. *Glad to see you, ma'am.* His torso bobbed awkwardly in a small bow. *I'm Chaz Green.*

Clare nodded and walked to him, stopped a little closer than she would with a live human. Zach joined her and put his hand on her shoulder.

Good evening, Mr. Green, she sent mentally to the ghost. *Have you decided to go on?*

He gave a short nod. *This is MY place, and I figger it's purtier'n Heaven would be and shure enough purtier than hell. I been happy here.* His chest went out. *Been strong and happy enough that I warn't sucked into that gray limbo most my kind go.* He turned his head and spit a stream of dark-looking liquid out.

An amused sound came from Zach.

Pardon, ma'am, the ghost said. He sighed and a small chill touched her face from his breath. His gaze went beyond her toward Creede. *I been concerned about that nasty one,* he said with traditional guy understatement. Then his form rippled as if in the wind. *Reckoned it might head down into the valley and get me next. I've thought and thought on it and thunk how to figger out who the thing could be—*

Thunder split the air and the snowstorm ghost was *there*! Fury struck at Clare, whirled her around, nipped at her with sharp teeth. The pain jolted her and she moved into the thing, trying to sense the core. Futility. She sucked in freezing-razor air, stopped breathing. *ENZO!* she shouted with her mind. *Enzo, come to me!*

I can't! whimpered Enzo. *I'm trapped. Get me out, Clare!*

With a snarl on the last of her breath, Clare stabbed with the sheathed knife, thought she heard silk ripping, didn't care.

She fought for her dog with her mind, too, sending sharp words. *You can't have him! You can't claim my Enzo.*

A shrieking giggle of mad laughter. *I can have him. He committed THE sin. He is MINE. My doggie. My pet. To torture.* Rippling laughter. *A dog ghost who is different than human, different taste.*

Clare shuddered. Ice pelleted her body. She swung and struck and blackness gathered as she tried to draw breath and nothing came to her nose, her mouth.

Bang! Bang! Bang! Zach's gun roared close. She felt hot fingers on her arm, was yanked aside and air shuddered into her gasping mouth, flowed into her lungs. The night air around her felt volcanic, burning. Her fingers unfroze and she dropped the knife.

Zach caught it, advanced with deliberate menace, plunging his cane into the snowstorm. The stick whirled away. He stabbed with the knife.

The cowboy ghost lifted, aimed, and shot a rifle, phantom bullets ripping the quiet, as loud as Zach's shots.

Then the apparition of the cowboy shuddered, rippled, became *more*. He—it—lifted his arms. *Begone, foul spirit!* Phrases in no language she'd ever heard, words too high to hear but that Clare could feel, peppered the air.

With an ululating shriek the swirling snow *thing* zoomed above them. *You are mine to eat! I WILL get you. I WILL be back. You can't hurt me yet!*

The cowboy turned to Clare and Zach, now appearing taller, more muscular, his purple eyes glaring at them with the Other's disgust. *I can interfere only once in one of your years. And I would not have done so but you ABUSE your tool!*

"Wha—" Clare began.

You FOOL! The Other raged. *You will be gone before the night is through. You TORE the silk! The protections will not work! The knife will call the ghost to you and you will die.*

Clare broke. *If I do it will be YOUR fault. You give me NO training, NO help, only obscure comments.* "Begone yourself!" She swept her knife from Zach's grip and thrust it at the Other.

Get the hell out of me! yelled the cowboy.

TWENTY-ONE

I— BEGAN THE Other.

Even I know there is rules. I didn't invite ya to use my shade, and I don't tolerate no bad-mouthing ladies. You just get outta me and onto your other concerns. Now. The cowboy's apparition waved as if in a strong wind . . . turned flat and two dimensional . . . faded in and out like electronics on the fritz, then stabilized into the shape Clare had first seen. He grunted, shifted his feet, shook out his limbs and rolled his head. No hint of any ghostly rifle showed.

He frowned, coughed, then nodded to Clare again. *Yep, I'm ready to go on. Think I hafta tell ya, though, that me and Albert Lord and Buddy Jemmings were friends as kids, and since Al witnessed O'Kelley murderin' Bob Ford, we talked about it a lot and he told that story often. I knowed that Buddy lived to a ripe ol' age.* The ghost paused to scratch his head under his hat. *His spirit dropped by, like, ta see me afore he crossed over. Anyways, Buddy talked to those who like to keep tracka old stories, so ya think about that.* Chaz's chest went in and out as if he breathed. He wiped his forehead with his sleeve. *And, yah, I'm ramb-*

lin' acuz I'm scared to my boot toes about crossin' over myself.

"I promise it's not painful," Clare said soberly, at least not as far as she knew, for the ghost. "And I have never seen a spirit go to hell." Of course she'd only helped six phantoms leave the gray dimension and head to whatever awaited, but she hadn't lied.

Chaz literally brightened. He shuffled his feet, hard to do since he floated about a foot above the ground. *Good to know, ma'am,* Chaz said. *I warn't a bad man, but I warn't much of a good 'un, either. Selfish, mostly.*

"All right," Clare said. "What happens is that I walk into you." She experienced bits and pieces of their lives. "And you, um, see where you need to go."

She handed the sheathed knife to Zach, then held out her hands. "So let's do this, all right?"

More fidgeting. *I guess.* He raised his hands slowly and she grasped them. Cold, but not too bad. She hurriedly stepped into the apparition, flashed on his deliberate and cherished solitary life, his love for the land more than anything else, an exceedingly brief vision of the two boys he'd talked about—Albert and Buddy, then Chaz gasped. *It's beautiful! Just like my spread but . . . but . . . MORE!*

Her vision turned sepia as Chaz poofed away.

Clare wobbled on her feet and Zach's warm arm went around her. Through chattering teeth, she said, "V-v-ver-y cold night, to-night."

"I am going to *destroy* that monster. It doesn't get to hurt people, living or dead, anymore." His voice seethed with anger and heat pumped off him, lifting her numbness.

"Did you really shoot it?"

"At it, into it, didn't look like it had any effect, but I didn't know that beforehand. But we got new data on the perp—perpetrator of crimes." He urged her a few steps toward the truck, then paused.

Parked behind them was a truck that even Clare recognized. She sighed. "It's the elder Pais, isn't it?"

"Yep," Zach confirmed, as the man opened his door and

shut it with a slam and strode to them. "I didn't see when he pulled up."

"Neither did I," said Clare. For a minute, embarrassment filtered through her at how she might have looked as she'd helped Chaz move on. She shook off the feeling. However crazy she appeared, she'd become a ghost seer and would have to become accustomed to looking strange—as soon as possible.

Pais tipped the cowboy hat back on his head. "You folks havin' any trouble?"

"No trouble at all," Zach said.

"Funny, I heard shots." He squinted through the night toward where their fight—no doubt invisible—had taken place. "When I drove up I heard shots and saw you shootin' at nothin'."

She didn't trust his friendly aw-shucks manner one little bit.

"That's right," Zach said, copying the man's manner. "Nothin' to worry about. No trouble."

Just as if they hadn't fought a ghost. The cold space, the wound within her ached. All of her ached. She shivered.

"Now if you don't mind, Clare is cold and I want her in the truck."

"Sorry, ma'am." Pais tipped his hat to her. "Sure, you go to your truck. But you, Zach Slade, come back and we'll check out those shots."

As if there'd be anything to see in the moonlit dark. Just an empty meadow. Clare didn't think any of the bullets had hit the fenceposts.

Since Zach didn't have his cane, they limped together to the vehicle and Zach opened the door. She climbed onto the seat. Zach leaned down and tucked the knife into the correct compartment of her purse.

She shivered as he turned and took his time walking back, then watched as he talked to Pais, argued about something and Zach refused . . . he touched his back so perhaps it was showing Pais his gun.

Then they began looking through the meadow. Zach would like his cane.

A noise, *not* a whimper, broke from her lips. He took the danger on himself, just naturally. Those broad shoulders shouldn't carry *her* burdens. And she sure didn't want the evil ghost coming for him. *Her* fight . . . first. She wiggled around until her fingers and toes stopped tingling and she could move well, hopped back out of the truck and strode over to where he picked up his cane and examined the battered stick.

"Looks like something chawed on that," Pais said.

The ex-sheriff was right. The cane had deep gouges, big splinters angled out from the staff, and the bottom was gone.

"Huh," Zach said.

"Huh," Clare echoed.

He frowned at her.

"I just needed to get warm." Though from now on, she'd consider toting around a thermos of hot coffee, or protein, chicken soup, perhaps. "How can I help?" she asked, too cheerfully. "I don't know what bullets look like." She tilted her head. "I wouldn't think you could find them." She stared at Pais with a guileless smile. "I'm not sure why you're looking."

His expression clouded, but he jutted a chin. "Just wanted to see that no animals got hurt."

Clare exaggeratedly looked around the empty landscape. "Well, chipmunks maybe. Rabbits? Maybe a coyote? No cows or sheep, for sure."

She thought the man grumbled under his breath. After letting fifteen seconds pass, she said, "Are we going to stand around here for long?" She widened her eyes and looked at Pais.

"No trouble here," Zach added softly.

"Yeah, yeah." Pais took off his hat and thumped it against his leg, like Clare had seen his grandson do.

Sticking his hat back on his head and adjusting it, Pais said, "You folks have a good evening."

"Same to you!" Clare caroled. She slipped her arm around Zach's waist and they stood and watched as Pais strode to his truck, sending a few glances back at them, then got in, stared at them, and finally drove away.

"He's suspicious," Zach said. He gave her the cane to carry as he put his hand on her shoulder and they proceeded slowly back to their vehicle.

"So what? I told him the truth up front this morning. Not our fault he doesn't believe it," Clare said belligerently. "There's nothing to see. Chaz Green moved on. The Other left. The evil apparition is banished for now." Memory flooded her and she recalled Enzo was lost. "Oh." Though she hadn't wanted to sob, that word came perilously close to being one.

"'Oh' what?" Zach asked.

Clare filled him in on the conversations she'd had with the evil revenant and what it had said about savoring Enzo. What the Other had said.

Zach appeared alarmed, and they hobbled faster. When they got to the truck, he looked at his cane before throwing it behind the seat. "Good thing I packed a heavy duty extendable metal cane that I can use for hiking."

She nodded and kissed his cheek. By the time he'd circled the truck and levered into the driver's side, she was studying the knife. He reached for it, and she withdrew it beyond his grasp.

"Clare—" he warned.

"My weapon," she said. Turning it over, she scrutinized the silk that had two long rips and several smaller ones. "The sooner we get back to the hotel and I mend these, the better."

"You can fix the sheath?"

"I always carry a small sewing kit in my luggage."

"Of course."

The empty hole inside her that the evil ghost had given her last night, and that had torn a little wider, froze instantly, and still throbbed all the way back to the hotel.

As they turned into Creede, Clare said, "I don't like having to do this at the hotel. It might be full."

Zach grunted. "People could be out at bars and restaurants, or the repertory theater."

"I looked earlier today. There isn't any show at the repertory theater tonight."

"No choice. We don't know any other place." Zach sounded frustrated.

"I could run up and get my kit and we could drive and I could sew in the truck . . ."

A short, seething silence. "We don't know what the ghost could do to a truck. I don't think I'd want to find out whether that storm and razor thing could take out a windshield. Especially if we're in the cab."

She sighed. "You're right."

"Did the Other say anything about you blooding the knife? It must be a good weapon now, able to kill the ghost."

"It may be good enough," Clare said. "But we need the ghost's name, its core identity." She thought, though, she could test that theory of Zach's . . .

"We haven't gone after it with the full power of the knife behind us," Zach said.

She paused, distressed by his choice of words, then decided to speak. "Zach, this fight is mine."

"We're a team."

"That's right and *I* am captain." She paused. "No, the Other didn't say anything about the knife but to scold me because I tore the sheath."

"Huh. Probably should consider it like a gun, then," Zach said. "Carry it only if you'll use it, and if you use it, don't screw around. Take both sheaths off and fight with it."

Her breath caught, but she nodded her head. "We'll figure out a good knot that I can yank and have it open." She bit her lower lip. "If I need to carry it around, the sheath is a liability." She breathed deeply. "Obviously that hasn't bothered anyone before me. If the metal sheath isn't good enough to protect me—us—people—from ghosts—"

"The metal sheath, and the knife itself, is unusual enough to attract attention."

"Then I will figure out something else." Her voice nearly

broke, so she took another little breath. "Maybe a tube, a leather tube. After all, it isn't as if I won't have the rest of my life." She stopped to scrub the bitterness from her tone. "If I survive this."

"Coming up on the hotel." Zach pulled in front and parked. Parking was difficult during the day, but easy at night.

Clare grimaced. "I'd rather not fight the ghost in a hotel full of occupants."

"Too bad," Zach said succinctly, turning off the engine and out of the door before Clare could say anything else.

As usual, he came around to her door and opened it. She got out, smelled something odd, stopped and sniffed.

"What?" asked Zach.

She frowned.

He angled his head and drew in a hefty breath. His nose wrinkled like hers. "Dust and old clothes and a metallic odor." His nostrils flared. "And . . . wet mold."

She hadn't scented that until he said it. "Yes. The ghost, I think. It's not up in the canyons." Her inner sore spot pulsed with a harder ache. "Over by the cemetery, I think."

"Logical."

"Yes, but it's closer."

"Still gotta do this." Zach shut her door, took the few strides to the hotel door and opened it for her.

"Yes, it may still be upset from our previous . . . contretemps . . . tonight."

Zach snorted, his eyes gleamed and he smiled. "Really, Clare? Contretemps?"

She flushed a little. "What would you call it?" She took the stairs fast, pulling out the ribbon in her purse that held the key, sticking it in the lock and jiggling it, opening the door.

Zach's voice shot up the stairs. "Confrontations."

"Oh," she muttered. She'd continued to move fast, flinging her coat off, letting it land on the floor. Yanking her empty suitcase up, she threw it on the bed, unzipped it, then unzipped the pocket that held her sewing kit. She opened the needle and thread packet up, praying that she already had a needle threaded. As far as she was concerned, color didn't matter as much as haste right now.

Closing the door behind him, Zach said, "Scuffles."

She spared him a glance. "*Scuffles.*"

"Yeah, doesn't seem like either one of them hurt either of you."

Her glance became a glare, and she tossed the kit aside. "Linda Boucher died."

His mouth flattened and he said with heavy irony, "I think the ghost had taken care of that little item beforehand. A good rock flung at the skull."

"Ugh." She refused to imagine that any further than the first image that had popped into her head.

Zach hung up his coat and hers, opened his suitcase, and retrieved a tube of metal that he extended into a sturdy cane. She jerked the sheathed knife from her purse, heard another little rip, and winced. With shaky fingers, she undid the knot, opened the sheath, tossed the knife on the bed. Zach scooped it up.

"My fight!" she growled, as she took a few precious seconds to study the cloth, pulled it inside out . . . better for mending . . . but she wanted to keep the darn patterns on the front as aligned as possible.

"Unless you want *me* to try and mend that, I'll stand guard." He moved around the bed toward the balcony door, took the step that kept him between the door and the window.

"Do you sew?" she asked, turning on the light on the wall over the bed and sitting beneath it, her back now to Zach and the outer wall.

"No." A beat of silence. "Black thread?"

"I'm thinking of it as yin and yang," Clare said, taking the first few stitches at one of the rips that didn't have a circle with lines in it. "I think I've seen these patterns before, series of broken and unbroken lines. Each different, though I can't recall when."

"Probably something woo-woo, and you weren't into that."

"Probably."

She set the stitches, focusing on the cloth. Not the time to go fast now. If those circles were protection, better that they were mended as perfectly as she could.

Ten minutes passed before she *felt* the ghost zooming their way. "It's coming, Zach," she said. It would probably come through the window . . . from behind her. She twitched, her needle caught a thread, pulled it, nearly across the whole tube. Darn it! A tiny sigh escaped her as she saw it didn't disturb any of the circles. She was doing okay with keeping them aligned and together with the tiniest of stitches. She had no clue what would happen if the six lines in the circle became five or four because she'd turned the material under, if a broken line became a solid one.

The wind whistled out on the balcony, rattled the windows so that the lace curtains shivered as if they were wraiths themselves. Rain poured on the roof.

"Come on in, *monster*, we are waiting for you," Zach taunted in a low and vicious voice.

Complete quiet . . . at least outside. Inside Clare could hear the raised voices of the couple next door in the Commodore room, the Jackpot beyond, and even some across the hall.

Fingers trembling, Clare bent her head and concentrated on her sewing, in and out, small stitches, as perfect as she could make them, but the nape of her neck prickled. Whispering, not knowing how much of regular speech the ghost could hear or comprehend, she said, "Ask it about Enzo. What it said about sin."

SIN, the ghost battered against the window. Clare whisked her head around for a glance. More than the shades, more than the curtains, showed white. The snowstorm looked a little like the lace.

"What sin?" asked Zach in a low tone.

The DOG'S sin!

TWENTY-TWO

"WHAT SIN?" ZACH persisted. Clare continued to sew. She was coming to the end of the longest tear in the tube. Did she dare switch out thread to white and try to repair the tiny lines? Hurriedly she knotted off the black thread, concentrated *only* on threading the needle with white, not on the conversation happening behind her.

And Zach *did* hear the monstrous spirit. She could tell from the flatness of his voice. Not because of her, but because of Enzo. Enzo heard and suffered, and she and Zach both felt that.

"Betrayal?" Zach asked casually.

BETRAAAYYYAAALLL! It shrieked through her brain and she *had* to pause in her mending to see, to watch. Zach rocked back on his heels, set his cane.

"Enzo betrayed no one!" Clare snapped. She steadied her hands. Her fingers had finally remembered sewing and she began trying to weave minuscule threads of the characters of one pattern together.

He betrayed! He was with the child.

"What?" Zach demanded.

He was with the child. He left his true companion for the child! the ghost spat . . . sleet hit the window, the door, slashed through the room. Clare hunched over the silk, then straightened as the words sank in.

She said, aloud and mind-to-mind, *I do not think that was betrayal.*

You hurt with the hurt of betrayal. I FELT you. He is mine now.

Clare put aside the silk. *No. I don't accept that as betrayal!*

Shrieking pummeled her ears, whipped through the room. *Only I make that judgment. Only me.*

"Give him *back*!" Clare yelled.

Zach made a slashing gesture. Clare bit her lip so no more shouts spewed from her. The hotel had quieted as if people were listening.

No! And no, and no! The phantom shrieked with the wind. The last "no" sounded accented . . . Spanish or something.

"What's your name? Tell me your name," Zach commanded.

Em— NO! You no catch ME. You no bind ME!

"We'll *extinguish* you," Zach promised savagely. "You killer ghost." He thrust at the thing hovering in the window with the sheathed knife.

A gasp, more than a gasp. All the air seemed sucked from the room. Clare panted, spots forming in front of her eyes. Zach leaned on his cane. His longish black hair blew away from his face. His jaw gritted.

Enzo wailed in her mind, then the coldness vanished just as quickly as it came. Clare sensed the phantom had withdrawn once again up to the start of Bachelor Loop and the confluence of the Willow creeks. The thing moved a little differently now. Slower if it wanted to bring wind and weather; faster if it just wanted to fight. Clare swallowed.

Zach's inhaled breath sounded as deep as the ghost's . . . well, it sounded, which was a blessing. He placed the knife carefully on the corner of the bed near him.

Clare heard the faint murmur of other voices, probably people next door. Yes, this was definitely a hotel built in 1905 without any soundproofing. She'd have to remember that next time they made love.

Zach cleared his throat, and Clare got the idea that the talk with the apparition, its manipulation of the atmosphere, had clogged him up some. A side of his mouth lifted. "We seem to be holding our own."

His words had her checking that inner wound of hers. Yes, it hurt . . . actually stung like it had ripped open even more, and ached. She didn't say anything, wasn't sure, now, what might possibly cure it. Perhaps the death of the ghost. Maybe.

She answered him. "Holding our own. That's important."

"Yes, it is." He zipped closed the inner pocket of her suitcase and the bag itself, set it upright back near the pole that held their hanging clothing, then sat next to her.

"You done with that—" He stopped abruptly. His mouth opened and closed. "You switched from the black thread to some that matched the silk." He stared at the ivory silk sheath, touched the tassels with a finger. They were sleek and silky as if new.

Glancing at the tube, she made a soundless, disbelieving noise. The sheath looked whole. Perfect. As if it had never been torn at all. She touched it with a finger, then pulled it close to knot and snip the white—white, not ivory—thread. The minute she did so, the small ends vanished. Now she had to clear her throat, too. "It's been a while since I mended anything. I pricked myself on the needle. I perspired a little bit, too. There . . . aren't any blood spots or stains on the cloth." In fact, every minute she looked at the ivory tube it looked nicer.

Zach leaned over and picked up the knife again, hissed through his teeth, and handed her the weapon.

He muttered something under his breath.

"What?" Clare asked.

He switched his intensity to her, flicked the cloth sheath with his finger, pointed to the knife. "Damn vampiric blade."

She jerked a little at the phrase. Picking it up, she stared at it, settled it back in the sheath and tied the tassels in a simple knot, got up and put it on the vanity.

"Looks like the sheath is blood-sucking, too," he grumbled. "You said that when the Other reamed you out, he-it-whatever called the knife a tool."

"And so it is."

Zach grunted, then said, "A weapon is a tool all right, but this is something more."

She returned to the bed and scooted back against the pillows. "Everything in my life is more, now." Her smile felt wobbly. "I have a fortune. I have a 'gift' of communicating with ghosts so they can pass on. I have a supernatural tutor who despises me. I don't have a real dog, I have a ghost—" she choked.

He rose and drew her up and into his arms, and they stood together. After a few seconds, he began to rock with her, and she forced *stupid* tears of self-pity back. Whispering, she said, "And I have a magnificent, larger-than-life lover, a man I wouldn't have dared to love in my previous life."

"Don't make me a hero," he said roughly.

"I'm not. You are, Zach, you simply are." To her horror, little whimpering sobs erupted from her. "G-g-good grief."

"You've been through a lot." He sat her on the bed.

Clare shrugged. "I'm just *not* prepared for this." She paused, couldn't help herself. "It would have been *so* much better if I'd had a few months of . . . this new vocation . . . under my belt. Or an easier monster to work with. Then I'd've known the requirements, how to discover a core identity. You did great, by the way."

"Thanks. Let's forget about the wraith now, and let your lover make love with you." He took off her vest, pulled her sweater and tank over her head, unclasped her bra, and his hands went to her breasts, caressing them.

With gratitude, she let her mind fuzz as her body clamored for release, and she undressed him. She participated wholeheartedly in the active and demanding sex, pleased when she made him groan, when they joined, when they reached rapture together.

They lay and she could see the window. The shades behind the thin lace curtains hung flat, relieving her. All too easily she could imagine an evil face pressed up against the window.

She feared seeing a face instead of a whirlwind of snow. Not that the opaque white roller shades had kept the thing out. Her imagination had come back online. Pity.

Zach stroked her side, draped his arm around her, his hand resting near her stomach.

Stress had tightened her muscles again, and tight muscles in bed were only good when you were making love. She remembered the relaxation exercise of her new yoga class, and began releasing every muscle . . .

"Would help if the Other wasn't such a jerk," Zach mumbled. "Guess it goes to show that spiritual-type beings aren't that much more evolved than we are."

"He said"—and Clare had always figured the Other for more male than female—"that he could only help me once a year." That just felt totally wrong. She'd had pretty much nonstop cases for the last month. In a year . . . But fear gnawed her that she wouldn't survive the week. Her body began to tremble.

Zach tightened his arm around her, grunted sleepily, and she kept quiet. The gush of feeling she'd had for him earlier had been absolutely sincere, but they'd had enough ups and downs for her to know he had faults just like her. Manlike— well, maybe humanlike—he didn't care for any over-the-top emotions, complimentary or the opposite.

Relax . . . every . . . muscle . . . Nothing stalking her, them, outside on the long balcony. No threat to their neighbors, in the next room, or the one beyond either.

At Wagon Wheel Gap the Other had sent the ghost on its way, and it hadn't fully manifested later. Zach had nearly sussed its name out of it. What a boon that would have been!

He was right. They were holding their own, and that was necessary until they had the ghost's core identity. Knew its name.

Though Clare had no doubt that the ghost would extract vengeance for this last fight. No, when doing the relaxing every muscle thing, you also banished negative thoughts. She began deep breathing, inhaled and smelled Zach and the tang of him, the hint of sage that she associated with him. His warmth comforted her back. His sheer presence comforted her heart, spirit, soul . . . whatever parts she had.

Flashes of the fights with the wraith highlighted her memory: the pain of tooth and razor-whip slices, the multi-mouths of half-consumed ghosts shrieking in fear and demanding she help end their torment, the quick sight of Enzo in a thinning bubble-capsule looking at her with doomed eyes . . . Her own eyes filled and she let the tears trickle down. She plucked a wadded tissue from under her pillow and wept into it.

Why hadn't she watched him better? Kept him closer? Sent him home to Denver so he wasn't at risk?

Now she'd lost the being who'd been with her from the very beginning and it tore her up.

Too much sadness, too many tears. She let her exhausted mind and emotions quiet, breathed deeply and regularly, relaxed muscle by muscle, and when, again, torturing thoughts and images paraded in front of her mind's eye, she let them pass and refused to dwell on them. Finally, even the indirect light of the moon faded as it rose too high to beam against the shade and sleep descended like a soft blanket.

It had taken Clare too long to fall asleep. Though Zach kept his breathing steady and his body loose around Clare—except for his dick, but *her* body was accustomed to that portion of him being stiff around her—fury raged in him, flooding his mind with a red haze. He was a much better actor than Clare, and he could lie with his body.

Circumstances were changing Clare and it riled him.

* * *

They woke later in the morning, spooned together and at the same time, and Zach was glad of it. Clare had needed the sleep, and he sensed that no nightmares had plagued her. Good.

She stiffened in his arms, made a small, grief-stricken sound.

He rubbed her back. "You remembered that we've lost Enzo—temporarily." He said it with all the calm confidence he had. Whether she knew it or not, Clare responded to that tone from him. It soothed her and supported her, and he was going to use every tool at his command to get them through this.

Sliding his hands down, he moved one to her breast and began to stroke her nipple; one he slipped between her legs and found her damp. She caught her breath and he gave her sweet, sweet attention, enjoying the hardening of his morning arousal.

Sighs and cries, soft moans and whimpers, and a soft rise to release and an even softer fall, together, holding each other, eased them into the morning. Clare rolled out of bed first, took the hotel robe and the key to the bathroom, and left.

Zach stretched out on the double bed and stacked his hands behind his head. It was Wednesday. They needed to keep moving on this case, and fast. Wrap it up Saturday morning at the latest, though from the fliers he'd seen, the first event of Cruisin' the Canyon took place Friday afternoon. Having it done by Friday would be better.

And he didn't have enough real facts to know that they could do that. They had the knife, the bloody, bloodthirsty knife. The weapon was ready. The person holding that weapon, Clare, might or might not be. Enzo being taken by the specter had been a bad mistake on its part. That made her even more determined. Of course she'd fight for Caden, but she'd only met him once. Enzo had been with her since her psychic gift had been dumped on her, had helped her through the first bad times. Clare would never forget that, and she'd fight all the harder because of it.

The piece of the puzzle that would be the difficult one was finding the dead sucker's name . . . Zach grunted. *Sucker* might be a word to keep in mind. Soapy Smith had been a con man, and Robert Ford had run a gang, too. They'd clashed, and later Ford had died. Plenty of leeway for betrayal in those circumstances.

Clare came back in and Zach took the other robe. "String of betrayals," he said, without thinking about it. He could talk to her about cases, bounce ideas off her. A woman he had sex with . . . cared for . . . unique in his relationship history.

Nodding, Clare said, "Robert Ford betrayed Jesse James and killed him. The Ford brothers themselves were betrayed in that they didn't get the bounty amount for killing James that was promised. Later, Ford probably felt betrayed when his older brother committed suicide. Most people think that Soapy Smith set Ford up to be killed."

"I'd considered that. I need to get up to speed on the legends."

Clare glanced out the window. "It looks like another mixed weather day." She gave him an unshadowed smile. "Always easier for me to read and do research on cloudy days. We have a meeting with one of the volunteers for the historical society at the archives this afternoon."

"I remember."

Once more when he returned, he found Clare dressed and sitting on the bed, her great-aunt Sandra's journal open. He wished Clare would listen to her gut more.

"Reading the story of how your great-aunt Sandra defeated her evil ghost again?"

Her mouth set stubbornly. "Sometimes you see new things."

"I don't figure one page can reveal new insights."

"You're being difficult."

"Maybe." He took off the robe, wanted to throw it on the floor, or the bed, but hung it on the stand instead. "I don't want you comparing yourself to your great-aunt Sandra and finding yourself lacking."

"I'm not."

He grunted and began dressing.

"Not much."

"And you're not regretting avoiding her, and not learning from her?"

"Not much."

"Really?" His sarcasm was heavy.

"Not. Much. I'm trying to ingrain the information into my head so all the concepts feel familiar when I think of them, not something I will doubt in the heat of the moment."

"Okay."

Clare closed the book and tapped it with her forefinger. "Great-Aunt Sandra's ghost had consumed two others."

Keeping his voice soft, Zach slid into the next question. "You know more about the monster ghost every time you check on it, don't you? You must have gotten an idea of how many ghosts it's taken over. Think, Clare, how many?"

A line twisted between her brows. She tipped her head as if listening. Her lips moved as if counting.

"Twenty."

Zach snapped his mouth shut so he couldn't shout the word, sucked in a breath and said, "Twenty."

"Yes, I think. She's consumed twenty."

"Clare!"

She jerked a little, looked at him. "Zach?"

"You said 'she.' *She* consumed twenty other ghosts."

TWENTY-THREE

CLARE'S EYES WENT large. "I did."

"The core identity of this ghost is female."

"Yes," Clare whispered. "Oh my God. Thank heavens. The ghost, *she* is female. We have something solid to go on!"

She appeared stunned. He finished dressing and came over to sit next to her and take her hand.

Relief washed through him, too. They had the gender of the ghost. So much easier to find a person, a historical person, if they had one good fact. And of the ten thousand people in Creede in the 1890s, a minority would be women. The case was looking up. Maybe they'd be able to solve it sooner than he'd thought.

They sat quietly for a good minute, then her breath whistled in, and her eyes met his and their gazes locked. "When we're talking about women in mining camps, it's unlikely that we're talking about wives."

"Whores."

"I don't like that word."

"Prostitutes."

Her lips pursed. "I don't like that one, either."

"Geez, what would you call them?"

Her chin lifted. "A phrase of the times, soiled doves."

"Hell."

"And only some men, some miners were recorded in history."

"That's right." Zach frowned. "Though the miners and business proprietors could have records—claims for the miners, at least."

"But the soiled doves sometimes used fake names, or were given nicknames. We might not even be able to discover her real name, not to mention just trying to track her down." A note of despair entered Clare's voice, damn it to hell. Yeah, damn the whore-ghost to hell.

Zach picked her up and moved her to his lap, said the first thing that came to his mind. "We have more information, just now. So let's leave it at that. Let it simmer in our subconscious."

He kissed her thoroughly, smiled at her. "Live in the moment."

She appeared a little dazed and he congratulated himself at how well he distracted her, and ignored his hardening dick.

"Cherish the moment," she said, and stroked his face.

"That's right. I'm hungry; let's eat."

"Yes."

The waitress showed up at their table by the window holding a pad and pencil and with a wide smile that wrinkled her face. She reeled off the specials.

"I'll have the oatmeal with nuts and dried fruits," Zach said. Sounded good and stick-to-his-ribs to him.

That wrenched Clare's attention from the passersby to him. "Seriously?" She sounded appalled. Glancing up at the waitress, she said, "No offense." Clare gave a tiny cough. "I just haven't met many adult . . . ," she stopped when Zach laughed. "All right, I'm funny." She glanced up at the waitress. "No offense to the chef."

"A lady like you who enjoys croissants might not understand the appeal of oatmeal," the waitress said comfortably. "I noticed you particularly liked the croissant yesterday."

She'd noticed that Clare had had designs on Zach's, but he hadn't let her have it.

"It takes a properly trained chef to make excellent croissants," Clare said stiffly.

Clare consumed her *two* croissants relatively quickly, played with her omelette more than ate it. She shifted in her seat, time and again, and Zach recollected their conversation about the seven deadly sins. Yes, she usually paid attention to her food. Not this morning. He finished his excellent oatmeal that Clare had been giving dirty looks. He could have finished her omelet, too, but the oatmeal was hearty—and tasty—enough.

She'd started pleating her napkin, so he stood, took out his wallet.

"I'll take care of the tip," Clare said. She laid cash on the table so fast he knew she'd had it ready.

"Thanks, Clare." He saw it was the exact amount he'd given the waitress yesterday. Clare watched her pennies.

Or, easier to say that she was a generous-spirited woman in other ways than giving money. She'd be one of those who'd spend a year teaching you to fish instead of giving you a fish. A bad analogy; he'd bet his whole disability pension the woman didn't fish.

"You're welcome," she said.

The minute he took her hand, he felt the thrumming tension in her, the need to act. He'd felt that himself before. He slowed her steps, bent his head to murmur in her ear, "What say we do some knife fighting practice?"

"Our room is too small."

"We'll find somewhere."

She squeezed his fingers. "Then I say let's do that."

They took the steep stairs slowly, then opened the door.

There, standing in the middle of the room, studying her bone knife, was the ex-sheriff, Mason Pais, Jr. Both sheaths, metal and silk, lay on the bed.

Clare lunged for him. "You don't know what you've done!"

As tall as his grandson, taller than Zach, the man held it over her head.

Anger washed through Zach. He controlled it. "Doing a little breaking and entering. Why?"

The guy shook his head. "Just can't get a good fix on you, Ms. Cermak. Jackson Zachary Slade, yeah. But you and that kooky ghost-psychic shtick? Not quite buying it. You're not like any kind of gypsy or medium I've ever run into."

"Here in Creede?" Clare said, scathing.

"I did my military duty. Spent some time in Denver. Nope, just not buying it. You look and act like an accountant."

Clare crossed her arms. "I am an accountant. I *was* at a very reputable firm, but someone else needed a good job that I didn't. You asked what we were doing here, and I told you."

"And you're pissed that I don't believe you're a flake."

"That does it." She reached into her purse, flicked on her phone, looked at Zach. "Do you know the number to the sheriff's office here?"

"Yeah." He gave her the number.

Her thumb moved as she began calling. "I am going to report you."

"I'll say you invited me in," the older man replied affably.

Clare gasped, stopped calling.

"Who do you think my grandson will believe?" Pais asked.

"Us," Zach said. "He knows you."

A crack of laughter came from Pais. "Yeah. Maybe. But what do you think he'd do?"

Zach sat on the bed, relaxed casually, signaling to the man that Zach didn't think he was any threat at all.

More head shaking from Pais. "You two are a couple of pistols." He turned the bone in his hand, glanced down at a fulminating Clare, met Zach's gaze. "Now we get calls from hikers and such, and I s'pose you did, too, about finding human remains. But the fact is, bear bones look a lot like human." He studied the knife. "Now, me, I can tell a human bone from bear. This looks like a femur to me."

"Please let me have it," Clare demanded.

"There are laws about obtaining and owning human bones, you know," Pais said genially. "The bones gotta be antique and . . . well, maybe I should talk about this with my grandson, the sheriff."

"You're right," Clare said. "It's an antique artifact. A *family* antique artifact. And I guarantee you that I will make a big fuss, here in Creede, and all the way to Denver if you confiscate my family heirloom."

She jutted out her chin, looked at Zach. "We're not going to let him get away with this, are we?"

Zach smiled one of his make-my-day-you're-going-down smiles. With teeth. "Nope. We're going to call his bluff." He sprang from the bed, knocked the guy off balance, and as he did, he broke the older man's grip on the weapon and threw the knife on the bed. Clare leapt to grab the silk sheath on the table even as Pais yelped and began to swear.

"Goddammit, Slade, you cut me."

"The knife turned in your hand as I freed it and it took a bite of you. It's particularly bloodthirsty, literally. It likes to soak up blood."

"You bastard," Pais said. His hand dripped blood on the floor, luckily on the wood and not the carpet.

"We have bandages," Clare said. "We'll take care of you before you and Zach have that little talk with the sheriff. But I want you to look here." She held out the pristine sheath. "Do you think you bled enough on the knife for it to be bloody?"

"Hell, yeah, I did—" He stopped as he stared at the ivory silk unmarred by any stains. He gulped. "Crap. This is crazy crap."

"Yes. It is." Clare smiled coolly. She drew out the knife, slipped it into the metal sheath, then back into the silk tube and tied a knot more complex than Zach had seen from her before.

Her head angled and she closed her eyes. Checking on the monster ghost, no doubt. A tiny sigh relaxed her body. "We're safe. This time."

"Crazy crap," Pais repeated.

Lifting her suitcase to the bed, she said, "You know I had this behind the lining of my suitcase. As far as I'm concerned, that's pretty extensive searching of my property." She looked at Zach. "You be sure to tell the sheriff that."

He swallowed an admiring smile. "I'll do that."

With quick efficiency, she had their first aid kit out and Pais's hand bandaged in a few minutes. "There, that's done. Now, as for you, Mister Mason Pais Junior," she said in freezing tones. "I give you permission, and the sheriff permission, to contact the last person I consulted with, Dennis Laurentine. I'm sure he'll give you an earful on me."

"On us," Zach said easily.

Clare sniffed. "Tell the sheriff that he can e-mail me the report or statement or whatever about last night at Pico's Patio." Her voice hitched so slightly, Zach didn't think Pais heard the hesitation. Clare was muscling through grief and fear with grace, not letting those emotions get her down. "I'll review the report and return it. If he needs me to come in, someone can call or e-mail me for an appointment." She waved at them. "Take Pais Junior away."

Zach was sure she wouldn't be surprised if he pulled out the cuffs he carried and snapped them around Pais's wrists. That would be satisfying, but over the top. "I'll be back in a while."

"That's fine." She sat down at the table and revved up her tablet, focused on it. Pais stared at her, but she paid absolutely no attention to them, as if they'd already left.

Zach stepped toward the door and opened it for Pais. When the guy passed him, Zach looked at the keyhole. No scratches. Interesting. The ex-sheriff might have a key.

The SeeAndTalk app on her phone jazzed the melody programmed for Desiree Rickman. Clare picked it up, tapped, saw the lovely woman and immediately felt plain.

"Is Zach there?" Desiree asked, peering as if checking out the room behind Clare.

"No. He's at the local sheriff's office."

Desiree's brows went up. "Tony will like that. He is very pleased with the law enforcement contacts Zach is making."

"Uh-huh," Clare replied. She didn't think she'd better go into detail.

"I'll be there in half an hour," Desiree said.

Clare felt her eyes bug. "What!"

"You won't tell Zach, will you? Tony has a hot case and thinks I'm skydiving today."

Clare opened her mouth and shut it.

"I flew into Alamosa and rented a van. I have your and Zach's armor, a gun and wheels for you."

Now Clare could see the interior of a vehicle . . . and both of Desiree's hands steering. Good.

"I don't know how to shoot a gun," Clare said.

"Damn. We'll take care of that when you return to Denver."

Clare was glad to hear "when," and not an "if."

"I won't come as far as the hotel. I'll stop at the cross street a block below and drive east one block. I'll meet you in the bar parking lot."

Clare didn't even know there was a bar at that location. "Wheels?" she asked. But the screen went dark.

She opened the door and went out onto the balcony, checking the county building catty-cornered across the street where Zach was, and the main street to the left, where Desiree would drive up. No people.

The sun had come out and the aspen on the hillside glittered golden in the slight breeze against the deep blue of the sky, a perfect autumn day in the mountains. The breathing exercise she'd learned in her beginning yoga class filtered into her mind and she stood, relaxed, soaking up the atmosphere, the beauty of the day, the quiet of the town, the freshness of the soft air against her cheek, and breathed.

Tension seeped away even as her lips curved and she held

tight to the sensory input, saving it as a cherished memory. Living in the moment, something she did all too rarely.

Perhaps a lesson of this case. Another lesson, a gentler lesson than learning how to destroy a killer ghost. The image of Caden's scared and tearful face rose in her mind and her jaw clenched and her shoulders tensed and her breath came choppy with fear and sorrow once more. Then, Enzo, big puppy-dog eyes lost and suffering, flashed in her memory.

She turned away and went to meet Desiree.

TWENTY-FOUR

CLARE'S TIMING WAS good. She got to the empty parking lot on the far side of the bar, Tappings, as a large, dark gray four-wheel drive van pulled in. The engine cut, and Desiree popped out of the cab, waved to Clare, then went around to the back, opened it up and leapt up into the rear space.

"Help me get this out," Desiree said, sliding out a metal ramp that Clare helped angle to the ground. The woman unlocked the wheels from its rack. Clare stood near the top of the ramp and rolled it down with her.

"What is it?" she asked. It wasn't that she didn't know, she just didn't believe it.

"Motor scooter," Desiree said with satisfaction, and shot her a glance from under enviable-long lashes. "You seem like a scooter kind of girl. It would get you to Alamosa. It's city and highway friendly."

"You brought me a motor scooter."

"And helmet." She gave Clare one that looked newer than the scooter, in a pattern of a universe with colorful galaxies and bright stars. Then Desiree dusted her hands. "Let me ask you this, Clare. What happens if Zach takes off in the truck?"

Clare glanced around the town, filling up with people for Cruisin' the Canyon, but still dead—no, not that word, never that word again—quiet. She couldn't imagine asking anyone for a ride. "Good point," she said.

Desiree jumped from the back of the van and sent her a serious look. "You have to remember to have *personal* backup plans."

If that was the woman's philosophy, no wonder she drove her husband crazy.

"I suppose so," Clare said. "I *am* an investigator, sort of."

"Yeah." Desiree swung out a bundle larger than the scooter seat storage compartment. "Here's your and Zach's body armor."

"Thank you."

"You can tell him it was couriered to you."

"That's the truth."

"Sure." Desiree narrowed her eyes and scanned Clare up and down. The woman's lips pressed together and she jerked a head at the bar. "Let's go in and get a soda or something. I want to look at you closer."

Clare's heart began to beat harder. She put her hand to her midriff. "You see it?"

"I see something. Some damage to you . . ." Desiree squinted and tilted her head. "That is also affecting your aura."

That didn't sound good.

Desiree shut the door of the van and locked it. Clare dropped her hand from her body and the inner wound, and fell into step with Desiree. "But the bar's closed."

"Tommy knows me. He lives behind it, he'll open it up for us." She smiled and looked even more beautiful. "He won't even mind if I don't buy liquor because I'm driving."

"I'm sure," Clare murmured.

"We'll leave him a large tip."

"That reminds me. How much do I owe you for the scooter rental?"

Desiree knocked on a door, hard, then whistled four notes and Clare heard stirring inside. Desiree gave her wide eyes. "I didn't rent it. I borrowed it."

Clare froze. "You borrowed it. Did you let the owner know you were borrowing it?"

With a cheeky grin, Desiree shook her head. "He's out of the country. It will be back in his garage in perfect shape by the time he gets back."

"I'll make sure of that," Clare said repressively. She had a creeping feeling that associating with Desiree Rickman would, on the whole, be expensive.

The door opened on a ripple of Desiree's laughter.

That was the last shared humor they had. A silent man with a belly, Tommy, grunted a greeting to them as he gave them a liter bottle of lemon-lime soda and two gin glasses as they sat at a table near the door. Then he retreated behind a huge and lovely bar to do set-up tasks.

They sipped their drinks in silence and Desiree scrutinized her. Then the smaller woman made Clare stand up as she circled her, humming to herself and tapping her lips with her forefinger. Finally she subsided back into her chair and took a large swig of pop.

"Well?" asked Clare, seating herself and keeping her hands still when they wanted to tug on a piece of her wildly curling hair.

"I haven't seen anything like it," Desiree admitted. "It looks like a nonphysical hurt, but a hurt all the same." She shrugged. "Not sure what to do to heal it, so we should hope it gets better on its own."

"Thanks."

Desiree frowned. "Do you know how it happened?"

"Maybe when I attacked a monster ghost trying to eat a little boy and it ripped through me."

Wide-eyed, Desiree nodded. "That could maybe do it. Be more careful."

Since Clare wasn't at all sure that she was going to survive, and that in trying to survive she'd have to risk everything, she just said, "Yes."

"So, can I see your knife up close and personal?" Desiree asked.

"It's back in the hotel room."

Desiree appeared shocked. "You don't carry it around with you?"

"No."

"You should do that."

"Uh-huh."

"Really," Desiree insisted.

"I'll keep that in mind. I'm not exactly accustomed to weapons."

"We *will* work on that." Desiree paused, said casually, "So how did the whole 'soaking in blood' thing go?"

"Surprisingly easy."

"Excellent."

"I just need to learn how to fight with it," Clare grumbled. A pressure at the top of her spine seemed to radiate warning throughout her body.

"Easy enough," Desiree said cheerfully.

Before she knew it, Clare stared at two wicked-looking blades on the table before her. She hadn't really seen Desiree move, let alone retrieve the knives from her person. They were smaller than Clare's weapon, but appeared more lethal.

Desiree smiled, and gestured to the wide space in the room, left for a band and dancing, Clare thought.

"We can do that right now." Desiree smiled. "The sooner the better, right?"

Clare frowned at her. Had Desiree heard Clare say that? Heaven knew, it was a phrase she often used.

So she wouldn't be distracted, she turned off her phone.

For extra space, they pushed back a few tables and chairs as Tommy watched them from behind the bar, continuing to work.

Clare faced Desiree with a knife and knew the smaller woman could slice her to bits, but wouldn't.

"I'm coming at you, Clare, we'll practice defensive first."

Clare didn't really want to; she'd rather go on the offense, attack instead of wait. She'd been waiting too long, trying to gather information so she'd be prepared for the final fight when she *could* destroy the ghost. But she learned a few defensive patterns, then stepped back and held up both hands.

"Um . . ." she said.

Desiree lifted her brows. "Yes?"

"Um." Clare glanced at Tommy sideways, then circled her finger in the air. "Um, the, um . . . what if my enemy came at me in a whirling motion?"

"Huh." Desiree stared at her.

Deciding to lay it all out on the line, Clare said, "You see auras, right?"

Desiree said, "Sure."

"Can you, um, expand your aura as if it were a sphere?"

The other woman's eyes widened. "Interesting concept." She tossed her head. "I can just about do anything with auras."

"Ah, okay. Then, could you, perhaps make it layered—" Like the evil ghost was layered . . . with other ghosts, with air, with supernatural stuff or whatever . . . with the nasty razors or teeth. "—and teach me how to penetrate each layer of your aura."

"While I'm whirling."

"Yes, while whirling."

"Wow. We can experiment." Another big grin.

Several minutes later Clare had learned the most effective way to thrust, slash, cut, and slice, moving ever closer to Desiree's body. And she and Desiree worked out a couple of sequential steps and patterns of attack.

Desiree's phone alarm beeped. She stood. "I have to leave in fifteen minutes to be back in Denver in time to meet Tony."

"I understand. Thanks for delivering the armor and the scooter, and most especially for helping me with knife fighting."

"I want to see you on the scooter."

"Okay." Clare left a fifty on the table, and Desiree gave Tommy a blinding smile that had him returning a melting grin.

Tommy and Desiree watched her take the scooter for a spin around a couple of blocks south and west—*not* near the county building. The vehicle handled just fine, though Clare didn't think she'd do well on an hours-long trip. But it was wheels, and enough to tool around town. Oddly, it gave her a sense of freedom she hadn't expected, as if in the back of her brain, she'd been anxious that she didn't have transportation of her own.

And her inner wound felt better, too. She thought part of that was because of the long, tight hug Desiree had given her. Clare had also sensed the woman sending her warmth and energy, and the thought of having a new, good, and supportive friend made Clare's eyes sting.

Then Desiree stood tip-toe to kiss Tommy on the cheek and got into the van. Clare waved good-bye to her and watched the vehicle turn back onto the road leading to the highway.

When the hefty guy led Clare to a shabby lean-to where she could store the scooter, he said, "You are two strange bitches."

That surprised a laugh out of Clare. She'd wondered what he'd thought of the whole thing, and now she knew.

He scrutinized Clare up and down. "Cute, but strange." He went back into his apartment without another word.

Since Desiree had asked for Clare's silence about her little side-trip—unless Zach specifically asked Clare—she left the scooter in Tommy's shed. The walk back to the hotel was only two long blocks, and the body armor was cumbersome, but not too heavy. Yet she grumbled as she walked up the steep stairway.

Once inside, she put them on her suitcase, which lay on the luggage stand.

Then she turned on her phone and saw that Zach had called three times and finally left a message. "The sheriff would like to speak with you regarding your statement of the events last night and this morning." Irritation laced his tones. "Please come ASAP. And bring the knife."

* * *

Time pressed on Clare. She'd been aware, in general, of a clock ticking in the back of her mind. Now she thought she felt every second, and not in an experience-and-treasure-every-moment sort of way.

She'd brought the knife, let the sheriff handle it. Filled out a permit form to carry it in her purse and gotten it approved. She'd told her story of last night at Pico's Patio, read the report, and approved it. Still they weren't done. She had to go through the events again and again.

She'd kept scrupulously to the truth, but hadn't told him of her gift, what she was doing here.

Neither Pais the elder nor Zach had mentioned that either. Some people just wouldn't listen, and Pais the fourth was one of those.

The longer she spent at the sheriff's office, answering questions that *couldn't* be rationally explained, the more she resented it. With each minute her nerves frayed until the fourth go-round, she lost it and stood. "I'm sorry, but I can't take this anymore. I have no additional information for you."

Zach gave her a dark glance, but one more minute and she would have said the words that would have made everything worse: "I'm calling my lawyer." Not that she had a lawyer that she could call in this sort of matter. She had consulted one for her will, and setting up a trust of her own, but nothing else. Another issue she'd have to address when she got home. If she got home. She'd ask Desiree Rickman for a name. *When* Clare got home.

The sheriff's expression fell grim. She didn't let that affect her. He grumbled and sighed, then waved toward the door. He looked at Zach, who somehow lounged in an old-fashioned wooden barrel–back chair, and Zach said, "Since you continue to believe you need more detail, sheriff, I'll stay."

Clare gritted her teeth, then added, "If you men and law enforcement guys had decided to accept my original statement and leave me out of the loop earlier, I would have appreciated it."

"Sorry, Ms. Cermak," the sheriff lied.

She couldn't leave the sheriff's office soon enough. Literally. She nodded coolly and, head up, marched from the department and the building.

As she stood on the curb for sporadic traffic to pass, her phone vibrated and she checked it, saw it was one of the archives volunteers. He had to cancel the appointment this afternoon; a family emergency had occurred and he was very sorry, but he wasn't even in Creede. He sounded apologetic, so maybe gossip about her and Zach hadn't affected him. She sure hoped that he wasn't related to any of the people the ghost had killed.

She asked if one of the other volunteers could meet her at the archives for just a few minutes, because she had the name of the man whose oral history she wanted to listen to.

The guy hesitated, asked the name. She gave him Buddy Jemmings, and the archivist let out a breath. He'd have another volunteer pick it up at the archives and run it by the hotel. Convenient for the both of them.

Clare accepted warmly, and made a note to send the Creede Historical Society a donation . . . and if the Buddy Jemmings oral history helped her, she'd consider adding them to a trust she was setting up for charities.

She was absolutely tired of waiting, and it didn't appear like she'd be able to initiate any positive steps soon.

Intolerable. Yes, her patience had definitely evaporated. She'd broken. Just plain snapped. She *would* do something. Now.

Enzo suffered, and she couldn't accept the failure to save her loving companion before time ran out.

She'd seen him in that thin capsule, so she tended to believe the Other, who had no liking for her.

It had occurred to her that the Other could lie. Or be mistaken? She kept hope alive in her heart, sent blessings to Enzo, prayers to Whoever might listen, and prepared to take action, to carry the fight to the ghost.

Perhaps she couldn't extinguish the specter, but Clare intended to save her dog.

She'd watched the town, the tourists, and picked the spot for her stand, near the canyon wall on the far side of the flume and to the north. That area, and the two old rental cabins, seemed empty.

So she passed behind the hotel, crossed over the open bridge, holding the handrail, and strode beyond even the farthest building. Not much space, but sufficient. And deserted, and not easily seen. That was important. She had a little qualm that Zach would not look for her here if anything happened to her . . . but if she died, it wouldn't matter, and if she freed Enzo, he could summon Zach. She preferred not to think of a middle ground, that she might live but not free Enzo . . . but Caden might be able to sense her, or Zach himself.

She studied the area, damp rather than dry from all the precipitation lately, with scrubby wild grass that grew in clumps. She checked to see that there weren't any dangerous-looking rocks around. Of course the whole canyon wall loomed beside her, but scrutinizing that, she didn't see any outcroppings to be easily broken off and dropped on her head. She hoped.

Yes, she *would* free Enzo!

Rolling her shoulders, stretching and loosening her muscles, she untied the knotted tassels of the ivory sheath with one jerk. That worked well. She scrunched the tube down and off, stuck it in her pocket, and looked at the metal sheath in the outdoor natural sunlight, just beautiful. But she hesitated to completely draw the bone knife. If she drew it, she'd have to use it, and she wanted to save the blade as a surprise for the final fight . . . after they knew the woman's name.

So she breathed deeply, sent her senses questing for the killer ghost, found her at the confluence of the Willow creeks, and yelled with her mind, *You BITCH!*

That felt good! *YOU BITCH!*

She didn't have to shout it again.

TWENTY-FIVE

THE STORM WHIRLED down the creek, the flume, onto land and straight for her. Incredibly fast! Quicker than she'd imagined, than she'd truly prepared for.

Crap.

Why hadn't she practiced *more*?

Because she was afraid.

Fear flooded her now, as the snowstorm bit and whipped and moved toward her. Forget that!

She shut her eyes—good grief, she could *see* it better, experience it—with her eyes shut, and plunged into it. A maelstrom of ghosts whirled and wept and shrieked around her like tattered banshees, mouths open, crying, crying, crying. Pleading for her to help, to set *them* free. A thick, black, monstrous negative-energy *oily* spot pulsed black in the middle. Hard to reach. Maybe.

And teeth bit her, claws scraped her side, but she ignored them, looking for Enzo. She *must* get him.

There! An encapsulated being, a dog, barked at her, pawed at the shield between them. Once he got his paw through it, the dark being snapped out and he took his foot back, dripping silver stuff, and cowered in his capsule—a capsule that showed cracks, and thin areas—like the one she now saw Enzo pushing his paw through.

No, Enzo. Be still.

Clare! You have come for me! He panted, turned his head toward her, and as he whizzed past in the funnel she saw huge, sad eyes. Not hopeful.

Go back, Clare! It WANTS you.

She didn't answer, set her feet, clenched her teeth, and remembered a knife-work pattern Desiree and she had done and began cutting, timing her strokes to when Enzo's capsule would circle to her.

She dismissed the creeping cold, standard when working with ghosts, though she sipped little panting breaths so her lungs wouldn't freeze.

One. Two. *Three*, and Enzo flashed near. Again she leapt, straight for him, slicing into his capsule, grabbing him— *yes,* she got him! She threw him from the storm, watched him fly free of it. The dark one moved toward him.

Opening her mouth, she screamed her own anger and fear in a war cry, continued with the stabbing, the weaving, the cutting . . . other spirits flung themselves at her, onto the knife. Yes, even sheathed it freed them!

They wailed as they vanished, hurt, but gone from this time and place. No longer tortured or finally absorbed by the central ghost.

That one whipped out nasty black tendrils. Those couldn't touch the knife. But they could cut Clare.

More and more ghosts thickened between her and the primary apparition, trying to impale themselves on the knife and move on from this hideous torture.

Clare took one step back, another. Heard the roar of loss from the monster in the middle as some of her chained ghosts vanished. Slowly, the core entity coalesced into female shape.

Think! Clare wouldn't last too long. She brought her hands together, stretched numb fingers to find the sheath, pulled the blade out. It stuck a moment, then freed a little and she saw an inch of red, red blade. She gasped; her mind seemed to crackle as thought broke from icy slowness. Then one of her feet, next her calf, felt autumn sun. Enzo pulling on her jeans.

And she was out of the whirling snowstorm, but continued to jab with her blade.

The specter compressed into a tight funnel, into a streak of gray-white-flashing-lightning. It shot up into the blue sky and was gone.

Clare fell. Enzo stood over her, his front paws in her. She felt nothing.

Zach comes! he yelled. Then he licked and licked and licked her face numb. *You SAVED me, Clare. From the big, evil, ghost thing. You can do ANYTHING!*

A large black shadow fell over her and instead of feeling even colder or more fear, she knew it was Zach, and it warmed her.

Then she passed out.

She came to consciousness when her stomach kept jostling against a hard surface. All her blood had rushed to her head and she found herself laid over Zach's shoulder as he limped with her back to the hotel.

"It's hard enough to keep my balance," Zach said through gritted teeth. He sounded steamed. "Keep still!"

"I can walk," she protested.

"Let's just get this done." He threaded through buildings and rocky ground to the closest open metal bridge over the flume.

He *did* have good balance as it was, even over the uneven ground. She tried a tiny shift.

"Stay still so I don't drop you on your hard head."

Just before they reached the hotel's back dining area, he lowered her, saving her the embarrassment of being seen like that, at least.

She knew her face was red, but he flushed with ruddy color, too.

"You scared the crap out of me. What the hell did you think you were doing?"

What spurted from her lips was, "Leave no man behind."

He sent her a fulminating, disgusted look. "You're not a damn marine. Or a ranger."

Enzo barked.

Zach froze.

Staring at the gamboling Lab, who didn't seem much hurt, Zach said, "You got Enzo back."

"I did." She nodded and took a step and had to lean on Zach.

"That does it. One damn fight too many for me. I'm taking you to the medical clinic to be checked out, and you're letting me."

Her mind swooped and spun in slow circles. Her face and body stung as if she had slashes. Her breath came too slowly.

"The knife helped," she said. Her fingers still clamped over it.

Propping her against his good side, Zach said, "Looks like the ghost ran away and is hiding and brooding, as usual."

"Uh-huh," she said, managed around cold tongue and lips. "I had to take action."

She thought she heard his teeth snap together, wasn't at an angle where she could see whether his jaw flexed. Then his body loosened a trifle. "I didn't see your breaking point coming. Shoulda."

"Eh. The ivory tube is in my pocket."

"See that, got it." He plucked it from her front pocket, wrestled the knife from her tight grip—and her fingers remained curved after it was gone. He stuck the knife in the sheath, tied the tassels, and placed it in a zipped compartment of her purse, which she realized she still wore with the strap across her body. Amazing. She hadn't given it a thought during the battle, and it hadn't bothered her during the fight, thrown her off balance. That was good to know since it made her better coordinated than she'd believed.

At the clinic, both Zach and Enzo stayed with her as she was treated for cuts, bruises, and scrapes. The nurses seemed to think she'd taken a tumble down a hiking path. Naturally, neither she nor Zach contradicted them, though one of them kept glancing at Enzo, then away. To take her mind off the pain, Clare wondered absently if that nurse had noticed when the regular ghosts had gotten gobbled up. And if she had, whether she'd liked that fact or not.

The nurse in charge gave her some antibacterial cream and recommended over-the-counter painkillers. As for Clare, she yearned for a nice hot shower.

She and Zach had a late and quiet lunch at the hotel that for both of them seemed to be nothing more than stoking up fuel. Enzo lay on her feet under the table. At the end of their meal, the hostess delivered the oral history Clare had been waiting for. It was on an old-fashioned CD.

When they went up, Clare headed for the shower, dragging butt. Again, Enzo followed, as devoted now as he'd been when he'd first come to her. Occasionally he whuffled, or licked her ankle, and always he watched her with adoring eyes. When she'd gently asked if he should go to Caden, the dog flickered wildly. *You SAVED me, and you are my companion. I didn't do my duty.* He lifted his head. *And the bad ghost got me because I was bad. Not gonna be bad again.*

At that she bent down to pet him and reassure him. "You're absolutely wrong. Caden needed you."

You wanted me with you.

Well, she couldn't deny that. "Yes, I was selfish, and I love you, so of course I wanted you with me. But you came when I blooded the knife, and I'm glad and grateful for that. *And* the reason the ghost caught you was because you were defending me from the zombie. You were a hero."

I WAS. And you are a hero TOO! We will be heroes together!

"Yes, we will."

I will stay with you. But that ghost is really, really mean and scary and crazy and I think you've made it MAD.

"I'm sure I have. I love you, Enzo."

I love you, Clare.

She'd already told Zach she'd need a nap to recharge, and

he'd agreed. What was going on in the man's head, she didn't quite know, but she figured he, too, had begun to reach the end of his patience and a breaking point.

She stood under a hot shower for a long time, wishing for even a built-in tub, and would have given a thousand dollars for a dip in a hot whirlpool. When the hot water began to cool and she realized guiltily that her indulgence might impact the rest of the guests, she hurriedly turned the water off, toweled dry, slipped on the robe, and headed for the room.

Once there, Enzo jumped on the end of the bed and she chuckled. She ignored the sunshine, Zach's shadow on the window shades as he stood at the rail outside on the balcony, and slipped between the sheets and then into the darkness of sleep.

After they returned from the medical center, Zach paced back and forth in the room until he couldn't take it anymore, then opened the balcony door and went out to stand near the rail in the sun to observe people, and to think.

He kneaded the tightness at the back of his neck. He should have seen Clare's break coming, but, so far, she'd been the most patient of women, proceeding slowly and steadily step-by-step in learning her new craft. Moving from one idea to the next when she felt totally sure of the solidity of the previous conclusion.

But she'd blindsided him with her actions. He'd forgotten the fiery gypsy in her.

She'd scared him spitless, especially since he was running to her, following an inner sense of where she was that had vanished the one other time in his life when he'd needed to depend on it.

He'd only seen a couple of minutes of the fight as he gimped to her, and they would sure talk about *that*, her moves, when she was recovered.

Gripping the square rail made his hands hurt, so he released it and, aware of any eyes watching, let himself lope to the end of the balcony and back. The far room of the three that shared it with them, the Jackpot, was empty. Zach sort of thought that they hadn't liked last night's unusual storm, which had hit the hotel and nowhere else in town. That had been the main buzz of a packed dining room at breakfast.

The people in the Commodore room were out Jeeping today—four-wheeling—following the Rio Grande to its headwaters.

For him, too, everything was taking too long, though he was more accustomed to slowly building a case than Clare.

He rubbed his face. He was getting lines, he knew it. No, he had the lines, they were just engraving deeper. That didn't matter except it showed the damn case gnawed at him. Not because of the woo-woo stuff. Not because he thought he saw crows at the edge of his vision or winging away, without being able to count them, which turned out to be way more frustrating than just *seeing* them. Like what were they? Possibilities of the future not set? Or could he only handle a couple of predictions at a time?

He hadn't seen any crows since the fulfillment of the *four for death* that had applied to Linda Boucher. But he had no problem admitting to himself that just the damned possibility of the dreaded four ate at the back of his mind. This case had turned rotten.

He was simply not scared of his death, and there was a time when living wasn't worth a good spit to him, though life had turned real sweet for him lately.

Clare might die, and that notion shivered his heart.

They'd made a little progress. First they'd found the trigger for the ghost going bad—the murder-suicide—then they'd determined the motive of the ghost—betrayal.

Blood the knife. Clare had done that and his blood was on the damned vampiric thing, too.

Discover the core identity. That item was the one hanging them up. They were close. He could feel it in the hairs on his nape, taste it on the back of his tongue like a word that should come but that he'd misplaced. Frustrating thing was, there just wasn't any solid evidence they could track down of such a person as an anonymous whore in a silver mining town of ten thousand. Em— Somebody. He felt a flare of pride that he'd gotten that much out of the thing.

Crap—and now he massaged his temples. If he couldn't get any info by regular means, then it had to be through the unusual and weird.

He went to their room door, opened it a crack, and glanced at a zonked out Clare, turned toward him and frowning in her sleep.

She wouldn't like what he was about to do, as much as he didn't like seeing the crows. He was, technically, he supposed, trespassing on her side of things. Not that she hadn't pushed him a few times . . .

Sitting at the table on the balcony, he took his phone and held it like the good prop it was.

Quietly, hoping he had this bit right and would reach only the dog and not Clare, he snapped a command in his mind: *Enzo, come here!*

The dog appeared, belly crawling across the wood floor with little whimpering sounds. *I am here, Zach. I know I spent too much time with Caden, but he needed me. He needed me more than Clare did. I thought. Clare had you.*

Zach said mentally, *And Caden and you were less likely to get eaten than Clare . . . or me.*

A small whine. *But I did GOOD! I attacked the evil ghost! I DID!*

Yes, you made a bad choice, then a good one. Good dog, Zach said. *I want to talk to the Other.*

Enzo gave him another fearful look, but before he could say anything, he sat tall and a different aspect came upon him and his muzzle curled. *You wish to speak to Me, man?*

Zach considered him—it—like he would a superior who he had to work with but disliked. Or the General, his father. Yeah—a light bulb went off in his head—the Other and the General shared several characteristics.

"What are you doing!" Clare stood just inside the balcony door, rumpled and too pale and holding her side, and necessary to him beyond all measure.

"Talking to a spirit. In private."

I am not here for you, the Other said. *I observe Clare.*

Clare gulped, but anger flushed her face. She disappeared for a few seconds while Zach and the Other had a stare down. She came back in new sweats that she'd consider barely acceptable for being seen in public. She took a chair closer to the dog than he, giving Zach a look that told him they'd be discussing this.

"If you're in on this conversation, you better look like you're talking to me," Zach told her.

Her mouth turned down, but she swung her chair toward him, wet her lips. "I could use coffee."

Zach gave her a guileless smile. "Good idea, why don't you make some?"

"No."

May as well start that discussion with her now, too. "The investigation is stalled. Time to shake things up."

She narrowed her eyes. Oh, yeah, he was shaking her up.

"So why don't you give us a clue, *Other.*"

The dog's spine straightened a little bit. So the *Other* liked that alias. Good information to have.

The Other looked at Clare.

I am here to observe Clare, not for You, man.

TWENTY-SIX

ZACH SLOUCHED IN his chair, fiddled with his phone prop. *I bet you know my name, nonetheless. I bet you know more about this situation than you're revealing . . . and I bet you don't like being called a "spirit guide." Well, we haven't been calling you that, you know, because you aren't helpful or guiding, but, me, I think that's part of your duties.*

The Other's eerie gaze slid away, and Zach knew what that meant, even with creepy supernatural beings. *What all aren't you telling me . . . us?* he snapped.

Forehead knit in a scowl, teeth showing, the Other snapped right back, *You must ASK. I cannot tell.* There was a hint of a sneer, of a lie.

Maybe I have to ask, but I think that you could be more forthcoming and you aren't. Too bad Clare got stuck with a prick for a spirit guide.

Clare gasped. Zach ignored her, went on in a considering tone. *I guess if you reward and punish Clare, and Enzo, that reward and punishment is part of the Big Scheme of Things by your Powers That Be. That there ARE rules. I can't hope to comprehend you—*

Of course not. The Other's mind voice was hollow, echoing, and, yeah, the chill that slithered down Zach's spine showed the intimidation worked, but what the hell, he had a point to make.

Eventually you, too, will be judged, won't you? On how well you worked with those you are supposed to guide. Maybe on such things as your help and compassion. Zach flicked a hand. *But that's your business and your choices. Back to what we need now. If this is a . . . balanced . . . universe with rules, there should be a way for us to discover Em's full name. She should not be able to rampage through a town, through a county, killing with no way to stop her.*

"Hmmph." That was Clare.

The phantom dog just stared at Zach with those scary eyes that, yeah, he had trouble meeting.

Then the dog's tail thrashed.

Zach continued, *So, there's a way for us to find this out. But we are running out of time. Give us a hint, dog, where we can find the damn name. Because, ya know, if we don't find the name in time, we might fail. A lot of people might die. Enzo might die. I might die. Clare might die, and I'm pretty sure that would reflect on your performance evaluation, huh?*

Zach ignored the little noises Clare was making.

The-Other-in-Enzo sniffed.

So tell us what you haven't before, Zach said silkily.

A long pause. *I could give you that information, but it would be best if Clare discovered it herself. Even she is smart enough to see the clue, if you allow her to rest, then to continue with her research.*

The thing just couldn't control his hubris and haughty manner, a flaw as far as Zach was concerned. He'd never thought the dictatorial worked well.

It began to fade, both Other and Enzo. So Zach asked the most vital question of them all. *Is Clare the only one who can dispose of the ghost?*

The Lab solidified again. *And live,* the Other said. *She is of the Cermak blood and so the knife will protect her as well as be her weapon. That is the reason for the blooding and the tuning. So she can extinguish evil beings that plague the world, and live.*

Zach's throat had dried, but this discussion had to be followed to the end. *So others might be able to use the knife.*

A haughty inclination of the head. *Yes, those whom the knife has tasted. They can destroy the evil, but they will not live.*

"All right," Zach said aloud. He waved a hand at the Other in dismissal. After forming the Lab's face into a scowl, lightning crackled from the spirit's eyes, then it flashed gone. The superior being vanished, leaving the dog blinking at Zach. *You have made it mad, speaking those true things,* Enzo said. *And making it talk when it didn't want to.*

"I think it's piss poor as a spirit guide."

"It's what I have," Clare said. She rose stiffly and opened the door to their room. "I'm making coffee."

He wanted to snag her hand, touch her, but she was out of his reach. "That's great. Come back out and sit in the sun while we have a chance."

She looked sternly at him. "I will, and I'll bring my laptop so I can listen to Buddy Jemmings's oral history again." Her forehead smoothed. "I *know* there's something in that."

When she returned with the coffee, she placed a mug before Zach, one at her plate, and set down her laptop that had an old-fashioned DVD player.

She didn't open up the computer, but sat and stared at Zach. "That was a very interesting conversation you had with the Other," she said coolly.

Zach shrugged.

She stared at him and he could almost see her deciding what issue she wanted to discuss first. "I can't believe that you think the universe is . . ." she seemed to struggle with the words "fair or balanced."

"Like an accounting ledger." He gave her his best smile.

She crossed her arms and scowled.

He drew his chair closer to hers, put his arm around her

waist, and leaned toward her. He stayed that way even when she remained stiff and her body didn't soften against his. Murmuring in her ear, he said, "I believe in justice. In the scales held by that lady. Good and evil. Evil shouldn't have an advantage."

Her head went back and forth in denial, though she didn't look up at him. "Life isn't fair. The universe isn't balanced. Evil isn't always defeated."

He moved a hand up over her lips. "Such an optimist, you are. So let's see, that is, listen, to the oral history again."

He angled the computer toward himself. She'd given him all her codes. But she put her hand over his. "I don't appreciate you contacting the Other—"

"Like I said, the investigation was stalled—"

She raised her voice and spoke right over him. "Without talking to me about it first."

He opened his mouth. Shut it. Then said, "Shoot."

"Right." She met his eyes wearing that serious look of hers. "We're partners in this case." Her brows came down. "And I'm the *senior* partner."

He gave her his flat cop look. She glanced away, toughened her body, and came back with an adorable scowl he didn't quite believe.

"Who's going to be killing this ghost?" she asked quietly.

He'd been scheming how he'd do that, but wasn't stupid enough to say so.

"I will be killing this ghost," Clare stated. "Therefore I am senior partner for this . . . project and you will run things by me."

Zach kept his cop face on. "I hear you."

Her face tightened more, probably since she didn't hear what she'd wanted from him.

"I most particularly did not like that talk about people whom the knife has tasted can kill the evil ghost and die."

"Clare . . ."

She turned and stared into his eyes. "This is *my* case, *my* job, Zach. I wouldn't tell you how to do your job, or interfere." She raised her index finger. "And even if you know how to fight better than I do. This is *my* case. I can survive the ghost. I *don't* want you fighting it."

Then she put both hands on his face. "I care deeply about you, Zach. It would . . . hurt me if *you* got hurt." She inhaled. "Me fighting this ghost doesn't mean I don't want you with me. Teamwork, Zach."

"Teamwork," he echoed.

Her eyes narrowed, her head angled. "Let me ask you this, Zach, do you have any outstanding crow prophecies? Particularly one that means death? Four for death?"

He let out his own breath. "No."

"Okay then." She took the computer and logged on; everything came up fast. Glancing at him, she said, "I can probably make you a copy of this and put it on your phone, if you want to listen, too."

Slightly conciliatory. He'd go with that. "Sure."

That was a mistake. Clare sat out at the table, her face knit in concentration, and he listened to an old and creaky guy's thready voice fade in and out, rambling about everything— his anger at his old cabin being modernized by his grandchildren, their lack of respect, how quiet Creede was compared to the old days . . . Zach went back into the room and propped himself on the bed pillows to listen to more of it . . . and the drone popped him right into sleep.

He woke, didn't think he'd been out long, since the guy still nattered, and decided to get some coffee, and refresh Clare's, too. He took the pot and limped to the open door to the balcony.

She was taking a break, too. She moved across the balcony, might have looked as if she were doing tai chi or one of those other exercise programs. She wasn't. She was practicing knife fighting. Poorly. Not aggressive enough, and that was a problem.

Her body didn't move with the suppleness that she should have. She favored her hurt ribs and sometimes put her hand on the wound she'd said the ghost had given her the first night.

The ghost had nearly gotten her earlier. In his mind's eye,

he could see the stupid fight she'd gone to alone, how the two had hurt each other, but it had sure looked to him that Clare was getting the worst of it. Sure she'd saved Enzo, but at what cost to herself? The whole thing riled him up again.

He withdrew and made some calls. No more than ten minutes later he went to the door, and saw whatever tiny skills she'd had, had deteriorated. It *did* look like lame exercising. And who had shown her such stupidity?

Stuff that could get her killed.

"What the hell are you doing?" he snapped.

"I was modifying—" Her lips pressed together.

"Modifying *what*?"

Clare stared at Zach, who'd apparently picked up her anger earlier, made it his, and simmered with it until this moment.

She shifted from foot to foot and knew even as she did that, it was the wrong thing to do. People serious about fighting didn't do that. Like it would put them off balance or something.

"Just where did you come up with that lame stuff?" he demanded.

TWENTY-SEVEN

CLEARING HER THROAT, and not wanting to go into an argument where everyone could see, Clare picked up her laptop and came to the door; he stepped back. She closed it behind her and gestured to the body armor atop her suitcase.

"What's that?"

Considering, she thought her promise to Desiree was null. Zach had asked, and there was really only one explanation. "Our body armor." She gave a little cough; she couldn't help herself. "Desiree Rickman delivered it and, um, taught me some knife fighting."

His blue green gaze arrowed to hers. "You think?"

"Why are you so upset?"

"Why?" He jutted his chin. "Because from what I saw out there, you would get yourself killed next time you went up against our favorite ghost."

She took offense, though her insides quaked at his opinion. "What? You think a soiled dove from the 1890s knows more about knife fighting than me?"

"Em-whoever."

"Emma." She scowled at him. "Didn't you listen to the history? He mentioned a prostitute named Emma was in Ford's Exchange, his business, along with other dance hall girls, when Ford was shot."

Zach raised a hand as if deflecting her words, the small clue.

"We can discuss that later." His tone was steel. "What we're talking about now is your extremely limited knife fighting technique."

"I thought I did pretty well."

"I saw the last of it." His jaw tightened. Yes, he ground his teeth now. With suppressed feeling that emphasized his words, he said, "I recognized some knife-fighting moves. A few."

They stared at each other. She breathed heavily in and out of her nose. "Why don't you tell me what's really eating you?"

"*Why*, by all that's reasonable, did you *do it by yourself*?!"

Instead of shifting her feet this time, she hunkered down into her balance like her yoga teacher had taught her. "I was worried about Enzo. He was . . . my responsibility, and time was running out!"

"Not buying this, Clare. More than an hour ago you talked about teamwork. Going to fight Emma-the-whore alone is not teamwork."

"Okay, okay! I had to do something! I just couldn't sit there, no matter what, waiting and waiting and waiting when I could try and save Enzo! Maybe I couldn't extinguish the specter, but I could, perhaps, free Enzo. And I *did*!" She found she was waving her arms and stopped. She couldn't recall the last time she'd waved her arms. Her knees gave out and she thumped onto the bed.

He rubbed his eyes. "You broke, you snapped, and I didn't see it coming." A slice of a hand. "That's done and past. I've rented a place for your knife-fighting training. Your *continued* knife-fighting training." He picked up her body armor and handed it to her. "We may as well try this out." With complete competence, he put his on, then he came over to her.

"I want to take my sweater off. I don't want to perspire in it."

His brows rose. "All right."

Clare studied him as she removed the cashmere and put on a soft button-down cotton shirt instead. "You're also irritated I asked Desiree to teach me a few moves. I think those helped, by the way."

He grunted. "They were better than nothing. My advice, don't even think of modifying them. Stick to what she—and I—teach you."

He shook his head. "I'm irritated that we didn't make the time to train you before."

"We've hardly had the time," she said. "We've been very busy."

"Well, we've slept and gone out for lunch and dinner."

"We've waited on information we couldn't find out ourselves. We've researched and worked out two of the three things necessary before terminating the ghost. We needed fuel and to recharge. We're human."

"That's right. I didn't like that you didn't tell me that Desiree was coming."

She huffed. "She called on the way from Alamosa, when you were at the sheriff's."

"Which is why you didn't pick up my call."

"That's right." He'd like it even less if he knew she was keeping the motor scooter from him. "Have you told me everything that you and the sheriff discussed?"

He gave her a stare of disbelief. "Do you want to know?"

"No." She really didn't think he hid anything, and the guys probably discussed aspects of the case that seemed like minutiae to her, like the hunters' injuries. "Do you want me to tell you everything Desiree and I talked about? We really got into auras—"

Zach cut her off with a gesture, sighed, and shook his head. "No."

They stared at each other for a few seconds.

"We should have made time for knife training before. I'm annoyed at myself that we didn't do so, among the other items we discussed."

"You don't really want me in this fight," Clare said.

"No."

"Zach," she reminded quietly, "it's *my* fight."

"And we return to cycling around this subject. I don't want to rehash that, do you?"

"No." She saw his cup of cold coffee, got it, and drank it down. "I don't like arguing with you."

"I don't either. I called two venues," he said coolly. "The community center—"

She choked and fear spurted through her. "That's north of town. Between here and the convergence of the Willow creeks where the ghost hangs out."

"That's right. It's underground, too." His smile was tight. "We haven't been to the mining museum next to it."

When she replied, her voice was a little high to her own ears. "I don't think it's going to have any information on soiled doves."

He shrugged. "Who knows?" Another quick, unamused smile. "I actually rented a community room in the chamber of commerce building. It's very new, modern, and in the south of town."

She picked up her purse and inserted her knife. "I'm not leaving my knife unattended in the room again."

"I don't blame you. But I have a couple we can practice with."

Her mouth flexed. "You and Desiree. Walking arsenals."

"We'll have to be careful, though, no mats." Then he frowned as he looked at her. "Your ribs are still sore, aren't they?"

"Yes. I could use help with this armor."

It took a lot less time to get it on her than she'd anticipated. She went over to the vanity mirror and studied the armor. Still ugly and flat and black.

This time she shifted her weight to try and get comfort-able with the heavy vest on her. At least it was her own, not Desiree's that she'd worn a week ago. Wait, no, not a week ago, four days ago. It was only a week ago that she'd started her second case.

She sniffed. "The armor smells."

"It's new," Zach said.

"Well, at least it doesn't smell like Desiree," Clare grumbled.

"You could spray some of that perfume I like on it," Zach offered. She thought he tried to lighten the conversation, move it back from their anger.

Clare made a face and rolled her eyes. "Heaven knows how the perfume would mix with the smell of this . . . ." She wasn't quite sure what the armor consisted of. ". . . stuff." She reached for her light windbreaker and put it on. She looked rectangular.

Zach zipped up his windbreaker, too. He looked virile. So not fair!

Chuckling, Zach came up to her and kissed her, a nice, deep kiss, though she didn't like the squeaky sound of their jackets rubbing against each other, and she couldn't feel any of his body but his mouth.

Then he stepped back and said, "Gorgeous."

She tossed her head and left the room, hung on to the rail as she descended the stairs. The armor definitely threw off her balance.

"How long did you rent the room for?" Clare gasped, dancing out of Zach's reach. He'd shown her some sword-work, canework, knifework . . . ancient patterns of attack and defense, then they'd settled on a couple of series of movements.

"Two hours."

"Okay." She swallowed. "I should have some good basic attacks solid by then, right?"

"One attack. Semi-solid."

She nodded. "Thank you for taking into consideration my concerns about working with a whirling, layered attacker."

His smile was thin. "If Desiree can do that, I can, too. And they aren't bad moves." He paused. "Unmodified."

"Give it a rest, Zach."

"I think we have rested, just now. Time to get back to practice."

"Get back to work."

"Practice."

A clatter came, and they looked over to see that her purse had fallen and the knife rolled out of the center pocket.

"Didn't you zip that center pocket?" Zach asked.

She gave him a cool look. "That was a rhetorical question, correct?"

"Ah. I suppose it wants to be used in training." He paused. "That could be beneficial, you know. Using the weapon you'll be fighting with."

It seemed to her that the knife, the ivory tube, the whole of it glowed a little brighter. And her temper broke again. She marched over and scooped it up. Didn't bother to take the blade itself from the silk, and held it so tightly her own knuckles showed bone. That seemed right somehow.

"A weapon and a protection. The metal sheath, and the patterns on the silk, should give us some protection. And I stipulate from now on that the knife will only draw the ghost when it's completely bare." She pressed her lips together, nodded with determination. "It's logical. It makes sense. I'm believing that." She inhaled. "And if *I* need to do anything now or in the future to make it *less* dangerous, I will."

She *sent* that determination and intention to the blade, and held it before her face, speaking to *it*. "You hear that *knife*, you hear me? You're crafted from the bone of my ancestress, so you *know me*?" She gave it a shake, continued, "First a ghostly Labrador dog bothering me until I loved him, a dog to take care of . . . and to lose." Her voice cracked. "That I had to fight—and I *did* fight—to retrieve him. Then that wretched, pompous, secretive, condescending—" She stopped the litany to take another breath. "Then that *Other*, spirit *guide*. More like a spirit dictator. Now a dam—, dam—, darn—, *stupid* bloodthirsty knife. Too many strange, strange things in my life trying to influence what I do. But listen to *me*, knife. I'm a good researcher and I *will* figure out how to limit you if you do not bend to *my* will, if you do not answer to *me*." To make sure it understood, she repeated herself in Hungarian, Romani, and a mixture of the two that her family used. When she'd finished she stuck the weapon back into her purse and rezipped the compartment.

Turning back to Zach, she saw him staring at her with admiration. "You are magnificent."

She hadn't had time to answer when the door pushed open forcefully and Michael LuCette spewed in followed by the elder Pais.

Michael lunged for Zach, who stepped aside and knocked him down. He leapt to his feet, chest pumping. "What did you do to him, you bastard?" His hands raised, fisted.

Zach snapped up his stick horizontally, held it out. "What are you talking about?"

"Caden's hurt!"

TWENTY-EIGHT

"WHAT!" CLARE GASPED. She shouldn't have been surprised. Enzo had said the ghost might want revenge and that had resonated with her. Even as weight settled hard on her shoulders and guilt flooded her, she glared at the elder Pais. She'd trusted that man to tell the LuCettes of her and Zach's concerns. Had he? Her words came out choppily. "Why do you think it was us? You sent us away. We went. We had *no* contact with Caden."

Mrs. LuCette stumbled in, tear tracks on her cheeks. "You sent that . . . that *thing* to him yesterday. I know it," she nearly screamed.

Her husband went to her, put his arms around her, and they both stared at Clare.

Mrs. Lucette said, "Caden won't wake up! He was tired, so I let him take a nap and now he won't wake up! We took him to the clinic, but Dr. Seares says there's nothing he can do for Caden. He's in a coma or something. They're talking about taking him to the hospital in Del Norte. We had to talk to you first!"

"Accuse us, you mean," Zach said. He looked at Clare,

lowered his stick and she moved to him, put her arm around his waist, one couple observing the other.

The elder Pais made sure the metal door that had slowly closed was completely shut and strolled over to get between them, letting the LuCettes focus on him. "Now, Mike and Jessica, when did this happen?"

"Just now!" Mrs. LuCette said. "About as much time as it took to find him and take him to the clinic."

Mr. LuCette helped his wife to one of the chairs against the wall. They sank down into them and he put his head in his hands, his fingers spearing his hair up in spikes. "A coupla hours ago."

The elder Pais pulled a chair over to them, but set it sideways as if he needed to keep an eye on Clare and Zach. He cleared his throat. "I—uh—we've been watchin' Zach and Clare and they weren't anywhere near your motel. So how could have they hurt Caden?" he asked gently, taking Mrs. LuCette's hand in his own, chafing it.

"They said . . . when they came, and when they looked so odd that first night . . . something would happen to Caden. And now it has," Mrs. LuCette sobbed.

"And you didn't believe us. You didn't believe Caden in the first place," Clare said tightly. Her whole body was tight, including her voice, compressed by anger at the ghost, and her own fear and guilt. She wasn't sure what more she could have done, but she should have tried *something*. She swallowed, then said, "Some people find . . . weird . . . stuff hard to believe."

Enzo appeared in front of Clare, tipped his head back and howled. She, Zach, and Mrs. LuCette flinched.

"It's the awful thing!" Mrs. LuCette wailed.

Pais appeared extremely uncomfortable.

"It's the guardian who tried to keep Caden safe. You sent him away, too." She looked at Pais. "So you were watching us. Was anyone keeping an eye on the LuCettes? *We* told you Caden was in danger."

The ex-sheriff's expression turned stony.

Now Enzo stalked back and forth, lashing his tail and

baring his teeth. *We will get that evil bitch. We will EXTIN-GUISH her. We can do it!*

Clare gritted her teeth. *Let's talk about this outside,* she said to Enzo. She was done being a display for people who didn't believe in her skills. She jerked her head at Pais. "We had nothing to do with Caden being hurt. You make them understand that."

Drawing away from Zach, she donned her windbreaker, got her purse, and opened the door. Zach grabbed his windbreaker and snagged her wrist, but she pulled on it, frowning at him. With raised brows, he gave in and walked beside her, limping a little more than usual, showing he was upset, too.

Enzo ran behind her, then breezed like chill winter through her legs and zoomed through the main doors. She followed and strode around to the side parking lot and stopped, blinking as the sun dazzled in the deep and cloudless blue autumn sky.

Drinking in a huge breath of sweet, thin, and cold mountain air, she let her shoulders rise and fall, relaxing the muscles as she did so. She hadn't realized how tight she'd gotten, and standing around after the strenuous knife training, not stretching, hadn't helped. For the first time since they'd left, she missed her beginning yoga class.

Enzo planted himself in front of her, just touching the tips of her shoes. *I love you, Clare. But I love Caden, too! We must help him.*

"We've been working on doing that all the time we're here." But she wrapped her arms around herself in guilt that she hadn't been faster, smarter.

Enzo's head tilted, his ears raised just a little. *The ghost has Caden, but she hasn't been able to eat him like she eats ghosts!*

"That's good news," Zach said.

Enzo whined. *Caden hurts.*

Clare shuddered. "We *will* save him," she promised. Just as she had when they'd first taken the case, though that vow was to protect him and she'd failed.

Yes, we WILL! I will go sneak and look at her. I will watch.

"Good idea," Zach said. "Come back if we call you."

I will! He stretched from doglike into a streaking gray spirit and zoomed north.

Voices had Clare's head coming up. Yes, those were the LuCettes and Pais; the couple had parked in the front. Car doors slammed and they drove away in the opposite direction so she didn't have to see them.

Pais Junior rounded the corner, his face hard. He studied them.

"So what are you going to do about this?"

Zach stepped in front of Clare. "What we have been doing about this. Fighting off the ghost, and working to find out her full name."

"Say what?"

Clare stepped away from Zach's bulk so she could face the ex-sheriff herself. "There are rules to this sort of matter. We have to find out the ghost's full name. And wait for the right time. We're hoping it is the full moon." She glanced in the sky, but it wasn't visible.

"Crazy crap."

"And we haven't had much help from anyone here so far." She was a little surprised by the amount of bitterness that came into her voice. "We know the ghost is from the 1890s."

"Wha-what?" Pais sputtered.

She gave him a look that told him she thought he was a slow student. "I wouldn't be here if it weren't in my time period." She waved that away. "We're pretty sure that this revenant ties in with the murder of Robert—"

"Ford," Pais ended for her, disgustedly. "As far as I can tell, that boy caused nothing but trouble."

"Yeah? Well, we have to find the name of the ghost or we can't terminate her," Zach said.

"The archivists have been as helpful as they can be, but they are volunteers, this is not their career." Clare paused. "Which reminds me that you are keeping me from listening again to an oral history that I think has a solid clue. *And* I spent a good two hours this morning in the sheriff's office instead of exploring other options online." A deep breath.

"You've complicated my task, Pais. So why don't you just get out of my way and let me do my job." She walked away, straight up the street. The hotel wasn't more than two miles, and though wind whipped the clouds close to the sun and the top of the hills, the air was plenty fresh and not too cold if she kept moving.

She had to keep moving or break down. Again. She had to keep moving forward, period. Nothing would stop her.

Something Buddy Jemmings said in his storytelling tugged at her. If she heard it again, she was certain she could follow that thread.

Once Zach had told her that he got a feeling when a case came close to being solved. She thought she felt something like that now, an itch that if she simply added up all the figures, she'd come to the right total—the correct conclusion.

Zach caught up with her, put an arm around her waist, and smoothly turned them back toward the parking lot and their truck.

"We need to eat."

Clare dug in her heels. "I'm not going anywhere in clunky body armor, and under it I'm just sweaty and icky." She eyed him. "You don't look sweaty and icky."

"I was teaching, not moving around as much." He opened the passenger door to the truck. "Hop on in. We'll go back to the Jimtown Inn, shower, and order room service."

"That sounds good." Clare climbed into the truck. Her stomach rumbled.

After the exquisite trout piccata, Clare and Zach settled against the bed pillows side by side. Both wore earphones, he listening to the history on his phone, she on her laptop that lay between them. She had a pad and pencil and her notes, and had circled the name, Emma.

As much as she wanted to just continue from where she'd left off before the knife-fighting training—and she glanced at the knife sitting on the vanity, appearing innocuous, or not glowing anyhow—she knew she had to start from the beginning. And concentrate harder. Terribly difficult when a young boy's life remained at risk. Her mouth dried at the thought.

"Ah'm Buddy Jemmings, an I lived here alla my life—"

She awoke more than two hours later. The windows were dark and a small lamp lit the room.

Gasping, she sat straight up. Looked at Zach who met her gaze with a compassionate one of his own. "You needed the sleep. You're still healing, physically and mentally."

"Caden?" she asked.

"He's in the hospital in Del Norte. I spoke with a nurse there not too long ago. No change. But Enzo reported back from watching our fiend Emma and said that 'Caden's little and slippery and tastes nasty to the ghost and can hide from her 'cuz she's not wound so tight and is not thinking right.'"

"Mad," Clare said. Zach had gotten Enzo's voice dead on. She winced. Completely right, Zach had gotten Enzo's voice completely right.

"You still look tired." Zach frowned.

Her hand went to her side where it felt inwardly icy, shriveled perhaps, from the ghost's freezing touch. She'd ignore that. Stretching from her huddle she asked, "Thanks for letting me know about Caden. Did you find anything while listening to Buddy Jemmings?"

He shook his head, mouth straight. "I did get the name Emma, the dance hall girl who'd become hysterical. Or more hysterical than the others. I also got the feeling that she'd been sleeping with Ford—and he with others, as well."

"Yes." Clare frowned. "There's something else, here. I know it."

He handed her the earbuds, got up and poured some coffee. The twitching of her nose told her it was freshly brewed and that the sounds of the making of it might have awoken her. Clare nodded her thanks at the mug, looked at her notes, and began listening again.

Two minutes later she stopped.

"What?"

"He's complaining about his grandchildren moving him

out of the cabin he lived in all his life, making him live with them because they said he was too old to handle himself, modernizing the cabin."

"Yeah, yeah." Zach nodded.

After a sip of the coffee, she set it aside to flip through her notes. "A little later he said he had some 'great stuff, some historical stuff.'"

Zach chuckled. "Hate to break it to you, Clare, but most old guys I know have great, historical stuff they're hoarding. I got the idea he'd hoarded, didn't you?"

She sighed. "Yes, but . . ." She frowned, found her notes, pulled up the audio program and moved through it to the notation of where he began talking about what his old friend Albert Lord had told him of the murder. She pulled the headphone jack out of her computer so Zach could listen, too. He glanced at her notes. "You put down the exact timing, minutes and seconds, of each of your comments."

"That's right. I'm organized, and, Mister Slade, it will pay off in efficiency, and saving time, just you listen."

"Albert Lord told us, me and Chaz Green, the story of Ford's murder. He told it many a time, got meals outta it many a time. And he told it the same and we did, too. Got it word for word."

"Yes, that's semi-reliable," Zach said. "Whatever inaccuracies that story had, it was from the beginning, if you could believe Jemmings . . . and Lord."

Not wanting to suffer through the whole gory story of the killing again, Clare skipped to another of her notes.

"Al said he'd picked up somethin' from the floor, a souvenir."

"Yes, I heard that," Zach commented.

Clare nodded, then rushed through most of the interview. "Now, this. Listen, Zach!"

"Those durn grandkids'a mine. Took me from my own place. Didn't even bring alla my stuff, an' I had good stuff. Coupla things I got from Albert Lord. They left them in the place, purtied up for God's sake."

"The souvenir," Zach said.

"The souvenir. Something that could lead us to Emma."

"You think because—"

She said, "Because *you* believe the universe is balanced. Because you wrung info from the Other that I was on the right track, and this is the right track."

"Got it." Zach moved from casual to primed for action. "I should have caught that, I'm the detective, and I didn't."

"The guy bored you," Clare said.

"Not a good excuse. Witnesses have bored me to tears before. It is different when I can't see the body language, though. Do we have any idea whether Jemmings's cabin is still in his family? Where it might be located?"

Clare got up and opened the top drawer of the vanity. "Phone book." She tossed it to him, came to the bed, and watched as he studied the entries. "One address, in town."

Opening the DVD tray, Clare looked at it, read the label. "This is the oral interview of Buddy Jemmings with his granddaughter, Marie Dermot, attending."

Zach snorted. "So he took a few shots at her during the interview. Dermot, yes, there're a couple of addresses in here. One address is to the west on one of the far ridges."

"Let's go." She felt energized.

"It might not be the right one."

"We can look. He described it in the interview."

"I've got a better idea," Zach said, grinning and pulling his phone off the charger. "We're going to call our good friend, the ex-sheriff, Mason Pais, Jr., and confirm with him that the cabin was Buddy Jemmings's and make getting into it his problem."

"It's nine ten at night." She stared at the clock; she'd slept a whole lot longer than she'd thought.

"If we're awake and up and working, he can be awake and up and working. He dropped the ball on protecting the LuCettes and Caden's in the hospital."

"Thanks for letting me know." She hadn't really forgotten the boy's plight, the excitement had caught her up in it.

Zach tapped the number. "Hey, Mason Junior . . ." he began genially.

TWENTY-NINE

ZACH WAITED WITH Clare in the truck for Mason Pais Junior to drive up. Zach'd applied a little judicious blackmail and the ex-sheriff had agreed to meet them and drive them to the old Jemmings cabin.

Getting a key wasn't a problem since the place was for sale, and Pais knew the lockbox code. Zach didn't ask how that was, but figured it might be the same way the man had entered their room. For an ex-lawman, the guy had more leeway in his morals than Zach did. On the other hand, the man probably considered the town, *his* town, and everyone in it, *his* people. And Zach reckoned Pais's curiosity was just as big as his own.

Enzo! Zach called.

Clare looked at him, startled. Seemed even more surprised when the dog appeared sitting between the two of them, weird eyes gleaming, tongue out, quivering with happiness.

We're on the HUNT! Enzo said, wiggling. *For the mean thing. To CHOMP her, to EXTINGUISH her.* He turned and slurped a long tongue up Clare's cheek and she shivered a little, but Clare could feel Enzo and Zach couldn't.

A line of worry twisted between her brows. Zach could guess that she was thinking Enzo had changed.

Zach agreed. The dog had become less domesticated, either by being in the hills with wild animals, or due to its time with the torturing ghost.

And, yeah, Zach agreed with Enzo, too. He wanted a piece of that thing for hurting Enzo, taking Caden, hurting Clare. He lusted for her blood—or whatever essence the monster might have—just as much as Enzo did.

Pais arrived, scowling, and gestured for them to follow him. The huge full harvest moon peeked in and out of trees, and from behind hills as they wound around old roads. Having Pais lead them was one of Zach's better ideas.

Soon they pulled up to a wide one-story cabin. The light, polished pine logs shone, and the chimney looked new, as did the front porch that ran the length of the front. A Realtor's sign sat perched on the rocky ground outside.

Pais got out first and waited for them at the front door. Zach liked his other cane better . . . well, he was more accustomed to using it as a weapon, knew the flexibility of the wood, liked the crook at the top to yank legs or arms. He'd just have to cope with this metal one. It could break bones, but the ghost had no bones.

"Stay with me, please, Enzo," Clare said, her voice a little shaky. When Zach walked with her up to the house, he could feel her excitement. Good, focused on the future and an excellent outcome, as she should be.

"I hope this is worth it," Pais grumbled, unlocking the door.

They stepped straight into a living room. Pais turned on the lights and Zach blinked. Before them he could see a door to the kitchen off-set to the left. To their right, the large end wall looked like one of the photographs of South Park City he'd seen—a full wall of newspapers behind Plexiglass.

Clare hurried to it.

A cold draft went through his calves . . . and back. Something tugged on his jeans, Enzo. For reasons known only to the ghost Lab, he wanted to show the clue to Zach and not Clare.

"Gotcha," Zach murmured under his breath, leaned a little on his cane since the ghost dog pulled him off balance as he walked—and how did that happen?

Though he'd noticed that ever since he'd called the Other, he'd been able to sense the phantom Lab more.

Pais stayed with Clare as she went over to the wall and began reading. Zach limped toward the opposite end of the cabin. When he reached the hallway, he flipped a switch, stood with tight shoulders to see if either of the other two had noticed. Neither of them said a word. To his right was a bathroom and straight ahead an open door revealed the bedroom—and another wall of papers behind glass.

As he walked toward it, a thump came against the window, a high horizontal one near the ceiling. Zach saw beady eyes. He shouldn't have been able to see outside, but that never seemed to bother his imaginary crows. They sat huddled in a circle on a large hanging bird feeder. Four sets of eyes.

Four for death.

Enzo made a sound in his throat, looked up at Zach.

"I'm not telling Clare about this," Zach said.

Enzo nodded.

"Unless she specifically asks," he added. But she'd wanted to know just that afternoon, so she might not pry further anytime soon.

The Lab glanced toward the far end of the cabin, and whined in his throat.

"You think Clare's in danger."

Enzo rolled his eyes.

"Got it. Of course she's in danger."

A whispery mental sentence came to his mind. *The bad, mean, awful ghost wants to hurt her really, really, bad. Extinguish CLARE! Not caring much about anything else.*

Zach's spit dried. He'd seen what happened when someone got lost in obsessive behavior, when they cared less about surviving than revenge.

Clare had been game but pitiful in the knife training, as if the only awareness she had of her body was during sex—and how talented she was then!—or when she dressed and undressed.

And anger flushed through him. Clare, too, was changing, would have to change, become aware, maybe even accustomed to violence, and that just seemed wrong to Zach. Not to mention the fact that he *liked* having a woman for whom the physical wasn't the be-all and end-all of their relationship, that working out wasn't the first priority in her life.

She might not be able to handle the ghost.

He could, but not without cost. Better that he pay the cost than Clare.

He turned on the bedroom light and scanned the collaged sheets of paper. Not just newspaper here, but other items. As he studied the wall he noticed that about a foot off the floor was a piece of paper, and stained brown . . . this time not from water, but old blood. Suddenly a red pawprint appeared on the sheet. Zach suppressed an oath and walked over and hunkered down.

I showed you, Enzo said. *Now I go back to help Caden.*

"You can do that?"

Yes! I learned how. I am learning more and more how to be a good spirit guide for Clare.

"Good."

The dog vanished and Zach scrutinized the paper. "My God," he said.

Clare ran in. "What have you found?" She came and stooped beside him.

"Ohmygod." She touched the handwriting at the top of the page. She didn't seem to see the red pawprint.

"This . . . this looks like the original Subscription List. The one everything written about the death of Robert Ford mentions. My God." Her finger went to the last entry, Ford's signature, and the notation "Charity covereth a multitude of sins."

"It's a real, valuable piece of history." She sounded awed.

Pais snorted from behind them. "I wouldn't give you a nickel for it."

"Hmm," Clare said. She put her finger on the line above Ford's name. "Jefferson Smith." Claire paused. "The subscription was for the burial of a prostitute—"

"A whore," Pais said.

"—who'd died the night before. To get enough money to take her body up to the cemetery and bury her."

"One of her friends was taking it around." Zach kept his voice calm. "Probably others in her same business were the first to subscribe."

"Peer pressure would—" Clare began, and stopped. When her voice came it was strained. "There it is. Twenty-five cents, Emma . . ." Clare stopped before she read the surname, Romano, aloud. She stood up, leaned against the other wall as if dizzy. "We have her full name. We can do this now. We can—"

Pais jerked and Clare must have seen him from the corner of her eye.

He put his thumbs in his belt and rocked. "Now I think it's time that you tell me *exactly* what is going on. You've given me bits and pieces, but nothin' good."

Zach leaned casually on his cane and shot Pais a big smile. "We've told you the truth, you just haven't believed it. So. All right, once more. Clare, here, is a ghost seer and communicator, and she helps them move on. You've got an evil ghost here in the canyon, one that's killing people, put Caden in the coma. This spirit originally associated with Robert Ford, probably betrayed him to Soapy Smith. The ghost was already here but finally gained critical mass when that murder-suicide occurred. The ghost is the one that's killing people with rock shards, or having them trip and fall into the flume, or drop dead in a local restaurant. That's it."

Clare rolled her eyes at the casual rundown.

Squinting at them a minute, Pais sighed. "Ya know, I think I finally believe that. What next?"

"Next we go back to the hotel and prepare to whip the ghost's ass."

"I'll go with you," Pais said.

"No," Clare said, at the same time as Zach growled, "I don't think so."

"Leave it to us," Clare said firmly.

"That's right." Zach nodded. "We're the experts here."

"This is my town—"

"How are the LuCettes doing?" Zach asked. It was a low blow and from the corner of his eye, he saw Clare wince.

"As well as can be expected," Pais said through his teeth.

"We'll take care of this." Zach used a soft tone laced with the command of back off. "Stay out of our business." He curved his fingers around Clare's upper arm and they left the house.

As they walked to the truck he heard the feathered beat of crow wings. No, they would not get Clare. Somehow he had to make her safe. Kill the ghost for her. She wouldn't like it, but he wouldn't be around for her to yell at him, would he?

"I don't like that expression of yours, Zach," Clare said when he got into the truck.

"What kind of expression is that?"

"Fierce, but something else—"

She was getting to know him. Now and again he'd faced imminent death and the fierce determination had hardened in him, set on his face then, too.

"Do you have the knife?"

She reached in her bag, caught her breath. "No." Now he heard anger at herself. "No. I left it at the hotel. How could I have done that?"

"Excitement."

"You have your weapons."

"Of course."

Her mouth thinned. "I must learn, too."

* * *

Clare hopped out of the truck nearly before Zach had killed the engine. He'd have to move fast to keep up with her . . . and outpace her.

Luckily, she had problems with the keys, both in the outside lock to the door and their room, though she'd taken the stairs at a run.

She'd thrown her purse on the bed and whirled to check out the room for her knife when Zach came in.

Her hair shone in the light, wild and free. Like he hoped she'd become. And every-damn-thing clamped inside him at the thought of giving her up. But an image rose in his mind of her as she'd been that morning after fighting the ghost: pale, unconscious. He'd thought she was dead.

Next time, *this* time, this fight they were going to, could make her dead.

The crows could be wrong, or not for her. But the predictions had always come true.

He hadn't yet figured out exactly what they meant. He didn't entirely trust them anyway, but if the universe had a slot for a death tonight in Creede, Zach would fill it instead of Clare.

"Clare." He stepped to her, into her space, against her, pulled her sweater from her jeans and slid one hand behind her to the small of her back, so he could keep her close and tight. His other hand trailed up her midriff to her breast. So full, so soft, perfect.

His dick was hard and ready.

"Clare," he whispered, his mouth close to her ear. He dipped his head so he could taste her under her ear. Clare. He didn't say it aloud, but let it sink clear through him, knew with a rightness that she was for him, no other woman.

He *must* protect her.

"We don't have time for this," she whispered, even as he stroked her nipple to tautness, even as her body arched and rubbed him right where he wanted.

"Where's Emma, Clare?"

"Up the canyon."

He nodded. "We can make it fast." He unclipped her front clasp bra. "You ever have sex with most of your clothes on, Clare?"

Her heart thumped fast under his hand, and if he knew his Clare, she'd match him in passion but have second thoughts about cleaning up afterward.

His mind emptied of everything but her. Smelling her, feeling her, tasting her.

THIRTY

HE SET HIS cane aside. Stood solid and strong before her. His Clare. He used both hands to unzip her jeans, move them and her panties—high-cut but white cotton—down.

Now her hands rubbed his dick behind his jeans and his breath came short and he'd about give everything he had in his life for this moment to last forever.

Wait. Not yet. Not this moment, but soon, soon.

Together they unzipped his own too-tight jeans and he groaned when she freed him and caressed him.

He had to have her mouth, found it slightly open and pressed his lips against her plump ones, probed his tongue into her mouth. Clare, Clare, Clare.

She fell back and took him with her and he felt her cashmere sweater against his dick and it was fine, but not as good as Clare. He pushed her upper garments above her breasts, then touched her lower, tested her, and she was wet and hot and she moaned. She couldn't open her legs wide, but there was space enough for him.

But he didn't enter her, got caught by the pure beauty of her . . . her eyes closed, her thin sweater and tank above her breasts, her bra fallen to her sides and showing rosy-tipped breasts.

That mass of hair spread on the quilt, framing her face full of straining passion.

He petted her, making her hotter, wetter, bent to kiss her lips, outline them with his tongue, sweep through her mouth again. Kissed and nibbled and listened to her whimper and slowly withdrew.

He'd put that sensual look on her face. She moaned for him. The most beautiful thing he'd ever seen and heard.

Her fingers quested, discovered him and tugged. He went over her. Paused until she opened wide, blurred eyes looked into his own.

Beautiful. Perfect for him. His.

He plunged into her and he said words he'd never said except to his family. "I love you."

She cried out and her body convulsed around him and that was the sweetest thing he'd ever felt, the best, the most fabulous, and he lost control and surged, and she tightened around him again, gasped, and he matched her gasps with groans of his own until they spun away into darkness.

"I love you," he said again.

For the second time that day, Clare thought she'd passed out, or at least her brain had gone definitely fuzzy. From pure pleasure and three orgasms . . . and from hearing Zach say he loved her. That had speared deep within her, to the bone, the words, the sounds, to be part of her and never forgotten. She didn't know what to do about them. Thought she should say she loved him, too. Because she did. But this didn't seem to be the time, because she'd want him naked in bed so she could cherish him and discuss every little detail.

She heard sloshing in the corner of the room, Zach using the basin to wash in. Considering it, she just didn't think she could, mostly because the water would be cold and she wanted warm . . . since she'd be going into coldness soon enough. The cold of the autumn night—a few degrees above freezing—and the petrifying ice of fighting the ghost—not to mention the basic chill of fear.

"Clare?" Zach said, standing fully dressed beside her. She glanced at the clock on the table. The whole explosive sex had taken less than ten minutes. Incredible.

With a little cough, she said, "Can you help me off with my boots."

His smile was quick and wicked. "Sure."

"I won't be longer than five minutes," she promised, then revised downward, "Three."

"Fine." His expression turned serious and she noticed lines on his thinner face. This case took its toll on him, too.

She found herself saying her standard platitude. "The sooner we get done, the better."

"Right." He knelt and tugged at the laces on her boots. She sat and realized he'd put a towel under her sometime and flushed because she hadn't noticed. She thought they'd left a towel on the bed, or maybe on the vanity that was within easy reach.

But her boots were gone and she yanked off the jeans, grabbed the hotel robe and bundled it on, swept up the key and shot into the hall and down it to the bathroom.

The faucet in the sink took a little time to run hot water, and she looked at the shower with longing, but absolutely no time for that.

Cleaning up and drying as fast as humanly possible, she bolted from the bathroom, stopped only to test that the lock had caught. Then returned to their room.

Zach was gone.

So was the knife.

Lunging across the room to the outside door and across the balcony, she looked for the truck. Didn't even see tail lights.

Goddammit!

He'd done it again. Left her. Infuriating.

This time, though, she figured, he left her not because he was troubled in mind and seeking answers for himself, but deliberately. To walk into danger instead of her.

A scrawl on the sheet of her notepad confirmed it. *I love you, Clare. Stay safe. Live well.*

Yes, infuriating. And terrifying.

They were supposed to be a team, and *she* the captain. *Goddammit!*

Now she knew what that look earlier had been about, their lovemaking. He planned on killing the ghost and dying himself.

Her heartbeat skipped in horror. Her breath simply stopped.

A bark had her blinking to see Enzo lying flat half-in, half-out of the plank floor. His tail wagged desultorily. *Zach called me. I am to stay with you,* he said mournfully.

"Zach called you." Clare flung on clothes, stuck on socks, and thrust her feet into boots. She sent her mind to check on the monster Emma. That one flowed down from the canyon, but instead of heading toward her and Main Street, angled west.

"Where *is* he? Not heading up to Bachelor's Loop. Emma would have stopped there." Clare stomped into her boots, tied her laces.

Anger sizzled all thought away. Her hand was on the door latch before she recalled the body armor. Whirling, she saw his was gone, a good sign. She fumbled her own on, leapt for the door, swiping the key off the vanity as she did and shot through it.

Enzo perked up. *We are going to hunt?*

She snarled, then hissed, "Yes!"

How?

"I've got wheels." Bless Desiree Rickman for her experience with hardheaded men. Clare jammed the scooter key into her pocket. "You go find Zach, now!"

Yes! I will, Clare. I will find him and come back—

"Stay with him." She ran down the stairs, carefully, quietly, holding on to the rail. She didn't dare fall. "Tell me where he is." She glanced at her watch. "Go fast!"

I can run FAST! Enzo said enthusiastically, joyously, and disappeared in a streak of spirit gray.

He sounded better. Healthier. More like the companion she knew, and that was great.

She *would* do this. Everything. Keep Zach from being killed. Save Caden. Save Creede. Save the goddam world.

Her breath puffing out steam in the frosty air, Clare flat out ran to Tappings bar and the scooter. Thank God for Desiree. Thank God.

Yes, Zach thought he'd stranded Clare. Protected her, was keeping her safe.

She didn't *want* to be safe. Not at the cost of his life. How could she live with that! Bad enough to try and live without him, a man who'd twined himself into her entire existence, let alone exist in a world where her lover had sacrificed himself for her. Impossible to survive with that knowledge weighing her down.

Her body shuddered with anger more than the cold. She was going to scream and yell at him for this. Something she hadn't done . . . in forever. Since she was a kid and hadn't gotten control of her temper. Throw a true tantrum. Let him know he'd done something nearly unforgivable.

I have found him! Enzo yelled into her mind. *He is at the old grave of Robert Ford.*

Yes, that might draw the wraith that had been Emma Romano. Surely her own unmarked grave would be in the cemetery just to the south of Ford's empty site.

Clare's anger barely had time to cool, even in the cold air, as her shaky hands opened the door of the shed and she rolled the scooter out. Since all of her trembled with rage, with terror, with adrenaline priming her for the fight—who knew what else?—she took the time to draw in three steadying breaths, let them out, center herself. She'd have to keep her balance while riding the scooter. Keep her head.

I will fight, too! Enzo yelled, then screamed with pain.

She roared out of the parking lot, followed the sense she had of the knife . . . and Emma, Enzo . . . the lost Caden. And Zach.

Tears froze on her face at the loss she'd already experienced, the hope she could save them all, herself, too. *Extinguish* Emma.

Leaning into a curve, her emotions settled into three strong ones. Anger at Zach, grief for Caden, and most of all, determination. This was *her* fight. How *dare* Zach take it from her.

How *dare* anyone believe that she wasn't up to the job, no matter how new she was at it. No matter what its demands or its costs.

Then she turned again, curved down over the machine for less wind resistance. Though she wanted to rip open the speed, she kept it at the upper limits of what she knew she could control . . . even as mist slicked the pavement.

Past the cemetery, heading north. There, there! A truck, two! *Two!* One was the elder Pais's!

She screeched to a stop, but the wind had picked up and swallowed the sound. Flinging herself off the scooter, she ran through the gate, up the gentle incline, slipping on the wet clumps of grass, stumbling as her boots caught dirt or rock.

Then she saw them beyond the gravesite, at the top of the ridge, lost in a flurry of a white cycling snowstorm that glinted silver. And lightning. "Goddammit!" she yelled. Two men. *Two*, were here before her, trying to fight the damn ghost. When it was her job. *Her* fight. Neither of them heard.

Zach stood closest to the evil ghost, taunting it. He waved Clare's knife at the specter, shouted, "Come on, Miss Emma Romano. Don't you want me?" His grin was reckless, baiting.

Clare stopped in her tracks. He looked like he enjoyed the danger, the fight. Because of the adrenaline rush, no doubt. And if she was thinking at all, she was lost. Pack the mind away, rely on instincts—baby ghost killing, ghost *seeing* instincts, but that's what she had now. She prayed as she ran up the hill.

"Don't you want me?" Zach danced, *danced*! How could he do that? "I betrayed my lover. I took *her* knife while she was gone. And I *planned* that. I stranded her, and I called you here. That's betrayal, right? No man ever leave you in bed when you still wanted him?"

That was *such* the wrong thing to say. Hell, why couldn't Clare run faster? Her ribs hurt, she put that out of her head.

"You know I can't kill you with this knife, don't you? I can . . . make you dissipate, but can't kill you. But you can take me. When was the last time you had a man?"

Zach lied with conviction. He *could* kill Emma. But not without dying himself. Sacrificing himself.

The funnel tightened, lengthened, swayed in no natural shape. Unnatural. Must be stopped. It flung itself at Zach. He held up some sort of shield. Where had he gotten that? And why didn't Clare have one of those?

She shrieked to get the monster's attention.

The snowstorm wobbled, aimed for her. Enzo harried it, Zach turned and froze, looking horrified.

And Pais leapt straight in front of it.

Time seemed stuck in slow motion as Clare raced toward Emma, though she could see, could hear the ghost as it lashed out at the ex-sheriff.

You betrayed MEEEE, one of your residents, one of your people! Emma shrieked as she rained blows on Pais.

He stood his ground, leaned into her wind, his face frosted over, and Clare saw bleeding *bite marks.*

Her running felt like lumbering.

"I heard that!" he yelled. "You are *not* one of my people. You *took* a child on my watch. You are an abomination!" With a blue and shaking hand, he raised his gun and fired.

The banshee shriek ice-picked through Clare's head, then rose beyond her hearing. She thought she heard a dog yelping. Enzo.

Act!

"Over here, Emma Romano! *Here!*" Clare screamed with everything she had.

Emma lashed out a serrated whip of snow, hit Pais in the chest, and wrapped around his torso.

He crumpled, dead.

YESSS!

Do you hear how crazy that sounds? Clare sent anger, scorn, disgust down their link. The storm hesitated, a shade seemed to drop out of the whirling mass, a small white wraith. Clare stepped into it, into the cold, gasped. Trying to keep this bit blocked from Emma, silent, she crooned, *Caden?*

Yes, it is me! You came for me, Clare. Enzo said you would. I am here, Clare, and not eaten. Help me get away!

Narrowing her eyes, she *saw* the small threads that held Caden to the ghost. Three threads that pulsed with red and sparkling life. Gritting her teeth, she touched one with the tip of her knife. It separated. Caden whimpered. Cold began to hit her like hail pellets, bruising her. She frayed the second, slit the third, and watched it tear away.

Nooooo! Emma cried, and bit Clare.

Agony took her breath, dimmed her vision. Propping the knife at an angle against her body she stepped further into the snowstorm that was Emma Romano, shuddered, then went numb. That freed Clare.

Bombarded by slicing hail and wretched, guilty memories from Emma, Clare slashed at the tethers that held other tattered, shrieking ghosts as they flew to her, then away—a World War I veteran, a barkeep from the mining days.

One quick punch of recent memories from Linda Boucher, the third of the recent love triangle. Sex triangle, truly, for she—and now Clare—knew that not one of those three had loved. No love, only power games.

Her arm and the knife swept through the bindings with no control from her, no awareness. The only thing she felt were frozen tear tracks on her face, her lips cold, cold, cold.

Then the snowstorm coalesced into a huge, lumpy ghost with shadows. Mostly Emma, and those she'd consumed before becoming free. "I know you, Emma Romano," Clare thought she whispered, put more effort into the words so she might hear them with her ears and not just her mind. "*I know you, Emma Romano!*" And she did. Emma had whispered to one of her clients that Robert Ford intended to kill

Edward Capehart O'Kelley, and that man had warned O'Kelley, who'd walked into the saloon and killed Ford.

I know why betrayal hurts you. Because you are guilty of the betrayal of your lover.

And finally Clare's mind and body connected and she recalled the right fighting pattern, took the first step.

Yes, he died because of meee! the specter screamed. *Because he used me and didn't see ME. Didn't care for me, and I loved him. And he barely noticed me.*

Clare wouldn't hesitate. Slash, slash. She couldn't tell if that hurt Emma, because the ghost continued to carry on. But Clare got closer and closer to the central mass.

I KILLED myself, Emma shrieked. *Now, during the full moon, now!*

"It's not now. It was then, over a hundred years ago," Clare stated.

It is NOW!"

"*Then,*" Clare insisted.

I killed myself. I died like Nellie Russell did, the one the subscription was for. But NOBODY NOTICED!

And the storm calmed, chilled to grimy frost, and Clare seemed to have stepped inside a snow globe—time out of time—the gray spirit dimension. She couldn't sense Zach or Enzo.

She saw the woman, a woman younger than she, heavier in body and features, long black hair as dull as her eyes. She wept and wailed and wiped her face with an end of the shawl she wore over a thin dress. Clare had to listen closely to words garbled by sobbing. "I left Creede and killed myself up Willow Creek and nobody even noticed I was gone!" She lifted chocolate brown eyes to Clare. "Do you know how that *feels*?"

"No," Clare replied quietly. "No. I'm so sorry."

Lonely sadness vanished in a flash, replaced by malicious glee. "It made me feel *murderous*!"

Clare held her ground, but let the knife fall by her side. Get close, within striking distance of Emma's heart. Clare knew how to deal a death blow, now. She thought she swallowed, but didn't feel it, her tongue, her mouth, the moving of her throat.

Cold, maybe too cold, and maybe this took too long. Usually helping ghosts on felt like it took too long. Perhaps this time her heart would stop.

She kept the knife by her side, hoping it didn't glow or hum or attract Emma's attention before Clare could strike.

Emma threw up her hands, paced a few steps, paced back. "No one noticed I was gone. No one noticed I was dead and I waited and waited and waited and got angrier and angrier and when those stupid *betrayers* had that fight near me, I *killed* them." She fisted her hands. "And it felt *good.*"

"So you went on killing."

"Yesss!" Emma hissed. "I felt potent and powerful and then I gobbled that bastard and bitch up and they tasted good and I went through the canyon and all the old towns that used to be here and *feasted.*" She licked her lips, and to Clare's horror, the woman's lips looked red with blood and it dribbled down from the corners of her mouth, to cover her chin. Her fingernail-claws shone richly red. "So many, many, many luscious ghosts. Those of my time—*now*— they know what happened to me. *Now* they regret my death, not finding me, not *missing* me. They regret it *deeply.*" She swiped her tongue over her mouth. "They didn't last long, so old and ragged as they were." She tossed her head. "Some I shredded and they took their sorry selves off to wherever." She flicked her hand and wet blood flew from her fingertips, then she smoothed her hands over her body. "Some are still with me." She smiled with triumph. "Made me a woman of *substance*, a force to be reckoned with."

"I can see that."

Emma sneered. "I swept up all the ghosts of all the times in my valley and my canyon. Then got hungry again and there was that boy . . . that nice-smelling, tender boy morsel."

"Caden," Clare said.

Emma shrugged. "Who cares about his name? But he

evaded me. Even within my power, he spun away." Her gaze grew intent. "You smell delicious. My mouth waters."

She floated toward Clare and her lips opened wider and wider and wider until all Clare saw was a huge mouth, sharp teeth, and Clare took one large stride and stabbed under her ribcage upward and into her heart.

Emma shrieked, screamed, wailed, the sound so high it hurt Clare's ears. She spun out of the storm that tried to keep cycling but couldn't . . . the world shattered and disintegrated around her as the snow globe flattened into two dimensions, turned to browns, blacks, and sepia, and fell apart and blew away in sheets.

Flat on her back, Clare saw murky, oily smoke fountain upward.

I will take her now. A sparkling net of stars wrapped around the diffuse spirit of Emma and she disappeared.

You did well, child. The soft and comforting voice came to Clare's mind. Her eyes focused on great blue crystalline eyes in the mist. More disembodied eyes. This time not the Other, was all she could think, since his/its had been purple.

You did well. You have been doing well. Remember.

Darkness fell across her vision, though she wasn't, quite, unconscious. She simply couldn't move.

Terrible swearing in a voice she didn't recognize as Zach's for a long minute, since he honored his promise to his dead brother and didn't usually curse.

Zach propped her shoulders up, held her. "Clare, Clare darling, wake up."

Yes, that was his breath, hot on her face, and she dragged in her own and it hurt and she realized she hadn't been breathing deeply. Ice seemed to fracture around her lungs.

Clare! Enzo. She felt the slight nudge of his nose. That, too, should have been cold, but wasn't, it was nearly warm.

Then Zach hauled her up, pulled her against him, and, yes! Heat. Her mouth opened, closed, then he stroked her face. Kissed her with warm lips, withdrew, and a tiny moan came from her.

"I love you, Clare."

She leaned against him and tears came to her eyes and dribbled down, hot, hot, hot, and all the ice around her, in her, crackled away, breaking off.

She didn't break with it. Surprising.

And she managed to turn her head and the night shifted from too dark to moonlit. Tipping her head up, she reveled in the sight of the full moon ringed with dark colors shining through the mist.

We WON. We WON! We are heroes. Enzo danced around them, zoomed into the hill and out.

Zach began slowly limping with her, and her feet dragged and stumbled, but he kept walking, one step at a time, and then she could lift and flex her feet and move stiffly. After a moment, she realized they headed for Pais's body.

"We won," Zach said, "at the cost of a good man."

More tears came; they still felt warm, so Clare let them run down her face. "Yes."

Enzo galloped to the dead Pais, sniffed him, then returned. *But he IS a hero, too. And he went fast and not much pain and to a good place.*

"Real-ly?" Clare asked. Her tongue felt thick.

Yes, Enzo said.

She gave him a sharp glance, as did Zach.

Enzo gave them back doggy eyes. Clare sighed.

You told him not to follow, and you told him to go away. He disobeyed, the phantom Lab said.

It wasn't like Enzo to make judgments, but Clare supposed that his own experience had shaded his personality. The Other could be a hard taskmaster, she was sure.

Zach squatted by the body. "Huh. Interesting."

"What?"

"He's wearing a body camera."

Standing by herself, she wobbled on her feet but didn't fall. "Yes. In-ter-est-ing."

Zach rose and took her arm. "Should sure let us off the hook for killing him. We weren't anywhere near him and the camera would show that."

Sirens screamed in the distance.

"And I'm thinking that he'd left a phone message or de-layed e-mail for his grandson, the sheriff."

"So hard."

The death of a hero was always hard, and dimmed the sheer glory of surviving.

Getting Clare warm and functioning came first for Zach and the deputies, then the sorting out of the vehicles. It didn't take more than a moment's thought to know Desiree Rick-man must have brought the scooter for Clare, and she'd kept quiet about that nugget of information.

Zach didn't know what he felt, except love for Clare and wrung out. He thought Clare might be numb, too, since she hadn't really reacted to his statement of love, and she sure hadn't reamed him out for betraying and stranding her. Yet.

Or she might be waiting for privacy to do that, and they didn't get any.

A several-hour interrogation by the deputies came first, then a worn sheriff who'd returned after handling the details of his grandfather's death, which was hard on them, too. Clare seemed nearly transparent to Zach, but she didn't fail, flinch, or walk out until the sheriff's office was done with them. She'd only smiled once, when a deputy told them that Caden had awakened in the hospital and demanded to go home—then to see the pair of them.

The video of the whole fight looked odd, but he and Clare were in the clear.

When they staggered back to the hotel, opened the door to see the lit room, the ordinariness of the small place hit Zach with the shock of disconnection.

"Tired," Clare said. Her sentences continued to be shorter than usual. She hadn't directly looked at him since the whole fight had gone down.

"Me, too." He hesitated. "Can I help you undress?"

She shrugged, stood head down, and moved slowly.

Soon they were together and spooned, facing the window that showed clear sky and bright stars.

Zach wanted to tell Clare he loved her again, but was afraid to hear any answer, or more silence.

They slept late, until the sunshine of the day made the quilt too hot and Zach grunted awake. Clare stayed curled up, not facing him. From what he could see, her face looked too pale. Dammit! These cases of hers—all three of them— were too hard on her. And next time he saw the effing Other, he'd tell it so.

She needed a break.

He needed one, too. This woo-woo stuff and relationship stuff sure took a man to the brink and back. Somehow he'd have to figure out how to slow it down.

His alarm pinged. He'd set it for an hour before the time the LuCettes had wanted to meet with them at their motel after the breakfast and morning rush.

Clare flailed. He wrapped his arms around her and pulled her back to him. She felt a little cool.

"Uhhnn," she said and rolled over, wiggled closer, felt his morning hard-on and her lashes snapped up, showing him pretty hazel eyes. Her fingers drifted across his dick, electrifying. A rush of pure, primitive instinct flashed through him. He wanted to take her, now, hard, imprint himself on her so she'd always remember what it felt like when he thrust into her, never want another man. Crap! He set his teeth and fought for control.

His emotions spiraled out of hand. God knew what he'd dreamed about, but it hadn't helped smooth the edges of the fight. He swept her fingers from him, rolled away himself, and gave her his back. He didn't want sex anymore. He wanted *loving*. And he couldn't handle it if she *only* wanted sex.

He'd break and tell her he loved her again and he still couldn't face anything she might say except a return of his declaration . . . and if she didn't say those words . . .

"We don't have much time before the restaurant closes for breakfast," he croaked.

He could feel her gaze, grabbed his sweats, fumbled on his foot brace and snatched the key for the bathroom and headed out.

A cold shower got his body under control, but not his emotions. They sat inside him, his head, his heart, compressing to diamond-like crystalized consistency with one question. What was he going to do about Clare if she didn't love him?

Zach had moved fast, faster than she'd seen him before. His disability had stopped slowing him down much. As for Clare, she sat up gingerly, wouldn't have been surprised to hear her tendons or bones creak. She wore a light cotton sleep shirt with short sleeves and rubbed her goose-bumped arms.

She didn't know what to think and her feelings felt turgid and frozen. Her body might be achy, but her emotions should be cheerful, optimistic, triumphant!

No.

Zach loved her. That hurt her heart and she rubbed her chest. He thought he loved her and she'd have given anything to have had him say that the night before last, because she surely loved him. She thought.

Aching body, aching heart, aching behind her eyes where tears should lurk.

Zach had told her he loved her. He'd told Emma that he'd betrayed her. He'd lied.

Except, not really. He had taken Clare's knife. She glanced at the weapon on the vanity that seemed . . . satisfied but not flashy, thank heavens.

He'd thought he'd left her stranded. Had planned on it.

Had planned on killing the phantom and dying in the process. Yes, tears welled up at that, a few.

She was worn out. So much drama. Finding the Subscription List, Zach telling her he loved her, discovering he'd left . . . to *die*! The fight and saving Caden and the loss of Pais the elder and . . .

One sobbing shudder. She waited for more but that was all that came. Emotions muffled, though she was glad her mind seemed to be working on all cylinders.

The alarm on Zach's phone pulsed again, and Clare snagged it . . . saw the list for today that he'd obviously entered when she was out of it: Breakfast, Meeting with LuCettes—her stomach clenched at that thought—get food basket for trip and check out of the hotel, turn in rental at Alamosa, depart for Denver.

She found her rapid breath slowed a little as she read the plans, and read them again, set them in her memory.

That simple list of events grounded her. Perhaps she couldn't experience great highs and huge lows right now. She could at least act like a normal, rational, decent person.

A cackle spilled from her lips, and her mouth felt chapped. Of course.

Hello, Clare! GOOD to see you, Clare. Here we are! We won! We are HEROES! Enzo zoomed in from the hall door, more manic and cheerful than ever. He leapt onto the bed, sat beside her wiggling, then opened his muzzle and gave her a cold, wet, sloppy lick.

She put her arms around him, let them sink into his freezing shadows. If he were real, she'd have buried her face in his fur. "Hey, Enzo. How are you?"

I am fine, Clare. Fine, Fine, FINE!

She dropped her arms, leaned away, found a smile for him. "That's wonderful."

Yes!

She got up and put on her robe, nodded to Zach as he came in, hesitated, stopped and kissed his jaw.

Relief showed in his eyes.

She touched her throat. "All my words that I need to say to you are blocked here. I can't—" She shook her head.

"You don't need to," he said stiffly.

"Yes. I do. We do. Just can't right now. I'll be back soon."

THIRTY-TWO

CADEN SAT WITH his parents on the couch in their apartment at the motel.

"Glad to see you're all right," Zach said.

"I'm glad I am all right." The boy's voice trembled and his father picked him up and plopped him on his lap. "It was scary being a part of the ghost, but Enzo told me what to do and we talked back and forth and I pretended I was dead and we was very, very, very quiet."

"*Were*, Caden," Mrs. LuCette said. "You and Enzo," her mouth pruned, "were quiet."

"Yus." He wiggled from his father who reluctantly let him go. Patted Enzo on the head, and turned to face his parents. "I do *too* see ghosts." He glanced at Clare. "The Other says they will send me a doggy companion like Enzo to help me. I'm glad."

He scowled at his parents, ran to his mother and climbed on her and kissed her cheek, crawled over her to his father and hugged and kissed him again and slipped back to the floor. "I *do* see ghosts. But since you told me I shouldn't talk about ghosts, I am going to my room for a time-out."

"You should say good-bye to Ms. Cermak and Mr. Slade," Michael said gruffly.

A smile broke across Caden's face and he looked all seven-year-old boy. He ran to Clare and she leaned down and got a hug from him. The hand he'd petted Enzo with was still cold. "Good-bye, Clare. Thank you for saving me from Emma."

"You're welcome."

"I love you, Clare!" He kissed her sloppily on her cheek.

She coughed a little. "I love you, too," she said. He felt good, a small boy, maybe a little too thin, in her arms. He withdrew first and walked over to Zach and stuck out his hand. "Good-bye, Zach. Thank you for helping me and Enzo and Clare."

"Always," Zach said, engulfing the child's hand in his, giving it a firm shake.

"Hasta la vista," Caden said and walked away with dignity.

"Hasta la vista," Zach replied. He held out his hand to her and she took it. When he stood, she rose with him. He didn't just tug at her hand, he helped draw her up.

In a low voice, Zach stared at the LuCettes. "I'd give anything to have my loving family back. Don't blow this." He glanced at Clare. "You say the piece you've been aching to talk about and we'll be gone."

"When do you leave?" asked Mrs. LuCette quickly, as if not wanting to hear what Clare had to say.

Zach answered, "Within the hour. Driving to Alamosa to return the truck. Your grandmother is sending a plane to pick us up."

Clare had second, third, fourth thoughts about speaking, but finally did. "I know you don't want to hear this, but Caden can see ghosts and you're going to have to deal with that." She met the two sets of stony eyes briefly. "Before I received my . . . talent . . . I wouldn't let myself believe in . . . psychic powers. I wouldn't visit my great-aunt Sandra. I lost her, or she lost me. It would have been so much easier if my mind had been open. Family . . ." She shook her head. "It's

the most important thing. Good-bye, Mrs. LuCette, good-
bye Mr. LuCette."

The pair stood, too. "We will keep your words in mind,"
Mr. LuCette said.

"We don't want him hurt by things he doesn't understand," Mrs. LuCette said.

"Too late." Zach nodded at them. "You . . . and he . . . can
talk to Barbara Flinton. You have Clare's number and See-
AndTalk info, and mine." He headed for the door and no one
said anything else.

When they reached the hotel, Clare went up to finish
packing and Zach crossed the street and walked up the block
to the county building.

People nodded at him as Zach strode through the county
HQ to the sheriff's office. To his surprise, the man's door
was open.

Pais the fourth stared down at documents on his desk
with the blank expression of loss that Zach had seen on his
own face and too many others. He knocked and the sheriff
looked up, face going flat.

"I got your text," Zach said. The place didn't much look
like the Cottonwood County Sheriff's Department that Zach
had left a month ago, but it smelled the same, felt the same
because a good man headed the office.

The sheriff glanced up at him. "The coroner says granddad died of heart failure." The man's jaw worked, then he
shook his head. "We don't have a history of that in our family." He stood, moved from behind his desk and walked over
to Zach, getting in his space. "What the fuck happened out
on that hillside by Robert Ford's gravesite?" Then Pais
hissed out a breath. "The video makes no sense. Or it didn't
when we looked at it as soon as we got it. Since then it's become nothing but fucking static. I—we've—done a search
and a check-up for any Emma Romanos and there aren't any
near here."

Zach scrutinized the hurting man in front of him. He'd
known cops, deputies, sheriffs who wouldn't look at the
truth if it held something weird. For himself, he hadn't liked

hearing the truth, but he'd rather he *knew* than not—than have something about a case sit in the back of his mind and itch, never go away.

Putting both his hands on his cane, he spoke quietly, but put a hint of Colorado drawl in his voice. "What you had here was a supernatural entity. A ghost that ate all the other ghosts in the valley and the canyons. She's gone now."

Pais stumbled back. Put a hand to his head as if his brain might explode.

Zach continued, "Young Caden LuCette can see ghosts . . . if they start occurring again. You recall that. I'm sorry for your loss, and your granddad . . . died a hero. I don't know if Clare and I could have taken down the monster without him." If they'd gotten their act together, *worked* together, probably. But they'd been at odds. "Hope that helps."

"Some." A shaky breath. "What now?"

"Now Clare and I are headed back to Denver and you and your town and your county heal. Cruisin' the Canyon will help with that."

"Yeah. No doubt. It's a busy time."

Zach turned and headed out.

"Wait, Slade," the sheriff said, catching up with him. Pais held out his hand. "Thanks." The muscles of his jaw flexed once more. "I owe you."

Zach shook. The man's palm was a little damp; Caden's had been drier. Losing someone you loved was worse than losing your own life. "Just keep an eye on Caden."

Clearing his throat, Pais said, "I checked you out as soon as you gave me your card."

"Figured."

"And later I found a few comments on the private Colorado police and sheriff's boards."

Zach rolled a shoulder.

"Denver cop talk, and Denver cops relaying what Wyoming and Montana deputies said . . . and Park County guys. You've got a pretty good rep, and you get around."

Zach grimaced. "It's been an . . . interesting . . . month

since I hooked up with Rickman." Since he'd hooked up with Clare . . . but Rickman and those associated with him had given them the last two cases.

"Good luck." The sheriff paused. "Come back anytime."

With a last glance, Zach met the sheriff's direct gaze, saw that the man actually meant his words. "Thanks."

He strode through the building and out, stopped a minute to let a couple of cars go by and admired the lavender-painted hotel a block down and across the street. The right-hand door to the balcony opened and Clare came out, carrying her tablet and a keyboard. He figured she'd be writing up her notes and cross-referencing everything six ways from Sunday. He pointed to the restaurant in the bottom of the hotel and she nodded.

He had no clue what she felt for him, and his insides twisted. After he got food for the trip, he opened the door to their room.

She'd tidied it up and the place looked nearly unlived in. Unloved in. As if they hadn't experienced so much as they had when they'd been there.

She sat on the balcony, her gaze toward the gap and the upper canyon. Her hand rested against her side. When he stood at the threshold, her head turned, but she didn't smile and he'd expected one. She gestured at the chair beside her and he came, shoved it closer to her, and sat.

"I'm ready to go." She sighed. "Such a pretty town, and a historic one of my time period that I could actually experience and appreciate, since there aren't any ghosts." She waved. "Like this hotel. I should like it more."

"We can always come back," Zach said. He didn't like this depressed Clare. He was the brooding one of the pair of them and didn't like seeing it on her. He took her free hand. Her fingers were cool but not cold. With a jerk of his head, he indicated the road up the canyon. "All the ghosts from your time period are gone, right? We can come back anytime you want."

"Oh." She blinked. "You're right." A small line set between

her brows and her eyes went distant once more. "All the mines up around Bachelor Loop, the site of Old Bachelor, too. No one's there."

"So we can come back. We'll always have Creede."

She looked at him askance. "Are you making a joke with regard to the film *Casablanca*?"

He nodded. "Lame. I know. Creede isn't Paris."

There was the hint of a smile. "No, but it's still beautiful in its own way."

"Uh-huh." She hadn't taken her other hand from her side. "Are your ribs bothering you?"

Her gaze met his. One of the things that first attracted him to her were the shadows in her eyes that might match his. Like she'd suffered through darker things in life and he wouldn't have to explain himself too much. Now the hazel had darkened, and there were more than shadows, there was torment. "I think she wounded me. Inside. It feels like I have a hole, or a lack . . . just some aching emptiness . . ." She shook her head. "I can't explain it."

Raising his brows, he said, "So I can't be the only wounded one of us? You have to be, too?" Leaning over, he kissed her lips. "I know all about working while wounded, handling that shi— stuff." Another kiss. "Clare, it's important to leave the past in the past." A tingle at the back of his neck, a shadowy bird on the wing, a crow? He couldn't tell. So it didn't count. But he got the feeling the words he just spoke would be coming back to haunt him. He didn't care. They were true, and true for now for Clare. "Let's leave what we can of this in the past."

Her lashes dipped down over her wide eyes, flirted up. She knew that particular look of hers tweaked his libido. This time her faint smile blossomed into more, though he thought she dug deep to produce it. She nodded. "It's a beautiful day, and I'm here with you in a pretty place. I should stop thinking ahead and cherish the moment."

"Good idea." He touched the hand she pressed at her side, collected her fingers and brought them to his lips. Her body eased and her eyes focused completely on him. Good.

He gathered both of her hands in his left one, placed his own hand where she'd kept hers, and tried to sense whatever she had. No go.

She stood, keeping one hand in his. A horn honked and she looked out over the balcony and so did Zach. A small procession of three antique cars drove up the street. The Texan couple they'd met whooped and waved at them. Clare waved back, met Zach's eyes and smiled. "Look at that—"

"Cheerfully unaware that anything other than slightly odd stuff was going on," Zach completed the sentence for her.

"*We* did that. We let them keep their peace of mind. Enjoy the moment, Zach. We won this battle, right? Wounded or not?"

He kept his eyes on hers. "Yeah, we did."

She took a breath and said, "Zach," and he knew his doom had come.

Stern and sad, she said, "How would you feel if I died when doing *your* job?"

The bottom fell out of his life, darkness edged his vision at the thought, the guilt that would eat him alive for the rest of his life, which he might just make recklessly short. As bad as a stupid man of the Old West who didn't think things through.

His knees weakened and he fell into the chair. Then his vision cleared a little as she came and sat on his lap, wrapped her arms around him and leaned against his chest, soft, womanly. His woman. In the clean, quiet mountain air he could hear her breathing, thought he might even hear her heart beat.

He said the only thing he could. "I had to protect you. I love you."

"You screwed up."

"I know."

"Don't do that again. We are partners. We are a *team*."

"Yeah." Action needed, groveling if necessary. "Do you forgive me?"

Her breath hefted from her. "Yes."

Words just came into his head and he said them. "Charity covereth a multitude of sins."

She frowned. "I'm not being charitable in forgiving you." Her head tilted and she paused. "I looked up that phrase, you know."

"Figured."

"It's from the Bible, the New Testament, Peter, I think, and that's a quote from the King James Version. The full verse is something like, 'And above all things have fervent charity among yourselves: for charity shall cover the multitude of sins.'" She pursed her lips. "I'm not persuaded that the King James Version is the best translation for this particular verse."

"No?" His heart, his body, had relaxed at the inflection of her voice, at the *feeling* that everything would be all right. His lips moved upward then spread into a smile. She'd forgiven him, and was treating him like a partner.

A very short discussion and stuff had been talked about and handled and they'd moved on.

And that pursing of her lips? He bent down and stole a quick kiss.

"No," she said softly, seriously, licked her lips as if to taste him. "I like the New International Version of the Bible better when I read that verse. 'Above all, love each other deeply, because love covers over a multitude of sins.' I love you, Zach."

"Yes." He had to squeeze her tightly against him. "Yes."

Author's Note and
Acknowledgments

All contemporary characters in this book are products of my imagination.

As Clare said, there is no definitive biography of Robert Ford, so a researcher must see him through the lens of someone writing about Jesse James, Soapy Smith, or even Edward Capehart O'Kelley (the man who killed him). The primary source for Ford in Creede is Cy Warman, the journalist and editor who ran the newspaper, the *Creede Candle*, and wrote stories of the Wild West. So the man's bias, and a storyteller's wish to make a good story, must be considered, but otherwise, I'd imagine the facts as related by him were true.

My sources:

Frontier Stories, by Cy Warman, New York, Charles
    Scribner's Sons, 1898
"Creede," by Cy Warman, in *The Colorado Magazine*,
    Volume 1, 1893

The later works I used most were:

Soapy Smith's Creede, by Leland Feitz.

I particularly liked Catherine Holder Spude's, *"That Fiend in Hell": Soapy Smith in Legend*, since it actually traced the making of the legend of Soapy Smith, compared it to what we know of the man, and brought up some interesting facts about his death. It's fascinating to see how a legend, any legend, can come into being, and it gave me insights on Cy Warman, my primary source.

And, of course, *The Assassination of Jesse James by the Coward Robert Ford* by Ron Hansen, which is fictional and lists no bibliography, but is very interesting all the same. The movie of that name was *not* filmed in Creede, but did snag a 2007 Best Performance by an Actor in a Supporting Role Oscar nomination for Casey Affleck, who portrayed Robert Ford.

Thank you to Johanna Gray and Jim Loud of the Creede Historical Society; the librarians, as always, of the Denver Public Library, and of the History Colorado Center (who have microfilmed issues of the *Creede Candle*).

Huge thanks to the ladies of the Creede Chamber of Commerce who let me use their phone, sheltered me during my time of snow, sleet, and rain there (Sound familiar? But it was May), and who pointed me to Robert Ford's first gravesite.

And who provide free Internet for travelers! We were doing cover conference (e-mail) at the time and we used one of the pics I took. I'm sure the ladies didn't expect to have their meeting room used for knife training (of *course* I looked into it . . . well, the door was open). But what can you do, I needed a venue!

A website that proved invaluable was *http://www.findagrave.com*, that I've used before and will continue to utilize.

Other figments of my imagination: the knife (though thank you to Sarah of NaturePunk Creations on Facebook for her information about a human femur as a prospective knife), and the Subscription List (though I do have a pic of the newspaper wall in South Park City on my Pinterest page).

Also fictional is the oral history of Buddy Jemmings. As far as I know, there is no oral history of anyone that might have been connected with Robert Ford's murder, though the Creede Historical Society does have some oral histories and interviews of people who were in the valley and canyon before the mining camp and town were founded.

A maverick lawman whose leg and life have been shattered...
A skeptical accountant who's inherited a psychic "gift" along
with a fortune...And the ghosts of Old West gunmen...

WELCOME TO THE GHOST SEER SERIES
BY RITA AWARD–WINNING AUTHOR

ROBIN D. OWENS

Available in the series:

GHOST SEER
GHOST LAYER
GHOST KILLER

"A nonstop romantic whirl...A terrific series."
—*Library Journal*

"Hot but grounded...paranormal action and a narration
that just won't let you put the book down."
—*Fresh Fiction*

robindowens.com
penguin.com

M1573AS1014

The Celta Novels by
Robin D. Owens

Available in the series:

"If you've been waiting for someone to do futuristic romance right...Robin D. Owens is the author for you."
—Jayne Castle, *New York Times* bestselling author

"Sexy, emotionally intense, and laced with humor."
—*Library Journal*

robindowens.com
penguin.com

M1574AS1014